The Eunuch

The Eunuch

A Novel

by

Charles H. Fischer

The
Gabbro Head

Wayzata, Minnesota
2022

Cover art : Copyright © 2022 by Chris Monroe. Front cover
inspired by a cedar wood statue of Priest Ka-aper, made circa
2465-2323 BCE, and now in the Egyptian Museum in Cairo.

ISBN: 978-1-7325799-4-1

Printed in the United States of America.

The Gabbro Head Press LLC

Email: editorial@gabbrohead.com
U.S. Mail: P.O. Box 53, Wayzata, Minnesota 55391

www.gabbrohead.com

for

✦   Lisa   ✦

✦

Acknowledgements

I would like to thank David Bosworth for letting me into his fiction workshop in the spring of 1995.

I would also like to thank the early readers of the manuscript—John Atkins, Michael McKim, and Paul Edmund Thomas—for their invaluable feedback.

And, without the patient edits of Robin Cruise, Sarah Flygare, Paul Edmund Thomas, and Lisa Wogan, *The Eunuch* would be more ill-conceived and sloppier than it is.

— Charles H. Fischer
August 2022

Contents

The way up and the way down are one and the same.

— Heraclitus of Ephesus
~ 500 BCE

Introduction
and
Note on the Translation

"The history of phallicism *is* the history of religion."[1] It may not be an exaggeration to say that Henry Poole's translation of *The Eunuch* illustrates G. R. Scott's axiom most persuasively. In the span of twenty-two cuneiform[†] tablets, Nergal the eunuch recounts the true story behind the madness of Nebuchadnezzar II and his decision to invade Judah, initiating what is known as the first Babylonian captivity. Apart from describing the origins of this decisive moment in history, *The Eunuch* also provides the modern reader with a rare, first-person account of Neo-Babylon, an ancient Mesopotamian imperium that was under the usual pressures of an empire in decline: drought, disease, famine, and war—as well as spiritual and moral exhaustion. Nergal's secret chronicle portrays a depressed mandarin class trapped in an untenable political environment, fighting and fornicating like their world is about to collapse. Unexceptional subject matter, some might argue, but *The Eunuch* is more than your typical 6th century BCE, end-of-the-world sex novel.

And yet critics in advance reviews have been unkind to Henry Poole's translation of *The Eunuch*. Kittelsby has called the work "obscene,"[2] while Thorson has labeled it, "a sad effort by a sad, little man."[3] To scholars of ancient Assyria, it will be clear that the translator knew little Akkadian and almost no Babylonian. *The Eunuch*, therefore, may strike readers as ill-conceived and ridiculous. How Henry Poole managed to capture the mind of a eunuch is a mystery to the editor of the present edition. In the following paragraphs, we will examine the origins of this strange work, for Henry Poole belonged to that unfortunate species of the contemporary university: the part-time adjunct. He was a man who was misunderstood by his times and hounded by his creditors until his regrettable commitment to, and subsequent death in, a psychiatric hospital in northern Minnesota.

In *The Eunuch*, Poole reconstructs the tale of a politically embattled King through the eyes of one of his court-members. Authorship is attributed to a Big Seraglio castrate and self-proclaimed "scribe" named Nergal who announces his intention to rewrite and revise the *Babylonian Chronicles*—another incomplete document—early in the text.[††] In the first tablet, Nergal claims that his work is an erratum, and scholars have interpreted this remark to mean that the original manuscript of *The Eunuch* was wedged as a secret and unauthorized addition to the author's copy of the *Babylonian Chronicles*. Yet no such copy of this section of the *Babylonian Chronicles* exists; or, if it does, it has not been found. Nergal's erratum recounts in intimate detail—often, in too intimate detail—the latter years of Nebuchadnezzar II and the unseemly realities behind the official court record. Here the reader will find all the usual suspects: the pomp and pageantry of the Eastern court, powerful priests, incompetent advisors, strange midnight rituals, and the hapless efforts of an aging and impotent King.

Fundamental questions about Henry Poole's reconstruction of the tablets remain unanswered. Little is known about Henry Poole (1961-2008), other than that he graduated from a small Norwegian-American liberal arts college in Minnesota, where he had his first of a series of emotional breakdowns. That he went on to pursue a graduate degree in religious studies at a renowned divinity school in New England, where he incurred a debt totaling well over two hundred thousand dollars, is only a minor footnote to the larger tragedy—some might say farce—of his academic life. After giving up on his dissertation, he toiled at various small jobs, picking up the occasional stint as a lecturer and attending classes in the school of Ancient Near Eastern Studies at his former university. Failing to secure a position in his chosen discipline, and after an unpleasant series of psychological troubles, Poole returned to the Midwest, where he obtained work in a used bookstore in Minneapolis, Minnesota. There he spent his days in long conversations with the clientele, which, according to his unpublished diaries, consisted of would-be poets, unemployed lecturers, and ex-seminarians.

Fate, happily, intervened when the U. S. Army invaded Baghdad in the spring of 2003, and the National Museum of Iraq was sacked. It is believed that in the post-invasion mayhem, *The Eunuch* was among the many antiquities and cuneiform tablets that were stolen and sold on the black market.[4] The extent to which the desecration of the Museum and the subsequent dispersal of its artifacts will impact generations of scholars is a matter of debate, but one thing is indisputable: Henry Poole would never have encountered *The Eunuch* if the government of the United States had not intervened in the affairs of the oldest civilization in the world. Who sold the tablets to whom remains unclear, but it is known that the final buyer was a bookman named K. E. Benson. Fearing prosecution, Benson hid the tablets in his office, where they languished, until one night, during the late shift, they came to the attention of Henry Poole. One can only surmise that here, among the dust and cat litter boxes of a used bookstore, the germ of *The Eunuch* was hatched.

Rejecting both the liberties of the paraphrast and the illusions of total similitude, Henry Poole may have adopted Steiner's notion of "literary enhancement."[5] Given the physical condition of the original text—a collection of twenty-two tablets, severely damaged by time and neglect—he pursued the

4

only methodology available to him, that of "corrective reconstitution." According to Steiner, this "corrective" is latent in the original text, and is an embodying forth of the "elemental energies" of the author, a spirit that can only be captured through emendation and linguistic excess. The fact that Poole realized that this translation method was ideal for expressing the mind of *homo eunuchus* is the subject of another essay.

The editor of the present edition was an old friend of Poole. We walked to junior high school during the cold, dark northern Minnesota winters, arguing about whether or not Bruce Lee's one-inch punch could kill Kwai Chang Caine or whether wasps could dream. Poole admitted reluctantly that they could, and these facts depressed him. Even for a sebaceous-faced adolescent, Poole was possessed of a melancholy and morbid mind, and this affliction, if it can be called such, followed him well into adulthood. Throughout his twenties, Poole's poor mental health interfered with his ability to complete his graduate studies. Moreover, he found the culture of academe to be uncongenial—the experience of which he compared to being strangled in your bed by a polyamorous dwarf who had forgotten the safe word. It goes without saying that over-indulgence in alcohol—as well as intermittent drug use—plagued him during these years, as did the penurious conditions of student life. He lived in a rented room with a hotplate, dined on cans of Dinty Moore, and read the *Upanishads*. Typical fare of the poor and lonely

5

academic. But Poole was not without literary ambition, however truncated by the times in which he lived.

It is now known that Poole's first readers, a small core of family and friends, thought his efforts to translate *The Eunuch* to be an act of a dangerous egotism, another version of the folly that caused him to pursue an advanced degree in the humanities. Admittedly, there were numerous times his friends supported him during these years in the wilderness: lending him a twenty-dollar bill to buy groceries, picking up the beer tab on the rare nights he socialized, and—on one ill-advised night while under the influence of psilocybin—promising to edit the literary project that no one thought he would finish. Yet few would deny his achievement. Poole has wrought a style fit for his elevated subject: the incarnation and withdrawal of a deity—Marduk, the god of the alluvial plain. Regardless of his methodology, it will become apparent to the casual reader that Poole intuited the deeper reservoirs of what can only be called "the eunuchoid mind" and, in the process, achieved a translation that will repel as many readers as it attracts. One might well accuse Poole of puerility, a charge he would no doubt embrace. It is a truism that *The Eunuch* exhibits an adolescent obsession towards human sexuality, but such arguments do little by way of actual criticism of the text. It is the editor's belief that *The Eunuch* embodies the spirit of Archilochus and has its roots deep in an ancient literature whose function can only be described as apotropaic—one designed to ward off evil and stimulate the fertility of the land.

When considered from this point of view, *The Eunuch* is not a piece of pornographic doggerel composed by a dead castrate and translated by a disaffected academic. On the contrary, it is art as magic, a ritual appeasement of the gods.

— Harris Bigg-Wither, editor

Moose Lake Archival Institute
Moose Lake, Minnesota
August 2022

† The term "cuneiform" refers to wedge-shaped characters impressed in tablets of mud or clay and used to write several languages spoken in the Ancient Near East between the Bronze Age and the beginning of the Common Era. For example — 𒀭𒈾𒆕𒌋𒂷𒌨 denotes "Nebuchadnezzar II."

†† Composed between the eighth and third centuries BCE, the *Babylonian Chronicles* are the official record of the acts of the Babylonian kings. Within this series of tablets, the Nebuchadnezzar Chronicle, also known as the Jerusalem Chronicle, is a partial record, for it narrates only the first conquest of Jerusalem, the struggle with Necho II and final subjection of Syria. Presumably, the second half of the narrative has been lost to history. Nergal's account, then, functions as a commentary on this lost text, and thus represents an extraordinary boon for scholars in the field. See Albert Kirk Grayson, *Assyrian and Babylonian Chronicles* (Locust Valley, NY: J. J. Augustin, 1975).

Tablet One –

By the Waters of Babel

I was born in the city of Nineveh, a breech birth. With buttocks forward I came into the world, and life hasn't changed much in my descent towards the House of Death. Even today, at this late hour, when I am allowed out of my cell, I back into the Big Seraglio rump-up to receive the warm and heavy hand of my King. Nebuchadnezzar, habitually uncomfortable in his role as Divine Plowman, likes to place his thick, ringed fingers on my hindquarters, and I can't say I blame him. A eunuch's backside, particularly if it is as large and succulent as mine, carries a potent magic.[1] The King is a lunatic, and our daily ritual seems to have a calming effect on his mood. Note the wedge *seems*. More to the point, a raised posterior is the eunuchoid style—we must always be ready to be ritually mounted by our masters and to ask for the condescension that is our birthright.

My parents never understood me, but they didn't live long enough to hear my complaints. A month after my conception, Mother attempted to abort her pregnancy. On the third day of Nisan, she drank root of moth and offered sacrifice to Moloch, and the hiss of the knife and the scream of the ewe remain imprinted on my prenatal memory. When the moon rose to its apex, she abjured the milk of kids and massaged eliminatory fluids on her stomach, and then, by the waters of Babel, she drew my birth chart and burned it in the fires of Uzumu. All of which, including Saturn, who squeezed himself into the heavens, augured badly for the malignant polyp germinating in her womb. Nothing, an unhappy prophet once lamented, could have prevented my arrival into the city of the plain. It was a difficult birth, I'm told, and Mother bled to death in about three hours.

Father's death, however, was more pedestrian. Swinging his scribal cane as if he were on a battlefield, Father stood just under four cubits, a petrified specimen of an earlier and, my brother would say, more erudite age. Smallpox had left deep gorges in his complexion; short tufts of white hair sprouted from his head. Father compensated for these physical disadvantages with his critical disposition: he was famous for disliking Babylon's most famous poem, of which he was the foremost copyist. A *Gilgamesh*-ian without peer, Father had rendered the poem over three-thousand and forty-two times with full critical apparati. Father was nothing if not critical, and it was said by Bel-uballit that Father's redactions were celebrated for their viciousness, and that his edits were so one-sided as to make the poet look malevolent or idiotic. As a teacher of the Royal Tablet House of Nineveh, Father's pedagogy was equally vicious: Father beat my brother and me when we failed to make our scribal quotas, and he beat us when we made our scribal quotas. Father said that the respect owed to a scribe was less than that owed to a dog, and that he was preparing us for our future. (Whenever I sit at my clay tablets, as I am doing now, I feel the sting of Father's cane upon my back.) My brother and I were at work on our tablets, and Father was in his library, when Nabopolassar's soldiers captured Nineveh. Father died when the walls collapsed around him—hit on the head by the tablet *On Divination*. He never looked up from his beer cup, at least when I was around, and so I doubt he saw it coming.

Summarily deported to Babylon, my brother Uruk and I experienced different fates, alternate destinies: Harpagus castrated me for the King's harem, while Uruk escaped the knife to become chief diviner to the King and augur of Marduk. These are fragments of memories, shards of the past. The story of my deballocking is untypical only insofar as I survived: two out of three boys died on the cutting rack. Gardeners prune an unruly hedge; botanists pinch back a young rose bush; harem scribes expurgate texts for heresy and obscenity. Castrate: "to deprive of the testicles, to emasculate, to geld."

My cell in the Ziggurat where I, Nergal the eunuch, wedge this tablet—in the forty-second year of my Lord's reign—is not as oppressive as one would think. Located in the bowels of the new palace, under the weight of brick and dung, buried in the slag heap of memory, my quarters are cool, dark, and mercifully silent, a place where an old castrate can nap for days without that fool, Bunt, telling him to stand up straight and watch the harem girls. And yet I miss my girls, all three hundred and two of them, clad in their diaphanous linens, gossiping around the foot pools with their soft pigeon breasts and long gazelle legs. I have two windows in my dank hole. One opens out on a courtyard full of emaciated lemon trees, and the other looks upon a bricked wall defaced by graffiti; some crony of Uruk's has misspelled the Sumerian term for eunuch in that unhappy phrase: "The demon curse all nut-less bastards." Even in my imprisonment, locked within the four mud walls of my room, I am surrounded by know-nothings and fools.

At my feet sits a clay water jar, decorated with young boys playing a game of Hounds and Jackals.[2] A small lute, which I play at night to fill the melancholy time before bed, rests in the corner. Alone in my room, what my old friend Chibby calls "the nights" bother me,

21

those empty, anxiety-filled hours, waiting for the final
gurgle of breath that may come at any hour. Death and
his Big Fat Prick are coming for me—and for Babylon.

I am afraid of death.

I am terrified of dying.

Marduk, protect the King!

In the Ugaritic recension of *The Book of the
Sumerian Dead*, the scribe Nim, son of Rod, listed
seventy-two causes of the King's demise: the collapse of
the Bull legions, the anger of the gods, the cowardice of
the Sovereign in battle—the usual qualities and
attributes of royal incompetence delineated in Nim's
predictably cranky style. He wedged with a touch of
condescension that only the practiced eye of a court-
scribe could discern, but Nim usually got things right. I
have witnessed many of Nebuchadnezzar's victories, as
both a slave and a servant of my master, and have tasted
the sweet and bitter fruits of his defeats, but nothing
prepared me for the disappointment that a successful
Babylonian orgy produced. While I was gratified by the
glorious climax of the Festival of the Golden Bull, and
was flattered by my intimate relationship with my Lord;
ultimately, it was merely that: a climax, a half intimacy,
the beginning of our end. However, it must be wedged
that the failures of the King were partially my own.

Depression plagues the middle-aged eunuch
slave-scribe who dares to wedge about the past. We
remember who we were in our youth, these timid, sexless
beings, filled with promise and light, hope and joy, and

we cringe with embarrassment. I recall my satisfaction the first time I held Nebuchadnezzar's staff of the Silver Serpent and recollect my fascination with the harem's rituals and cults: the smell of patchouli and pomegranate, the bird sacrifices at dawn, the room of the green lizards, and the fire pits where reluctant concubines' hands were burned—but such things bore me now, and, were it possible (it is not), I would forget the glory of the peacock feather. We of the royal College of Eunuchs wear bird feathers in our urethras as a privileged sign of our status, and the peacock is the bird traditionally associated with castrates, but only that ass, Chief Eunuch Bunt, is allowed to wear the splendid male plumage. The feather of the male peacock! How luminous its blue-and-green ocelli, how iridescent its green-and-gold erectile train! I must confess that in my youth, I was gripped by a lust to possess it. Lower caste castrates favor the goose or, in some cases, the partridge, but I myself wear, have always worn, the quill of the vulture. Black is a color suitable for all occasions, and the elegance, as well as the reserve it signifies, bestows upon me a great dignity.

By the happy dispensation of the gods, my room smells of mud and erudition. Here I spend my hours lying on my daybed, reading about the worst that has been said, thought, and done in Babylon. In my unnaturally protracted adolescence, I filled my cubby with over a thousand tablets and styli. Messily stacked along one wall, the wedged and lined texts testify to a thwarted scribal ambition: there is a miscellaneous victory stele, an inscription cone of my father's, cylinders of unknown provenance, poorly inscribed bricks, and a rather impressive royal seal. The latter I borrowed and never returned to the King one night when he had typically—all too typically I must wedge—passed out in his own vomit. The seal depicts our Dread Sovereign receiving the decapitated heads of Egyptian swine: the wet, shrunken skulls, the beards matted with blood, the white, pulpy eyes. An unknown scribe wedges somewhere—I believe it is in the magisterial *On Deportation*—that the decapitated head knows that it is a decapitated head: consciousness survives long enough for it to realize its horrible state. Truer wedges were never wedged, of course; the absence of a limb is always keenly felt, particularly at the oddest times. To wit: at this very moment, as I push my stylus in the mud tablet, I experience a twinge in my stumpie, a whispery suggestion of lust; it's not the full bray of the hound, mind you—it's more like a plaintive howl.

O Nabû, give my stylus strength!

I gaze at my reflection in a cracked glass and note with pleasure my large, curved, and aristocratic nose. A gift from my grandfather and his august family line of scribes, astrologers, and diviners. We all have this nose: my father, myself, and that toad, Uruk. In all, I must wedge that I look almost handsome for a member of the neutered class; few castrates—in these dangerous and tumultuous times—make it past their thirtieth year.

14

Yes, there are thick bags under my eyes, filled with fat and grief, and yes, my trunk has thickened appreciably, and, like most eunuchs, I am beardless, and my once vigorous, full head of hair has become patchy and thin— which is unusual, for eunuchs are rarely bald. I have a persistent cough, a sore hip, a bad lung, and, the doctors tell me, a poor heart. My voice, however, is not that high, whiny timbre typical of a castrate, but rather low and throaty, and, I am told, sonorous enough to be that of a singer of poetry. My hands are not as strong as they once were, but my eyes are remarkably keen—surprising, for eunuchs generally have poor eyesight—and I can still wield a stylus.

In the three generations in which the House of Nabû has occupied the Throne of the Golden Bull, Nebuchadnezzar's reputation as a lover has been unprecedented, and I have been forced to watch him indulge every whim and gorge every appetite. The beard[3] has been insatiable. He was and is considered a god. Sexual hagiographies circulating in the streets of Babylon describe the experience of the King's largess as a vale of soul-making. I encountered one of the so-called "sacred" tablets quite by accident one day in the month of Ululu. On an errand for Uruk (he had sent me out for a crow wing to be divined for the razing of Judah), I loitered at a tablet stall on the right bank of the Euphrates, where I picked up a small tablet faintly smelling of mud and dung. It was one of those commonplace, overwritten pseudo-mystery texts that have covered our fair City like locusts during the past decade, one that described in intimate detail the experience of the King's prerogative. The initiate (no doubt an ex-concubine trying to shekel in on her years of service) had wedged: "Our bodies exploded into the stars of heaven, and I felt myself to be part of the shuddering, groaning fecundity of all creation." I paused, impressed by the artless sincerity of the declaration, and reflected on the possible truth of the account. It is rumored among the women at Court that merely being in the King's presence can produce an involuntary vaginal contraction. Long theoretical tablets, ponderously filled with jargon, were written by my brother's scribal hacks to justify such epiphenomena, and I might dismiss such stories as no more than Uruk's Court agitprop had I not seen the King indulge himself, without inhibition, in fifty threesomes, female impersonation, and—to the extent his bad back allowed him—autofellatio.

A eunuch's pleasures, however, are humble compared to those of a king. I delight in food, sleep, reading, and wedging *errata*[4] to tablets, in that order. Oh, the simple life of a eunuch slave-scribe cannot be wedged about, nor can its joys and satisfactions! How can I explain reading and wedging to the uninitiated? *Errata!* It is the work of the gods, the pastime of scholar-kings, and the patient labor of all good eunuch slave-scribes. I enjoy no deeper gratification than commenting on the stylus efforts of other wedgers, noting their obscure allusions, delineating definitions, and, best of all, observing mistakes. I have wedged an erratum on almost all the tablets in my room: words behind words, tablets next to tablets, worlds beside worlds. When I am not sleeping or eating one of Slosh's incomparable roast mutton shanks, I may be found in my cell, stylus in fat hand, wedging observations, noting errors, and carrying on arguments with my tablets.

In regard to genre, I have commented on syllabaries, dictionaries, annuals, conjurations, panegyrics, lamentations, prayers, wills, letters, proverbs, elegies, king lists and chronicles. I have composed a fantastically long footnote to an index of Babylonian and Egyptian tax accounts, written in old temple Sumerian, of which Murkik's was perhaps the most distinguished. I have provided the final word to cuneiform inscriptions of Babylonians who hunted the wild ass on the hills of Jarmuth, starved to death in upper Bactria, and fought the Hurrian beast at Nuzi. I have composed beautifully wedged annotations to Canaanite accounts of prisoners sold from the death pits of Mari, only to be slaughtered in the valley of Mot by the Israelites. I have wedged copious notes on the stele of men who knelt before Marduk in the plains of Anatolia, sacrificed bulls in the Zagros Mountains, and took the heads of their enemies along the Greater Zab. I have rewritten a number of histories of the world, each differing from the others on all the significant facts.

Tablet One

On the floor, next to *The Deluge*, and between a wonderfully rare Aramaic papyrus from Elephantine, lie Tablets I-XXIII of *The Babylonian Chronicles*, dense and forbidding with their promise of tedium and indignation. Widely known as the standard history of our doomed empire, the *Chronicles* narrate the triumphs, but not the tribulations, of our hapless King, Nebuchadnezzar, or "Nebbie," as he is sometimes called by his intimates. Those wedges and lines, composed by my brother and copied down by the most elite scribes in our Tablet House, are lies, of course; much that was officially written about Nebuchadnezzar or, for that matter, Babylon, bears little relation to the reality. Most of it, in fact, is trash, a fantastic political delusion dreamed up by the King's chief diviner, my brother Uruk.

It is the fortieth year of my Lord Nebuchadnezzar's reign, and I sit and watch a cloud of dust roll down the Processional Way, the headland of another sandstorm, the seventh in the past month. Wind from the Zagros mountain scrapes generations of mud off the plains. Swirling clouds of dirt and sand tumble through the City, engulfing temple and palace. Horses rear. Doors and windows slam closed. Rugs and rags are jammed into crevasses. After a brief respite of rain, the drought has returned more virulently than ever. We have lost the battle of water and earth, despite the labors of Enuggi the Irrigator, whose magnificent canals thread through the City. Locusts have decimated our wheat and

18

barley fields, leaving them brown and dead. The desert creeps over the walls, begriming everything and everyone. My room darkens as the storm of grit tumbles by, thundering down alley and road.

The King fails to feed his citizens. The granaries lie empty. Revolt breaks out in the desert. Our survival is a matter of months, weeks, or even days, and the portents are dire. In the past month, a blackbird shadowed my window, a hyena's spine broke apart in my hands, the herbs' magic distilled only bitterness. Can the King survive another year? Ur has collapsed, Sippar has betrayed us, and only Borsippa remains loyal to the throne.

Lighting my lamp, I settle down to a night's work. My musty, tablet-lined room comforts me. I am in the mood for wedging an *erratum*, but I must work swiftly. I take a quick sip of watery beer, sharpen my stylus, and pull the thick mud tablet of Uruk's chronology toward the light, savoring the opportunity to comment on and annotate the undeserving text. It is a squarish piece of mud with about four dozen wedges, tiny triangles, and parallel lines. Heavy in my hand, the tablet feels good, solid, and reliable. This is an illusion. Most of what is written on it will turn out to be rubbish. Unlike Uruk, however, I am not trapped in urgent omen meetings with contentious astrologers or under the financial thumb of venal temple administrators. Beyond the reach and pressures of a panicked King and a fickle, ignorant Court, I am entirely at liberty, free to scratch my ghost balls,[5] free to see the armies gather on the horizon, and free to wedge whatever I damn well please.

Reading the first line of my brother's chronology, I snort with contempt; it is exactly what I had come to expect from him. Narrating a grand religious ritual in which Nebuchadnezzar secured the fertility of Babylon for a thousand years, the tablet is about two hundred wedges too long, and the tone is not quite right either: a tad too confident in its assumptions about Babylonian dominance and its position within the wider Mediterranean political reality. As I scan the first column, my suspicions about my brother's prose are confirmed: *The Babylonian Chronicles* are nothing more than a false scribe abusing himself at the keyhole of life. And now I shall do with Uruk's history what that butcher Harpagus did to me: extirpate its lies, root and branch.

O Moon God, accept my prayer!

Tablet Two –

Climbing the Ziggurat

> In the year of [...], the King paid homage to
> the might of the gods, and (he) remained in Babylon
> offering first fruits and fresh lambs to [...]
> His cries were heard and the City was
> delivered a great victory.
> His might as over-lord was a terror to all.
> Our Lord [...] is without peer in the land.
> (He lays) waste his enemies and their women know no
> end to their lamentations.
>
> —*The Babylonian Chronicles*

Officially, seven major staircases spun up the
Ziggurat, each inlaid with onyx, ivory, and gold, but I
preferred a lonely and little-used back route, which
originated in the castrates' quarters and, while more
toilsome, exhibited a humbler style. Above the entrance

was the carved and bearded head of a bull, and I touched its horns for luck. Placing a foot on the first step, my ankle wincing (eunuchs have weak ankles), I anticipated a nervous ascent.

On that fateful day, now over two decades ago, I brushed away the cobwebs that had appeared overnight with their brittle detritus—the dried thoraxes of flies mixed promiscuously with the exoskeletons of dung beetles—and began my trek up the dark passage. In all, there were seventy-two hundred steps, each named after a Babylonian god, a happy celebration of our former polytheism: Enlil, Ninurta, Marduk, Ea, Nabû, Tammuz—although, what was the point in naming those indifferent bastards? They had never honored the sacrifices of the King's harem scribe nor listened to his cries from the bottom of the Ziggurat—yet each morning before I mounted the stairs, I kept strangling chickens or dripping rat's blood on my sandals. Habits of piety are difficult to break, and dangerous, too. The goddess of love and war, that cunning bitch, Ishtar, resided on the sixty-eighth floor, where I planned on taking a break. One could not climb the Ziggurat without a short respite. Not on eunuch legs.

It took about ten minutes to go around the Ziggurat once, stepping on smooth, worn brick after smooth, worn brick, holding my torch toward the high ceilings. My ascent was slow, spiraling round the building, circling its dark ramparts, rising higher to the penultimate floor—where next week the King would be joined in sacred marriage to his "holy bride."[1] The air was musty, and the walls were cracked with age. Traffic was light on the back staircase. Early on, I encountered a barber, a vendor selling oranges, and a mad, one-eyed Jew ranting about vile figs that cannot be eaten, false prophets, and fire consuming Judah, the usual end-of-time rubbish. The fellow was a strange being, covered in a beautiful robe and with long curls running down his cheeks, and his mouth hardened into a grimace as I passed. Every fifty cubits the staircase would open up to a pandemonium of voices, shadows, and sounds. Merchants hawking dead camel hearts. The swish of a barber's sheers. The infernal noise of a street musician's lute.

While the Ziggurat was revered for its height—at seventy-two floors, it was almost too enormous to describe accurately—few outside of Babylon were aware of its considerable girth. The heavy brown bricks of the tower were dug out of the famous mud pits of the Drudgers, a destitute class of ex-scribes and out-of-work beards who lived south of the City, and who were known for their prodigious capacity for beer drinking. Twisting upward toward the heavens, stacked terraces of mud narrowed into a pockmarked cone, as if they had been designed by a spastic, malevolent child. Blackbirds circled its walls; their cries echoed throughout the galleries. There were scribes in the Tablet House and diviners in the Omnia who theorized that the Ziggurat represented many things: the intersection of the celestial

23

spheres with the wet mud of the wheat field, a symbol of the three hundred and sixty-five days the earth takes to revolve around the sun, the foundation of heaven and earth. But those views were mostly crap. To me, the Ziggurat resembled nothing so much as the venereal limb of a devil.

I wound my way around the circumference like a gnat in the airy spheres of Babylon, buzzing into this gallery and flitting into that cubbyhole. I passed channels of the tax scribes and grain-counters, slipped by the tracts of cattle offices and the department of water works, skulked by the holes of the royal barber and chief courtier, and sneaked around that horrid place of the overseer of worker slaves. The floors were cool. While there was a feeling of metaphysical ascent as I mounted stairwell after stairwell, I knew that was a lie. I was in the middle parts of that catamite, Power—in the dank galleries and sub-galleries of the City's royal infrastructure, which stank of the greed and lust of men.

Up, up the Ziggurat. My legs were tired, my heart was weak. Fissures lined the stairs; some of them were large cracks, some a half cubit in length, that I had to negotiate carefully. Many of the individual bricks were loose, and I had to know which ones might precipitate a fall, so as to avoid them. I had developed a system of counting the faulty steps, memorizing them through a technique I had learned from my father, the eminent scribe, Drab the Indignant. Father always said that if you turned numbers into letters and letters into names, then you could remember the numbers more easily—and all too predictably, my father's theory proved to be true. My acronyms for the dangerous steps up the Ziggurat were numerous. Early on in my climb, ALTAR worked for stairwells two and four, and KNIFE served my purposes nicely on stairwells seven and eight, but for stairwells fourteen through twenty I had nothing—there was no pattern to the crumbling treads and broken risers. I had to lower my torch above each step and move carefully, picking my way up the stairs through the wobbly tower. One wrong step, and a nearsighted eunuch could tumble down the abyss, never to place his stylus in a mud tablet again. Whenever I experienced this fear of falling, there was a twinge of anxiety in my stumpie—that scarred mound of flesh where my loins once reigned.

Weary from my climb, I paused on the fiftieth floor, which was little more than a brothel of merchants pandering their wares: from watered-down beer to a thin-hipped boy. Hippopotami, crocodiles, and snakes were for sale to improve male potency, as were rats' blood to remove pimples and unguents of cedar to heal groin rot. In the far end of the alcove, a group of pilgrims had just come from their ablutions at the Temple, the bull's blood still streaking their faces and hands. A group of young scribes chattered mindlessly next to me, happily oblivious to my presence. One of the imbeciles opened his mouth when I passed, displaying a masticated ball of bread. Another laughed idiotically.

That's when I saw it. Above a beer stall, some fool had scrawled a disgusting pun: a wild slander about the King's organ of regeneration. Etched crudely into the wood beam, the wedges and lines were amateurish, as if they had been composed by one of the illiterate slaves or tower swabbies, whose job was to clean up after pilgrims. Etymologically the phrase derived from a Sumerian pictograph, which roughly translated "the ants no longer stick to the aardvark's tongue,"[2] but its meaning in the original was far more derogatory, much more blasphemous in its intention to ridicule and degrade our holy Sovereign. With the possible exception of Harpagus the Mede, my Lord Nebuchadnezzar was the most vigorous man in Babylon, or at least that was the official line. Harpagus was a formidable enemy of the King, and would, without doubt, use this type of graffiti to his advantage. Was it possible that some execrable slave knew the truth?

Godsdamn Harpagus. Lewd deballocker of boys. Son of priests. The only child of an only child. The Mede was unmovable as only a man with seventy-two Bull Legions at his command could be. It was rumored that he marshaled twenty-five thousand infantrymen from Media to supplement the King's army. His tyranny over the other generals was the thing of which legends were constructed. The Mede possessed a terrible hold over my Lord—not even his mother, Samas-iddina, who had buried six husbands in her day, could make him fawn and cringe, as he did in the run-up to the war on Judah, in so disgusting a manner. Harpagus knew his worth on the market of Babylonian power politics and, when the time was right, would crush the hydra of foolish reform that had recently gripped his fellow members of the Court. If the King failed to generate eight bastards in this calendar cycle, it was all but certain that Harpagus the Mede would benefit handsomely. He knew the Big Beard was weak. He smelled spiritual and political weakness. It was well known that Harpagus believed that Nebuchadnezzar did not possess either the stiff plow or the seed to fertilize the land and restore it to green abundance. That he lusted after the throne of the Golden Bull was common knowledge among the eunuchs of the harem, most of whom he had castrated himself. That he advocated an end both to the King's flailing in the harem and to his ineffectual bachelorhood with a marriage to Princess Amytis of Media—who just happened to be the general's niece—was also a commonplace among scribes and eunuchs of the Tablet House. If that marriage happened and Harpagus became a member of the royal family of Babylon, he would attain a position of great influence in the Court, and if Nebuchadnezzar's fortunes fell too precipitously, perhaps, even become King himself. Then Babylon would wage war like it was supposed to be waged: viciously and without quarter. Eliminate the swine and dog, that was Harpagus's motto.

And yet the treacherous Mede was not wrong. Undoubtedly the weather had been hot and dry. Unbearably so. Our priests and scribes claimed a direct connection between the lack of rain and the King's poor performance in the sack, and I will not deny that it had been a season of overcast skies, humidity, and high temperatures. My tunic always stuck to my chest. My rooms were suffocating, oppressive, dull. There were months and months when it seemed that the clouds were attempting rain but could not complete the act. Every morning, dark cumuli assembled on the horizon and threatened to deluge the City, but invariably nothing happened—and the beards and ladies of the Court were anxious with an anticipation that was never relieved. In the Ziggurat, marketplace, and field, anxiety infected every encounter. Slaves dropped dead at their plows; urchins fainted in alleys; even the camels complained. Bread prices had been allowed to rise to ten and a half shekels, and for the first time in a generation, hunger threatened the City.

Darkness descended from the east. The dying sun twitched in the window. Godsdamn Tek. Uruk's mouse-faced lackey. Two weeks before the New Year's Festival, he had shown up at my room, holding a torch. "What do you want, you stupid boy?" I rasped, heartburn biting my chest. "The most eminent scribe requires your presence in the Omnia," he mumbled, his tiny rodent teeth flashing in the light. Tek's head was about the size of a late-summer melon, and for a moment, I had thought about bashing it on the floor, but we the truncated generally avoid violence, so I merely gave him my iciest smile. "Tell the most eminent scribe, as he calls himself these days, to go fuck himself." Tek spat a thick gob of mucus at my feet and scurried away, the disgusting little brute. I would deal with him later. But the shape and texture of the mucus gave me pause—flaked in black blood and ending precipitously with a ridge—and it signaled, at the very least, some sort of imperial indigestion. Perhaps a larger spasm of misfortune lay in the City's future, something catastrophic that would shake the foundations of my brother's grand ambitions.

Now, while I was almost sure Uruk was aware of what I was doing with the harem tablets—jacking up the bastard numbers, constructing fantastic scenes of pleasure and predation—he had never asked me to wedge blatant forgeries. He had requested that I help the King, and I was helping him. The Ministry of Illegitimacy—that incompetent cabal of priests, astrologers, and eunuchs who presided over our water canals and granaries—was intractable on this point. The numbers had to add up. The numbers had to be correct. Strictly controlling to a beard—they would not even allow carrots or zucchinis around the girls—the Illegitimates had a horror of Things Going Wrong in The Harem, and the threat of failure or betrayal was genuine, for how could one man keep three-hundred or so women—most of them slaves and, moreover, resentful, petulant slaves—satisfied? It was an impossible task, a dangerous task, and they knew it. Nebuchadnezzar had trouble even selecting one girl for the night. When I complained to Uruk, all he would say was "do what you must."

The most eminent scribe! What was it that bothered me about my brother's summons to climb the Ziggurat? His golden stylus? The smugness of his scribal smile? The proud manner in which he wore his robes, which were luxuriously long and embroidered with mauve geometric figures shaped in the figure of the god Nabû? Yes, yes, and yes. Undeniably, Uruk had climbed the Ziggurat. As a second-year scribe, he had published his first monograph *Against Heresies.* And moreover, he put it out on papyrus—just to spite our father Drab. Papyrus![3] That ephemera of ephemera, and the latest fashion of the Tablet House! Without question, the exuberant reception of *Heresies* had led to a promotion to the Omnia where, among the blood and entrails, he fingered the sheep stomach that sent Nebuchadnezzar to war against Egypt and Judah. A year later, my brother read a pimple on the tip of Nebuchadnezzar's nose, a crafty political move that enabled the despot to conquer the Elamites, and Uruk's position was secured, as the feckless scribes in the Tablet House would say.

Without knowing exactly how I got there—time squeezed in upon itself like a lemon when one climbed the Ziggurat—I found myself on the sixty-eighth floor, standing before the harem doors. Pausing more out of duty than respect, I genuflected before a makeshift altar. One of the more fanatical girls (I think it was Anunit), had placed dead flowers—juniper, mulberry, apple, and willow branches—at the entrance, no doubt in the hopes of placating the gods or obviating undue criticism from a harem chronicler. Warning inscriptions were tacked above the entryway, curses against interlopers, promising a lifetime of impotence and frustration to the transgressor. The door of the abode of happiness was composed of broad planes of cedar, overlaid with copper and ornamented with the silver carvings of Ishtar. Her winged figure stood demurely in its perch above the harem entrance in a way that did not quite do justice to her fantastic powers. The stories and rumors about the harem, however, were true: the place vibrated with sexual possibility. Within its walls could be heard the purring of dozens and dozens of girl slaves of all imaginable shapes, colors, and sizes— girls, by the way, who had been deported from a smoldering city or pulled from a burning village. I had breached those walls a number of times, of course, both in my official and unofficial capacities for the King; often my Lord merely wanted my company, as he dipped for his nightly ladle of flesh, tasting the soft carrots and succulent peas of that swollen and richly flavored soup.

The King's harem!

Past the bejeweled entrance, and down a series of narrow halls, resided Madame Grape. The Prodigious

One. She who had birthed Nabopolassar's seventy-two bastards.

Entering Madame Grape's apartment with my head down in mock submission, I twirled my black feather. It was our standard greeting.

"Ha, ha, ha! Nerggie, you better put that feather away. You're going to poke somebody's eye out!"

Old, immense, with the pathos of a former beauty, Madame Grape resembled a shambling, louse-ridden dog. She sat on a bed wrought of bronze, picking her teeth with a short knife. In her day, she had been the concubine of concubines, the sovereign's alpha, but age had seen a considerable diminishment of her allure. The old Ishtarian had ballooned into a three-hundred-pound creature, an immense wrinkle of flesh who now presided over the King's harem. Garish red paint encircled her eyes. Her lips opened and closed like two fat grubs. Many of the girls liked her, but an equal number found her repellant.

"Come here, Nerggie. Come closer to old Grapie, so I can see you." Madame Grape's gaze, as aged as the earth itself, pulled me into her orbit, an atmosphere of old-woman creams and unguents. An encounter with Madame Grape was like drinking a rare wine: sweet, complex, and dangerously potent. My being cowered before her mass, trembled at the thought of her watermelon breasts, which were veined, pale, and imperious. In the uncertain light of evening, she appeared as a huge clay oven—with the smell of soft, warm bread beckoning—and part of me wanted to climb in and die.

"Nerggie, do you know that my oil rations are low? Do you know that we live in near total darkness at night? Be a dear and see if you can get them raised. That old bitch Sammas-iddina receives more oil than I do. In fact, she receives more of everything, and I am sick of it. Sick of it." The rivalry between the Dowager Queen and her husband's old concubine was as strong as ever.

"She never got over his coronation. No, I was the one who curled his beard—with the tongs of Nimrud—and greased his hair with myrrh. He looked splendid. She may have been at the ceremony, but it was me he went home to—that night and every night. Did you know what she said about me last week? I heard it from one of my girls. She said that I am common." As if to demonstrate the soundness of the remark, Madame Grape emitted a long and capacious fart. "That's what I think of Sammas-iddina, ha, ha, oooh, hah!" She cackled and squeezed my leg, not expecting a reply.

"But you don't care about an old woman's problems, or, for that matter, an old woman's gas, do you Nerggie? Oh, by the way, you're in luck. The Swans are about to practice their latest entertainment for the King."

Rolling deftly from her couch, Madame Grape led me to The Bird Room, where a dance was scheduled to take place. Cedar beams spanned the ceiling and three hundred and two blue swallows, embalmed in jars of honey, hung from the rafters on thin wires, under which overfed cats lolled about in sleep. Madame Grape whistled happily as her feet boomed down the halls. As queen of the harem, she was invested with the holiness of the place, and its sacerdotal powers had settled on her immense legs. Marbled with fat, they resembled the two cosmic pillars that held up the world. Her hips rotated like the earth revolving around the sun, pulling me behind her with a force that was as inevitable as it was timeless. Purple and blue linens wrapped around her torso, while her dress, beaded in lapis lazuli, was surprisingly short. With each pounding step, I found my gaze involuntarily inch up the back of her thigh toward the mighty crevice of her massive behind. The whole performance, and it was a performance (the old concubine was a skilled actress), was staged for my benefit. I did not know whether to applaud or run from the theater.

"Girlies! Girlies! Girlies! Come out of your warrens, you little rabbits! We have a special visitor today. We hardly have time to dress and make pretty. Where are you? Come, my lovelies! Nobody's here? Where could they be? They must be in The Booty Room, fitting themselves for the dance. Come, Nerggie!" Madame Grape clapped her hands, and we wound our way through the various holes and sub-holes of the harem, each of them more private than the last. There were innumerable lounges, filled with silk pillows and sturdy wood benches, each of them equipped with a hookah.

We entered the costume room, a sub-gallery that contained the concubine's jewelry: beads, pendants, headbands, breast ornaments, hairpins, armlets, and bangles the girls deployed when entertaining the King. The room was almost as spacious as the Great Hall; there must have been fifty girls milling about the place, picking at garments and fingering blouses, linens, wools, and silks. They were bored, listless, sniffing the goodies like they were stale cheese.

"This is where it all begins, Nerggie. Booty for the booty! Backstage where my babies transform themselves into royal harlots. Look at them, so pale and unremarkable, so stupid; they're really just overgrown children. I wouldn't fuck them, and in my day, I would fuck anything, and often did. But wait, watch, as I transform them into magical birds. Anat! Quit picking at your face. Get over here!"

Anat drifted slowly to the fitting area. A small, morose child with almond eyes, no older than sixteen, she suffered from a fatal disease. There were spots the size of shekels all over her face. She stood shivering before Madame Grape, her breath rasping through her thin lips.

"See those bumps? The poor thing is sick with river fever. She'll be dead in six months. It's a pity. But while she's here, we must use her. There will be no malingerers in my harem. Not while I am still pissing

35

into my piss cup. Which reminds me, hold this, while I help her with her outfit. When your bladder is as weak as mine, you have to take these things everywhere." Madame Grape passed me her piss cup, an elaborately carved chamber pot, depicting that most venerable motif—the destruction of the earth by water.

Pulling Anat in front of a mirror, Madame Grape fussed her hair back over her ears and wiped her lips with a handkerchief. Anat's eyes watered at the ghost she saw in the glazed surface.

She wrapped a linen skirt around Anat's waist "It was stripped off the corpse of a dead matron in Aleppo, and there was hardly any blood on it when it first came in. We'll place these feather bands around her neck, and there she is: a rare bird, ready to be plucked by the King! . . . Well," Madame Grape said, stepping back for a reappraisal, "maybe not. Where is the bead bin? Here it is. Perhaps this bull pendant? No? Too masculine? These were taken at the siege of Tyre. Wait, I know what we'll do." Madame Grape stuck her fist into a large urn and pulled out a handful of beads. "Jewels to gild the lily while she is still alive." The lily looked at her jewels and sighed. Anat knew this was her last time in The Booty Room, and seemed relieved that her duties, as well as her sorrows, would soon be over.

"She will be playing a small part in the entertainment the Swans are putting on for the King next week, and she must look perfect or, at least, as best as she can, the poor dear. Now, as a last touch, we'll put this fine leaf headdress on her. Isn't it a sumptuous piece of work? That's it, girl, now don't you look regal? The headdress previously belonged to the Queen of Mari, who reputedly had her husband poisoned. Anat, straighten your toggle pin, your dress is coming down. I can see your bubbies. Nerggie, I think I am finished. Behold the beauty, Anat. Ready to meet her King!"

I had to admit that Anat, covered in a crown of golden rosettes and silver leaves, and shining forth like the goddess under whom she served, looked good. It was an extraordinary transformation. Death had been painted over by the arts of Madame Grape.

"You see, this is what we do all day. Dress up for the King. But does he come to see us? Does he? Most of the time, he doesn't. It is scandalous. I suppose we should be content with the little he gives us. Come, line up girls. Let's get into our Lamb groups, and do some exercises. We want to look our best for our Lord and master."

Madame Grape clapped her hands, and the girls filed out of The Booty Room. While she drilled the girls through the various tropes of Babylonian harlotry—the Lugubrious Ox, the Ram in the Thicket, and the King's favorite, Shaking the Donkey's Tail, I took a seat on my scribe stool, feeling like a crab under a rock, its pale claws twitching helplessly. The dance preparation was exhausting for the girls, stretching their limbs into strange, ritual contortions not seen outside the heavens. They grunted and groaned, their legs spread and knees bent, their arms arched backward and mouths twisted in feigned passion. The girls seemed tired, or perhaps they were merely anxious in my presence—to me, they resembled a flock of river birds preparing for their winter flight.

After the initial warm-up, Madame Grape had the concubines practice singing "The No Song" to Nebuchadnezzar: a ritual that enticed him into a frenzied state, what my brother called the "fecund mind."

A knowledgeable scribe once wrote that the history of the harem could never be written, yet that was exactly what my brother had asked me to do. The King had not made a bastard in over two years, and Uruk was panicking and perhaps, for the first time in his life, afraid for his job. The Ministry of Illegitimacy was on him about the numbers: production rates, rainfall over square cubits of plain, quarterly grain and barley yields, possibilities of drought and famine, fear of starvation, number of bastards born per annum, etc. And so it was vital for him to produce something tangible, something to get them off his back—or so he claimed in my evaluation a few days ago. And yet, as our priests have long maintained in their hymns and lamentations, the presence of a god cannot be captured in a tablet, and any account of the harem—with its subterranean cults and elaborate subcultures—could be only a partial one. It was nasty and difficult work, this harem thing.

How can a eunuch capture the tedium of a harem's afternoons or the sadness of its evenings? Housing dozens of rooms, the harem was a confusing labyrinth of halls, nooks, and cubbies. Each of the larger rooms was dominated by a different motif: the serpent room contained a thousand vipers that writhed over the rafters (punishment for the reluctant concubine), while the cat room housed a tiger—as a symbol of the harem's importance for the health of the City. He was, alas, old and toothless now, and occasionally I took him out for a walk on the streets of Babylon. And not for nothing was the Big Seraglio called "Big"—there were over ninety-seven spoken languages, fourteen religions, and sixty skirt styles in the harem. Any attempt to capture its texture was impossible. There were cliques, and there were claques, and there were cliques within claques, and claques within cliques. Even my knowledge of the four harem girls I knew best—Madame Grape, Pea, Anunit, and Tutu—was at best fragmentary, accumulated over many years, by cross-checking their stories, one against the others.

Orange and red petals carpeted the floor. Cardamom incense burned from torches, and on the blue tiles stood an ingathering of the first and last fruits of the King's foreign policy. I counted about fifty girls. All were perfumed in balms and anointed with oils, and their smells and odors were as diverse as their origins. Every battle and skirmish of Nebuchadnezzar's bull legions was represented—Carchemish, Nineveh, Kalhu,

Hamath, and Judah—and in each of the girls' faces, Nabû, god of scribes, had wedged a tale of pain and suffering. Although most of them would deny it, the harem girls were all shaken by their deportations, rattled by the mauling of their guards and soldiers, which, to a girl, had been more or less violent. The light infantry beards of Harpagus's First Legion had dragged Medi screaming from her family's burning farm—they slashed her grandmother's throat and left her on the floor of the grain silo where they had hidden; the Mede's siege boys pulled Astarte down the wall of a battlement, breaking both her arms; Eudoxia watched as her parents were hacked to death by the sword beards of the King's Second Bull Legion; and, after the chariots rode through her village and burned its crops, Anunit avoided starvation by eating tree bark and drinking her urine. Pea and her younger sister were enslaved by a gang of spearman of the Second Western Legion and endured the repeated rapes by child soldiers. The stories of the harem girls, and I had heard most of them, were enough to curl your beard, if you had one. It was my task to know the overall stability of the King's concubines, for he liked them madder than a bag of scorpions, which created its own problems. It was difficult to gauge the right emotional temperature for a successful assignation, and I was no longer enjoying my job.

I must wedge a caveat: the sight of big-breasted harem girls, stripping and slapping each other's bottoms, left me cold. It was not the bouncing of their flesh, nor

the red blotches on their backsides that bothered me—
no, I could ignore the water fights, turn a blind eye from
their embraces, even forget their half-naked bodies.
What I objected to was the cretinism of it all. Oh, the
dullness of the harem! I was bored with the bounce, tired
of the supposedly "erotic" and "provocative" situations
the girls provided the King for his edification. It had
become all too predictable. The mind of
Nebuchadnezzar—and sad to wedge, I came to this
knowledge late in my story—was limited to the most
pedestrian sexual tableaux, confined to the most
primitive erotic narratives: "strip, slap, and flop" was
what the girls called this latest obsession, and it was one
that I found most wearisome. I scoffed at the so-called
rigor of the concubine's art and deplored the
consistently low culture of the place. Twenty-five young
women were now repeating the same phrase—"the
beams of your house are made of cedar, and your rafters
are made of fir"—while another set of concubines were
learning how to conceal one portion of their anatomy
only: linen skirts were lifted, bellies partially revealed.
One sacred harlot draped her legs in carnelian beads.
Another wide-eyed creature practiced a vulgar smile, her
chapped lips pushing out toward me and saying, "Does
your dew cover the spring grass?"

  "Time for High Holy Day poses!" called out
Madame Grape. The girls disrobed and assumed what
in the harem was known as the Scuttling Crustacean, a
posture that held, I knew from long experience, a fierce

spell over my Lord. When I looked at Nebuchadnezzar, and it was my job to look, I felt only pity—embroiled as he was in the business of copulating with strange young girls all day. Who would aspire to such a life? Certainly not the first eunuch of the black feather, and yet anything was better than the dreariness of my job and the long, dull days of wedging my harem tablets. Running the numbers on the girl slaves wasn't easy; oh no, recording Nebuchadnezzar's nightly assignation with concubine x or y—or in earlier, better days, tabulating his commingling with concubines x, y, and z—was difficult.

Although I would never admit this to my brother, tracking the King's tastes wasn't easy. The number of girls overwhelmed me. There were tall, skinny girls who shimmered across the harem like the ghosts who dwelt upon the shoals of the Great Underworld, and short, fat girls who sang hymns to Enki in low throaty voices. There were brown-eyed maids who mourned the deaths of their mothers from plague, and green-eyed wonders who saw visions of the end of the world by darkness and fire. There were goddesses who had jumped off the rocks of Sidon, and there were nymphs deported from the siege of Tyre in wooden crates. There were concubines who marched together in iron neck braces from the sack of Kish, girlfriends offered to the temple of Aa, and girl children found abandoned by their families on the necropolis of Ur. There was Mintani of the honey breath and

melancholy eyes; Lirisi, who loved the bad poetry of
Bagoas the eunuch scribe; Candle-wax, who liked to eat
spicy mutton sandwiches in bed; Arret of the lanky legs;
Jip the moralist; Milie the complainer, and Rasp, who
would die later that summer from wet lung. There were
more, of course, many more, too many to track in my
harem tablets, and most of them found my presence
oppressive.

On any given day, there were roughly three
hundred concubines in the harem: this number
fluctuated between twenty and thirty harem girls,
depending on Uruk's deportation numbers, and I had
difficulty knowing who was who—who had bedded the
King, who had not bedded the King, and whom the King
had refused to bed. For example, Siduri of Megiddo—
whose hair was dark and thickly curled, whose eyes were
like the deep green sea, and whose mouth was painted in
the most provocative pigments—had been in the harem
for eighteen months before I had ever heard of her, and
I only came to know her name because Anunit had
mentioned as much, on that one morning she "caught"
me in the undergarment room stealing undergarments—
a bogus claim that I refuted in several tablets. When it
came to the harem, I was horrible with details, which was
a problem, particularly given the fact that my job was
about getting the numbers right. The number of harem
girls was supposed to be organized into a complex
schema designed by Uruk to track the King's production
rates, and this schema charted things such a home city,

hair color, bed-talent, and a host of feminine arcana that would fill encyclopedias. The whole thing was impossible!

There were over two hundred hairstyles—and I was supposed to know which the King liked and didn't like. Anunit wore her hair up in a bun; Tutu wore hers in braids wrapped around her forehead; Shebe shaved her head, while Delphebe never cut her hair—and as far as I knew Nebuchadnezzar never slept with any of those girls. And whom the King slept with on a regular basis was important to my brother. Essential, in fact. Uruk was interested in what he called a harem girl's "point of origin"; he demanded to know what city or town the girls came from, and again, he was insistent that I get this fact right. My brother believed if he could pinpoint the origin of girls attractive to the King (it was a poorly kept secret that few women actually attracted him), he would then know where to send the armies. For example, if, in the month of Sitas, the King achieved a successful assignation with a Syrian or Jew, and a healthy bastard resulted from their union, then to Jerusalem the army would go: as long as I had been in the harem, there was always, always a direct correlation between the King's tastes in concubines and the imperial army's movements—as my chronicle will demonstrate.

O mystery of the King's harem!

The heat in the narrow hall closed in on me, and the dust from the latest storm—one that my brother had failed to predict from his gall-blasted oracles—covered my harem tablets. Crouched on my scribe stool, I watched the Swans practice the Dance of the Two Rivers, a laughably bad re-creation of our creation story in which Marduk slayed the serpent of the waters, and one that I had seen many times. Performing their parts with plausible vigor, the girls made a go at what for them must have been a hopelessly arcane subject. Siduri of Megiddo—O sweet goddess, nightly I dripped wax and sprinkled rosemary on your altars—played the sea serpent, Tiamat, while Eudoxia played Marduk the dragon. It was slow going at first as the girls gestured and buffooned about, and I more or less ignored the preamble with its elaborate disrobing rite, and the various gymnastics performed with long and lithe limbs: yes, I know that my brother would say that there was the power of the god in that, and yes, I know that Chibby would claim that I was buried in denial of my "true" eunuchoid nature, but I remained untouched by their provocations. The clichés simply overwhelmed me: the pantomimes of milk flowing from their breasts, the honey bursting from their loins—who really cared? Certainly not I, Nergal the eunuch, or so I said to myself at the time. Siduri opened her maw to swallow Eudoxia, and the other girls, who played the waves, joined in the action, and before long, the mock fight degenerated into a pseudo-orgy, complete with tongue kisses and breast caresses—an all too obvious interpolation by the harem girls, who were clearly trying to provoke me. It was a new wrinkle in the moldering corpse of harem games, and I confess that the slap and flop of their divine plums did make an impact, although it was a slight one, a stirring around the edges of my stumpie—a sick and searing feeling—and, for a moment, I wanted to find a private place where I could be alone and rub up against a chair.

But I insist that this feeling lasted only a moment, and soon it was the details of the dance that captured my attention. The Swans—Siduri, Annat, Millie, Eudoxia, Gula, Kin, and Nantura—made swimming motions across the room with their blue and red scarves, which I thought was overdone and silly. It was strange, but I couldn't shake the feeling that the girls were trying to entice me, that they were not dancing for Madame Grape so much as they were turning and leaping for a certain eunuch across the room. Often, I would catch one of them looking in my direction. Siduri of Megiddo was the worst of the offenders. Siduri of Megiddo. Brown hair like thistles. Eyes like thorns. Her breath smelled like panther sweat.

Siduri weaved in and among the other girls, pulling at her garments, crawling on her hands and knees, imitating the serpent pursued by a jackal, twisting her neck to avoid capture, twirling her body in my direction with her serpent tail. Moving nimbly through the room, she dispensed wild orchids over the floor, arranging her arms and hands in arcane geometric positions—symbols of Marduk slaying Tiamat in the waters. Now the standard line on the dance was that the earth burst with a cornucopia of milk, beer, and the nectar of bees, and Uruk was always nattering on about how a concubine's power must evoke a pleasurable madness, but I never really understood what he was talking about until I witnessed Siduri practice her dance. She possessed something, a quality I could not put my eunuchoid finger on. It has been divined by our liver men and prophesied by our seers that the appearance of a goddess would purge the harem of its complacencies, and I must wedge that when I saw Siduri dance the Dance of the Seven Swans, I knew that time had come.

Gazing at me knowingly, Siduri danced toward the foot pools, bowing before me, which got a big laugh out of Anunit and Tutu, who supposedly hated her. As she darted her head between my legs like a common garden snake, inching her way up my thighs, she grabbed my tunic and pulled me into the orbit of her flesh. She had three faint freckles on her nose.

"You will be my husband, and I will be your wife," she snarled. "I will let you seize kingship over the wide earth—you will be master, and I will be mistress!" That got a bigger laugh out of Anunit and Tutu. The girls thought it was funny, and it was funny in a cruel way, but I got another of those odd feelings when she said those words to me—a painful tingling where my you-know-what was supposed to be—and she stared at me strangely. While I was rapidly becoming aware of Siduri's harem magic, I was not aware of her ironies— which were manifold in their complexities—and for a

47

moment, I thought she was serious. It was odd, but I stood there, embarrassed before the girls, feeling more vulnerable than usual. Her performance was a success, but the daughter of the moon was not finished with me, oh no, for she raised her leg in a long and slow arabesque, pointing a stubby toe toward the heavens. Her lily—which glowed with the radiance of Ishtar herself—revealed its wonders within half a cubit of my nose. Leering Nergal. I ogled her like a common adolescent.

Tablet Three –

Let Us Build a Tower Whose Top May Reach unto Heaven

After my encounter in the harem—Marduk protect me!—I bounded up the final steps to my brother's diviner's shop. I paused to collect myself and gazed out the window. Located on the seventieth floor of the Ziggurat, the Omnia, as it was officially known, had a fantastic view of the City, one that almost penetrated the heavens. Note the wedge *almost*. A hard wind had picked up from the west. Short bursts whirled across the plains, blowing sand upward toward the vast, extirpating sky. Amid the orange light, I experienced a momentary bout of dread.

On this night, Uruk's fiefdom—that hoary place where our mages and augurs performed their bodings and foretokenings for the King—appeared more spacious than ever. While I had little but distaste for my brother's profession and its daily butcheries, I was not unaware that the Omnia was an impressive place with low, cedar-beam ceilings and ancient papyri charts like "How to Read a Gall Bladder" and "On the Importance of Liver" tacked to the walls. In the back rooms, birds of the air and beasts of the field awoke in their wooden cages, awaiting their fates. The lambs bleated, and the ravens croaked. They knew that an immense sandstorm was about to engulf Babylon, and that the gods were tired of screwing around and were about to demand fresh blood and burnt bone on a sacrifice long overdue.

Wandering around the Omnia, I was struck anew by the officiousness of the place. Its many tablets, detailing monthly prophecies, were judiciously dispatched to every outpost in the empire. Following the promptings of the stumpie, which was expanding and contracting with urgency, I entered the work room. A number of low-level Omnia flunkies were on their dinner-break, slurping up bowls of steaming mutton broth, munching on potato dumplings. One particularly dirty scribe was licking his bowl in a disgusting manner that filled me with an unnamable loathing, and under any other circumstance, I would have retreated to my room for a simple loaf of bread and a side of cheese. But I could not ignore the promptings of the stumpie, whose tractive pull had increased in ferocity. I quickly made my way past the oil diviners, bird augurists, dream readers, and that acme of the Chaldean arts: the scatomants.

They were a wily bunch, the scatomants, and possessed a terrible wisdom—for they insisted upon a divine correspondence between the will of the heavens and the dung of a sheep and believed that the color and texture of goat droppings determined the fate and destiny of men on the alluvial plain.

But we the castrated have our own knowledge!

The stumpie was—with its tender scar tissue and rough mound of hard flesh—more accurate than any snaggle-toothed dung-reader. It was one of the central ironies of my life that my gelding did not, despite what my critics allege, cut me off from the heart of life. On the contrary, my castration produced a clairvoyance in my soul, an inclination towards the prophetic.

Whenever a storm blasted from the west, as it was doing now, and covered the City in its brown clouds, swallowing beard and slave alike, just as the great leviathan of the deep dispatches a school of scuttling fish, the stumpie awoke from its dogmatic slumber. It always began with a slight tingling in my loins, which would turn into a throbbing contraction of muscle tissue and then work its way through my stomach and into my throat, where it would lodge like a bolus of undigested bull meat. My whole being would come alive with the possibilities inherent in things. Liberated from the tyranny of the body's demands, I was free to contemplate its mysteries.

Slipping into my brother's quarters, I ran into that rodent Tek, who was rinsing out the duodenal tract of a pig. I was about to box his ears, when my brother appeared from behind a panel. He was surrounded by Enuggi the Irrigator and Taps the Grainman who bustled about him like worker ants around a bulbous queen. Enuggi ignored me, as was his custom. A talented waterman who comported himself as if he was the author of *Gilgamesh*, Enuggi the Irrigator was an impressive self-promoter who wielded a disproportionate amount of power within the Court. His face was brown, and his hands were gnarled by years of chiseling victory stelae on desert rocks and outcroppings. An ex-army scribe, his booty lists were lessons in sycophancy, although of late he had turned his not inconsiderable energies to the City's vast water works and their relation to the Fecundity Rite.

Taps, however, greeted me with a kindly nod. An irascible, old scribe, Taps the Grainman's central contribution to the world of wedges and lines was a monograph entitled *Dust*, which in turn was followed up by the much acclaimed *More Dust*. Taps was a beard after my own heart. Residing on the twentieth floor of the Ziggurat in a one room cubby, he was responsible for keeping track of the wheat and barley reserves of the City. Three grubby son-scribes worked directly under him—boys from the Tablet House who subsisted on old bread and beer—and they hadn't left the Ziggurat in months. Dear, old Taps. He was a worrier, and lately, he had had much to worry about.

Tablet Three

My brother pretended to ignore me. No doubt he resented my presence at important meetings, although he would never admit such feelings to me. Uruk's silences signaled many things—envy, loathing, disapproval—mostly the negatives. In our youth, we did not agree on anything, other than our mutual antipathy for each other. Politics, religion, the correct length of the stylus, all were areas of bitter contention between us.

Uruk took a papyrus scroll from his tunic and spread it out on the tiles of the Ziggurat. The papyrus scroll was a much-copied fragment of Tablet XXIV of the *Corpus Fecundicum*. Uruk rapped his diviner's stick on the first line: and pronounced the words slowly, "The liver is the foundation of manifold reality." The text was reputed to be an encyclopedia of every variation of chicken bladder, pig intestine, bull stomach, or sheep lung known to the mortal, bearded race. He proceeded to guide the ministers through its salient points. Here were the traces of old-world diviners engaged in predicting the will of the heavens—all of which portended well for Babylon.

"These images before you," Uruk said, pointing to a cancerous stomach, "are not just pictures of animal guts and their abnormalities, but actually they contain within them an echo, or, if you will, a taste and substance of the divine being. And when you examine the images, you will see that our current so-called lack of rain is only a temporary condition. It is a physical situation—which has a spiritual corollary to a larger and more important reality, one in which the waters overflow the riverbanks, and the green wheat covers the valleys in winter."

"Cut the crap, Uruk. Just tell us why you called the meeting." Taps the Grainman stood to his full stooped height, arms crossed over his chest. He was not impressed with Uruk's homily on heaven and earth. He had seen too many droughts in his day to rely on the authority of tablets or, for that matter, sheep intestines, and this hostility registered in a slight hoarseness, as if he had swallowed a spider and was now trying, without success, to cough it up.

"Well, Taps, we are here for what we are always here for: to report on the state of the City. And you, Taps, will do what you always do. You will give your grain report. Good Enuggi will do what he always does. He will provide us with a reading of the water supply. And Nergal—who has an unseemly beer stain on his tunic—will give us the latest from the harem. And then, with your permission, Taps, we will wedge a report for the Ministry of Illegitimacy. Why do we do this, Taps? Because we are committed to the Greater Fecundity, that's why. The King is committed to putting a loaf of bread on the table of every Babylonian household. It's that simple—but the Ministry of Illegitimacy is on our asses right now. They are worried, and some of them accuse us of actively spreading lies about the King. Yes, that's right. There are those in the Ziggurat who believe we are not entirely truthful about the King's vigor and its effect on the crops. But despite their opposition to the Greater Bastardy, things are not as bad as they seem. Not even close. I am confident that things will work out. Things are really pretty good. Did you have bread for breakfast this morning, Taps? A cool cup of water? That's right. Yes and yes to both questions. But you have to be committed, Taps. And if you're not committed, Taps, then, by all means, continue to waste our time with your stupid interruptions."

Duly—though only temporarily—humbled, Taps the Grainman bowed his head. Although he disliked my brother and his dissimulations, he wasn't one to argue with the Haruspex of the Golden Bull, who could have him skinned alive for having an untimely bout of flatulence in the King's presence. Enuggi smirked. He thought Taps to be a reactionary bore, and often told him so.

"Well then, I won't waste, as you say, any more of our time," Taps said, rubbing his pock-marked chin, where a few, sad whiskers of a once fulsome beard remained. "I shall begin with the grain figures from the north of the City. There has been a slight downturn in the production numbers, as I'm sure you are all aware. With the lack of . . . with the precipitation *lessening*, both the wheat and the barley numbers are not what they were last year. But the difference is, again—and I say this with all due respect to the Greater Fecundity—only a slight one. The real differences emerge when we compare the production numbers to five and ten years ago. That's when you can observe the extent of the drought."

"Thank you, Taps, for the history lesson, and although I hate to inform you of the facts, there is no drought, not if you look at the grain numbers going back to the reigns of Esarhaddon and Shamash-shum-ukin. They show—and I believe you will certainly agree with me—that the differences in grain production, which when viewed from the vantage point of a few months or years may seem significant, but when compared to fifty or a hundred years ago, are nugatory."

"What do you suggest we call this then?" Taps had brought in a field sample—a handful of soil—which he squeezed in his fist, the sand and dust sifting to the ground.

Uruk stared at the fallen dirt with a practiced eye. A great and wise bureaucrat, my brother was responsible for implementing the controversial Bastard Laws, which required Nebuchadnezzar to produce the bountiful royal issue of twelve bastards a year. And while this number did not sound particularly impressive, generating twelve bastards a year was not easy. The pressure was enormous for a man in middle age, and our King did not respond well to pressure. It was an unfortunate truism that our Babylonian priesthood had always insisted upon a divine correlation between the number of bastards the Sovereign produced and the general health of our grain fields. For, along with the speed of our chariots and the accuracy of our bowmen, the City's grain stocks constituted the foundation of our dominance within the river valley, a dominance linked— a little too dogmatically in my opinion—to the King's revels.

O Great Nebuchadnezzar!

The agricultural year was a long one, and the King often complained that his yoke was heavy. Under normal circumstances, and given the right conditions— with an annual rainfall of thirty to forty inches and a robust and healthy king—our agricultural successes were the envy of the alluvial valley and appreciably richer than those of the so-called grain producers in the Levant. After the rainy season, teams of plowmen converged on the fields of Babylon, vast tracts of arable land encircling the City that our priests declared to be good. Large oxen pulled the plows from morning to evening. During the month of Nisannu, sweet and succulent onions were brought into the City by the cartload, soon to be followed by lentils, field peas, grass peas, leeks, cucumbers, and radishes. After a week of eating vegetables (I preferred them salted and soaked in vinegar), the farmers slaughtered the lambs for the Festival of the Golden Bull, where the beer and wine would overflow Babylon's cup.

"I don't care what you call it," my brother said, swinging his stick in the air. "But it is not a drought. *It is not a drought.* Enuggi, Taps thinks we are having a *drought.* Tell him he's wrong."

"Well, it's no secret that canal levels are low, dangerously low, as low as they have ever been, in fact," Enuggi replied. "If my calculations are correct, the canals will run dry, if the gods curse us, in six months—or perhaps, if the gods favor us, twelve months."

Enuggi nervously fumbled with his tunic belt, as befitted a bureaucrat in charge of the City water in the midst of a catastrophic drought. His father had been a general in Nabopolassar's army, which had sacked my beloved Nineveh, and was a genuine hero in the Babylonian ascendancy, as it was then called. After the conquest of Assyria, his father had become wealthy, as had most of the high command. He had spent the rest of his days—in all, there were about sixty of them before the King had him strangled—in great dissipation. Enuggi's father had never forgiven him for going into the Tablet House, and Enuggi finished his report with a perfunctory bow, moving like a man who was uncomfortable in his own beard, anxiously touching his curls.

"Twelve months," scoffed Taps the Grainman. "That's assuming Harpagus has the patience to wait that long." It was well known that the general planned to launch a violent *coup* if the King could not fulfill his role as Divine Plowman. Most of the eunuchs in the harem hoped that Harpagus would usurp the King's prerogative and end the drought once and for all with his formidable battering ram. Why this was so, I cannot explain, but it was. I never fanned such hope because it seemed to me that if the Mede went through with what he had so often drunkenly promised, we would all be tossed off the Ziggurat.

My brother smacked the *Corpus Fecundicum* again with his diviner's stick. He had dealt with Taps's unseemly interjection concerning the Median danger by pretending that Taps had not spoken at all. He instead turned back to Enuggi and dismissed the Irrigator with a wave of his hand, as he placed an index finger on his nose and shot a line of crusty, green mucus onto the tiles to punctuate the point he was about to make. A swarm of ants descended on the hard, little orbs, carrying them away for their evening dinner.

"If I'm hearing you clearly, Enuggi, and I think I'm hearing you clearly, we are almost out of water. And this is affecting our grain production, how?"

"Well, bread prices have doubled from last year," Enuggi replied evenly. "One and a half shekels per loaf."

"Yes, but no one is exactly starving, are they?" Uruk asked.

"There have been no fatalities yet," said Enuggi," except for the hundred or so Amorites who were trampled to death in the bread riots last week."

"That's good news, gentlemen," said Uruk. "We must never forget to focus on the larger picture. Drought, famine, death: these are merely the simple facts of life. We've had three droughts in the past fifty years, but there is no hard evidence that we are in the midst of another. *No hard evidence.* Usually, if there is a drought, ten to fifteen thousand die. We haven't seen any deaths that can attributed to the lack of rain. Taps, how many starved to death during the last drought? I assume you have the figures on that."

"One hundred and fifty thousand."

"One hundred and fifty thousand is hardly a figure to complain about. Particularly when one realizes that when droughts come—and I'm not saying we are in a drought; rather, I'm just making a theoretical point—they are cleansing. Droughts actually help purge the system of its excesses. Famines, too, are curative. Come talk to me when the City's deaths reach three hundred and fifty thousand. Then we can talk about drought, but until then, let's stop the grumbling. It's boring. It's also blasphemous."

Enuggi exchanged a woolly glance with Taps, who gestured in my direction with a ringed forefinger. I nodded. We were all in agreement: My brother was not to be dissuaded.

"Now, of course," Uruk continued in the nasal accents of the Tablet House, "I am aware that things are not where they should be. We need rain. Nobody is arguing with you on that front. Much will depend on the King's performance in the next two ritual cycles. We need some bastards. And I am expecting more bastards. The King is expecting bastards. The Ministry of Illegitimacy, as you know, is expecting bastards."

"What condition is the King in these days? Is the Big Beard strong enough for the Bull?" It was Taps again, whose eyes muddied in the late-afternoon light. No doubt he had heard about the King's unfortunate habit in the Hanging Gardens. Nebuchadnezzar had taken to a strange ritual involving ropes and trees and lewd drawings, and it was a practice that I, fearing for my survival, hid from my brother. Taps's question, however, was simple and direct. He turned toward me, shuffled a step forward and crooked a hairy ear in my direction.

"Yes, Nergal, please tell us about the King," Uruk commanded. "Is he up for the Bull?"

"He's good, he's good." I said.

"How's his surfeiting?" Uruk persisted.

"Surfeiting? He's surfeited all right. Quite … surfeit."

"His drunkenness?"

"Overall, I would say excellent. He's drunk most of the time."

There were murmurs of approval and much beard-stroking from Uruk and Enuggi. Taps shook his head incredulously, and, for a moment, I thought he was going to strike me for my impudence.

"What about his vigor?" asked Taps.

"The beard is strong, as I believe, my harem tablets will indicate."

"Excellent," said Uruk. "What about his prodigious appetite?"

"Holding steady, as they say. His appetite is more than adequately prodigious."

"And how are his bastard numbers?" asked Taps with a menace that surprised me.

"Um, yeah, well, yes," I stammered. "His numbers are, well, yes, they are, as we say, respectable. Very respectable. His numbers are uncommonly respectable."

"Go ahead, Nergal, read your harem tablet for Enuggi and Taps," Uruk instructed me. "Disabuse these beards of their lack of faith."

I pulled out Bastard Tablet XVII, which Tablet House critics have called "important" and "magisterial," and I read in my best harem voice:

"On the last half-moon, Nebuchadnezzar arrived in the harem at nightfall. Concubine Pea vigorously fellated the King. Nebuchadnezzar ordered an impromptu feast and consumed an entire ox. The month of Kislev has been most propitious. The King plowed the furrows of seventeen concubines. There were fourteen pregnancies to record. Only three stillbirths. A good sign."

"That will be enough Nergal," Uruk advised. "And there you have it, gentlemen, straight from the Sovereign's harem scribe. The King is fit and ready for the Grand Seeding. The signs, as you see, are solid. If things go as expected at the Ritual of the Golden Bull, the rains will come, and the Harvest will be bountiful. It will be a cinch."

It will be a cinch.

Before I descended the seventy-two hundred steps of the Ziggurat, I walked over to the rampart wall of the mammoth structure—its crenellated sills and broad views were the best in Babylon—and yet despite its impressive vista, my mood darkened. Seventy-two floors below me, the men and women of our great City appeared as beetles on a dung heap, crawling over the latest chimera of pleasure and burrowing into the next illusion that promised relief from the chronic fecklessness of their lives. The Euphrates, dark and forbidding, wound around the Temple of Esagila, past the old palace, through the Samas Gate, only to pass silently into the desert plains. In the distance, the buzzing was getting louder: thousands of dispossessed farmers had overrun the City and were decimating our wheat and barley reserves like locusts. Twenty thousand hungry beards barking for their share of Babylon's loaf marched through the streets, while beating pots with sticks, chanting slogans, and demanding redress. Soon, possibly very soon, they would scale the Tower walls and cut our throats in our sheets.

It was common knowledge that it took seven seconds for a body to reach the ground from the top of the Ziggurat. Last spring, during the time of Egipar, the neuties in the College of Eunuchs timed the fall of my predecessor, the harem scribe Bel-u-ball-it who had *misrepresented the facts* on his harem tablets, to quote Uruk's official report. Bel-u-ball-it's appendages flapped helplessly as he spun downward, growing visibly larger to witnesses on the ground, until his fatal splat on the bricks—in an unsavory pudding of organs, blood, and bone. Seven seconds in all.

Tablet Four –

His Might as Over-lord Was a Terror to All

> [Pe]ople of both sexes, donkeys, camels, [cattle]
> and small [cattle] without number I brought to
> Babylon.
> —*The Babylonian Chronicles*

Sitting stoutly on his royal toilet, Nebuchadnezzar, my Lord and Master, emitted a bat-squeak of gas from his primary fundament. He was constipated. Again. Yet the discharge was clearly a sign of hope, a cautious portent of the weightier act. He looked up from his hands, his thin lips touching his beak-like nose and sighed, "Oh Nerggie, what does Uruk want from me? What? What?" he cried in his smooth Babylonian accent. We were in his magnificent privy, and I could hear the murmur of birds outside the window.

"How's your stomach, my Lord? Is the pressure bad?"

"Ooooohhhh!" whimpered the King. "Could you press down on my tummy again, Nerggie? I need it bad tonight."

I leaned forward and placed each of my palms on the sides of his massive, mottled stomach, pressing down on the two beating veins that crossed his abdomen like thin and nervous lizards. Nebuchadnezzar's belly—round and quivering in the torchlight—was most holy, and its bulk was the result of calibrated gluttony, one that feasted on the choicest of fatty pig shank, the aged lamb chop, and the marbled beef steak. I admired it immensely.

He moaned softly, motioning me with his hand to move closer. "Wait, I think something happened. Yes, wait, would you check? Please look, Nerggie. I think something happened. Did anything happen?"

I peered into the cavernousness of the royal vessel. It was dark, and I could see no evidence of royal effort, no excretal deposit from he who sat upon the Throne of the Winged Bull. A quick sniff was all that was needed.

"Nothing happened, my Lord."

"Could you tickle my back again, please Nerggie?" he said, his brown eyes pleading like a child for his mother's breast.

Since the onset of drought, I had begun spending the night with my Lord, sleeping in his over-sized bed, tickling his back. The King was afraid of the dark and feared the silence of the night. Too many voices, he said, of the dead, of the fallen, of the men, women, and children he had put to the sword in the cities he had de-bricked and the towns he had razed. It was well known that his victims were innumerable as the stars in heaven. Moreover, he didn't like sleeping alone. The harem girls were out of the question. Too much pressure. Too much expectation. It wasn't easy being the Divine Plowman in a time of severe drought, and he felt his limitations keenly.

The King's bachelor apartments consisted of several large, over-decorated rooms, jammed with second- and third-rate booty taken during his first military campaigns in the West. Indeed, his rooms were a peculiar combination of blood and bad taste, kitsch and killing, the gauche and the garrote. Like the concubines in his harem, each piece of woeful furniture told the story of pillage and siege. Evidence of the King's dominion was all around him. for Numerous basalt monoliths and rock stelae proclaimed his divinity. I STORMED AND CONQUERED announced one. I SLEW WITH THE SWORD, said another.

To make him forget his troubles, I would tell him the latest foolish joke that was going around the College of Eunuchs—"what is the most useless thing on a woman? A eunuch"—which unfortunately made him only more depressed. He would wander up and down the torch-lit halls of his apartment, muttering profanities, whining about his bad luck. Our priests believed him to be stricken with a strange melancholy; Uruk suspected witchcraft by foreign elements in the Court. But I knew that was untrue. Nebuchadnezzar, a beard coddled by the gods and deluded by luxury, had awakened to the essential misery of being a divinity on earth. He had become aware of his every failure—the botched slaughter of the Carians in the deserts of Anatolia, his chronic inability to fill the Bastard Hall, his poor judgment in choosing counselors. Was he regretting his choice of Uruk as augur of Marduk? I believe he was. I believe he was.

In the early days of his malaise, I was not unaware that I had been overly critical of my Master, and perhaps harder still on my brother, Uruk. The King could be charmingly vulnerable, when he didn't have a mutton leg in his mouth and an amphora of beer in the crook of his arm. But I could afford this generosity of spirit, because my "life situation," to quote my predecessor, Bel-u-ball-it, was directly opposed to the poor beard sitting without hope of a credible bowel movement.

"What does he want from me? What?" he cried.

My brother didn't think I had the balls to break it to him (I didn't), and I admit my abbreviated state made me pause, yet in a moment of sympathy, I told my Lord about Uruk's latest scheme to stimulate the agrarian economy, but I dumbed it down, leaving out the tendentiously theoretical parts that I knew would only annoy him. He nodded and said, "Yes, yes, go on."

A cool wind blew through the apartment, one that I took to be a favorable portent. The Court slaves, six naked and ritually bald attendants who were quick with fan and tankard of beer, stared dumbly into space. I had a habit of ignoring slaves who were not eunuchs, but one of them—that malcontent, Flea, I think his name was, who once corrected my reading of the poem, *Enuma Elish*, accusing me of bungling the rhythm—motioned to me to speed up my explanation to the King, for he was tired of standing, the shirker. So I slowed it down. I began simply at first, and then with greater conceptual rigor, explained the details to Nebuchadnezzar.

Uruk's plan, provisionally entitled *Fecundity, Hope, and Mud*, was to institute a city-wide *imitatione Nebuchadnezzi*, a command to all good Babylonians within the parameters of our blue-glazed bricked walls, to base their lives—their beliefs, thoughts, actions—on the King's. *He* would be the gold brick standard for all human behavior, the God whom our great horde of shopkeepers and wheat merchants would aspire to emulate. It wasn't a bad plan, such as it was. Uruk hoped that if he could convince the average beard that he had a right, nay a duty, to fight and fornicate with impunity, he might achieve his larger vision—of an empire dedicated to profligacy, of a grand imperium of doing *whatever one wanted, whenever one wanted*. His ideas were not particularly profound nor complicated, but they were totalizing, and this, I think, constituted their chief strength. A Ziggurat in every city, a Starman on every corner. A permanent brothel-state. Again, and I must stress this point, *it sounded like a good idea at the time*, but—and I believe, apart from Taps the Grainman, I was the only one in the mighty Tower who was fully aware of this—it would never work, precisely because the King was out of his mind. He was the soft underbelly of the Imperial Dragon, that smooth, baby-scaled spot ripe for the sword, but try telling *that* to my brother.

"Oh, Nerggie, my whole life has been a failure; everything has turned to shit."

"Not everything, my Lord," I said, trying to cheer him up.

"That's not funny. You know what I mean." He shimmied his back so I would remember to caress above the hallowed crevasse.

The poor beard had finally realized that there was more pain in life than gladness. He had become obsessed with time's fatal scythe. He moaned about his weight gain—in the last year, he had thickened like a toad—and he complained about his receding hairline.

Apart from his "agricultural difficulties" (I believe that was the euphemism of the week), it was his constipation that bothered him the most. My Lord's irregularity in this regard was so complete, so comprehensive, that not a single excretion, not a sole elimination, not a singular effusion nor partial voidance, not even a tight little turd had been recorded in the past three weeks by yours truly, and, frankly, I was worried.

"I'm being smashed to black bits!" he whined with his customary exaggeration.

I began to tickle his lower back—that soft mound of flesh, full of baby down and located above his impressively large buttocks. He slept for a while, purring like kitten.

He startled awake. "That's it for tonight," he said dejectedly after his nap. I can't sit on the winged lion cub any longer. It's time to go to the harem again. I suppose I will have to choose a girl tonight. How I hate decisions."

Although none of the King's ministers and priests in the Court of the Great-Winged Bullman would admit it, the King was fucked out. In this way, I suppose, Nebuchadnezzar's problems in the harem were symptomatic of the agricultural and religious crisis—drought had blighted the wheat fields, and cankerworms had devoured our barley reserves. A habitual melancholic, a soul who labored perpetually under Saturn, the King elicited smiles of pity from the eunuchs along the wall whenever he entered the harem. Our priests and astrologers referred to the King's condition as "The Big Slump," and there was a great deal of beard-wringing and tunic-twisting in the Ministry of Illegitimacy. It was godsdamn depressing. I hate to wedge this, but it was true: in the eighth year of his reign, his reputation as the Divine Plowman deflated before our eyes, and then came the situation with Siduri of Megiddo. Incarnation of Ishtar and queen of the daggers. She only made things worse.

It would be wrong to suggest that Nebuchadnezzar was abandoned by his ministers and priests who consulted the livers and stars each time he had a blocked sinus passage or an irregular bowel movement. They tried to help him. They really did. Anodynes were offered. Ablutions given. Cures were proffered and discarded. Uruk scrambled from *The Fecundity Tablets* to Enuggi the Irrigator for advice about the royal condition, but nothing seemed to work. Nothing.

I find it difficult to piece together accurately all the attempts to revive the Sovereign, for the total mass of the written record overwhelms the faithful eunuch scribe.

On my desk, in front of my beer cup, and next to my dirty feet on the floor, are small mountains of tablets, composed in all the languages of the empire: old temple Sumerian, late Ugaritic, low Akkadian, high Hebrew, demotic Egyptian, and a bastardized version of Elamitic spoken in the swamp regions of that country—

and most of these are more or less readable. The record of this sad tale is available to any beard who wants to read it. Here is my record of the Court's efforts to save the King in the eighteenth year of his reign, a combination of political folly and metaphysical despair, and I present it now for posterity with a heaviness in my heart. May the infernal gods have mercy on Babylon.

Under the half-moon of the twelfth heaven, Nebuchadnezzar drank the blood of a thousand bulls, spilling the liquid over his bloated belly and hairless thighs. That was in the month of Shabattu when Uruk accused me of sedition and poisoning the King's relationship with Siduri of Megiddo. But those entirely baseless attacks on my character were parried by my work on the bastard tablets, and, in the month of Addaru, I was spared the knifey fate of Taps the Grainman.

Later that year, the King bathed in the blood of warriors slain in battle, but every beard in the Big Seraglio knew they were four garden-variety sectarians taken from the City jail: idolaters and apostates who were hewn hip and thigh and burned in the Valley of Shem. As Lord of Light and Dark, Nebuchadnezzar devoured raw goat testicles, and as Scourge of the Plain, he swallowed pig bollocks the size of babies' heads. In his incarnation as Anubis, he ingested sheep rounds, but when he assumed the mantle of Nudimmud, he ate the balls of a three-headed dog.

During the month of Nisannu, incense was burned under the genitals of the Divine Plowman, while he wore a gonad of a beer-drinking donkey around his neck. This revived him temporarily, and he sired a lone bastard, a scrawny pup who later died of water in his lungs in the third moon of the year of the Invasion of Judah. Yet the Sovereign's Great Awakening, as it was later called in the Ministry of Illegitimacy, was no more than a brief and drool-filled hiccup in a long night of imperial indigestion. At the suggestion of Bunt, my Lord ate the bark of the Great Cedar of Lebanon and snorted the wings of a dung beetle. But nothing happened.

On a war party in the mountains of Zagros, he was given a hallucinogenic enema from a one-armed priest that left him wandering the steppes for a week, spitting and groaning. Again, nothing.

I made numerous compilations of Nebuchadnezzar's efforts in the harem during this period, and most of them have been lost or destroyed. In the months of Simannu and Du'uzu, the King tied concubines up in pseudo-slave-auctions, and when that yielded nothing, the concubines tied him up in pseudo-palace-revolts. He abducted virgins. He abducted wives. He imported amputees. He exported eunuchs (for a time I was with the army, tabulating decapitated hands and numbering severed noses for general Harpagus's field reports). He attempted statuephilia, violating a sculpture of Ishtar in the Temple of Nippur twice a day for a week. He practiced self-mutilation, making tiny incisions across his doughy chest. He degraded his lovers and was degraded by them. During the month of Abu, the King staged his own death and masturbated over his mock corpse.

During the months of Ululu, Tasritu, and Arahsamna, much toil was devoted to the King's member of regeneration—*holy, holy is the Lord*—in an effort to enlarge mass and enhance tactile gratification. Priests modified his C—k by inserting pins in its tip, and when that failed to regenerate his spirit, astrologers sewed chicken bells, stones of ivory, gold triangles, and shells of azure into its shaft—swelling the divine member to untold proportions.

Now a brief wedge about the King's C—k. (May the gods strike me down for the liberty in which I am about to indulge, but in the six months that followed Uruk's meeting on the drought in the Omnia, I became quite familiar with the said instrument.) No mortal or scribe is supposed to make a direct reference to the King's C—k: there were laws for how and when a harem eunuch referred to the King's C—k. Uruk simply referred to the King's C—k as "the wedge" or "the line," while the eunuchs in the College of Eunuchs called it "the wedge and line." The King's C—k was a sign of the ineffable, a symbol of the divine, and it could not be captured in language.

I was told by a reliable source (a cupbearer who was later strangled in Judah) that Uruk engaged a witch to cut the tendon of said sacred instrument, which caused it to hang forward, thereby giving the appearance of greater length—not that it appeared any longer to me. It was relayed to me by Siduri, who said she heard it from Bunt (although I have never confirmed her story): the King, in a fit of pique, ordered the Court butcher to cut his foreskin off and then, before it healed, demanded that the royal hood be restored. In *The Fecundity Tablets*, winds are symbolic,[1] and a soft north wind blew without result when Nebuchadnezzar had a nipple pierced and his Scrotum tattooed. Bull men branded Nebuchadnezzar's chest and marked his abdomen to impart fertility. Cock rings—made from goat's eyelids—were embraced and abandoned. The King drank cups of blood and semen. The King employed flatuphiles. The King embraced frottage. And nothing happened. Nothing.

My brother blamed me.

Tablet Five –

The Festival of the Golden Bull

Marduk, the mighty Bull,
          embraced his concubine Ishtar
He marched through the Valley and […]
Bread and water he provided the m[ultitude]

—*The Babylonian Chronicles*

"We shall eat until we vomit" had been the motto for the Festival of the Golden Bull[1] for as long as I could remember, and the feast that night exceeded the expectations of all but the most gluttonous. Torches flared from the walls, lending a contented glow to the sweaty, red-faced exertions of the eaters. Smiling slaves bustled in and out of doorways, clearing emptied plates and presenting new courses amid the murmured approval of the eaters. A stooped servant staggered beneath a platter heaped with peaches, while his tattoo-covered assistant trudged across the Hall, carrying a serving tray of two-hundred deviled sheep kidneys. Thus far the Court had dined on eleven roast oxen and a half-dozen other dishes: sweet mutton, red goat, pickled sheep's liver, goose giblets, chicken feet, and hoof-of-bull marinated in a creamy leek sauce. The hour was still early, however, and the real delicacies lay ahead: ox stomach soup served in gilded swan's heads, poached river fish, and blood-thickened lamb shanks. And then, after the digestion wines, Slosh's royal entrée, which was usually a rare dish such as roast African rhinoceros or braised songbirds in spiced soup. One year a whole camel had been roasted over a fire with its slave rider—dipped in a batter of breadcrumbs, parsley, and sesame oil—still sitting on its hump. It had been over a decade since Slosh had made this dish, and the eunuchs of Babylon still spoke of Roast Camel Rider in hushed tones of reverence and awe.

Twenty-four feasting tables filled the Great Hall. Long accustomed to these affairs, the eunuchs along the wall endured the gastronomical exertions of their masters with a spirit that was equal part pleasure and pain. Moil, Chibby, and I—we made an unhappy trinity— stood behind the first table, watching men and women stuff and gorge their way through four hours of heavy eating.

"Harpagus the Mede's doing a marvelous job with that bull bone, I think," said Moil thoughtfully, pulling at a stray piece of wool on his tunic. "When you consider the pressure he is under. Now that he has settled the score with Elam, the Illegitimates hope he will shore up the Babylonian presence in the West."

"He's nothing but a thug," rasped Chibby. "A thug with no table manners."

Licking his fingers carefully, Harpagus the Mede reached for another bull bone from his plate and slapped a wide-eyed lady-in-waiting on her backside. She bit off a chunk of bread and made a lewd gesture with her mouth.

"Yes, but he's a thug with great numbers," said Moil. "He's killing the numbers." If the College of Eunuchs had a Gilgamesh of the gelded, a Lord of Dullness leading the castrates up and over the wall of boredom, it was Moil. Early in his life—he hadn't been castrated until he was seventeen, which gave him a decidedly more masculine and bearded appearance—he had studied with the proverb men in Philistia. From these withered and dung-smeared ascetics, he'd learned the rudiments of magic, astrology, and divination. Yet to me, Moil was little more than a tablet of commonplaces, an anthology of cant, a summary of all that passed for brains in Babylon. He was also the most officious castrate I had ever known.[2]

"I wish I were dead," said Chibby.

"Bunt believes the King to be healthy again," said Moil. "That's at least some good news. I'm looking forward to a successful seeding tonight, aren't you Chibby? Last year," continued Moil, ignoring the disdain on Chibby's face, "General Harpagus brought over a thousand cedar-and-gold boxes for the King from the campaign in Lebanon, and that's not even mentioning the five thousand cattle and six hundred sheep. What about all those beautiful prostitutes he dedicated to the Temple of Ishtar, and what about the girls he practically gave to the royal harem? What were there, sixty or so? If we had a legion of Harpaguses, our problems with the drought would be over. The beard makes a contribution. There's no denying it."

"Look at all that grease on his beard," said Chibby. "That man disgusts me."

Clad in the russet leather and blue wools of his imperial armor, Harpagus the Mede surveyed the room with the contempt of a man who regularly put whole villages to the sword. Harpagus the Mede. Lord of Deportation. Castrator of Boys. Commander of the King's Bull Legions. He had not aged much since the day he deballocked me in the basement of the Ziggurat, ushering me into a perpetual agony of desire—with its soft, sallow flesh and eternal peach fuzz on the chin. Harpagus munched on his beef bone, lost in the transport of fat, salt, and gristle, although perhaps he dreamed about his latest victory in the fields of Carchemish, where he had left twenty thousand of his soldiers lying face down in the marshes. He spat on the floor and fingered the castration clamp around his neck. The clamp was a long, thin shearing knife with an ivory head shaped in the form of a horned goat. I still felt its cold, iron grip around my loins. Indeed, Harpagus had snipped the plums off of most of the neuties in the Great Hall: Moil and myself, of course, but also Nook, Stub, and Bagoas, who stood along the opposite wall, greedily watching the feasters now spooning buttery quail porridge into their mouths.

Time and space prohibit me from wedging a full account of the Festival of the Golden Bull, but let me remark that the usual orgy-goers were present and accounted for that night—aristocrats mostly, the courtiers and ministers of Nebuchadnezzar's Court, princes of the realm, ladies of the Dowager Queen, as well as the odd priest and scribe. There were also three dozen courtesans, prostitutes, and harlots lounging about the Hall, and it was they who would make merry over the Bull of Heaven's haunch later in the evening.

Sitting on a daybed was the fair-haired lady Belit, a Court matron of minor status. She was dressed in the amber silks and linens befitting a woman of her class, and on her head sat a diadem of small rubies. She scanned the room, and her smile hardened into envy. Although she possessed the right conversational skills of a Babylonian lady, she was not as beautiful or smart as her archrival Gula the Assyrian. Belit, however, was a formidable intriguer of the old school. Pear-shaped.

81

Bitchy. Constitutionally unhappy with her surroundings. I was confident that one day, with the right lover, she would penetrate the musky inner folds of Court power. Currently, she was sleeping with the King's cupbearer, Nabu-zer-ibni. As the King's cupbearer, Nabu-zer-ibni was perhaps the least important beard in the King's ministry, but he was also one of the City's great libertines. His eyes widened as he watched Mummu the Harlot bite into an enormous apple. Nabu-zer-ibni lusted after her openly, much to the aggravation of lady Belit, who dug her nails into his bony thighs.

There were another half dozen Court lackeys, just out of earshot of the proceedings, but frankly, I find them too repulsive to describe. All were present. All were waiting on the King to roll the rock of ritual orgy up the hill.

Chibby snorted with disapproval when the majordomo wheeled out a roast boar on a cart. It was a large, obese creature who had been fattened on the King's barley in the stalls of Adab, and one that had slept in Slosh's own bed for six months. Blackened by Slosh's hot fires and fiercely spiced with pepper, the roast boar elicited the predictable *oohs* and *ahhs* from the eunuchs along the wall. The majordomo steadied the highly seasoned roast by pressing a large carving stick in the topmost bone, so that its juices overflowed its marbled banks. He carefully and swiftly carved up the snout, tail, and trotters first, giving these savory delicacies to Harpagus the Mede. As the general placed a trotter in his mouth, sucking the flesh through his teeth, Chibby sighed deeply.

"I can hardly bear it when he smacks his lips like that," he said. "It's sickening."

The old eunuch watched members of the Court carefully when they were at plate, observing gluttony, appraising food greed. He noted when Hanunu the merchant stuffed a bundle of figs into his mouth awkwardly and marked when Pharnabasus the Persian slurped his pigeon soup too loudly. Chibby's keen ability to hear the beards' feasting was the central torment of his life: knives scraping bone to free a tasty bit of marrow, throats clearing after ingesting a fatty joint of mutton, sneezes provoked by over-peppered porridge. Nothing at a feast was lost on the old castrate. Admittedly, listening to the beards feed and fornicate was thankless work, but it was Chibby's constant need to disparage them, his desperate urge to criticize his betters that I found so tiresome, though I kept my feelings to myself. He was quick to find fault with unorthodox attitudes and to perceive moral weakness in a eunuch who had nothing negative to say about the New Year's rite.

"The bastard can't stop eating. Something is wrong with him," said Chibby, eyeing the Mede. Tall and spindly-legged, Chibby resembled a dead cactus in a dead land.

"It's going to be a great orgy," Moil gasped. "I can feel it. The feast is starting out magnificently."

"These new orgies are crap; that's what they are," said Chibby. "They're crap." With his cane, the old eunuch pointed to a dendrophile copulating with a knotty hole in one of the King's potted orange trees. "Look at that beard. In my day, he would have been thrown off the Ziggurat for that kind of thing. And look at those neuties standing next to the wall. They don't know how to behave at an orgy anymore. Things are going to shit. Godsdamn Stub. Good-for-nothing Nook.

"So, you liked the old orgies?" said Moil.

"No, the old orgies were crap, too," said Chibby, sighing again.

Across the room, the two bulbous testicles of Nabu-zer-ibni swung back and forth, slapping the ample bottom of the lady Belit. It was the first coupling of the night, and usually the eunuchs along the wall noted this fact with a snigger and a leer, but Nabu-zer-ibni was a wily beard, lifting Belit's skirt before the digestion wines had been served. And Belit seemed to be enjoying it, salaciously declaiming the usual pieties of "oh no, oh no, oh no," but you never knew. Babylonian ladies said all sorts of things, and I was struck by the way the top of her teeth bit into her lips, which were chapped from the sandstorm that had engulfed the City all week. She seemed in pain, or what approximated pain. Nabu-zer-ibni's testicles were unusually long and wrinkled—even for a cupbearer—like a pair of turtle heads that had stewed for a week too long in one of Slosh's marinades.

To the untrained ear, the slapping was dull and monotonous, but it provided a rhythmic counterpoint to the music that floated from the far end of the room.

Goodly Nabu-zer-ibni. Ibby, as he was known to his drinking mates. Nobody would accuse him of not doing his bit to help my brother's program for the Greater Fecundity—that cuddly political baby Uruk liked to bathe in the unguents of Ishtar and swaddle in the soft wools of Marduk. Nabu-zer-ibni had just finished up with lady Belit, dispatching her with an all too predictable whack on her bottom. He now gazed about the smoke-filled room, looking for the next gazelle to take down. As the King's cupbearer, Nabu-zer-ibni was perhaps the most lecherous man in a lecherous City and, given the City's political climate, was prospering fulsomely. In the past year and a half, he had reputedly given Babylon eight bastards, and this, even more than the fact he was the King's cupbearer, explained his presence in the Great Hall. Tall, big-nosed, and with a repugnant leer, Nabu-zer-ibni resembled a degenerate camel, and, somehow, he used his grotesque physical appearance to great advantage.

My stomach rumbled with hunger as I watched, with a modicum of interest, a minor drama playout on a pile of silk pillows. One of the lesser temple priestesses was attempting to placate the anger of her boyfriend, a court ululator named Allamu, who was a decent beard, but until recently knew nothing of her many infidelities. Huddled in a corner, they were fighting, or I thought they were fighting, because they whispered in that tense voice couples use in public when they really wanted to strangle each other with a garrote. I couldn't hear what they were saying, although from the gossip of the Court, I could guess. The priestess was having what from all accounts was a passionate affair with the majordomo, Silik-mu-lu-dug, for the past year and a half, or that's what Bunt told me, and it had reached that culminating point where the newness and pleasure had worn thin, and something had to be done. They'd been banging each other silly—in the palace, temples, and stairwells of the Ziggurat. She felt guilty, and some this guilt registered on her face as enthusiasm, that bogus intimacy you put on for the person you are betraying. She touched Allamu's arm, scratched behind his head with her long fingernails, chatted to him about his favorite music— Allamu was obsessed with a rare form of Sumerian flute hymns. I sympathized with her. She felt bad, but for whatever reason, wasn't willing to give up the majordomo and was forced to live with her betrayal. Yet when she wiggled her bottom at Allamu, all I could think of was that pot of Slosh's oyster-pepper soup that was waiting for me at the end of the night.

"Do you think the King will successfully copulate with the holy bride tonight?" Chibby asked, while scratching a spider bite on the back of his neck.

"He'd better," said Moil. "The Illegitimates will have plenty to say about it if he doesn't. I must say the eating and drinking rites have gone amazingly well. Now it's up to him. Not that I'm worried. I'm not. The King has my full confidence."

"How many bastards were born last year," I asked, wondering how much Chibby and Moil knew about the truth of the King's condition. Our condition.

"Well, there's debate about that," said Chibby.

"I heard there were four born," said Moil. "I suppose that suggests a permanent decline in overall productivity rates, what with the lack of rain, and there is a lot of negative talk in the College of Eunuchs, but it's just talk. Four bastards per year, while not ideal, is not the end of the world."

Chibby shook his head and gestured toward the ululator, Allamu, who was now aggressively paddling the priestess with a cedar cane. It appeared the unhappy couple had made up or settled whatever difficulties they were having.

"Look at them. He's hitting her pretty hard, and she is blubbering like it's the end of the world. But I wonder? It's all so godsdamned predictable and depressing. What's the point?"

Allamu spanked the priestess with real force, reddening her buttocks with each swing of his stick, causing her pendulous breasts to slap together in the most vulgar manner. He struck her bottom again, and the priestess's screams sounded like a small mouse running from a hungry cat.

"I don't suspect you know what I'm talking about," said Chibby, turning to face me. "Why would you? You're still young. Moreover, you have a good position in the Big Seraglio." Chibby shifted his weight, uncomfortable in his role as melancholic castrate at an orgy of beards.

"There are many in Court who feel as you do," I said."

"Do you think so? I'm not so sure. I mean look at those eunuchs along the wall. Bit, Grub, Stub, Bagoas. Gods, they're pathetic. So fat and feckless. Fucking castrates, they're all the same. Counting the hours until the orgy is over and they can get their hands on a half-eaten chicken wing. Do know what Grub said to me the other day when I caught him pulling the meat off of a wing that had been thrown to the floor?"

"No idea," I said.

"One of the concubines, I think it was Mater, had tossed the chicken wing over the table, and he picked the wing up and snuck off to the cupboard room. That's where I saw him, gnawing on the thing. It disgusted me, and I told him so. 'That's no way for a eunuch to behave. There's no dignity in that.' But do you know what he said? He told me that if he'd be willing to eat a concubine's pussy, he'd gladly eat the food off her plate any day, no matter what its condition. Can you believe that? What a vile thing to say. Grub has never eaten pussy in his life. Never will, either. Am I boring you?"

"Not at all. I find your general good spirits heartening," I said.

Ham the Grammarian was now stroking the lettuce box of Nanshe, a sacred prostitute from the Temple. He was deploying a technique I had never seen before, a kind of over-and-under-motion that was hard to describe. Nanshe was a grumpy wench who had been pulled mute from a poorly camouflaged hiding pit in a cattle raid about five years ago. Ham was the King's tablet man and a fool. The pair coupled vigorously for about a minute, maybe a minute and a half. Wrapping her immense legs around Ham's equally immense buttocks, she ground her hips into his loins, arching her back, leaning on her hands and arms, jamming her pelvis into his belly, a mound of flesh that consumed about six heaping plates of deep-fried pig's intestines a day. Alas, given the weight of the participants, such an athletic position could not be sustained. Now Ham was a hungry tiger in the bush; now Nanshe was on her hands and knees like an anxious fawn, hands reaching back between her legs, cupping Ham's testicles, which were shaved and goose-bumped, and a tad on the smallish size. Sadly, eunuchs spend a lot of time at an orgy noticing the gonads of our bearded masters, commenting on their size and shape, comparing, contrasting, and judging for length and weight. It was a hobby of ours, and when we were genuinely bored, we would count the undescended testicles in the room. That night there were four.

Tablet Five
[Lacuna: tablet damaged:
unknown number of lines lost.]

[...] I may have erred when I grabbed the Dragon's tail. Overwhelmed by the death-haunted acts of my fellow Babylonians and subsequent untimely reflections they caused me, and also, I confess, by the amphora of beer I chugged, I overreacted to the King's impotence. It will be obvious to anyone who reads this tablet that I am a far less credulous eunuch than I was in the days before the invasion of Judah, when I sat on my buttocks for twelve hours a day, wedging and lining the pleasures of my bearded betters, and I hope my newly regenerate attitude will be appreciated by my Lord and King.

May the Great Winged Bullman live forever!

I will send thee to the land of no return, said the Queen of Time. Twenty-five years of war and siege, twenty-five years of mourning for the concubine who haunts my dreams (chiefly by not appearing in them), I was not completely of the King's party. Back in the callow days of my so-called youth, when I lacked all ambition for myself, I had a tendency toward skepticism, doubting earthly prodigies and heavenly signs in equal measure, laughing at a quivering bile duct, scoffing at a shooting star with same amount of contempt I usually reserved for Moil or Tek. The royal lion hunt disgusted me, the healing in the desert made me want to puke. I despised the harem and loathed the orgy. Unhappy with my job, I found fault with others. What can I wedge? We Babylonians have so little by the way of immortality insurance, so little help in fighting the struggle against oblivion, that the full weight of drowning time rests on our sagging flesh, on our not-so-furtive pleasures of table and orgy. Only an idiot would quibble with a few hours of forgetfulness in the arms of a drunken and semi-attractive stranger. The cold void over my head, the infinite stretch of sand around the Ziggurat, the emptiness of my heart—all speak to this general condition.

On the whole, however, I must wedge that the quality of Babylon's orgies had declined during my tenure as harem scribe. Even before the drought and bread riots—partly caused by my brother's risible, agricultural reforms, which have deserved the scorn heaped upon them—Nebuchadnezzar's debauches were little more than exercises in aristocratic bombast and bad taste. They were loud and pretentious affairs, where the best beers flowed like the Euphrates after the rains, and elaborate dishes were served by well-oiled and perfumed slaves who had been marked for execution (seven red dots tattooed below the left eye). Part of the problem was that there were too many of them, and because of my brother's reforms, there were more. Many more. On the half moon, beefy kitchen slaves hauled braised carcasses of roast mutton or bull up the Ziggurat, where they were served on elaborate platters of silver and gold, and the next day, piles of bones, gnawed clean by a sickly general or drunk lady-in-waiting, were thrown off the Tower, spinning downward like the autumnal leaves onto the banks of the river. Concubines slipped in and among the guests, dispensing their usual cup of charm and anguish. Old men flogged themselves with long reed whips. Young men stabbed their prodigious members into sobbing matrons whose husbands sat in the corners wildly abusing themselves. It was always, always the same old stuff: the breast bondage, the incest games, the coprophilia, etc., etc. Oh, the tedium! For harem eunuchs, the dullness of orgies cannot be expressed in wedges and lines, but invariably, all the beards had a "great time" and found the evening to be "amazing."

[Lacuna: tablet damaged:
approximately sixty lines lost.]

It was as if my boredom had conjured a spirit, for the King, Nebuchadnezzar, Lord of the Four Rims, appeared in the Great Hall. Standing modestly before the Court, he held a lion cub in his arms, gently stroking its whiskers, smiling his nervous half-smile. I knew immediately that we were in trouble. Wearing his multi-horned triple tiara, my Lord seemed more wall-eyed than usual, if that were possible. Then the lion cub urinated on my Lord's tunic: yellow on gold, which was a bad sign.

I placed a half-shekel under my tongue for luck and waited. The King hesitated in the door, caressing the cat's whiskers, seemingly unaware of the piss stain spreading on his tunic. He nodded at the assembly of orgiasts: the drunk beards, courtiers, and courtesans, who had all scrambled from their debaucheries to prostrate themselves before him, the hypocrites. They lay like salted mackerel at the bottom of a fish barrel. I knew their resentments and jealousies better than they did themselves. All of them, if they examined their sooty hearts, were hoping he would fail in his attempt to make a bastard tonight, and why this was so is difficult to explain, but it was so.

Statues of lion-bodied men with curled beards glared down from the walls, and the air smelled of the great river that wound through our City. I whispered a prayer to the goddess—*Holy Lady, giver of life, protect my Lord from the wind demon!*—but my anxiety was nearly unbearable. When the trumpets blasted, I knelt and touched my forehead to the cold floor. Raising the staff of the red serpent high above his head, that loathsome priest Bi-Reed called out: "Make way for Nebuchadnezzar! Lord of the Four Rims!"

My Lord approached the altar with uncharacteristic brusqueness, dropping the cat, which wisely scrambled out of the Hall. Strewn with flowers and covered in wax, the altar stood in the northwest quadrant of the Great Hall, and above its arch was the great figure of Fecundity herself, carved in gold and shining with rubies. The goddess of love had many names—Iskur, Nin-anna, and Astarte—but all good

Babylonians bowed humbly before her round womb and pumpkin-sized breasts. As my Lord made his way down the center lane of the Great Hall, suppliants and ministers competed to catch his eye or touch the fringe of his skirt. Iron Rod of Marduk. He Who Hunted the Wild Ass.

Let me wedge that Nebuchadnezzar looked and behaved exactly as one would think a Winged Bullman who was considered a god all of his life would behave, that is, if the god-man was a balding drunk frequently troubled by constipation. Dressed in his ceremonial linens, he wore his once-thick beard curled and oiled in the Assyrian style. He possessed the neck of an emaciated pig and the body of a pregnant cow. His eyes were bloodshot with fatigue. His nose resembled a half-moon pocked with lesions and scarred with acne. Syphilis? Probably.

Nebuchadnezzar touched his gold breastplate and touched it again. Anxious King. Walking past the groveling members of the Court, Nebuchadnezzar surveyed the room. I counted ten rows of raised posteriors, two hundred buttocks: all undoubtedly had been heavily powdered and perfumed for the festivities of the evening. Enuggi the Irrigator bowed his head piously. Madame Grape, whose allure had dominated the late King, grinned. She leaned forward from her perch, her lizard eyes blinking, her generous cleavage closing like the doors of the underworld. The Ministry of Illegitimacy—or what was left of it, poor Taps the

Grainman had fallen early in a drinking game—knelt before the King. As Nebuchadnezzar paused before Harpagus, he condescended to place his hand on the general's muscular bottom, signaling the red-faced soldier to rise. The Mede stood proudly. It was only to be expected that the other three ministers—the Dowager Samas-iddina, Bunt the chief eunuch, and Enuggi the Irrigator—would receive this condescension, but he merely waved his hand. A palpable slight.

Holding his royal whip, Nebuchadnezzar strolled over the rumps of the lesser aristocracy, acknowledging their ritual chants of "Great King, Mighty Lord." He muttered a profanity to himself, and his black eyes narrowed at the largeness of the crowd assembled before him.

The King was in the center of the Hall now. He pulled a silk cord around his waist, loosening all his linens. With the exception of his doughy chest, which was covered under a pectoral plate emblazoned with a gold falcon, the King was naked, and as a naked beard, he was understandably uncomfortable standing before two hundred drunk Babylonians. The Divine Sun. He had changed during his sixteen years on the throne. He had become more pomegranate-shaped, and his belly sagged with greater weight than it had since the last Festival of the Golden Bull. I thought I had caught his eye, but couldn't be sure. As his trusted eunuch, I occupied a small but dangerous point on his inner circle, and he always acknowledged my presence before he penetrated one of the temple priestesses for the ritual marriage. Always.

There was a moment of silence, and the Court prayed aloud for the King's strength, as all members lifted their hands to the heavens. The incantation lasted two minutes, and the air thickened with the heat. The prayer was dull: it was the usual thing about the King's incarnation in the form of a rampant bull, the typical bloated oratory that my brother wedged and lined for ritual occasions.

At the altar, the "bride," Siduri of Megiddo, greeted our Lord; she was a last minute replacement arranged by Uruk, the clever beard. It was a commonplace that Ishtar was the ablest of the gods, and from the manner in which she stood on the altar—like the bejeweled finger of fate—I knew that Siduri was the ablest of the King's concubines.

Siduri offered the King a twig of rosemary, while bowing low. The Court shouted, "With the cut of His plow He created the sea!"

Examining her round figure—thick legs, wide, childbearing hips—I detected Uruk's preferences at work, for the priest within him favored the numinous powers of a barley-fed beauty. "To ward off evil," he said.

The King's hands shook as he approached his bride, and thin lines of worry formed around his temples. My brother checked his figures: noting the moon and stars. My Lord's breasts jiggled womanishly.

Sad to wedge, but I always thought Nebuchadnezzar to be an unattractive beard, and middle age had not served him well. Thick black hairs sprouted from his nose and ears. Innumerable warts and moles dotted his back, chest, arms, and neck. He smiled apologetically.

"O, who will plow my vulva?" Siduri asked the heavens.

"O lady, the King will plow it for you," replied the Court.

"Plow my vulva, man of my heart!" she cried.

Kneeling before Nebuchadnezzar—eye level with the Sovereign's massive wrinkled scrotum—Siduri offered him a libation cup upon which the figure of a dog-king had been carved. Accepting the offering, the King poured the contents of the cup on the floor, where the wine spread into a tiny maroon sea, which his real-life and wolfish hound rushed to lap up. Whether at work or play, and from a legitimate fear of poison, the King always had his dogs taste his food and drink. Splashing the wine on Uruk's sandals, the animal wagged its tail happily. At least he was unaware of the pressure the King was under.

"I have my spice," intoned Nebuchadnezzar.

"Many rivers cannot quench my thirst," said Siduri, spreading apart her legs like a butcher parting a pair of smoked hams hanging in the marketplace.

The music picked up its mournful tune. Moil held his breath. Chibby yawned. With one or two tentative thrusts, the Holy Bridegroom mounted the

Holy Bride. The drummer beat out a faster beat, and the King picked up his rhythm—one, two, three more thrusts. But, inexplicably, my Lord stopped. Leaning over his bride, hanging his head, he sucked wind, his chest heaving as he gasped loudly. The Great Hall went silent. Nebuchadnezzar's whole body had slumped almost immediately upon contact with the great priestess. It was like watching the juice drain out of a large and ripe tomato.

However, Siduri was savvy enough to hide Nebuchadnezzar's—how shall I wedge this?—lack of certitude. Moaning softly, she displayed her manicured fingernails to advantage as her hands fluttered up and down the King's back. She spoke words of encouragement. She spoke words of love. He was her Lord, her Mighty Farmer, her Great Husband. And she was his lusty maiden, his sweet consort. In the furrow of her vulva, the King's plow would seed the land.

The beards and ladies leaned forward in anticipation of my Lord's humiliation. And Nebuchadnezzar glanced down at his flagging staff and despaired. Yes—I am not ashamed to wedge the line— the poor beard despaired. Raising his head, my Lord looked at me, and—regardless of what Moil alleges— caught the eye of his favorite eunuch for a second time, grimacing in supplication. I nodded encouragement. My King shrugged.

Lying before him like a lamb before the knife, Siduri whispered suggestively to the King. I was too far away to hear what she said, but it was obvious that he liked what he heard, and he responded enthusiastically. He pulled her toward him by grabbing her hips. She laughed and slapped his face, and he didn't seem to mind a bit. Indeed, he made love to Siduri with a sensitivity that surprised me, and I was struck by the passion of the act. The King entered her slowly, easing himself into her with a sigh of relief. He was gentle as he lay on top of her. Fearful of crushing her, he held himself up on one arm as he caressed her hair, cheek and neck with his hand. His buttocks strained and contracted with each movement. Groaning like a young deer in rut, for a brief moment, I actually thought he was going to finish the job. It was rare for the Big Beard to transcend the purely physical act, but he was experiencing something like real feeling with the concubine. He was tearing up—the sentimental fool—pushing his face into hers, whispering, "I need this, I need this."

I have had a number of years to reflect on what happened that night, too many, as a matter of fact, and my thoughts are well-marinated in regret, but it's a regret that is seasoned with my own particular kind of knowledge. How does one explain a mediocre love affair? Describe the meeting of two individuals who decide on a whim to bring down an empire? Was it two pneumatic waves that crashed together under the moon and stars? Or a case of one soul impressing itself on the innermost parts of another soul? No and no. It is my humble opinion that the King's infatuation for the girl from Megiddo lay in the nexus between dream and desire, a fatal meeting between a fatty slice of beef and a hunk of baked bread, all of which was slathered in Slosh's famous pepper sauce. That's it. Of course, neither Siduri nor the King possessed what I would call the supernormal faculties of a eunuch; they did not understand what happened to them that night. For that, they would need a third party: a harem slave with a stylus and a dose of late empire melancholy. To wit: Siduri had awakened the King from his undogmatic slumber, and it would be my role to explain it to her.

The ritual consummation, then. Siduri, for her part, played along gamely with the King's attentions, encircling his hips with her thick thighs, a gesture that was done completely by the tablet. Nebuchadnezzar's kisses, however, were too long and labored, it seemed to me, but it was a fair enough performance, as far as these things go, and a great improvement on last year's disaster. It was percolating along, until Siduri ventured a remark about a stray freckle on a technically unmentionable place. Nebuchadnezzar cursed loudly. No soul within or without the harem was supposed to make a direct statement about the King's holy instrument—*glory, glory be to the Lord*—it was an interdiction that none dared violate. Not even Uruk could get away with it. There were edicts and decrees wedged about this stuff. It was bad form. It was worse luck. It was also blasphemous. I closed my eyes and waited for the Ziggurat to implode.

"A little help here!" Nebuchadnezzar shouted imperiously.

I looked at my brother and shook my head. Uruk bared his camel teeth.

"A little help here!" my Lord again implored.

Uruk made a fist with his diviner's hand and shook it up and down. I knew what he was asking for and hesitated. My brother nodded his head again, this time more vigorously. I ignored him. Sagacious haruspex. It was highly improbable that he had ever had to insert his physical person into the King's ritual function at a New Year's orgy, but he was more than happy to have a eunuch-slave scribe do the job. However, I was not unaware of the importance of the King's request. The prospects of a successful seeding were, to say the least, ambiguous. The Bull must gambol with the lamb, as the prophet said. Something had to be done.

"A little help here!"

Placing my stylus and tablets on the floor, I tip-toed to the divine couple and stood for a moment over the King. His nose reddened appreciably.

"Do you think I'm kidding? Let's go," he ordered.

"Holy Is the Lord. Your Rank Lustiness is Great Indeed," I replied in the formal address of eunuch-scribe for his King.

Nebuchadnezzar had requested—for all to hear—the Three-Legged Jackal, a delicate and dangerous operation of mutual obligation between master and slave with a long and unfortunate history in the Big Seraglio. It has been alleged that I did not care for my brother and therefore desired the Festival of the Golden Bull to fail, and while those charges have been answered, and answered most definitively, I will wedge this: Ibbatum the eunuch, a castrate of great ability and extensive learning, and reportedly a master of the Three-Legged Jackal, did not live past twenty-four. He fumbled during an important assignation with the King's favorite during the month of Du'uzu in the year three of my Lord's reign. Some say he was starved to death on a rock.

It is difficult to describe the sexual act without degenerating into pornography, or worse, sentimentality, and so I will limit the following account to the essentials. Nebuchadnezzar, erudite and lofty in the field of love, turned his head toward me. He grinned without the least suggestion of embarrassment.

"For the gods' sake," he said again.

"Thy Voluptuousness is the Strength and Foundation of Babylon, my Lord," I whispered hoarsely.

The King hovered over Siduri, whose breasts flattened on either side of her rib-cage like two of Slosh's deflated egg soufflés (which were light, creamy, with just a touch of leek butter). Leaning forward, I extended first my right arm and then my left, sliding them along Nebuchadnezzar's immense belly, grabbing the base of his holy member—*how excellent is Thy Name in all*

Earth!—with both hands, thus initiating the Three-Legged Jackal. This move had to be done carefully, because if one showed any disrespect to the King's efforts, one would be felled by the chthonic forces of dread earth, or worse, ripped apart by a mob of rabid priests and scribes. Holding the Sovereign's most reverend instrument tightly—*Thou art the glory of Babylon!*—I watched it inflate to its proper and most sacred size. I said a short prayer of thanks:

> *Let your heart rejoice,*
> *Let your spirits be happy,*
> *I will swell large as a dog!*

Let it be wedged that there is an art to the Three-Legged Jackal: a eunuch must neither grip the King's blessed tool—*holy, holy is Thy Name!*—too hard, and thereby damage my Lord's *membrum virile*, nor hold on to the staff of Adad—*great is our Lord Nebuchadnezzar, He can move mountains!*—too loosely, and thereby defeat the whole purpose of the technique. It was a game for a natural moderate, and my trick was to hold it tightly in the beginning and then loosen it periodically, timing my movements to those of the King. There were those in the College of Eunuchs who assumed that the King's Plow—*my strength, my rock!*—would kill any eunuch who dared to approach its magnificence. But they were wrong. It felt like a skewer of undercooked chicken.

"Thank you, Nerggie."

And then the King—with the help of his favorite eunuch-slave-scribe—proceeded to make love to Siduri of Megiddo, and the act went, more or less, as expected. The Divine Bull commenced with a few thrusts into the ready loins of the concubine, and Siduri, blessed harlot, responded like the true priestess of Ishtar that she was. She welcomed him heartily, her eyes rolling backward into her skull. She rocked up and down upon the altar. It was a better than an adequate performance, but then she reached up and cupped the King's testicles with her patchouli-scented palms—and, for a blessed moment—our hands touched. It was a quick touch, but I felt a slight tingle of fire pass through my limbs. Her green eyes met mine and held my gaze as I melted into what can only be described as ecstasy. I almost lost my grip. My being vibrated in this pleasant burn, as My Lord Nebuchadnezzar pounded away on the poor girl. Later that tingle of fire turned into a funeral pyre as high as the temple of Marduk, and nearly consumed my being, but for now it was nothing short of divine. I thought: tonight is the first and quite possibly the last time that I will make love to a woman. I was wrong, of course, horribly wrong.

O Siduri!

The happiest moments of my life were spent as I held on to the King's member—O, *Wrath of Humbaba!* [3] —and my hand would graze your chubby legs, your puffy stomach, your chapped lips. Dear, sweet

Siduri! In your arms, I found rest from the burden of climbing the Ziggurat. Your soft brown curls shook gently under our gentle and not-so-gentle ministrations. You possessed a birthmark on the back of your left thigh that resembled a walnut. Your hands trembled as you held the King's arms. Your eyes sparkled when you cried out, "O Enhil, without you, the beasts would not want to copulate!"

O Siduri!

The initial action, if I may call it that, lasted about five minutes. After his tentative opening, the Big Beard was back in good form, switching to his middle game, a variation of the Aardvark and the Anthill, which I never had much confidence in. Stout-hearted Nebuchadnezzar! With every push of the King's buttocks, I was wrenched forward into the depths of Siduri. Kneeling next to my Lord, I held on tightly to his sacred plow—*Holy, Holy is the Divine Bull*—for the Kingdom depended upon it. But then the King started to improvise, as he performed a series of moves with his hips with which I was unfamiliar. My forearms were jerked behind my back, and I almost lost hold, but I soon recovered my grip on the Royal Sword—*Wondrous Art Thy Powers*—although I must wedge that it was as slippery as a treacherous eel. The pain in my wrists was acute, but I did not care, for nothing mattered more than a successful insemination, or that was the official line. I closed my eyes to see if I could penetrate through the unseen realities that hovered over

105

my actions—the invisible presence of Ishtar and her train of demi-goddesses, demons, and spirits who presided over Holy Copulation—but I saw nothing.

A City of Bastards! To this end, I remained faithful. As the pain became more unbearable, I sang to myself the old song about the bar-maid, a song, by the way, that our father, Drab the Indignant, used to sing when he was in his cups:

> My wool is lettuce and he will water it,[4]
> My mound is box-lettuce and he will water it,
> And touch the dubdub bird in its hole!

As I half-hummed and half-chanted this song, Siduri smiled. She recognized the ditty; it was a great favorite among the harem girls, and, as a token of thanks, perhaps, she placed a foot on my chest. Pushing against my sternum for leverage—for the King was sweating profusely now—the touch of her foot sent waves of anguished pleasure through my limbs. I nearly wept with gratitude. The experience had the fierceness and clarity of a hallucination. It was lucid madness, blessed lunacy. I knew, absolutely so, that I had been touched by the goddess. Ishtar herself had manifested.

To Nergal the eunuch!

Paradoxes abounded. Despite her reputation as queen of the harem, I always judged Siduri to be a "B+" in the looks department—and, obviously, she possessed more than the average concubine's guile and treachery, as her promiscuous history of love suggests—but when I looked at her big, calloused foot on my chest, I swooned. Yes, I "swooned," godsdamn it, and I am not embarrassed to wedge such a cliché, particularly after what happened. There was no other word to describe this experience but as a revealing—an opening out of spirit to spirit, flesh to flesh. *My heart unbudded like a wildflower during the spring rains.* These were the phrases that I used at the time. What more can I wedge?

When her dirty, rough, adorable foot touched my chest, color turned into sound, and sound into color. I felt an exhilaration that can only be comparable to falling off a Ziggurat. Time stopped, and the Great Hall struck me not as an empty symbol of the King's failures, a painful reminder of all that was wrong with Babylon, but it buzzed with possibility, became pregnant again with all that was good about being alive, all that was good about living, if that makes sense. A tear descended my cheek, and landed on Siduri's sublimely fat thigh, and within this tear, I was convinced that I was looking at an entire world, our world, as a matter of fact, and it was good. Ovoid and translucent, within its prismatic walls there shimmered a tiny City set on two rivers where beards and eunuchs and harem girls happily went about the gods' business. Life seemed to burst from the tear: a painted bas-relief of fields of barley and wheat rimmed with gold, and a reaper swung his scythe, cutting down the stalks, as the seed was separated from chaff in time's eternal whirling.

What I am trying and failing to wedge was that these images—as hackneyed as they are to the unwashed ear—possessed a real pedagogic function: they made me feel good to be alive, and moreover, they made me feel good to be alive and to be a Babylonian, a feeling I had never felt before. But soon, too soon, the initial wild golds and sublime blues, colors that had hinted at a glorious ethereal sphere of being, quickly dulled and contracted into murky browns and grays.

The King faltered.

In the days of the Big Slump, as it was later called by the chroniclers, my job was to support the Staff of Adad and follow where the King led, and Nebuchadnezzar, the Good and True Farmer, was about to throw his Plough away. His member—*holy, holy, holy is the Lord!*—was entering a phase of what can only be wedged as de-tumescence. It felt like I was trying to coax a terrified snail out of its shell. Something had to be done. I decided that the only way to prevent ritual failure was to reverse the position of my hands: that is, replace my left with my right hand and vice-versa. Timing my movements with the upward thrusts of Siduri's watermelon-sized buttocks (How I loved watermelon!—particularly with a pinch of salt on a hot day), I carefully replaced one hand with the other, and here I can only record what I remembered, and what I remembered was that as I was shifting my right hand underneath my left, finger by finger, thumb by thumb, my hold loosened for a moment, but a moment was all it took. In this brief loosening of my hands and fingers, the King's member responded with a slight dilation, which turned into a more significant dilation. I felt it. The King felt it, too. A blast of blood, and then another, surged into the veins of the great serpent Marduk. It surged! It surged!—I could feel it, yes, and so could Siduri, who laughed her devilish laugh, bright big horse teeth gleaming in the torchlight of the Great Hall. She looked at me with gratitude, and oh, what a fine feeling to be finally appreciated, to be seen finally for whom I really was! Siduri's kind smile, her all-knowing eyes illuminated by pleasure, confirmed what I had always secretly known. I was a good eunuch. A decent castrate. A worthy steer.

The Holy Serpent surged!

As I held on to the Sovereign's staff with both hands, the King's body shuddered and shook like a man struck by lightning. He strained and groaned like a god. Siduri pumped with greater vigor now, and the steady and faithful hand of Nergal held fast to the King, and Nebuchadnezzar—our King and my Lord—he lay on his back and gazed at the concubine as if he could not believe his good fortune. Up and down, up and down, up and down, up and down: it was the rhythm of the universe, the eternal drumbeat of the order of things, and this cosmic rhythm, this metaphysical enactment of the truth about life, hypnotically entranced the room.

O mystical surge of life!

All creation groaned as the goddess impaled herself on the King's rod of the Euphrates. His pockmarked face empurpled; the vein in his neck swelled and pulsed dangerously, near bursting from the strain. Siduri began urging him on, calling him first *Enki* and then *Enlil*, exalted *Master of heaven and earth*, and then plaintively asked the ram to provide the ewe with a lamb. And then Nebuchadnezzar stood up like an attacking bull, lifted his holy spout and filled the Euphrates with water. There was a sudden gush of air, a shot of light, and a stream of glorious elixir flowed and then overflowed from the cup of life. My hands were sticky with the stuff. All hail Most Fecund King!

The naked dancers danced, the smooth-skinned harp-players played, and the Nubian singers sang:

> *The Dragon of Marduk has manifested!*
> *He has made an appearance!*
> *Sweet Return of the Mighty Serpent!*

And a eunuch wept.

The King collapsed on the floor like a bull who had just been slaughtered for the winter sacrifice. His eyes were closed, but he was laughing—ripples of his laughter echoed from the ceiling to the floor. The King's laughter! The King's laughter had not been heard in the palace for five years. It moved through the Great Hall like one of the seven winds of Ea,[5] as the members of the Court who lined its walls—from Harpagus to

110

Uruk—all nodded and grinned approvingly, the phony bastards. Even the eunuchs Chibby and Moil managed a smile. Only Madame Grape seemed skeptical—she loved me and knew Siduri, of course, so she tried not to show it.

"May my long phallus be praised!" I shouted.

Tablet Six ~

O Fence of Reed, O Wall of Brick

Now, the reader must keep in mind how fatally my youth was marked by the day of my castration. A poison entered my soul, and although it would take years to course through my body, course it did. Tonight, as I stare at my brother's laughable account of the events that led to the Judaean war (see Tablet II of *The Babylonian Chronicles*), I recall two dead fathers: each—may Queen Ereshkigal be merciful—taught me how to be a good eunuch slave-scribe. The first was my natural father, the eminent Drab the Indignant, who gave much but required much in return. The second father was Harpagus the Mede, whom I no longer blame for removing my tender boyhood, a deed he performed with clumsy, drunken efficiency, but the score, and we're all keeping score, has been settled. Though all of that lay in the future. For the moment, I am concerned with capturing the past, with wedging precisely in my *erratum* the story of my extirpation at the hands of Babylon's most powerful general. Of course, the Mede was not a general in year two of Nebuchadnezzar's reign. He was merely a competent, low-level captain in the King's legions, assigned to the netherworld of the Ziggurat, biding his time, doing bureaucratic hackwork in the castration corps. What I recall of that day, I remember in the fragment of memory and shard of the past: the death of my Father, the long, flea-bitten march to Babylon, the cold and corrugated iron of The Clamp.

Father's death, then. We had been sitting on our bench in a shaded corner of the yard. It was an off-day at the school, but Father insisted that his sons practice their copying exercises from sunup to noon, regardless of the schedule. Carrying the cane of Nabû, Father shambled into the garden, his sandals clicking as he carefully stepped over the pig turds that lay in the grass. It was a few hours before his death, and the famous scribe was attempting to work up an enthusiasm for a discipline for which he had grown tired. He genuflected before the altar of scribes and murmured the proverb of all scribes everywhere: *"what is stronger than the braying of an ass? The load."*[1] The altar was a small bronze statue of Nabû, god of stylo-and-mud-men everywhere—a dirty and chipped remonstrance to all that Father had not accomplished in his professional life.

Perched in the back of the garden, the altar was hidden among overgrown weeds and small apple trees. Goats whinnied and pigs snouted around the remnants of burnt offerings, the scraps of bone and bits of juniper that Father deposited weekly before his beloved tyrant. The bricked walls of the garden were high but had eroded over the years of his tenure in the house. Part of the south wall had crumbled and lay in pieces of mortar and half bricks in the dirt, a harbinger of our fate.

Father ignored us. Excitedly pacing up and down the garden in his threadbare robes, he grumbled under his breath, "the mud's not right, the mud's off," for he had just acquired a poorly copied tablet of *The King's Chronicle*. Father's habit of reading reflected a larger love of exegesis, and this love had left its mark on his face, which resembled an old piece of papyrus— Father despised papyrus—that had been crumpled in an act of critical outrage and then smoothed out again. Lurking behind his cloudy eyes lay a restless, brooding intensity that found satisfaction only in pointing out the errors of other scribes. When Father came upon an offensive passage, he whistled, and it was a sound not unlike the vulture of the desert, which, according to *The Annals of Ea*, sings its song only after picking the skin off the remains of a dead child.

"How are you, Father?" Uruk asked, hoping to bait Father into one of his famous bouts of indignation.

"How am I? How am I?! What do you mean by that phrase?" If Father had possessed eyebrows, he would have raised them pointedly. Like many members of the scribal class, Father was almost hairless, and to compensate for this state, he grew a few hairs below his chin, which made him resemble the goat that gnawed at the corncob beneath his feet.

"I dunno," Uruk replied.

"Cut the crap," Father said, smacking my brother's head with the side of his hand: *Swat!*

"How do you think I am?"

Uruk said nothing. I lowered my eyes and pretended to copy a wedge on my tablet.

"Out with it, boy!" he said, cuffing Uruk's head a second time: *Swat!* "This is not the Tablet House. You can say it. I look like shit!"

And with that, Father boxed my brother's ears again, this time harder: *Swat!!*

Father was right, of course—he did look like shit. Tall and cadaverous, his bony frame sprouted bumps, cysts, warts, and various waxy protuberances. A large spleen wart, emboldened by years of neglect, swelled on the back of his neck: its cauliflowery surface was dotted with tiny, black spots in geometric patterns. His feet were infected with ulcers and covered in corns. A nasty fungus had set in under his toenails. The forty years Father had spent in the Tablet House had made him gravely ill, despite the fact he had produced little.

"Okay, boys. Shall we review first principles? Are you paying attention? Good. If you apply yourselves dutifully to your lessons, and by that, I mean if you read

115

and copy out your tablets carefully, if you do all that is asked of you by your father-scribes, if you show loyalty, work hard, and do your job capably, what will happen?"

"You will be consigned to a life of poverty, toil, and ill-pay!" Uruk and I shouted in unison. We were careful students of our Father's pedagogy.

"But if you do not perform your jobs capably, what will happen then?" Father asked, twirling his cane of Nabû.

"You will be consigned to a life of poverty, toil, and ill-pay!"

"Exactly, boys. Work or sloth, it's all the same," Father said, knocking each of us with his cane for good measure: *Swat! Swat!* "The life of the scribe is as immutable as the rising sun. Today brings the drudgery of the tablet, tomorrow brings the drudgery of the tablet; today arrives with the inevitability of our daily quota of copying tablets. And tomorrow? What will tomorrow bring? Out with it! Out with it!" Father demanded, raising the cane of Nabû.

"A day like today!" Uruk and I shouted. Father nodded his head and hit us again: *Swat! Swat!*

It was a sad fact, but daily and vicious beatings were an important part of Father's pedagogic vision, and Father was nothing if not pedagogic. Father insisted, as I have wedged elsewhere, that the rewards of a scribe's life were so meager that a strict regimen of humiliation and violence was the only way to prepare him for his future. "A dog has more respect than a scribe," he would say often. "I am merely giving you a foretaste of what is to come."

The origins of Father's violent pedagogy were rooted in the woolly undergarment of his past. For the last ten years, Father had been a minor clerk in Ashurbanipal's Library, a post he had assumed after a long and undistinguished career in the Tablet House. Until, one day, after a contentious committee meeting of library scribes, where his rival, the much-loathed Bilshidi, presented his tablet on slave transactions of the third empire, Father was, without warning or ceremony, told to pack up his muds and styluses and never return. Father's dismissal from the Library was a blow from which he never recovered. The reason Drab was removed has always been a matter of contention among those who knew him. Uruk argued Drab had, in all probability, offended the powerful administrator Susani with an untimely bad joke. His colleague Not the Gouty cited his lack of work ethic, for, in the latter years of his employment, he hadn't produced anything of note, other than the justly revered *Enigma of the Tablet*. Indeed, Father was one of his generation's great underachievers, which made him proud. "Ambition and hard work," he was fond of saying, "did more harm in the world than laziness and inaction."

Regardless of our speculations on why Father had been dismissed, the why didn't matter, such was the depth of his indignation. Poor, angry Father. He had never forgiven the Royal Library for becoming a viper's nest of administrators and bureaucrats who, in his unfortunate phrase, "didn't know fuck-all." After his dismissal, Father spent more than three years brooding in his mud hut, where he stared blankly out the window and obsessed over his enemies. On the fourth anniversary of his expulsion, he decided to open up a small Tablet House school for boys. Located in the center of the scribal district of Nineveh, Father's school—The Illustrious Pedagogue's School for Young Laggards—had become popular among the sons of the priests and scribes of the royal Tablet House.

"Now take a look at this king's chronicle," Father said. "It's just been placed in the Tablet House library, and it looks to be the work of a former colleague of mine, the justly famous Bit the Wedger. I thought I might have you boys make twenty copies, so you could get the feel of Bit's style. Bit may be a scoundrel, but as a copyist, he's achieved the true scribal manner. Uruk, bring me the mud bucket." Father reached into the bucket of mud and began to shape two mud squares for copying. "I thought that Zagros mud would serve Bit's chronology best. Its mountain source reflects the breadth of the ages, don't you think?" Father asked, probing a sore on his ear with a finger. A cancer was eating away his left ear like a rat nibbling cheese. The lower lobe had tooth marks up and down its base, and had Father not died prematurely that day, he no doubt would have been dead within months.

"Uruk, would you read for us this morning?" Father asked, handing my brother the tablet of Bit's chronology. "You are a much better reader than your brother. Nergal, and I am only going to say this once, if you yawn one more time, and if I have to look at your disgusting mouth again and those grimy teeth, I am going to feed you to the pigs. Uruk, don't forget to read slowly and watch your tempo and pauses."

Uruk harrumphed, for even in our adolescence, he possessed a formidable scribal harrumph—and read the passage in a voice of great seriousness:

I, ASHURBANIPAL, KING OF THE FOUR RIMS, BUILT A PILLAR NEAR THE CITY GATE, AND I FLAYED ALL THE CHIEFS WHO HAD REVOLTED, AND I COVERED THE PILLAR WITH THEIR SKIN. SOME I WALLED UP WITHIN THE PILLAR, SOME I IMPALED UPON THE PILLAR ON STAKES, AND OTHERS I BOUND TO STAKES ABOUT THE PILLAR. AND I CUT OFF THE LIMBS OF THE OFFICERS, OF THE ROYAL OFFICERS WHO HAD REBELLED. MANY CAPTIVES FROM AMONG THEM I BURNED WITH FIRE, AND MANY I TOOK AS LIVING CAPTIVES. FROM SOME I CUT THEIR NOSES, EARS AND FINGERS; OF MANY I PUT OUT THE EYES. I MADE ONE PILLAR OF THE LIVING AND ANOTHER OF HEADS, AND BOUND THEIR HEADS TO TREE TRUNKS ROUND ABOUT THE CITY. THEIR YOUNG MEN AND MAIDENS I BURNED IN THE FIRE. TWENTY MEN I CAPTURED ALIVE AND IMMURED IN THE WALLS OF MY PALACE. THE REST OF THE WARRIORS I CONDEMNED TO BE CONSUMED WITH THIRST IN THE DESERT OF THE EUPHRATES.

O magnificent King! Ashurbanipal was a mighty conqueror and great tablet thief. He was no underachiever. Our great King wielded a stylus as powerfully as he wielded a sword, which was a rare talent in a despot. He was revered in the world of scribes—the worthy beard had stolen, appropriated, and borrowed (without returning) tens of thousands of tablets from his enemies to build the great library of Nineveh. Eminent scholar! When it came to getting the tablets he desired, Ashurbanipal would raze entire cities and reduce them to rubble. Father admired him greatly.

"Well, boys? What do you think?" Father barked irascibly, readying the cane of Nabû. A tiny wood tick crabbed up Father's leg and into his skirt for a morning feeding.

"He is a most dread king! A godlike sovereign whose will is law!" shouted Uruk, whose respect for royal authority was in its incipient and, perhaps, most fanatical phase.

"He is a cruel thief and murderer," I said for no reason but to contradict my brother. Father liked it when we fought. He encouraged scribal dissension. A good scribe, he always said, was a contentious scribe.

As Father pondered our answers, and also, perhaps to take a break from swinging his cane, he walked over to one of his beloved she-goats. An old, stinking creature that had been in the family for twelve years, the she-goat had long and hairy ears. Father cooed as he pulled a corncob from his pocket and fed the nanny. She gripped the cob with her teeth and munched deliberately. The nanny had given birth to a litter of kids the previous week, and her udder swelled with milk.

Father loved his she-goat almost as much as he loved a rare Egyptian treatise on demotic hieroglyphic usage. He kissed the she-goat on the nose.

"Interesting replies, boys, interesting replies. I don't doubt that each of you is correct, in his way, but both of you cannot be right. That would be a logical impossibility. So, which is it? A thief or a god? A murderer or a divinity?" he asked as he rubbed the she-goat's nipples, massaging her pimpled teats to increase her milk supply. Father liked a good cup of she-goat's milk before he lectured us on his pedagogic method.

Uruk smirked as if the question was beneath him. Father hit his forearm viciously: *Swat!*

"Remember, all good tablets hide more than they reveal. Nergal, stop picking your nose. It's disgusting." Quietly milking the she-goat now, pulling on its empurpled teats, Father grabbed a cup and squirted warm milk into its hollows. He took a deep drink and addressed us again. "Come now, you're making it harder than it is."

"The King is both Father!" I shouted. "A murderer and a god!"

"No right answers!" howled Father, swatting my shoulder blade with his cane: *Swat.* Father practiced an esoteric brand, both in his work and his pedagogy, of Sumerian cryptography: all right answers were wrong answers, just as all wrong answers were right answers. During our lessons, Father would ask us, "Is the sun shining?"—it always was—and our "yes" would elicit a severe beating from the reputable tabletman, and our "no" would be rewarded with praise and fresh goat's milk. The lesson was a simple one: Father wanted to impart "indignancy" to his students, to give them the gift of a morbid and unhealthy mind, and teach them to view the phenomenal world with the hostility and suspicion it deserved.

In early days of my son-scribeship, I was shocked to discover that the scribal class secretly despised the texts they worked so hard to preserve. Chained to their benches all day, copying out tablet after tablet, they moaned and complained about their drudgery. I now realize that Father's famous indignancy—his embattled condition, his general sourness, his waxy complexion, his reeking limbs and greasy robes—was an outgrowth of his boredom over copying tablets, a condition that infected the orbit around him. The backyard of our modest home looked and smelled like the midden heap. A colony of spiders occupied the corner of the north wall, weaving webs over the bricks and crevices. Broken shards lay scattered across Father's worktable; mildew sprouted in the dirt. Whole orchards of orange peels littered the grass, remnants of Father's fight against an intractable indigestion.

Father clenched the robe at his belly and skittered into his library, while Uruk and I made copies of Ashurbanipal's chronicle. Each day, Father attended a bowel movement between seven and eight o'clock in the morning. His exertions would last a full hour, and these sufferings—diffident whimpers and cautious groans—could be heard from our practice bench.

Uruk sniggered, "smelly bastard."

I ignored him, lost as I was in the soothing warmth of the sun. A soft wind bringing morning smells from the alley blew into the yard: somewhere someone was baking bread. I heard children playing a game of Master and Slave across the avenue. Copying out *The King's Chronicle* was tedious work, of course, and soon Uruk was up to his usual tricks—he wedged notes to himself in the margins of his tablet about Father's bodily habits, which we both found interesting, not in their own right, but for what they revealed of the man. In the years of our son-scribe training with Father, my brother had become fascinated with the old tableman's body, its rhythms and peculiarities, counting all the hairs on the celebrated scribe's ear (the good one), calculating the circumference of the boil on the back of his neck, and measuring the bunions on his toes. Uruk noted these physical peculiarities on his tablet: a Drab list, a Drab chronicle, a tablet of Drab—a Drab tablet.

When Father returned to the garden, he found Uruk's Drab tablet and laughed. "Now, this is exactly what I have been trying to teach you," he said, swatting the back of my brother's head with his cane. *Swat!* "This is it, exactly. I give you *The King's Chronicle* to copy, and you give me a list of my bodily complaints and bad habits. Most interesting. Now the question is—what is the connection between the two? On the surface, the relationship between a king who inters his enemies in a brick wall and the bunion on my left big toe appears entirely arbitrary. But that is the job of the scribe: making connections where they don't exist."

"I don't see anything that could be remotely described as a connection," Uruk said, genuinely baffled.

"Good. Good," replied Father. "That's the first step. There isn't a link. None whatsoever. You have to imagine one. This is where the priestly mode of writing I have been trying to teach you comes into the picture. As you will remember, it is based on the deliberate inversion of characters, the esoteric substitution of signs. Let's, for example, take another look at *The King's Chronicle* you were supposed to copy out. The first line reads, 'I Ashurbanipal, King of the Four Rims.' Impressive, isn't it? But let's examine it more closely. See the ideograph Bil-gi? Traditionally, we read that for "king" right? But let's apply my law of opposites to it and see what we get."

"That would be Gi-bil," I said, happy to beat my brother to the answer, but I was also worried about Father's reaction—for Drab was now swinging his cane through the air, as if he were fighting an imaginary army of Tablet House administrators.

"Which means?" Father asked. "What is that noise in the alley? Silence! I need silence!"

The playing children now ceased their game of Master and Slave. Father was not above going into the alley and thrashing them, too. A mother's voice shouted for them to come in from their play.

"It means liar or thief," interjected Uruk.

"Exactly. But we're not done, not by any stretch. What if we reverse the signs again. What then? Silence! Silence! I need silence!" There seemed to be a great commotion down the block. It was a sound like thunder or drums. Father heard it, too, and dismissed it as an unwanted distraction from the lesson.

"You would have Lib-ig," I said.

"Which is Hittite for—" he asked.

"Scribe. Lib-ig is Hittite demotic for scribe."

"That's right, my boy. That's right. And who do you think is more important—the king who crushes the city, or the scribe who records the killing?"

As I contemplated my answer, a strange and powerful new feeling gripped my chest. It was as if a comet blazed across the evening sky, or the stars in heaven sang a divine song of earthly triumph and life everlasting. A smile spread over my face, and Father hit the side of my head: *Swat.*

"I will show a scribal mystery," Father said, holding Bit's chronology in the air before our now eager faces. "Here, boys, as you know, is the chronicle of our great King, Ashurbanipal. A smallish square with wedges and lines, made of dung and grass. What does the tablet tell us? The tablet tells us that the god-King has smitten his enemies with his sword. The tablet tells us that he has put his sandal on the necks of the vanquished and trampled their cities. The tablet tells us that entire populations were put to sword before breakfast and lunch. And do you know what else the tablet tells us? The tablet tells us that the scribe who wedged this tablet believed he wedged in the divine idiom." And then Father did something extraordinary: he flung the tablet forcefully on the ground, and it broke into dozens of shards and fragments.

"I set before you the mystery of the broken tablet. It was once a coherent account of a mighty king, and now all that remains of it is fragments and dust."

As Father discoursed on the mystery of the broken tablet, his beloved pigs congregated at their trough, which was next to our workbench. It was lunchtime, and the swine gorged on wheat mullet and old carrots, snouting and wheezing in the happy oblivion of their meal. I should have been listening to Father's lecture, but the pigs were defecating—quite loudly—as they ate, and the smell was horrible. The pigs' small tails wiggled impertinently as they gorged at the trough. Uruk stuck his stylus in the mound of excrement and made pig sounds. Father ignored him, proceeding with his dissertation.

"The tablet is broken. That is a fact. No use mourning its demise. But what of the fragments? How many fragments are there? How many? How many pieces manifested in the fall? I want you to count them, boys. Count them all, and I don't have all day."

Kneeling next to the pigs, Uruk and I counted the broken bits of Bit the scribe's chronicle. It was an unhappy task because the pieces and fragments were now mixed up with the pig's dung, and the pigs continued to eat and defecate as we labored. We worked quietly in the chaos of tablet shards and dung, which I suppose was one of Father's points. I sorted carefully and deliberately, pulling out the pieces and chips of the tablet from the pig dung, wiping the excrement on my tunic, and then placing the clean shards in a small pile at my side. Uruk, however, only pretended to work. He refused to perform any task unless it had a direct bearing on his own advancement. He scoffed at my earnestness and whispered, "We are never going to be able to count all these shards, so let's just make up a number, huh? Come on, tell the old man something. Hurry."

"Seventy-two, Father, there are seventy-two," I said nervously.

"Seventy-two? Is that what you found?" Father asked. "A most wily answer. No doubt you are lying. You did not count them. But do you know something, you little rodents? You will be happy to know that that is the correct answer. *Swat! Swat!* A lucky guess? Perhaps. In all probability, you have read my treatise on *The Perfection of the World*. Assuming that you have read it, you will remember that seventy-two is a divine number. A number set apart and reserved for Ashur. Do you know what those seventy-two mud fragments represent? What the broken shards signify? Come on, come on. I haven't all morning to play with you young baboons. Nergal, you have pig dung on your hands. You disgust me."

"Sorry Father," I said, embarrassed by the mess on my hands. "But no, I don't know what the shards represent." I felt ashamed for going along with Uruk's trick, and it was the sort of thing he did all of the time, but I tried to set a higher standard for myself. I prepared myself for the next round of blows from Father's cane, but they never came. Father was smiling at me, although he could have been enraged. With Father, it was difficult to distinguish between the two.

"Those are the seventy-two names of the gods, Nergal. Uruk, don't stare at me like I am a wart on a donkey's testicle," he said, rapping my brother on his hands. *Swat!* "Ask me a question, ask me a question!"

"And why might that be important, Father?" Uruk asked, rubbing his hands and silently cursing Father under his breath. How my brother hated the old tabletman!

"I cannot answer that, you conceited little plague-sore. At least not directly. But I will show you something. Observe and learn. Do you see those fragments in the pile at your brother's feet? Yes? Good. Now pick one up. Come on Uruk, stop playing around. That's it. What you hold in your hand is a fragment of a tablet. A part of the King's chronology. A piece, as it were, of the larger whole. And do you know what that means?

"No, I don't know what it means, you old goat fart!" shouted Uruk.

Raising one's voice to the Illustrious Pedagogue was a capital offense, and, for a moment, I thought Father was going to beat Uruk to death. Father's face reddened as he fingered his cane of Nabû. But Father did not beat Uruk; he only smoothed the wrinkles of his tunic and said in his calmest, most pedantic voice: "Uruk, you are an ignorant bull's pizzle, and it is a good thing for you that I am feeling merciful today, despite, or rather because of, your impudence. Now please listen to what I have to teach you. The divine unity of the good tablet has been broken. Broken. And, as goes the tablet, so goes the world. Everything in this world is broken. All is vulgar dissension. Father-scribes beat son-scribes. Son-scribes despise father-scribes. On that much, I think we are in agreement. But there is more. Confusion and chaos are not just the way of the Tablet House, but they are also the way of the court, harem, and army. In this world, nobody agrees on first principles. Argument. Controversy. Sectarianism. Division. Wars and rumors of wars, storms and eclipses, disease, disaster, and drought. It is all lies, lies, and more lies. Everything is broken. Scattered and forgotten. Just like the tablet. *Who* will put it all back together, I ask? Who? Who? Who?"

"No one cares, Father," Uruk said.

"Barbarian!" Father struck him on his back. *Swat!* He then turned his angry countenance to me.

"And what is perhaps more important, Nergal, *how* will someone put it back together? Can you answer that?"

"By copying another one?" I said.

"No, you little pig turd, not by copying another one. What a stupid answer." *Swat!*

"You, Father. You will put it back together," Uruk said. "Are you not the eminent Drab the Indignant? The great scribe of Ashurbanipal's most eminent Tablet House? You shall do it."

"You honestly think that *I* will do it? Have you been paying attention? Look at me! I loathe a scribe's work! I will also be dead soon." Father uttered these last words with a touch of melancholy in his voice. But it was only a touch. He then stood to his full height and said with all of his authority, pointing to me: "I will tell you who will put it back together. *You.*"

As the swine waddled from their trough and into Father's library, Uruk struck me in the ribs with his elbow and snarled out the hated epithet of all scribes in the Tablet House, "Bench-minded!" That he despised Father's beatings had never been in question. For his part, Father appeared serene as he followed the pigs to the library, hogging their way through dirt and dead grass. He loved his pigs and goats and gave them the freedom of his garden and library. Father turned his head and smiled at both of us—there was something bordering on pride and perhaps, even affection in his rheumy eyes.

"You had better get started, boys. Gather ye fragments! Gather ye fragments! It will take a long time, a good long time!" he said with a malicious laugh.

[Lacuna: tablet cracked;
approximately 40 lines lost.]

We heard a violent noise outside our garden. Against the wall, there were shadowed movements, as if ghosts had risen from the netherworld, or a battalion of rogues had been let out of the tavern early, drunk with wine and sodomy. The will of beards, without restraint of custom or law, was a bloody thing, and my brother and I would soon discover how wide-ranging and vicious it could be. Fearful sounds of bronze and leather trampled across the brick alleyway, and a cadre of armed men marched through our doors. Shouts of "Death to Ashur!" and "The most lofty one!" rang out. Nabopolassar's soldiers appeared in the midst of the garden. Rank and vile, ready to make dark mischief. And there was a crash, as if Enlil had conjured a storm in the heavens and drowned the inhabitants of the alluvial plain.

Dropping our mud tablets, we ran to Father's library—which was little more than a hovel set behind our house next to the alleyway.

Originally Father's plan had been to model his study on the famous library in Smyrna, which resembled a smallish Ziggurat, but Father had come up short with the building costs—Father was always coming up short—and it looked exactly like what it was: a poor mud shack in the scribal district of Nineveh. Yet Father loved his library, for it was his one true sanctuary from all the disappointments of his life and profession, housing a collection he had spent a life accumulating from obscure used tablet shops and down-on-their-luck scribes. Whenever Father was not beating his charges or tending his pigs and chickens, he was in his library, reading arcane accounts of Tiglath-Pileser III's harem practices or wedging unreadable omen texts.

When we found Father, he was alone, and his library had been sacked with great force. Uruk checked the window while I knelt beside him. Drab was dead, lying on the floor—with the fragments and shards of his "muds" around his body. It was all but certain that his beloved tablet shelf had collapsed over him, killing him instantly. Like the broken chronicle tablet, Father had been reduced to nothing. He had spent a lifetime copying the tablets on that shelf, and it would not be too much to wedge that his collection—now scattered across the floor—was the result of long years of labor, and, given his disinclination to work, more prodigious than I had expected.

Father's tastes were peculiarly negative—along his upper buttocks was a divination manual whose predictions had failed to manifest, along with a recently copied medical tablet that recommended dying for a whole spectrum of maladies, including drunkenness.

Next to Father's calloused and grass-stained feet was a Sumerian theodicy that claimed the gods did not exist. I leaned down and read one of the verses: "Grief has come upon me ..." but then it broke off in unreadable lines. Across Father's bruised and broken back lay the remains of the *Encyclopedia of Omen Texts* in four volumes. It had been, according to Father, a very good copy. There were also a number of minor divine revelations that covered his forearms and a decent copy of a Babylonian Theogony over his legs.

The tablet that likely killed Father was the first copy Father had made as a young-scribe: Ur-idinna-nabuk's *On Divination*. The worthy omen tablet had crushed Father's head, leaving craters of blood and gore across the back of his bald dome. It was curious, but most of the texts on and around his head appeared to be magic and ritual tablets, those mud squares devoted to warding off evil and calling for divine help. Father's death was inflected with just the type of tablet-house irony in which he trafficked, and in the end, one could wedge that it was the wisdom of Nabû that killed him. He would have been happy about that, I suppose.

I fell on the ground and wept. Beloved Father was gone, and I was left alone with a ruthless brother. Uruk was a cool one. Sorting through Father's desk, going through his belongings, looking for a few gold coins, perhaps to bribe the soldiers who would soon be back, he did not even acknowledge Father's death. At least not openly. Who knew what was going on in the depths of his cramped soul?

I should have helped Uruk, should have done something, should have, in fact, tried to escape Father's library when we still had a chance, but I just sat next to Father's dead body, stroking his curled beard lovingly, pulling out the remains of his lunch, a cold porridge of barley and dates which had congealed around his chin. Father had been a handsome man in his youth. His dead, brown eyes stared at the tablets around his head. I picked up a shard of the tablet that killed him and fingered its sharp edges, felt its broken ends. Death was a knot that was difficult to untangle—its threads refused to yield its mysteries. I gripped the shard fiercely, piercing my palm until blood trickled, and the blood, as a sacrifice to memory or offering to the gods, flowed down my hand and wrist. I thought of many things—Father's violence as a pedagogue, his vicious and daily beatings, his inordinate love for beer, and the occasional kindness he bestowed on me when he was drinking.

How I loved Father when he was drinking!

He was most loving when he was in his cups. In his library, and after an amphora of beer, his entire manner would change. Putting down his cane of Nabû, he would smile, and a gentleness would envelope his waxy, boil-covered frame. The constant physical beatings and verbal abuse he administered in his role as Drab the Indignant disappeared, as did the more severe peculiarities of his pedagogic method. In their place was simply a lonely old man who desired the affection of his favorite son. "Come to Drabbie, Nerggie, my boy!" he would bellow and kiss me on my forehead. Father would tell me stories of his childhood, regale me with tales of the Tablet House, flatter me with bits of Court gossip he had overheard in the marketplace. Father smelled of old soap and mud. Apart from his lectures, he said little to me that was of a personal nature or suggested emotional intimacy, and yet what I remember best about Father was his physical presence: his scribal sloth, his short, dark brown hair, the way he held a stylus, clutching its end with four fingers and thumb. But mostly, during our moments alone together, I would sit quietly in the corner of his tablet-filled room, as he poured cup after cup of his favorite scribe's piss down his gullet.

Had Father consulted his omen texts that afternoon instead of getting drunk, he might still be alive today, beating Uruk and me with the cane of Nabû. Uruk is in desperate need of a sound thrashing, and I could use a father. It was my brother's theory that Father knew of his fate and pulled a last tablet from his shelf with the intention of killing himself. He claimed that Father was aware of the company of Babylonian thugs who were crashing through Nineveh, neighborhood by neighborhood, and had deliberately abandoned us. I cannot and will not believe this slander. Father was not always an indignant beard. That he was a kind drunk proved quite otherwise. When he was in his cups, he would allow me a sip of his beer—a good, solid Assyrian ale. I would gulp from his cup, and a peace that surpasses all understanding would infuse my being. I would sit on Father's lap, and he would laugh and sing, and tell tales of his young scribe-ship. He would even declaim from the loathed epic:

> *Gilgamesh, why do you rove so?*
> *The life that you seek, you shall not find.*

"Truer lines were never wedged, my boy," he would say, rubbing my hair, and he would down another cup of beer.

Father would often lie on his daybed while holding up a tablet to the afternoon light, and his bony ribs would quiver with pleasure as he savored a misplaced word or solecism. How Father loved to correct the tablets he read! Little in life gave him greater pleasure than exposing the idiotic thoughts and muddled style of other scribes. With his pigs sleeping in the corner—a sow on her back, ten little piglets feeding greedily, and a belly full of beer—Father experienced the closest thing to happiness that he was capable of feeling, and, apropos of nothing, he would turn to me and say: "Nerggie, I worry sometimes that I have not taught you enough about the world. It's a cruel, violent, godless place. Someday, I am going to send you into it."

Tablet Six

"Father is dead," Uruk said, placing his hand on my shoulder, waking me from my sad reverie. "Get up, we must go!"

After Uruk shouted those words, a truncheon struck my head, and all went black. Minutes or perhaps hours later, I awoke to sounds of grunts and groans, and a bronze-armored thug, all muscle and hate, was violently sodomizing Uruk like a rampant stag, leaning over his skinny frame and pumping away with a look of brute, animal purpose on his face. We were still in the library, surrounded by Father's broken tablets. As Uruk's head jerked forward and back to the thrusts of the beast behind him, he whimpered and moaned. The line on the vile beard's forehead folded darkly, his mouth opening with a leering gape as he squeezed out the final spasm. Uruk stared directly into me, and his eyes spoke tablets of fear. I have often wondered about the effect of this experience on my brother, this invasion of body and spirit, this physical manifestation of the monster Humbaba in the loins of a soldier. I took no consolation from Uruk's violation that day, and we have never spoken of it.

There were six Babylonian infantry-beards in the library and the garden, burning and looting, defecating and pissing, commandeering the goats and pigs, slaughtering the chickens for lunch. Armed with spears and bows, they wore belted leather tunics emblazoned with a bull—the divine Babylonian Bull of which their King was incarnate—and they had small leather greaves

137

on their shins. Burly, sweaty, boy-raping beards. I said something about the vulgarity of their appearance, and a stinking Chaldean slapped my face. Two large-headed goons grabbed us; we panted and shuddered like small animals to be drowned in the river. The soldiers bound us with leather straps around our wrists and ankles, trussed us up like pigeons for the cook's fire. They clamped iron manacles around our necks and forced us to march out of the city. I am still marked with a slight, whitish scar ...

Babylon. The very name causes me to [...]

[Tablet damaged:
all subsequent lines lost.]

Tablet Seven –

They Took Me and Forced Me to Reside
Far Away at the Mouth of Two Rivers

There is a very good rock stele in the City square, commissioned by Nabopolassar and carved by the late Bel-u-ball-it years before his untimely jump from the Ziggurat. It's a tall, narrow triangle made out of black basalt and stands next to the temple of Esagila and behind the old palace. On its north face, the sculptor has fashioned a testament to the late King's victory over the Assyrians. There are lines of marching soldiers and horse-drawn chariots, and, behind them, rows of bulls and sheep, chickens and goats, carts full of boxwood and cedar, and gold and silver ingots. Next to the booty, and below the soldiers, stands a line of slave boys shuffling in single file, manacled neck by neck, heads down, hearts despairing, as they march through the Ishtar Gate. If you observe closely, you will see a smallish boy in the corner of that victory rock, clutching a tablet and gazing up at the tower of Babylon. His bones are delicate, his expression soft-eyed and intelligent. A pointy-helmeted thug, truncheon in hand, pushes him forward.

It is a fair representation of my first day in the Gate of the Gods, now over thirty years ago, but there was more that the sculptor left out: the blue bulls and gold aurochs emblazoned on the walls of the Processional Way had come alive to the boy, shimmering in the sun, whispering intimations of his fate. The great sun burned down from the sky, blistering his back and neck, and the crowd, filthy with drink, chanted, "Powerful King! Powerful King!" Every few minutes, the boy falls and is beaten by the soldier, that shit-for-brains Salmat. The boy is fearful and thirsty. From a window above, a withered hag places a finger on her nose and ejaculates a fusillade of snot upon him.

A fine layer of dust covered the inhabitants. A camel urinated a thick stream of piss into the dirt on my left, and a priest vomited into a sewer on my right. Flies the size of shekels stung my legs and arms, and dust blew into my eyes and mouth. People on the street shouted profanities, strange foreign tongues to my Assyrian ears. There were Africans with scarred faces, Jews in curls, Elamites in beautifully colored tunics, and Medes on horses. The beards seemed to be drunk. The women were mostly naked—later, I would discover the women were sacred prostitutes, baring their breasts and legs to the leers of field workers and irrigation men as merchants hawked the decapitated heads of Babylon's foes as souvenirs.

Past the temples of Nabû, Ishtar, and Ashratum, we were thrust deep into the Imperial City. Stepping on the brick tiles, I tried to conduct myself with dignity, but the chains were too heavy for my small frame, and I collapsed in the filth of the street. "The heavens are shaped like a bowl," a humpbacked guard shouted in my ear. "They are filled with milk and raisins. I like a good raisin." He smiled a gummy smile and yanked me to my feet.

Soldiers pushed us forward. Beggars, wild-eyed and gap-toothed, skulked alongside our train of captives and whispered intimations of our future. While Babylon was a City of great riches, it was also a City of great want. Whole neighborhoods had deteriorated into sinkholes for the destitute—men and women who spent their nights in their own dung, like oxen in the stable. A derelict dressed in rags sneered at us. A bony old woman pulled her skirt down to reveal her withered parts. A young hooligan burped in my face, pressing his collapsed cheeks and horrible mouth into mine. Dirt-faced miscreants of

141

every race and creed shadowed us as we marched into the center of serpent-god's dominion. The line of boys threaded its way through merchant stalls, took turns down strange lanes and moved past faceless mud huts, until the great Etemenanki rose before us like a malarial sun.

The Ziggurat!

Nebuchadnezzar's grand project to transform the City rested on the success of this overbuilt temple to Marduk. A mere seventy thousand slaves died during its construction. Long-stepped ramps thrust upward to the main entrance, flanked on either side by two massive marble-winged bulls. Winding upward to the heavens, at seventy-two stories, the tower of Babylon was a brick-and-mud architectural calamity, a woeful and mighty celebration of the Sovereign's might. O Great King! O terrible gods! We trembled before its might.

"Fuck them. I'm not going in there," said Uruk, stopping for a moment while our guards beat another boy, who had complained of thirst, with a leather stick.

"What are you going to do?" I asked, holding on to the iron manacle around my neck, for its edge dug into my skin, and I had begun to bleed. "Just walk away?"

"Something bad is going to happen in that place. I want no part of it."

Three beards, clad in the vestments of scribes who had fallen on hard times, approached our line.

"They're going to cut off your pecker!" said the first ape-necked mendicant.

"What?" I asked.

"They'll be doing ye a favor!" a second scribe yelled.

"I can't keep my hands off mine," a third old scribe said.

"But my voice has not even broken!" I shouted back to him.

"No worry about that ever happening." He laughed.

Like a leviathan's mouth, the entrance of Etemenanki swallowed us whole. The guards shoved Uruk and me forward, and a chain of weary boys spiraled downstairs into darkness, down, down, down to our destination: the College of Eunuchs or, as it was known in the idiom of our strange new City, the Hall of Felicity. It took our line of hungry and tired boys an hour to descend to the basement, and when we emerged from the darkness, we found ourselves in a vast circular room. Marked with age and decay, the stone floors of that dome-like room were slick with brownish slime. Walking was difficult. I remember the sound of dripping water, or what I thought to be dripping water, although I was later to learn it was blood, the blood of boys who had preceded our group in the previous days. The leakage echoed off the high ceiling and filled us with fear. Torch light reflected off the sebum-faced boys in the middle of the room. One fellow cried openly, but the majority of us endured our unknown fate with a reserve that, I would later learn, is customary of those in the eunuchoid class.

After another head-count, we were then herded through a large door and proceeded through the College of Eunuchs, down additional staircases that led us to the very bowels of the holy tower. At last, we reached the Hall of Felicity, where about twenty-five boys were obviated every hour. It was not really a hall at all; it was more like a labyrinth of halls, a brick-and-mud maze through which we wound, our silence broken by the occasional sniffle. We stumbled single-file through a corridor that turned every ten cubits, an architectural trick that prevented us from divining our future. Along this hall, as I would later learn, were the seven stations of castration: strappers, swabbers, cutters, cleaners, tie-ers, knotters, disinfectors, and featherers—the division of labor in the hall was designed to maximize speed and efficiency.

A slave named Rad-adan came down the backstairs. He tied our wrists and ankles with leather straps, binding us to beams, which leaned against the wall and down the hall as far as I could see. I counted eighteen boys, hanging from ladders, and no doubt there were more beyond: a city of incipient castrates buttressing the hoary underbelly of Babylon.

What an odd fellow was Rad-adan! One of his tasks was to console us in the hour of our ascension— for the operation was, according to him, a kind of promotion. No longer would we be limited, he told us, to a life in the grubby mud fields or pressed into military service. Not for the eunuch was a life of physical labor. Most of the boys, he said, those that survived extirpation, were to be taught the rudiments of literacy in the Tablet House.

"We prune about two dozen of ye a fortnight. And they will charge ye a hefty toll for it."

"Are we going to die?" Uruk asked.

Due to a morbid revulsion of darkness, I had difficulty stifling the panic that was swelling and sloshing against the banksides of my reserve.

"Die? Hopefully not, my little mouse," replied Rad-adan, "ye are going into debt. The pruning tax is the worst thing about it. One hundred-thousand shekels. It'll take ye the rest of your life to pay off. It's quite a good deal, really. They provide the service immediately and ye get to pay it off gradually. That way, ye won't strain yer budget."

"What are you talking about?" Uruk asked.

"For the privilege of matriculating."

"Matriculating? What is that?" he hissed.

145

"Ye are going to join the College of Eunuchs! Ye, my little mouse, are entering into quite a select body. I wish I was in yer manacles. You have no idea of the power ye will possess, that is, if ye work hard and mind your wedges and lines. Ye are a lucky fellow, that's what ye are, and I would stop yer blubbering, if I were ye." Rad-adan looked down the line, where a commotion could be heard, as if a winged colossus had descended into our midst.

"How does one matriculate?" I asked. Uruk and I exchanged looks of dread.

"Oh, I wouldn't worry myself too hard about that. Ye will find out soon enough. After the ceremony, that's when the fun starts. There are only two doors that lead out of this dungeon. One leads to the harem; the other to the Tablet House. If ye enter into the latter, ye will receive a small, annual stipend of three shekels a year. That is what all slave-scribes receive for their labors, regardless of their ability. Of that wage, one shekel pays for room and board. Everyone needs a spot to shit, bathe, and curl his beard, doesn't he? But, of course, ye won't have to worry about a beard. Be that as it may, one and a half shekels is due to the god of the Mud—our lord and protector, Marduk. That leaves ye with a half-shekel to pay yer Gelder. The Gelder has to be paid, my little mouse. But I wouldn't worry too much. Most neuties don't live to admire their pruned branch."

Another slave entered the room. He carried a sloshing wooden bucket from which he swabbed both Uruk's and my perineum with a berry-hued liquid. "It'll be over before ye know it" was all he said, as he washed us with the sponge. Soon, we were surrounded by the sounds of castration—the *"No! No! No! Please!"* of pleading boys before us—and the anxious questions—*"What's going on? Tell us!"*—of fearful boys behind. I closed my eyes and tried not to think about how painful the Gelder's blade would be. It was dark, with only erratic torchlight to illumine our exposure. Laid out like a criminal before the executioner's sword, I couldn't see a thing until the slave thrust a burning stick in my face.

Harpagus the Mede! Father of the everlasting twilight, I lift a cup to your fanatical dreams!

Harpagus's face was blotchy and shaped like a kidney. He was a stocky, dark-complexioned beard with intense black eyes, and it was these eyes that grabbed you by your throat and pulled you into his charismatic, murderous orbit. The Mede possessed a terrible charm. Covered in imperial blue leather armor and armed with his bronze clamp, he examined Uruk and me with the eye of a seasoned castrator. He picked at our tunics, looking for contraband. His touch was casual, as he if were a friend or a parent who did not beat you regularly. I had a feeling he was looking for tablets, some clue to explain our urbanity, that smoothness of scribal demeanor that can only manifest from a childhood spent around tablets and styluses. For the Mede was a Babylonian anomaly, a soldier with a passion for tablets, a violent beard who enjoyed reading an *Enuma Elish*. And, like a good autodidact, Harpagus the Mede particularly loathed those whose path to knowledge had taken more established routes. He disliked all professions—priest, astrologer, haruspex—having to do with the Tablet House, especially those that claimed a metaphysical provenance. He was also drunk—reeling and stinking of beer—and whistling too, I might add, an insipid tune about a lamented girl from Lagash. When I reflect on that moment, it was not his drunkenness that disturbed me so much; it was his castration theory, an ill-tasting porridge of half-digested ideas that were currently in vogue at Court. Harpagus had read selectively—picking at this mediocre wisdom list and plucking at that poorly wedged astrology guide. He had memorized the hack philosophers, digested the lesser hymns, and misunderstood the minor poets. But his alpha tablet, his sacred document, the foundation of his intellectual edifice, was the *Codex Castratum*, a barbarous treatise on the deballocking of young boys.

"Do not fear the operation," he said in the uncertain tones of his self-educated accent, "standardization is the golden rule of our *Codex*

Castratum. Each individual cut is required by order of Nebuchadnezzar to measure 2.2 micro cubits from the tip of your scrotal sac to the base of your perineum. We aim at quality extirpation here at the College of Eunuchs, and I am proud to say that, with the help of the *Codex Castratum*, we accomplish our goals, more or less."

He wiped a wick of spittle that had congealed on the corners of his mouth. "We are not butchers. No, more like midwives, I should think. Our esteemed King needs eunuchs of ability to run his empire. And you want to help the King run his empire, don't you boys?"

I did not answer Harpagus at the time. None of the boys did. How could we interrupt the Master Gelder, who would soon apply the clamp to our tiny cocks? Who could argue against the axioms of the *Codex Castratum* ? I looked at the boy next to me—I think his name was Sisit—who was trembling on the ladder. He seemed to be only half-aware of the travesty that was about to be visited upon him. Another boy named Alam had fallen asleep, while Uruk stared contemptuously at the blank space before his eyes. He turned his head and refused to look at the Mede.

"And what is your name?" Harpagus asked.

"Nergal, sir," I replied.

"Nergal? That's a stupid name. And what a pretentious accent you have! Are you a special boy? Are you a scribe's son? I'll bet you are. I've killed many scribes in my life, Nergal boy. And what's this?" Harpagus pulled a tablet out of my robes, a tablet I had grabbed from my father's library, as our house was burning.

"This is contraband."

"It's Shalimar's study," I said nervously, "of rainfall in the river valley during the reign of Marduk-apla-iddina II."

He scanned the lines and snorted. "You're reading Shalimar, are you?" he asked, throwing the tablet on the ground. "I read Shalimar once. He's a fool. Irrigation scribes are nothing but a bunch of charlatans. I mean, I could do a better job with the canals than half these educated men. Tablet-house flunkies, all of them." He spat in his hand and looked at me intensely.

"I much prefer Syrac the Ammonite's tablet on rainfall rates. It's subtler. The Ammonites have a talent for that stuff. Hezekiah the Jew is also quite good on the subject. Have you read Hezekiah? Tsk. Tsk. Didn't think so."

Harpagus was not the last self-taught beard I would meet in Babylon, but he was the most intransigent. He had taken an immediate disliking to me, angered by my formal, scribal manner. What's more, he suspected, given the presence of the tablet in my tunic and curve of my long, aristocratic nose, that I possessed an educated boy's knowledge of Sumerian and Akkadian. He hated educated boys. He thought they were conceited. A cultural despiser of the meaner sort, he picked up the tablet again and dangled it in front of my face.

"This smells like a monkey's bottom," Harpagus said, pleased at his witticism. He was a crude beard and knew how to humiliate the weak. Pulling out his obscenely large member—embedded with thick, copper beads—he micturated on the text's beautifully wedged triangles and lines. It was not the first penis I had seen, nor would it be the last, but it was the largest: long and thick and full of repulsive, worm-like veins. The Mede caught me looking and winked.

Turning to Uruk, he paused, studying his placid countenance. "You're a bit of an enigma, aren't you? You probably don't know what that word means. It's a good word. If you looked up enigma in the dictionary, you'd see that it comes from the Sumerian word for riddle. Do you know what a riddle is? No? It is a—what do ye call it?—an inscrutability. Do you find me inscrutable, Nergal boy?" he said, giving up on my brother. Gripping the castration clamp tightly, Harpagus delivered this digression in a voice that approximated irony, but it was an irony coupled with

a soldier's rage. The Mede was working himself up for
his task, throwing wood on the fires of intellectual
vanity until the flames licked his trembling lips.
Taking his sword out of its scabbard, he scrawled the
ideograph C-A-S-T-R-A-T-E on the mud floor.
"Here's a riddle for you, and it's going to be the most
important riddle of your lives. Once a year, on Ishtar's
day, we free one of the boys. That's right. One of you
lads is going to keep his little ballocks. Why? Because,
in addition to being—how shall I say this—a crazy
bitch, Ishtar is also a merciful goddess. So, here's how
it's going to be. The boy who answers the question to
my satisfaction keeps his manhood, such as it is. Now,
boys, what do you say to that?" Harpagus pointed to
the ideogram, his kidney face contracting in a passable
imitation of scribal condescension.

Having sized up Harpagus for the mad beard
that he was, Uruk plotted his strategy carefully. Too
carefully, some might say, although I was impressed
by his self-control. He refused to answer. I should
have known this basic fact—for I was father's best
student—but my bastard of a brother was applying
Drab's pedagogy to Harpagus's riddle: All right
answers were wrong answers, and all wrong answers
were right answers. Yet Uruk, the clever son-scribe,
did it with a twist. Instead of giving a false reply, he
refused to answer the question at all. It was brilliant.
He knew the importance of not angering Harpagus—

don't ask me how he knew, but he knew. He also knew that if he was to escape castration, it would be by flattering the Mede's prejudices, which were many.

"What does this mean?" Harpagus barked again, pointing to the scrawl on the floor.

"Don't know, sir!" said Uruk, adopting a bogus accent of the army barracks, "nor do I care." He leaned forward and spit onto the tablet. "That's what I think of tablets, sir!" he said, grinning stupidly, pretending to be ignorant and dumb. It was a shoddy, amateurish performance, but Harpagus bought it, the moron.

Now Harpagus's question was a pivotal moment in our lives, when the whole of our futures, the very shape and texture of our days, would be set in the stars of the heavens forever, and I made a mistake, a horrible mistake. Had I kept my mouth shut, had I listened to my better instincts, had I remained silent, it would have been me rather than Uruk who would be sitting on the pomegranate-scented seat of the Haruspex of the Golden Bull.

"It's old-temple Sumerian for 'beardless eunuch, sir!'" I said.

Why? I have asked the gods, repeatedly and *ad infinitum* in my darkest moments, here in my snug, little hate-hole. Why did I answer so quickly? Why didn't I channel our father's wisdom in that most necessary hour? It was I, after all, who revered his method and contemplated its mysteries. There is no answer to that question, other than my compulsive desire to outperform my brother. Father always was happy when we degraded each other's intelligence. He said it made us better scribes, gave us sharper styluses. I speak, of course, in metaphors.

"It's your happy day, young one. I can't stand competitive scribe-boys," Harpagus said, staring at me, as he untied my brother from the ladder. "You think you're so superior to these poor fuckers," he gestured to the line of simpering and soon-to-be-castrated boys tied to the racks along the hallway. "Always have to be the best, always have to get the highest marks and always have to outshine the others. It's pathetic. And you all grow up to be big shot diviners and astrologers. Fucking know-it-alls. It makes me puke! What you don't understand is that you know nothing that I can't learn myself. I don't have to sit on a bench all day long. I can read tablets in the open plain, on my horse, before a battle. Do you think you're superior, Nergal?"

"No, sir," I said, lying.

"Well, Nergal, you will be quite happy as a castrate. And you," he said to Uruk, "I'm going to send you to the Tablet-House. That should fuck those bastards up, giving them an idiot like you. Now off you go, you young, stupid ass, off you go. You're too small for the army. Otherwise, we might have you.

Rad-adan, take this boy down to the Tablet House. They can try to mold him into one of their bum-licking wedgers. He should be quite unhappy there. Sorry boy."

And with that, Uruk was gone. Vanished. It would be half a decade before I would see him again, and although our destinies were tangled together like the greasy hairs of Nebuchadnezzar's beard, I despised him for out-smarting me. He scampered quickly down the hall and up the stairs, his laughter echoing off the walls. I still hear his laughter today as I wedge this tablet: it sits in my belly every night and congeals into bile.

Harpagus began sharpening his shears on a rock blade attached to the wall, and, because of his drunkenness, he had a difficult job of it. He dropped the knife three times before giving up altogether. The Mede stooped and picked up the clamp, and the prodigious amount of beer in his stomach was now making him even more inebriated. His mood darkened, his features compressed themselves into his lips, now thin with resentment. Harpagus straightened to his full height. He was preparing himself for the ritual cutting, an act he had done a thousand times in the last year. He held the *Codex Castratum* in his hand like he was a priest of Ishtar, which I suppose, in a way, he was. He was casual, off-hand, bored, and a little disappointed at the quality of his charges. Yet, you could tell he took his job seriously in so far as it allowed him to discourse on his pet topics, indulge his wild paradoxes, declaim his mad theories, which were mostly rationales for his own life, as the King's castrator in the bottom of the Ziggurat.

"Do you know what this fucking accomplishes?" Harpagus asked, as if he were an old philosopher querying recalcitrant pupils.

The boys on the ladders hung like ripe fruit on cold fall day. They looked at him confusedly and hoped he would not be too long.

"Of course, you don't. I will tell you. Not a godsdamn thing," he said. "Men succeed only in passing on their miserable fucking suffering to their fucking miserable children. And it has always been fucking thus. The world is fucking old, boys, very fucking old, indeed. Imagine the fucking countless generations of fucking unhappy men and fucking unhappy women that have trod the fucking plains under the fucking hot sun. Can you fucking imagine that? No, I don't suppose you fucking can. Men are like the fucking wildebeest of the flatland or the fucking river fish swimming up the fucking stream. Once their fucking journey has ended, they fucking lie down and fucking die. It is a sad, sad, fucking state of affairs. What I'm trying to say is that we, here in the fucking College of Eunuchs, are offering you freedom from this fucking cycle of fucking futility. Freedom—

how shall I say this?—from fucking. It is a fucking gift, if that makes any sense, though I don't suppose it does. Fuck it. You'll have to fucking trust me on this. Today you are going to walk through the fucking Gate of the fucking Gods. Free from fucking. You fucking trust me, don't you boys? Fucking good."

While we were too young to see through the stock *contemptus mundi* by which Harpagus the Mede attempted to console us in the hour of our deballocking, we were close enough to smell the mutton and onions that rose from his breath. He had burped as if to punctuate his oration.

In the years between my castration and my present imprisonment, I have misplaced many memories, and one of them is the moment before our castration, when my predecessors, Sisit and Alam, exchanged a series of glances that were too awful to describe. Alam was not a handsome boy; his eyes were too close together, and one cheekbone was higher than the other, a structural defect which had the effect of making him look like a poorly executed sculpture. His body shrunk before his fate, like a tree struck by lightning and instantly burned to a stump. The Mede approached with his clamp and Alam reached out to Sisit, grabbing his hand, and then the autodidact smoothed the boy's hair, told him he would be better off, happier without his little aardvark between his legs. Alam nodded his head and said, "do it."

Harpagus butchered Alam with an incompetent efficiency, stabbing him in an artery of his thigh: his end, at least retrospectively, was mercifully quick. He was dead within two minutes. We were not boys to Harpagus, not ordinary twelve or thirteen-year olds who liked to play Hounds and Jackals, nor were we children who played at war in the daytime and slept in our mother's arms at night. He saw us as symptoms of a larger metaphysical disease, one which he was trying to eradicate: to Harpagus, we were mere steps in the road of his larger vision.

But what was genuinely original to Harpagus was not his philosophy, which was, as I have wedged, an unhappy blend of commonplaces that circulated around the City at that time. What was genuinely individual to the man was his castration style. He boasted of never cutting a boy against his will, and I have no reason to doubt his claim. Harpagus would never put the clamp on until a boy said yes, and this yes had to be genuine; this yes had to be enthusiastic. He would only castrate you if you yielded to him, if you agreed that life as a eunuch was not only the best possible life, it was the only life worth living, the only way to be in the world. It was a trick, of course, but what a trick!

Alam was dead, yet I felt nothing. But Sisit was a good-looking boy, or I thought so at the time, a period of my life when such adolescent crushes were standard among our set in pre-burned-to-the-ground Nineveh, and his anguish and vulnerability had a great effect upon me. Now I am a eunuch who loathes the sentimentality that is currently in vogue among Babylonian poets and Court scribes, and I am in no way indulging in that amateur trick of feeling for feeling's sake when I wedge that when Harpagus raised his knife above Sisit, who was nodding his head, as if to say let's get this finished quickly, I felt as if *I were being castrated.* By the god of scribes, Nabû, I wept! I wept! Turning my head (I could no longer watch the horrid farce), I felt the rack rattle as Sisit struggled, heard his screams and saw his blood spatter on the floor. Ten minutes later, little Sisit was dead. He had quietly bled to death on the ladder.

When it was my turn to experience the knife, and enter through the Gate of the Gods, I gripped the sides of my ladder. Approaching quickly, swinging his castration clamp around his finger and still whistling his dull tune, Harpagus knocked my ladder with the damn thing, causing me to cringe and whimper. Dedicated to an obsolescent fertility goddess, the castration clamp was topped with a goat's head, and its curled horns were made of ivory. He held the clamp in my face, smiled, and put it down.

"Nergal, you are an exceptional one, are you not? Yes, I thought so. It's the harem for you, my friend. You'll enjoy the harem, boy. All those girls. Do you like girls?"

"Yes, I like girls," I said. It was another of his ruses, and I fell for it.

"That's all I need to hear. Happy travels, Nergal."

And with that, the Mede maneuvered—miraculously, because he was not paying attention, having noticed a stray spot of grime on his soldier's leather—the oval ring into its proper place. My boyhood retracted like a frightened turtle.

"Now these testicles shears are not really fuccckkking shears at all," he slurred, his drunkenness now infecting his speech. "This may hurt a little."

The autodidact lied. The clamps bit down with brutal force, and my bearded future was excised from the tablet of life forever: the hurt—part pull, part tear (for the clamp was very dull)—was more than a little. Much more. It hurt a lot, or as Harpagus would say, a fucccckkking lot. My throat closed, and I couldn't breathe. Blood washed over my thighs, pooling in the shallow grooves along the wood rack.

Rad-adan had returned from the Tablet House just in time to see me gasping for my life on the ladder. He shook his head, as if to say, this one's time is up, he's finished, he's dead on the rack, but Harpagus, contrary to all my assumptions, ignored him. While it was a commonly known secret that few boys survived their matriculation to the College of Eunuchs, the actual number of deaths was a statistic that the Tablet House never published. Perhaps Harpagus was aware of the failure rate, and the soldier in him was trying to improve the numbers. I don't know the reason, but he stayed by my side, administering what he called "fuccckkking unguents" and tying "fuccckkking tourniquets." He whispered smooth words in my ears, rubbed my sweaty hair gently with his hand. Oh, the beard was a paradox of paradoxes, he was an inscrutable one, to quote his self-description: full of big words and gutter-talk, and the source of his unexpected kindness has been a mystery to this day.

When the bleeding finally stopped, I was carried out of the Ziggurat and into a courtyard by Rad-adan, where he summarily stuffed me into a fresh dung-hill over ten-cubits high. Goat manure that had been blessed by a priest of Marduk was believed to expedite the healing process—quite the reverse, of course, but most things in Babylon would prove to be a lie. It is a truism to wedge that fields of excrement smelled like shit, but I will wedge it anyway: they smelled like shit. I was covered in dung, from head to toe, for three days. During this period, swaddled in goat and sheep dung, I drifted in and out of consciousness, surrounded by my brother-eunuchs, we the castrated, who one day would guard the King's harem.

The heartbreak of lying in forty bushels of excrement was not lost on the half-dozen freshly cut boys, who were like the lilies on the trash heap of that old song I can't remember; both the tune and its lyrics escape me. I do recall singing the song, as flies landed on my nose and laid their eggs in the craters of my nostrils, and I swore that if I survived, I would try to understand what happened to me that day in the bottom of the King's Ziggurat.

I was wrecked.

Tablet Eight –

They Laid the Booty at the Altar of his Feet

In the same year the King of Babylon wed
The lady of Ishtar,
He went up to Akkad
Plundered Rabbilu and Hamranu
And abducted the gods of Shapazza.
                    —*The Babylonian Chronicles*

It was early afternoon in the Hanging Gardens, and Nebuchadnezzar gazed about the lush green terraces with the muted satisfaction that only living gods achieve in middle age. Lolling under a parasol, protected from the spasms of heat that burned a bald eunuch's head, the

King and his alpha-haremite were receiving tribute in that cool, prickly bower of love. They appeared delighted with their new role as royal lovers, and I wedge "appeared" because even the happiest of couples teeter on the abyss of an unconfessed malaise. Siduri sat with her legs up on the Garden Throne, thin arms wrapped around her knees, purring like a cat. My Lord kissed her hand. She nodded her head happily as the wind ruffled her lovely brown curls. It was a bas-relief of pastoral bliss, warm zephyr winds that carried faint odors of the diviner's shop—of freshly filleted liver and gut—from down the lane.

And where was the third leg of the mighty Jackal, that faithful and true dog, Nergal? He was where he always was in those days of innocence before the Judaean war and his banishment to his damp and cockroach-filled hole: at the feet of the royal couple, tablet and reed in hand, on his hairy back, wagging his tail.

Wearing their stiffest wool robes, courtiers presented ceremonial pears to the divine couple, while ushers introduced a line of supplicants to be rebuked and a group of evil-doers to be scorned. It was a confirmation of all that the King had proclaimed.

"Muwatalli, King of the Hittites, bows before your divine effulgence!"

"Hail, Nebuchadnezzar, Lord of the Four Rims!"

"O, August One, please accept these gifts as recompense for your royal condescension!"

The princes of the earth lay prostrate before Nebuchadnezzar and offered choice cedar boxes with ivory-inlay, a dozen sun discs, seventy-two bronze bathing tubs, and a gift of one thousand deportees to be used at his discretion—as draftsman, quarrymen, painters, or scribes. There were bowing Ninevehans, lisping Nippurians, and submissive Marians who presented flocks of goats, baskets of wheat, bins of barley, and measures of flour and meal. There were two thousand sheep, four hundred chickens, straw for a thousand horses, chairs of ebony, and linen garments of every color. There were men-singers and women singers, she-assess and he-asses, and three hundred yokes of oxen.

Taxes and tribute for the King—and much tribulation for a eunuch whose job was to wedge it all down on a clay tablet. I noted the number of wheat bushels (twenty-three), estimated the amount of bread the City could expect in the next week (about two thousand loaves), and waited expectantly for the next line of supplicants. I was happy to observe that Nebuchadnezzar exuded an uncharacteristic confidence with one arm curled around Siduri's breast. He demanded more beer from his lithe and well-greased slaves and requested for another whole roast ox to be carried up the green hill. Gone was the anguish and turmoil of his lost years, the vicissitudes and uncertainty of the days spent in the wilderness, the anxiety and sorrow over a misspent youth. He had struggled with a heavy anointing from the gods, he had been burdened by an immense destiny, and he was no longer the beard his father had once dismissed as a wastrel. As he stroked Siduri's hair and nibbled a pear, I felt pride at my achievement, at our achievement.

"Is not this great Babylon?" my Lord shouted a little too loudly to his mistress. "Pigeon, I have built these Gardens for the house of the Kingdom, by the might of my power, and for the honor of your majesty!" As the Big Beard spoke, he raised his buttocks and emitted a long, aqueous fart.

The Hanging Gardens were the biggest plot of green in the City, filled with trees, flowers, and plants, many of which had been uprooted from the torn lands of the vanquished. Seven, stepped terraces rose up the hills of Ashur that had recently been brown stumps of grass. There were exotic blue roses that wound around bejeweled trellises and fruit trees in abundance—fig, date, melon, pear, quince, and pomegranate. Built as a concession to one of Siduri's frequent bouts of melancholy, the Gardens were said to resemble the hills of Megiddo in springtime: when the hill waters overflowed their banks, and the rocky, brown glades were transformed into lush, green slopes full of wild yellow flowers. It was a scribal truism, but the King's orchards spoke of the vigils of Ishtar: round pears hung low on the branches; apple trees shined with ripeness;

the fig and olive trees blossomed fruitfully, and clusters of currants spotted the vines that twisted and curled their green fingers around the vulnerable and unsuspecting trees.

As guards pulled long lines of captured soldiers before the King and concubine, I made wedges and lines in my tablet. The prisoners had the appearance of men whose lives were over: ashen faces and eyes like the cobalt sea. Soon they would be flayed alive or, if my Lord was in a good mood, decapitated. Clad in a gold breastplate, executed in the bold, repoussé style of old Babylonia, the King was said to embody a Rampaging Bull in his person, and I had to give the beard credit where credit was due. Nebuchadnezzar had always given a passable imitation of a warrior-king, and I admired his guts. With Harpagus's latest incursion into Aram, we had lost soldiers by the thousands to disease and other depredations of a protracted desert campaign, and yet the King never wavered. He simply raised his hand to the sun, and a thousand men died of river fever, five hundred souls were immured in a brick pillar.

O Nebuchadnezzar, your hand mixes clay with water! Your finger wedges the tablet of life!

Yet the King seemed off on that day in the Garden. He ignored the shouts of "thy decree is unrivaled" and "we await the chastisement of thy holy pleasure!" He perked up, however, when a minor prince

167

of the north presented him with a cart of heads and limbs collected during recent uprising in the West that had swept across the empire. From my brief tenure with the army, I had learned how to count the severed parts of our enemy, and I made a quick estimate. The pile contained fifty-two hands, dirtied and bruised by the revolt, sixty-some arms, forty-four feet, and about thirty heads. Each hand was hacked above the wrist. Some were tattooed with strange signs: faint arabesques or triangles. Others were too filthy with dried blood and mud to be recognizable as hands. And the heads were laid neatly in a row next to the pile of arms. The eyes of the decapitated always had that certain look. It was a look of surprise. A look that said, "How did this happen to me?"

"Pigeon, I have conquered the nations of the earth for you, by the power of my armies and for the glory of your name!"

"Oh yes, my Lord. You manifested this Great Abundance for You Will Be Who You Will Be," said Siduri, stretching her arm in the sun and gazing happily at the ruby wristband I had just removed from a lonely hand. Moments before, I had been rummaging among the limbs, looking for swag, swatting flies off the stinking flesh, when I had come upon the band, glittering in the afternoon light. The trinket had encircled a small wrist, a child's wrist, perhaps one of the standard-bearers of an Egyptian legion or a daughter of a Judaean zealot. When I gave it to her, she waggled her hand in front of the King, who grunted appreciatively.

"You are like Enlil, who delivered the mountain town to the shepherd. You subjugated the nations of the earth," she said.

"Hey, Nerggie, you know the virgins love thee! You know it! Hey, I am feeling particularly smiteful today! Who's got a bull ballock? I'm starved. And bring me some more beer!"

During a lull in the tribute line, the King spotted a ring on a hand he thought Siduri would like. It was a double-spiral, gold signet ring, and he ordered me to fetch it for his concubine. Flies continued to buzz on the stumps, crawling over the hands, covering them in a black mass. I reached through pile and twisted off the ring from a fat thumb. When I gave Siduri the ring, she gazed quizzically at the object, trying it on and taking it off (it was too big), and then, when the King wasn't looking, placing it in her pocket. When I returned to my place below my Lord's throne, Nebuchadnezzar raised a finger of gratification to the heavens and stroked my backside.

"Hey, Nerggie, I think you missed a bracelet on that hand," the King said as he took a cup of beer from a servant. "The hand on the bottom. Yeah, that's the one. Hey, this beer is damn fine. Are you thirsty, Nerggie? You're doing a good job with those hands, a damn fine job. I'm drinking another tankard of beer. You want one?"

"You are the heavens who provide the gentle rain, my Lord," I said.

"Now, this is a goodly and proper hand, Nerggie," said the King, taking a fresh hand from the pile. "No calluses. Soft and womanish. Perhaps he was a scribe like you?" Stroking my face gently with the hand, the King traced my cheek line from ear to jowl, pushing a dead fingernail into my face until he drew blood. He was a real jokester, my Nebuchadnezzar. He liked to find the weakest spot in a eunuch's soul, locate his deepest anxiety, and place a dead hand on it.

"Do you like that, Nerggie? Do you like my caresses? Hey, Pigeon, Nerggie likes it." The King stroked my face harder, slapping it slowly at first, with one dead hand and then another dead hand, and soon he was slapping my face faster and harder with both dead hands until I was on my knees. Holding the dead hands above his head, each flopping lifelessly to one side, my Lord danced a jig.

"I'm the hands of the gods," he sang, as his feet capered about the Garden. "I am the hands of the gods who mold and shape the world."

When my Lord finished his song, he placed both of the hands around my neck to mock-strangle me. The hands were cold and smelled like rotten beef. I feared he was going to toss me down the Garden stairs and so said a prayer to Nabû. "Oh, relax, Nerggie," he said. "I'm just playing with you. You know our love is better than beer. You know it!"

The King was not wrong, I thought. I picked up a hand with a small, green star tattooed on its thumb. Their love was better than beer.

A day after the Festival of the Golden Bull, Siduri had moved out of the harem and into Nebuchadnezzar's dark, smoky apartment. She didn't bring much with her, one or two temple skirts and a tiny silver band that had once belonged to her grandmother, which she wore on her little finger. The garrison-like atmosphere of the King's apartment was not to her liking, so she soon set about making plans for redecoration. She would replace the stone-winged griffins at the entrance with something less intimidating, and redo the brickwork in their bedroom. Their relationship was a miracle to them both. Nebuchadnezzar loved how Siduri oiled her legs after bathing, marveled over the way her comb lay on the floor after her toilette. He adored the smell of her hair after she had washed it in the pools of the Hanging Gardens. Long summer nights were spent playing Hounds and Jackals, gambling for small amounts of shekels that Siduri would always win, for she liked to cheat, and this, too, the King found adorable. The King couldn't believe that he could live with a woman so easily in his private quarters, and was pleased with himself. The one or two times he had done so in the past had ended disastrously—he banished the first to starve in the desert, and the fate of the second was too gruesome to record. When they were alone, Nebuchadnezzar hand-fed dates into the mouth of Siduri of Megiddo, and she poked him lovingly in his belly. Getting blind drunk was another thing the King and his concubine had in common; most nights, they drank two or three amphorae of wine and smoked copious amounts of Dream Dog that turned their brains into a thick porridge. It must be noted that Siduri's face had been transformed since the Festival of the Golden Bull: She had shed much of her habitual sadness. Her mouth was like a cork in an amphora of the finest beer—a cork the King liked to pull before and after dinner.

And yet there were problems—the proverbial flies in the ointment of their coupling. While heart, liver, spleen, and womb were pledged by Nebuchadnezzar and moon, stars, plenum, and greater plenum were invoked by Siduri, the concubine was plagued by fears that their words lacked divine substance. "Our love is greater than the Zargros Mountains and more powerful than the Euphrates," Nebuchadnezzar would say, while Siduri fanned herself on the throne of the Sacred Consort and privately fretted. But these fears were quieted by their nightly revels, the expensive clothes in which my Lord dressed Siduri, the places they visited—touring, for example, the mud pits where the City's bricks were made. They feasted nightly on roast oxen and beer, and I crouched expectantly by the couple as they nibbled beef bone and sipped from Marduk's cup, waiting for my call, waiting for my Lord to tap me on my shoulder and say, "Arise and go to Nineveh!" It was what he called our moment in the royal bedroll, a half-teasing, half-serious reference to my city of origin. "Arise and go to Nineveh!" my Lord would command, and I would arise and go to Nineveh.

When the lovers were both fully naked, Siduri would feign tears, and this was part of a game they played. Siduri would say she didn't want to make love. She would say that she wasn't ready, that she hardly knew him, that she wanted to take it slow. And the King would agree with her. He would say that he, too, wanted to wait, that all of his life had been spent looking for his one true passion, his one true love, and he didn't want to ruin it by sleeping with her prematurely (although, according to my harem tablets, they had already copulated vigorously seventy-two times). When the moment was right, my Lord would ease his heavy frame over her soft flesh, like a gigantic tapir slipping into the river, and the little dog Nergal would grip his reddish C—k between his thumb and forefinger, and Siduri's eyes would roll back as we slipped into her "happy place."

As harem scribe, I had never seen a concubine submit to Nebuchadnezzar's requests with such shameless abandon. She kissed his fungal toe, stroked his swollen face, pulled his fat and hairy belly upon her smooth, lemon-scented belly. With each congress, the Ziggurat would shake, and I knew that something big was happening, and one day she told the King that he was "the One." Lying on a lambskin rug on the floor of his apartment, Nebuchadnezzar stared at a mosaic of Ishtar on the ceiling, smiling his dumb post-coital smile. The divine barmaid played fitfully with the thick, matted hair on his chest and hummed a tune I didn't recognize.

"I think you're the One," she said, smiling slyly.

"Of course I am the One," he said, placing a grape in Siduri's mouth. "I have always been the One. All my subjects know that I am the Great I AM."

"And don't forget Gargantuan of the Plain," I offered.

"That goes without saying," he said, slapping the bottom of his exhausted eunuch. In many ways this is how I prefer to remember my Lord, before the dark philter of Siduri's love seeped into his veins. He was happy and confident in his role as Divine Plowman, yet relatively free of the obsession that would come to dominate him.

As more deportees paraded before us, Nebuchadnezzar remarked on the solidity of my backside, something about how he had once lost one of his gold rings on a tear in my woolen skirt, but Siduri didn't laugh, or she didn't laugh loud enough. That's when I saw it. That's when the King had his first attack or the beginnings of what our doctors called the madness of Nebuchadnezzar. This shift was subtle: his brown eyes turned black, and a panic seemed to slam into his chest like one of Harpagus's battering rams. He stared at my lips, which had wrapped themselves around a beer straw, a straw that Siduri had passed to me from her lips. It was an innocent gesture, or so I thought at the time, though now I am not so sure. She had opened her mouth and handed me the straw, reddened with her lipstick, and I had placed my mouth where her lips had been. Normally eunuchs were considered beneath notice by the concubine class, and the thought of sharing a beer straw between harem girl and castrate would have been a serious offense, but I had been granted a dispensation by the King from this ancient and foolish prejudice. Nebuchadnezzar choked on his beer as if it was a locust.

"I've got something I want to say," said the King, grabbing a sun fan from one of his attendants.

"What is it, my Lord?" asked Siduri.

"When we look through the heap of human hands, I feel I lose you."

"What do you mean?"

"I said that when we look through the heap of human hands, I feel I lose you," he said. "When I pick up a hand from the pile, you go someplace else."

"I go to the spirit world and dream of the gods," she said, reaching for her drinking cup, which I had been holding for her. Our hands touched for a moment, and I thought of her lying on my Lord's bed, surrounded by tapestries and fine linen. I thought of the auburn curl of her pubic hair. I loved that curl.

"It's not just when we examine the hands for booty," said the King, who twirled the sun fan aggressively in his hand. "Sometimes, when we watch an execution, too. It's like you're not there. Like you go someplace else. I can't really describe it another way. Do you remember when I crushed that sower of scorn's head on a rock? And I was trying to tell you about the history of rock execution, how my father instituted rock crushing as the last decree of his kingship, as a legacy and gift to me, so I could have my prisoners' heads crushed by a rock. Do you remember that? How only rocks hewed from quarries from Babylon were to be allowed when dispensing with an enemy? And that's why whenever I witness a prisoner getting crushed by a rock, it makes me think of my father. Do you remember? Do you? You see, you don't even know what I'm talking about."

"I am not sure I like the sound of this," Siduri said, her voice rising in anger.

The unhappy couple was fighting now. He complained about her on-the-shekel mood swings and wintery silences. She called him a blunderer and a fool.

Egyptian lilies fluttered in the breeze. Sheep, unshepherded, wandered amid the lush grass. There was a time when Siduri and the King nibbled on quail eggs stuffed with figs, rubbed unguents of palm and nut oil on each other's chests. But not today. Outside the Garden walls lay crusted fields and stiff furrows. There were granaries half-full. You could smell the burnt corn and barley left to rot in the field.

"Nerggie," the King implored me. "You understand what I am saying, don't you? Look at her.

Her silences are formidable. She becomes like snow on the mountains. And stubborn, too. Like a general. I haven't experienced stubbornness like that on the battlefield. It's her Megiddogian background. They're all like that. It comes from living on dung-heaps."

Siduri was a seasoned foot soldier in the field of love. She enjoyed a good fight and used silence to a brilliant tactical advantage. A stupid remark by Nebuchadnezzar—such as "where were you last night, honey-pot?"—and then the abyss of Siduri's silence. Siduri's silences were deep and cold. No life could survive there. Her silences were like rocks of heaven that sometimes strike the earth.

"I am just wondering what's going on with you. You are never really there for me when I need you," said the King.

Siduri reapplied red paint to her lips. Gods, she was depressed. That's what she whispered to me one afternoon in the Hanging Gardens, after I had awoken from a nap—from a happy dream in which I had stabbed my brother in his bedsheets. She said she was so depressed she felt like killing herself. In the last month, Siduri had been nostalgic for her home city and had entered a deep sadness over her exile in Babylon. And she was drinking more than ever.

Exile is the central sorrow in our City. To uproot a concubine or a eunuch, for that matter— pulling them from their smoldering cities—was like hacking off a limb. We mainly were exiles in Babylon, cut off from tribe and clan, lonely, and mystified at our rage toward the Gate of the Gods. Moreover, Siduri's melancholy wasn't merely the sadness of the stranger in a foreign land. Her sadness was a sadness compounded by the harem. The concubines were an unhappy lot, or as the apostate Pea once said: "Who wouldn't be depressed after a lifetime smelling that beard's ballocks?" Sadly, most of the girls were unbelievers, and if her remark sounded heretical, let me wedge that I personally liked the way the King's ballocks smelled.

They smelled like a god.

"And lately, lately," the King sobbed, "after we make love, you never seem to be wholly mine. You seem to be withholding. Isn't that right, Nerggie? Tell her. She's not there. Tell her she's withholding!"

"Nerggie, what is this asshole talking about?" Siduri asked. "What in the gods' names? Are you two talking about me behind my back? I won't put up with that kind of betrayal. Nerggie, answer my question."

"My lady …" I said. A strong wind blew through the fig trees.

"Don't answer her, Nerggie. Siddie, leave Nergal out of this. He has nothing to do with what I am talking about. You are trying to avoid my question. When we make love, you don't nuzzle my neck with your nose anymore. How come you never nose-nuzzle my neck anymore? How come?"

"I nuzzle your neck," she said.

178

"No, you don't. Not the way you used to. Nerggie will back me up on this. Nerggie, tell her that she never nuzzles me with her nose."

"But, my Lord," I said, "I saw her nuzzle your neck with her nose this afternoon."

"Yes, but that was different. There is something different about her nuzzling. I can't explain it. Why won't anyone believe me?"

"Nebbie, what are you talking about? You know that I nuzzle your neck all the time. You are making this up. Admit it. It's all in your head," Siduri said.

"I dunno," the King said meekly, backing down. "It's just that I worry sometimes. I get the worries. Tell her, Nerggie, about how I can't sleep at night. Nerggie?"

"My lady, the King, as you well know, suffers from sleeplessness, and—"

"That's it. I will not put up with you two talking behind my back. I am done with this conversation." Siduri raised her hand in my face, stopping me midsentence. I smiled, bowed, and said nothing.

"You go someplace else. Admit it," said the King, who was crying now. "You're not there. You're never there for me. Why won't you just admit it?"

"Are you saying I don't love you?" said Siduri. "How could you say that? I thought that you loved *me*. If you loved me, you wouldn't be saying that."

"But I do love you," said the King. "That's what I'm trying to tell you."

"That's not what I am hearing." Siduri unexpectedly took my hand, and her touch burned like the fires of Ereshkigal. "Come on, Nergal, let's go. I don't want to talk about this anymore."

The King picked up an amphora of wine, a heavy Grecian import, depicting two beautiful boys in an embrace, and poured it over her head. The red liquid covered her hair, face, and blouse, matting her eyelashes, now thick with tears and rage.

"I have just about had it with your childishness," she said, her voice quivering.

"And I have had it with your . . . er, er . . ." the Lord of hosts searched and failed to find the right words to express himself. Lately, the King walked around the Great Hall as if there were an ax lodged in his chest. He didn't know why he was so unhappy. Whenever he was not with Siduri, he succumbed to an overwhelming anxiety. He said love wasn't supposed to feel like a worm in his stomach. He said that he felt like the seal on his heart was cracked and that he was going to die. And nothing, he said, could wash away the fear or panic of losing his beloved.

"Why won't you talk to me?" he pleaded. "Why? Why? Why?"

Silence.

"Siddie! Just talk to me! Please!"

Silence.

"Please, just tell me, what did I do? Just tell me!"

More silence.

Tablet Eight

Siduri sat down on the grass, folded her arms, and refused to speak. Instead of telling the King how she had never recovered from her deportation, instead of telling him that the pain of seeing Megiddo in flames and hearing the cries of her younger brother lying under the collapsed wall was too much to bear, she picked up a desolate hand and threw it across the Garden. The hand whirled over a row of courtiers like a fireball shot by one of the King's battalions on the walls of a besieged city. The miserable lackeys sought refuge under the pear trees. And while Siduri's behavior angered Nebuchadnezzar—he lifted the sun fan again and raised it above his head—she didn't give a damn. She was just warming up to her waste-laying and destruction-making. She took another hand and threw it at the King. He ducked, and the hideous appendage hit my face. I fell to the grass, stunned.

The doors of the underworld opened as dismembered hands, feet, and heads flew across the Garden. Siduri hoisted two bloodied heads and tossed them both at the King, who deflected the first with the sun fan, while the other struck a lady-in-waiting. Siduri's rage was a lamentation, a windstorm offering to the god of the storm, Enlil. Crying uncontrollably, Siduri dug into the pile of heads. She beaned me with an old man's putrid head, knocking me nearly unconscious. Siduri enjoyed getting worked up. I could tell by the way she picked up one hand after another and hurled each at the Bull King, who had crawled under his throne. She seemed more alive angry than happy. Her final act was to pull out a small clay tablet from her blouse, a tablet in which she had recorded all of the small secrets the King had shared with her about himself and smashed it into innumerable pieces at his feet.

Nebuchadnezzar was weeping. He was on his knees, gathering the stray bits of anatomy, and tucking them under his arms. He grabbed a foot from under a rosebush and pulled a hand from an apricot tree. Lost in his tears, he clambered across the terrace, collecting sundry body parts. His plan for the dead appendages was unclear, but he appeared to be reconstructing or building a person or what seemed to be a person—it was too grotesque to be an actual beard. But my Lord was too upset to realize what he was doing. His labor finished, the King stood up and beheld the unseemly thing he had made. The monstrous figure had three heads and seven arms, twelve feet and six hands.

I have often wondered what exactly motivated my Lord that day in the Garden. Was the hideous, disfigured being a self-portrait? Perhaps. Although at times, lying in my sweaty sheets at night, filled with regret and unable to sleep, I think it was his relationship with Siduri that he was putting back together—the intimacy that he once described to me as like water on water.

Nebuchadnezzar blubbered over a final hand, trying and failing to fit it onto an arm. The hand was too small, and he couldn't make it work. Then, when he realized that it was a child's hand, he sobbed more violently.

Tablet Nine –

The Dew of Heaven

Three days after his breakup with Siduri, I found Nebuchadnezzar suspended from a cedar branch with an elaborate system of ropes wrapped around his chest and neck, his skirt around his ankles, and a thick stream of ejaculate spattering his sandals. The tree was old, dead, and gnarled, with its bark mostly stripped off. The rope around his neck had twisted his features into a dullish-blue death mask.

When things were going badly with Siduri, Nebuchadnezzar would take up this little-known and esoteric practice—what Moil and the neuties called "scarfing"—and boy, did it have a terrible effect on our weather. I could always tell when the King was scarfing because the skies, as if by strange alchemical magic, would transform. If they had been clear and calm, clouds would gather and the winds would pick up. If the sun was at its apex, the sky would darken. One time, after a particularly gratifying session with his ropes, there was a report of a partial eclipse of the moon. Unfortunately, the King's scarfing, and the resulting reversals of the heavens, were unpredictable and hard to control. After one violent fight with the Megiddogian—my Lord wanted to know why she had refused to come to bed (she was drinking wine with his favorite eunuch)—the King went missing for a week, which he spent indulging in this desperate practice.

When I lifted Nebuchadnezzar from the ground, the sun retreated behind a cloud—blackening the sky. Oh, the power of my Lord's shameful habit! Had my brother only known about the potency of this mysterious act, perhaps the fate of Babylon would have been different. To the seasoned eunuch, however, the gods work in inscrutable ways.

The ligature strapped around the King's body was difficult to remove. Half rope, half leather, the apparatus was designed to induce a state of ecstasy known only to our mystics and priests. This practice, while theologically untenable, was not without its adherents in the Omnia. Bel-u-ball-it wrote a strenuous monograph on the subject, although I confess I have never read it. In those first days of their tumultuous love affair, I read very little. I was too busy running interference between Siduri and the King, assuaging her fears about being swallowed whole by my Lord's desperate need and placating his anxieties over her perceived abandonment. The King, however, must have had someone read this mysterious and dangerously potent tablet to him. His position bore all the usual signs of Bel-u-ball-it's treatise on fertility: the quarter moons carved into the leather straps around his chest, the rag soaked in vinegar balled up in his hand for reviving himself, and the crudely drawn and rather vulgar pictographs of naked concubines in lewd positions at his feet. How many times in the past week had Nebuchadnezzar auto-strangulated? It was a question worth pursuing, given the extremes in weather we had been having. If the King's body *was* closely tied to the land, as our priests and mages insisted, then that would explain the skies last week: wind and heat followed by sandstorm, followed by wind and heat again. But never rain.

With great effort, I untied the ropes and slipped off the straps from his shoulders; he was still breathing, thank Marduk, and once he hit the ground soon woke up, spitting blood and saliva from his chapped lips. My Lord groaned miserably. Crumpled in the grass, he strained to lift his once-regal head, which now resembled a fat tick just pulled from a dog. Nebuchadnezzar was almost hairless. In a fit of desperation, the King had cut off his beard and yanked the hair from his head, leaving little bloody stubs on his scalp. He was caked with mud and smeared with filth. When I asked him how he was feeling, my Lord burrowed back into the dirt, fingering a pimple on his nose like an adolescent who dislikes himself only slightly more than he dislikes the world. A dry wind blew through the weeds and dead bushes. Flies plagued the blisters on the King's arms and legs.

Sad to wedge, but in the days following his fight with Siduri, Nebuchadnezzar lost his shit. The poor fool had been unmanned, to borrow a phrase from Chibby. Siduri had trimmed his beard, alright. Ripped it out by the roots. The divine barmaid's dangerously subversive doctrines of "my soul's delight" and "you're the One" had opened a void within his bronze-plated breast and revealed a sniveling, miserable lunatic. He didn't like it. Nobody did. Fear spread among the royal scribes like a buzzing horde of locusts on a field of wheat; a careful listener could hear the munch-munch-munch of "Will I be the next to be skinned alive?" or "Will he crush Bi-reed under a rock?" throughout the Tablet House. We in the College of Eunuchs expected the usual bad behavior—the terror and mayhem one usually associated with a mad tyrant, the wild and not entirely baseless accusations of betrayal, the slow midnight garroting and casual savageries that were characteristic of a despot's fall. Moil put a body-count pool together, arranging the game around which scribal lackey or sandal-licker would be executed first. Chibby predicted that it would be me, but I placed sixty shekels on my brother.

Our worries, however, were misplaced. Instead of piking a counselor's head on a rampart or tossing a eunuch down the terraced stairs of the Hanging Gardens, the King had disappeared. Vanished. The tumultuous affair with Siduri had shaken the foundation of Nebuchadnezzar's already tenuous being. It had been a real decline and fall, as Love and its handmaiden, Desolation, crashed the gates of his empire and put his cities to the torch and slew their inhabitants. But those banal, imperial metaphors in no way did justice to his anxiety over their relationship—one minute they were coupling sloppily in a Ziggurat stairwell, and the next, they were throwing votives at each other's heads. It was of course technically difficult for a concubine to break up with the King. That said, Siduri did a better job than most. It had been tried by one or two naïve harem girls; they were invariably tied to crags in the desert and eaten by scorpions. Few girls, at least to my knowledge, had ever said no to Nebuchadnezzar. If you were the King's girl, your job was to take it. But not Siduri of Megiddo. Siduri didn't take it from anyone.

Things were bad and getting worse. The complaints from the Illegitimates grew louder by the hour, as did the grumblings in the harem, and the long bread lines that wound around Ésagila night and day could no longer be ignored. The Court, however, remained ignorant of Nebuchadnezzar's problems with his concubine. My brother had seen to that by telling them that the King was indisposed with river fever, but few believed him. Moil sniggered when I told him I was bringing a hot cloth to my Lord. Bunt cornered me in the harem one morning and threatened me with his stylus if I refused to provide information. I spat on his slave-made sandals.

Mounting my mule, I rode through the Ishtar gate to search for my Lord—for I was as miserable as the King without the Jackal. The sky opened before me. The smell of gypsum and salt thickened the air, aggravating my allergies, which made my eyes water. Would that my tears could water the earth! The desert crouched under the sun like a hapless eunuch before his King, with vast spaces where no life dwelt. I knew all about the arid plains; the longing of lifeless hills and dead valleys, the desolation of wind-blasted land.

My mule was ornery, giving the lie to the belief that mules were docile and easy to guide. The mule's thick torso and long ears were ugly, but I liked him nonetheless. A superior species, possessing the sobriety and solidness of the ass and the strength and valor of the horse, the mule was bred primarily in Babylon as a pack-animal, but eunuchs knew the value of a hybrid being and rode them for everyday use.

I searched the plains for a few hours and found nothing—other than a group of Diggers shuffling about the dead fields, looking up to the sky, muttering about the heat. There had always been a multitude of down-and-out beards outside the City's gates: paupers, ex-prisoners, out-of-work laborers, down-and-out scribes who couldn't hack it in the Tablet House. These and other malcontents lived on what they could scavenge, and most were refugees from the vanquished peoples my Lord had rent into submission: Scythians, Cimmerians, Syrians, Jews and other victims of the Babylonian Bull legions. They were known as Diggers, a subgroup of the derelicts who eked out an existence by fashioning bricks for the King's numerous building projects.

The Diggers' village consisted of hundreds of huts made out of dung and mud. Dry mud encrusted hovels that heated up to one hundred and sixty degrees during the day. Lying to the right of the town, the "mud fields" stretched out beyond the horizon: cubit upon cubit of clay, which, when combined with sand, dung and water, were used to fashion the bricks that built our cities. Every brick in the Ziggurat was reputed to come from these fields. Every brick! In a tablet presented to the Gelded Society of Good Fellows, Moil estimated that there were seventy-two hundred thousand bricks in the Tower. All that mud, dung, and straw mixed diligently by human hands, fired by the rays of Shamash. It was a privilege to climb its sacred steps, but I am digressing.

Circling back to Babylon, I found my Lord in a barren wheat field. Six oxen had gathered around him like the scoffing prophets of Israel, ankle-deep in dust, chewing boluses of cud. They were miserable animals: thin, bony, and depressed by the drought. An old cowherd stood in what was left of the field of lilies.

When I asked him why he did not try to save the King, he smiled and shrugged his shoulders.

"Because he ordered me not to, that's why," the cowherd said. "He's been out here for a few days now. Sometimes he weeps like a baby. Other times he rages at the stars. And then there is that thing there with the ropes. But mostly he just stares at the grass."

"Has anyone else been out here?" I asked. "Anyone at all? Anyone else seen him like this? Say, like a tall, ginger-bearded fellow with a funny way of speaking?"

"Just me and these cows," he said, gesturing to the emaciated beasts. "They've seen everything, but don't you worry none; they don't mind what he does. It's all the same to them, you know. As long as they have grass to eat, they're happy. Not like that poor fellow over there. No, no one's been here, except you."

"*Necromantia,*" said the King when he saw me. "It's a word I learned from your brother. Summoning the dead. Are you dead, Nergal? My father is dead. Your father is dead. My Siduri's love is dead. But I am not dead. I am a god. Forgive me my constipation."

"My Lord, we have been worried about you. Siduri is worried about you."

"I am He who causes the green herb to sprout up. Did you know, Nergal, that the length of the Euphrates from its source in the mountains is five million cubits by boat," the King said, touching his face where his beard should have been. "The 'serpent river' is what the Sumerians called it. And did you know that complete agrarian collapse is imminent? Starve and die, I say."

"My Lord."

"All trees are not frankincense," he said, staring into my eyes. "The scent of your garments is treachery. Did you know that the sun has a flock of ewes? He has seventy-two ewes."

"My Lord, it is Nergal."

Among the thorns and nettles, I caressed Nebuchadnezzar's head and told him it was time to come home. He stared, as if in a trance. For some time we sat quietly together on the dead grass. He rubbed the swollen rope burns on his throat, and I brooded upon this apoplexy of his soul. All men think their burdens are the heaviest, but my Lord was not all men.

How shall I describe the King's condition? Unhorsed? Unbearded? Unsworded? As a child, I had once witnessed a spider kill a wasp. After winding her prey in a silky thread, she stuck the insect with her poisoned stinger. It was an action she repeated numerous times, until the wasp was paralyzed. The spider then removed the insides from the creature, leaving a vacant, pellucid shell. That is what Nebuchadnezzar had become in the wake of his affair with the golden queen—a husk of himself, a translucent mass that rattled in the wind. The King offered me something to eat from his leather sack. Within the small bag were four roasted goat testicles. I chose the smallest one, and we sat munching in the sun. The gonad was salty and pliant in my mouth.

"My Lord," I said, "it's time to get back to the Ziggurat."

"In my lifetime, I have seen rivers of blood," whispered Nebuchadnezzar. "Rivers that have flowed into seas, and seas that have flowed into oceans. Oceans of red. Sometimes I dream in red. Do you ever dream in color? My dreams are bathed in crimson. I am surrounded by enemies and betrayers. I have put entire populations to the sword with a wave of my hand, or merely because of indigestion, without losing a wink of sleep. No, no, no, this desperate feeling I have is no idle trifling." My Lord spoke quickly to suppress a cough.

A rumble of thunder, sweet with its suggestions of metaphysical relief, rolled in the distance, and I thought I heard the patter of rain on the dirt, but no, it was only the blackbirds squabbling. Their skinny claws sprang up and down on a willow branch, beaks squawking and spitting, as they fought for position. One of them had dropped a dead mouse at the base of the tree, its neck twisted, broken and bloodied, and the other birds squawked threateningly. In a moment, they all began to toss small stones at the mouse, a curious practice that I had once witnessed in Nineveh as a child. One bird would pick up a pebble and drop it on the ground, and the others, heads turned curiously as if they were being solicited to a new game or strange religious ritual, would follow suit—ping, ping, ping.

"You know," he said. "I was getting just a teensy-bit bored with her, too. I needed another month for the heat to cool off, and then I would have gotten rid of her. I would have been fine. Look at this."

Handing me a broken, marble shard, my Lord brightened a moment. It was part of a palace bas-relief that the King, in a fit of anger, had destroyed the day Siduri had thrown him out of their apartment. In the picture, a chiseled and stout-hearted Nebuchadnezzar, Conqueror of Judah, leads a line of naked and bound prisoners into the City. While the piece was only a fragment, muddied and broken around the edges, it was nevertheless impressive, conveying the sublimity of his military exploits, and I told him so.

"Yeah, that's me," he said. "And do you see that one there? The fourth in line? The one with the iron collar around her neck and bound hands?"

"My Lord, your beard, you're bleeding. We need to get you back home."

"That's her. That's my Siduri."

"You look good together."

"Happier times, I guess," the King sighed.

Pebble on rock. Ping, ping, ping. A blackbird squawked at us and dropped a claw full of pellets. It sounded like the fusillade three months ago at the siege of Elam, where our great King's armies flung down thousands of sling bullets and round clay balls upon a pacified populace, entombing them in their homes, suffocating them in the dust of broken brick and mortar.

194

Buried in blackened rubble used to be a fate visited on the peoples of the valley fairly regularly—when Nebuchadnezzar was healthy and feeling up to the snuff, and soon, too soon, thanks to the strange magic of his favorite eunuch, he'd be doing it again.

"They are blaming me for this so-called drought, you know," he said, a tad defensively.

"No one is blaming you, my Lord."

He reached out and took my hand, blubbering words of affection. "You are my rose, you are my gazelle that leaps in spring, you are my everything," he gasped. His eyes brimmed with tears, and he pulled me into his arms, which were strong and speckled with light hair. "Because it would be a pity if you were to betray me, Nerggie," he said, an arm curled around my back as he rubbed my bottom.

"I am an ever-faithful eunuch." The sun's rays warmed our backs. A small, blue butterfly landed on the King's shoulder, twitched its wings, and took off again.

"Ha! Good answer. So am I. Gods, I'm depressed living in this stinking City! Oh, Nerggie. My body is dying. But my soul"—and he took my hand and placed it on his chest, which heaved with emotion— "still craves the consolations of love. You think I'm ridiculous, don't you? But you, too, will grow old one day," he said, his fingers winding themselves around my throat, gently but with the promise of pain. The King did not strangle me that day, as so many frustrated lovers do. He did not wrap his weathered fingers around my windpipe and close them like Ereshkigal's door to the underworld. He did something more surprising—he confided in me. Again.

"All of my ministers think they know what is wrong, and they think they have the solution. Ignorant asses! They don't. I will tell you the problem. They breathe too loudly at the table. The harem girls breathe too loudly when they eat. I can't stand loud breathers or loud eaters, and I loathe the pairing. Enlil shall have his revenge."

What was the origin of my Lord's unhappiness? He was broken-hearted over his affair with Siduri, and yes, the ministers and priests were blaming him for the drought, but it was more than that. Much more. It is my belief that my Lord Nebuchadnezzar had awakened to the fundamental misery of being a beard. He had reached that place in life where his limitations outstripped his abilities. A spoiled prince, he despised the responsibilities of the Bull Throne, and it would not be unfair to wedge that Nebuchadnezzar lacked the basic tools of kingship. The lion hunt no longer interested him, and he waved off healings in the desert with an irritated hand. Last week he had confessed to me in the middle of a constipated night that he was bored by deporting whole populations, and besieging towns was completely out of the question, what with his bad legs and chronic shingles. As far as erecting his image in the desert—well, forget it.

"My gods, Nerggie! I am so tired of their prudery and small-mindedness! Nobody understands why I chose Siduri rather than Inanna, Mater, or Urshe. Why her, they ask? Why settle on one? Well, I'm tired of the harem. The gods know how hard I try to make a bastard, Nergal. You know how hard I have tried this past year."

"Your labors have been formidable, my Lord."

"I have tried every combination, Nergal, every combination known to Nabû. The Elamite with the Amorite with the Moabite with the Assyrian with the Mede with the Jew with the Greek. There is only so much variation. Do you know how difficult it is for a Moabite to achieve orgasm? I believe I have a disproportionate number of Moabites in my harem."

It took me a while to realize that Nebuchadnezzar wasn't as mad as I had initially believed. The bloody scalp, the long fingernails, and hollow eyes had fooled me. He was depressed, and I don't think he had ever been depressed before in his life. Not my Lord. Oh no, he had always, always been the immovable one. Nothing ever pulled his chariot; he wasn't capable of being affected by other people's sufferings. Ten thousand of his subjects could perish of river fever, and he'd be out javelining a lion or hawking with his generals in the fields of greater Babylon. But when he began to cry, I knew that I had a whole new tyrant on my hands: a blubbering, whimpering tyrant. Anything could happen.

"I have not slept in a week. My bowels are gummed up. I'm having thoughts, wild thoughts of Ashur and Telepinu, Tiamat and the rest. They come to me in the night and chastise my armies for destroying their temples. I'm afraid the gods are having their revenge upon me, Nergal, and I am powerless before their wrath. Powerless! Do know what that feels like? Of course, you do. But I, Nebuchadnezzar, King of the Four Rims and Scythe of the Wheat and Chaff—have never felt fear, not until recently, and do you know something? I don't like it." He then grabbed my buttocks hard to emphasize his misery. "I'm having thoughts about Siduri, Nerggie. Terrible thoughts about her. Why did she say all those things to me if she didn't mean them?" The King gasped like a spear had just be screwed into his chest by a wild-eyed Bactrian. "She said that I was the One. *The One.*"

"You will always be the One with me, my Lord," I said.

"We had picked out the names of our children," he said, waving a fat bull ballock in my face.

"My Lord, we need to get out of the heat."

"We were like Ulligarra and Zalgarra. Newly created and divine."

When a King gets sacked by a concubine, there is only one thing he desires more than "getting back together." He wants to grab a poor eunuch by his buttocks and tell him about it. From the beginning. I tried and failed to mask my boredom, but

198

Nebuchadnezzar didn't notice; he was even more oblivious to others than before, if that were possible. He blubbered on and on about how when Siduri held him for the first time, he experienced joy, an emotion—to hear him tell it—entirely new to him.

"It began with an exchange of letters," he said. "She can read and wedge, you know."

I knew. Siduri and I had exchanged letters; in fact, my tablets—wedged in impeccable Akkadian—may well have contributed to her latest break-up with the King. After reading my letters, she had come to find Nebuchadnezzar dull. She complained that he had "nothing to say" and that his mind was "so conventional."

"She said that I was her true and only love. Why would she say that, if she didn't mean it?" he asked again.

"True and only love" for Siduri meant different things at different times. For she indulged this "true and only love" with dozens of lovers: broken-hearted harem girls, carping eunuchs, and a variety of mud-smeared rulers of the world.

While I ruminated over the antinomies of the concubine, the King began a detailed monologue on Siduri's charms and imperfections. He was fixated on how "sweet" she was, the little things she did for him to make each day "more cozy." That was the phrase he used, too, "more cozy." While my Lord was never known for his verbal wizardry, he never had, as far as I could recall, sunk to the insipidity of harem-talk. But there he was, with tears and mucus covering his face, using the word "cozy" to describe everything from a rare strain of Eastern tea to the flaying alive of a lapsed Mardukian.

He listed the pet names they had for each other. Most of the King's began with the phonetic "s," an all-too-obvious variation on the concubine's first name: Sibby, Sooby, Silly, Sibby-Sooby, Silly-Dibby-Sooby. Others took their charm from a one-stress rhyme: Pip, Whip, Jip. But there were still other names whose origins were more recondite: Mistress of the Wheat and Tares and Lady Sow and Reap.

He detailed their intimacies in elaborate narratives that left nothing to speculation. These I shall pass over in silence, condescending only to remark that the lust-infatuate couple had devised code names for their favorite positions. He described Siduri's one-thousand-and-one pairs of undergarments, the pearl-beaded skirts that sent him into antic fits, the embroidered silks that he had stolen after the Dance of the Serpents, an undergarment that he now wore.

The scene of Nebuchadnezzar's passion smelled of butchery and blood. That was clear enough from the infested howls emitted from the poor beard's mouth. He wailed about her mood swings. He despaired over her muteness. It appeared that, like a god, Siduri could often only be experienced negatively. One moment she was wedging poetry on what she had for breakfast, and the next, she was slamming doors and throwing cats across the room.

"And now, it is all over," the King whimpered.

"Your generals have been requesting reinforcements in the West, my Lord. The Egyptian hordes are threatening Palestine again. They require—nay, demand—an answer."

"She locked herself in a room for three days. When she finally came out, she still wouldn't speak to me," he moaned.

"Uruk believes additional troops can be levied in Media," I said. "The generals have signaled that they might be amenable to such an action. What do you think?" I said, trying to draw him to other subjects. My Lord was very keen on all things having to do with his imperial army.

"That cunt Harpagus. He's behind this. Oh, I just had a terrible thought, Nerggie. I'm going to ask you a question, and if you know the truth, I want you to tell me. Siduri's never been with Harpagus, has she? He brought her into the harem, and I know that bastard too well. He always samples the booty, from guzzling purloined wine to burning and eating a stolen bull. The thought of her with Harpagus makes me physically ill. I know what a sick bastard he is. By Ea, I can't get the images out of my head. It's agony. Oh, Nerggie! Tell me she's never been with him! Please, don't spare me."

"There are tax levies that need to be signed, my Lord," I said, visualizing those same images that now pained the King, and feeling slightly nauseous myself. "Come, my Lord, I believe those are rain clouds on the horizon, and the winds are picking up. Perhaps the gods are sending you a sign."

"She has, hasn't she? I knew it. That fucker! Oh, he's going to pay for that breach of trust. Where is he?"

Looking back now, I am now certain that something had broken within the King that day, one could almost hear the tendon of his blindness snap. That's the thing about concubines. They were never safe from the lusting and insatiate eyes of other beards. Eunuchs were notoriously easy to bribe. A half-shekel and a roasted goat's joint could get a beard a bit of harem flesh on any feast day of the week. If Nebuchadnezzar could not possess his beloved, he knew that some beard, sooner or later, but probably sooner, would penetrate the walls of the harem, and subsequently, Siduri, and it was that thought, more than any other, that sealed Babylon's watery end—and hers.

"Nerggie," he said, pulling me around to get a better grip on my buttocks. "Did you know the Ziggurat was burned to the ground by fire three times? Twice inundated by water? Did you? It was swallowed by sand ... let's see, twice, if I am not mistaken. It was a good thing, too. Because each time the Ziggurat was rebuilt, it was bigger. Will you tickle my back?"

As I pushed down on his soft upper buttocks with my palms and lightly scratched his spine, he moaned softly. Poor Nebuchadnezzar. My Lord's problems were not merely of a religious nature, although they were that too. A lifetime of excess had taken its toll: his bald head and depressed spirits all signified a life on the wane; his remaining years were less than those he had lived, and he was taking stock, reassessing his position as Lord of Destruction. It is sad to wedge, but he had reached that time in his life when a beard preferred a backrub from his trusted eunuch to turning a city into a mound of potsherds.

"Mar-nabu added forty floors to the top floor of the Ziggurat, three of jade. Tel-war constructed the magnificent Temple of the Two Lions. As you know, my father built the tile pools in the harem, pools that are said to be visited by the ghosts of his favorite three concubines—they died of lung fever, I think, after the invasion of Nineveh. Just think what I can do if the Ziggurat is overrun by the Egyptian swine—the Elamites could betray us, and the Median alliance could dissolve the second Harpagus believes it to be to his advantage. It's my only consolation. I can rebuild."

"My King," I said, "you are He Who Builds Ziggurats that Reach unto the Heavens. You shall ever sit on the Throne of the Golden Bull."

"Could you tickle a little lower, Nerggie? Could you please? Ooh, that's it, that's it."

Tablet Ten –

When His Navel-Cord Was Cut,
for Him She Was Destined

She scribbled her first letter on papyrus, in Aramaic script, which I had mastered enough to read her beautifully formed yodhs, nuns, and samkaths. But it wasn't the script that impressed me. It was the sound of her voice coming through the marks with sacred intensity: low, sweet, strangely matter-of-fact, as if she was perched on an eternal lounge-bed. Siduri's voice, with its slight Aramaic accent, could raise the dead. Like the mantic utterances I would later learn from Madame Grape in the desert, Siduri's voice could regenerate a eunuch and return him to an undreamed state of potency. She could make a blind beard see, a deaf beard hear. Through our letters, night after night, I would slither, dreamlike, on my belly across the cold tiles of the King's apartment and wrap myself around her thighs, where Siduri would feed me a few dying flies before placing me in a wicker basket next to the bed. Then she would proceed to violently couple with my Lord. Shamaness. Priestess. Mystical concubine. You crushed me like a bed louse between your thumb and forefinger!

Why did I wedge her back? It was Siduri's letters—more than my brother's phony haruspexing—that brought Babylon to its knees. Nebuchadnezzar was terrible at small talk; all the ministers at Court knew that. He was a living god, yet the truth is that living gods sometimes have trouble expressing themselves. Because of this uncomfortable fact, the King had tasked me with the emotional heavy lifting of the relationship. It wasn't serious. Siduri and I exchanged letters, nothing more than that. There's no need to deny that it was I who did the hard time of late-night pillow talk. It was I who had to take a moment from my busy harem schedule to wedge little notes to explain where he was and what he was doing. It was I who listened to her complaints when she and the King were fighting, and they were always fighting. Nebuchadnezzar wanted to know what she liked (a Jewish prophet named Moses, gold basket earrings, past-life experiences, beer, her likeness on a bas-relief, lion cubs) and what she didn't like (Amytis's hairstyle, Uruk's breath); what she ate for lunch (extremely spicy beef sandwiches without the bread); where she came from (a small town outside of Megiddo), and who she was before her deportation to Babylon (a child). But most of all, my Lord wanted to know whom she had fucked before she had met him.

He wanted the details. All of them. And I delivered. I got the information. One might be tempted—and some scribes and diviners have not resisted the temptation—to trace the origin of our subsequent invasion of Judah back to this crisis.

I have a tiny confession to make. It was around the time of the Three-Legged Jackal that I noticed a lone, curly hair sprouting from my chin. Alas, the origin of this black beast, and others that soon followed, is no mystery. Since my miraculous performance at the Festival of the Golden Bull, I had been consuming between one and two dozen of Slosh's bull ballocks[1] a day, eating the King's leftovers when he tired of eating, stealing them when no one was about the Big Seraglio. Squatting like fat, meaty oysters on a small bronze tray in the foyer, I would filch three or four of them before they were taken away. I could not get enough of their tart, sinewy fleshiness. I needed my strength. The King needed my strength, for the pressure on Nebuchadnezzar to make bastards was great. Slosh cooked them in a number of different ways. He marinated them in green pepper sauce, flash grilled them over a cedar wood fire, or ground them into a salty cream soup. Around nine in the morning, I began to dream of their spicy flavor, deciding on how many I would have for lunch (usually seven or eight but sometimes as many as fifteen or sixteen), what beer I would wash them down with (an Assyrian ale). By eleven o'clock, I would be hunting around in Slosh's kitchen for the little buggers, popping three or four in my mouth at a time. And my raging appetite was not just for bull ballocks. I had become addicted to goat jewels,[2] pig balls, and when I was in the mood, horse rounds.[3] The latter I preferred with a bowl of soft cheese and a slice of fresh cucumber. Each week, per the orders of Uruk, who mistakenly believed they might invigorate the King, Slosh made batch after batch of these sweaty miracles. Meanwhile, my craving became obsessive, as if a demon had taken control of my stomach and was demanding daily sacrifices. And the hairs on my chin continued to grow. I feared my brother or the King might notice, so I took to plucking them out as soon they appeared. Within a few months, I had plucked seven nasty, thick hairs.

Yet my incipient beard did not bother me as much as the hair on my imaginary testicles, and I only wedge imaginary because while I knew there was nothing below my waist, it did not feel that way. My ghost balls, as it were, attained a reality that was difficult to deny.[4] To wit, in the past month, the natural and healthy exhibitionism of the harem girls—they walked around the baths and pools of the harem sporting nothing but their nipple rings—oppressed me like the dust of a late-spring sandstorm, whipping a nasty grime of lust into the folds of my tunic, blowing brown chaos up my skirt. My desire had never been without its problems. Most castrates are infected with a sliver of lasciviousness, but, with my regimen of bull ballocks, that sliver festered and swelled into a malignant boil, one that was ready to rupture. O Ishtar! I was unaware of the ballocks' potency, their dark magic, their alchemical powers. I simply and honestly did not know. How could I? Subsequently, during my daily routine in the harem, I began to fetishize like a loutish beard who skulks the back alleys of Babylon's worst neighborhoods, shrinking each girl down to her principal sexual parts. A girls' feet, previously of only minor interest, now compelled my attention the way tax treatises in the age of Sargon the Great once did. Instead of wedging about interest computations of wheat versus barley, I cataloged my fascination with ankles, toes, arches, and heels in my tablets. Sneaking into the bath of the seven pools, I observed the girls wash and gossip. Isis had toes like red Persian peppers. Astarte's feet were fat and stubby, like round half-shekels. And Siduri's feet, when she raised them in the air during the Jackal, resembled the drooping flowers of late summer. She had an enticing mole on her pinky toe. I wanted to kiss it and die.

For a time, the girls' noses drove me to despair. I loved a big nose the way most beards loved big breasts. Overbites also drove me mad. I was attracted to a harem girl's overbite not just by the variety of ornaments with which she decorated her teeth, but also by the way in which she exhibited her teeth: partly revealing, partly concealing, teasing lovers by opening her mouth wide and then closing it quickly. Big teeth—suggestive of a predatory cat and a compulsion to dominate a poor eunuch slave-scribe—for a time demanded all of my attention, and then, one day without warning, small teeth invaded my thoughts. I sat enraptured on my harem stool as I watched Pea or Anunit demolish a good joint of braised bull in front of a fire on a winter's night.

It also must be noted that the girls' laughter eviscerated my repose, undermined what self-respect I still possessed. Siduri's laugh began deep in her belly and burst out of her mouth like lilies in springtime. Whenever she laughed, all I heard was the sound of white, soft petals settling on the floor.

A difficult equation had established itself: I craved ballocks, particularly horse rounds, rolled in shredded goat cheese and barley breadcrumbs, then fried in pig fat; yet, the more I feasted on these delicacies, the more I gorged on their spicy muscle-y-ness, the more I suffered in the harem. Walking through the pool room on bathing day was agony. And yet, when I wasn't lingering in the undergarment room—yes, the harem had an entire floor of the Ziggurat dedicated to the silk contraptions designed to caress and kiss the soft bottoms of the King's girlfriends—I was in the kitchen, feasting on Slosh's daily miracles. There was a demonic connection between the number of horse rounds I ingested and the time spent on my knees staring through the low door hole of the harem baths. I couldn't stop myself. I had to stop. I dreamed of both in a feverish blend of cardamom yogurt sauce and Siduri's soft brown feet. I wasted entire afternoons at my desk attempting but failing to compose the King's response to Siduri's latest letter, while thinking about stuffing a garlic-infused dog testicle in my mouth and spanking Pea with a hairbrush. What was wrong with me?

My thoughts became wild. Perhaps Slosh was not the greasy, mutton-stained genius I had taken him to be but was, in truth, an anti-Jackalist, a dangerous mage who plotted to destroy the King's hope for making bastards and thereby undermine any chance of the drought's lifting.

"What's in these things?" I asked him after I found myself repeatedly, for weeks, in the kitchen, my hands covered in the grease of sheep balls.

"Have a smoke. This stuff is pretty good," said Slosh. Sweating profusely and covered in flour, he resembled a thick slab of roast pork, heavily peppered, with the juices dribbling down its sides. He sat on his kitchen bench, next to his fire, smoking from an old hookah.

"I need to know what's in the bull ballocks. You haven't dipped them in baby's blood or anything, have you?"

"Baby's blood? We stopped doing that years ago. Naaaaah, a little lemon juice, some salt, that's all. It's simplicity, my boy. Simplicity is the key to cooking, as it is the key to life. And you're in luck. I've just cooked up a fresh couple of dozen. Try these—I've coated them in pig lard and rolled them in a turmeric rub that I think you will find delectable. Go ahead, have one." Slosh's porcine features darkened as he pushed the tray of ballocks in my direction.

"Did Uruk pray or chant over them?"

"Oh no. I just brought them out myself. I sprinkled a little parsley on them for color."

"There are no curses or magic associated with these things?" I asked. "You'll swear to that?"

"Just a pinch of coriander. You don't want to overwhelm the natural flavor," he said, blowing a thin bluish plume from his lips.

"Whenever I eat these ballocks, a strange feeling comes over me. It's like a restlessness in my legs. Well, it starts in my legs, but soon it's all over my body. In my head, too. I can't think anymore. I just want to break something."

"Well, I do cook them for about five minutes a side over high heat. You see that was one of my early mistakes. I was always using too low a heat. It's the high heat that sears the outside nice and crispy while sealing in the natural juices."

"Slosh, you must help me. I'm becoming a beard," I said, pointing to three black hairs that had recently sprouted from my chin. "And look at this." Pulling up my tunic, I showed him a lotus flower of black hair curling up my abdomen. "Where is this coming from?"

"I'm not in the business of divination, Nerggie boy. That's your brother's job. I just cook 'em and serve 'em. Here, try this Libyan beer. It leaves a bitter-sweet aftertaste that rounds off the game-y-ness."

The Grand Betrayal—as it was later called by my brother—started with Slosh's bull ballocks, but soon became a delicate game of stylus and tablet between the harem girl and me—passed in secret under feast tables and over Nebuchadnezzar's sleeping corpse—letters in which we discoursed on the King's failings as a lover. There is no need to enumerate them all here, but let me wedge that Siduri held nothing back. She had kept a secret record, written in her most secret hand, of every botched caress, every bungled kiss, every unexpected bout of flatulence. She mocked my Lord's poor attempts at poetry, laughed at his stammered declarations of love, and wondered why he was spending long days playing Spirits Speak[5] with his mother.

Since their big fight in the Hanging Gardens, my Lord's behavior had grown increasingly peculiar: He roasted and ate his pet dog, tied sycophants up by their wrists and struck them with his horse-hair whips, and often he would sit on his favorite eunuch's back for hours. While his most outrageous murders were yet to come—for a time he enjoyed a repose, and he had won over the City by opening the final wheat reserves— Siduri said she could no longer abide his madness. I empathized with her, telling her what she wanted to hear, listening to her fears over their inevitable breakup, easing her anxieties as to whether she was capable of ever trusting another beard. Oh, I rationalized my treachery, telling myself that Uruk's policies were nothing more than sad attempts to bureaucratize libertinage. Now I am less certain.

The first letter, then:

My dear Nerggie,

Oh, you big Snout Head!!![6] why does he ask such questions of his Siddie? Poor Nebbie. He is mired in the veil of illusion that blinds us all. well, here is a tablet containing the list of my lovers [...] He asked for it ...

[Lacuna: tablet badly damaged;
approximately 5 lines lost]

My beloveds to me are bags of myrrh . . .

My first was a large and ugly goatherd from [...] and his name was [...]. He liked to [...] quite frequently. And then there was a great deal of time I spent in [...] harem. He was a terrible man. And after [...] there was [...] who was followed by [...] and then for a brief time I was with [...] Oh and then there was [...] but don't tell him about that. How this matters, I don't [...] why does he want to know about [...] or [...]? That's disgusting. But if you must tell him about [...] tell him that he meant nothing to me. It was more like a strange [...]. And then there was

Tablet Ten
[Lacuna: tablet damaged;
approximately 72 lines lost]

and, of course, I could never forget
[...]. He had a prodigious [...] not that it made a
difference. Tell the King that it makes no difference in
my pleasure. My heart, your heart, his heart, our
hearts are part of the All and All.

[Lacuna: tablet damaged;
approximately 14 lines lost]

Oh, ·Nerggie, you are my little dog. Remember these
words. I am the wife. I am the virgin. It is my
husband who bore me, and I who am his mother. It is
I who shall be pregnant. It is I who shall be the
midwife. I am she who received revelation from the
Pleroma of Imperishability.
I must see you. Alone. In your rooms.

There were many corpses in the meadow of her ardor,
moldering bitterly of abandonment and betrayal, and I
had heard a few stories from the other girls in the harem,
too, and I knew several of the names from her past: big,
powerful beards who rained fire down on cities of the
plain, although I never told Nebuchadnezzar about
them. Before she arrived in Assyria—where Harpagus
found her in a soldier's brothel—she was in the King of
Media's harem. He had purchased her from an obscure
Hebrew prince. Or so she claimed. For a time, she

214

became the lover of the Median king's sister and the sister's son, Astyages, who was sixteen, but only just sixteen. What our priests call the soul in paraphrase. All of which augured well because she bore King Cyaxares three bastards, his brother two, and Astyages one. She was perfect. Ideal for the purposes of Uruk and his ministers who were always barking about the King's numbers. She liked to tip the wine cup and spend a lot of shekels. So what? The girl had a history, had plucked a couple of grapes in her time. Who hadn't? That was what made her what she was: charismatic, gods-besotted Siduri. Did I show the King this letter? No. I would have been an idiot to show him the letter. I kept quiet.

Here is a recension of Siduri's twenty-sixth letter, which found its way to my basement room from an unknown hand. It was this letter, more than her angry denunciations of the King, that sealed our fates:

Nerggie,
When I had not heard from you—for two whole days, you rat!—I realized something important. I am falling in love with you. O Nerggie! You are my everything, my heart. I was despondent when you had not wedged a letter back to me. I look forward to our little correspondence. I have never felt this way about anyone in my life. Not Harpagus who captured me for the King nor that loathsome you-know-who, and anyway, what are you doing right now? I imagine you in your room with your reed in hand, a tablet in front of you. You are a handsome scholar! How did this

happen? The gods have willed it. I know it. We knew each other in a past life. Nergal, I cannot believe I am wedging these words to you, but I love you and long to hear those words from your mouth. Will you wedge it? Please do so and more. I long for you to say something bold—tell me that you cannot live without me, that you would rather die than betray our feelings. Tell me, tell me. Say something really risky.

I am, always and forever, your

Siduri

       That night and I wedged something risky. I wedged that I would gladly cut off my hands for her. I wedged that I would dress up as a woman and move into the harem—so we could spend the days in a silken, beaded embrace. I spoke of her intense fragility, compared her fingers to the petals of a flower, mused on opening the drapes of her being, composed a conversation between two lovers, one of them married. I conjured our glistering bodies and her gentle touch. Hearts and eyes were mentioned, as were moons and maidenheads—mine, of course, not hers. I compared her face to a garden. I believe that I also used the word *eternity*, or maybe it was *forever*, as in *I will love you forever*. I said these things, and, the lamentable thing was, I meant them in earnest. It felt good to wedge *My soul is enamored with your soul*, but now I know that it is a dangerous thing to possess a soul, and, moreover, a dangerous thing to possess a soul that is capable of being enamored.

In the early days of our acquaintance, I saw her in the harem and feigned indifference while she flirted dangerously with me and without regard to who was watching. Splashing about the foot pools, Siduri's feet looked smaller than I remembered, like a newborn calf's hooves.

"Put your reed down," she said. "Your tablets are vanity."

Siduri wore a thin, green gown with silver arm bracelets in the shape of the dragons of Marduk, and I sensed the soft form of her breasts through the garment. She looked splendid, but there was always a touch of sadness about her. Taken from her village on the Syrian coast, her family slaughtered, Siduri had endured enslavement, deportation, and humiliation at a young age. I had only heard parts of her story, and what I had heard was horrible.

"Why do you squander so much of your time reading tablets?"

"Why do you smoke so much Dream Dog?" I asked.

"Are you here for an oracle? I am feeling wonderfully sibylline this morning,"

"No, I am collecting my daily information for the harem list," I mumbled, lying of course. I was still nervous in the harem: the strange smells; the secret idiolect the girls spoke around each other, part word, part gesture, all of which caused my stumpie to clutch helplessly.

"I have a question for you. How many times have you been in the King's bed in the last week? My calculations say one and a half. Is that correct?"

"What kind of number is one and a half?" she asked.

"I need the number for my harem tablets."

"I wouldn't tell you, even if it had been twenty-two and half." She laughed, taking my hand and running her fingers up and down my forearm.

"I actually need to know. You can tell me."

"The King's a dipshit. End of story. We are his slaves. You present your bottom to him every day, he rubs it nicely, and you thank him for his attentions. I, on the other hand, have to fuck him twice a week. And, by the way, you are consistently amazing in that regard. Without you, I really don't know what I would do."

"But that's not the point," I said. "My tablets are checked and rechecked by Uruk. He is really picky about their accuracy. Don't laugh at me. He is one of the ablest men in the Kingdom. But he's unscrupulous. Have you ever seen a eunuch pushed off the Ziggurat? The sound when he hits the bricks is memorable."

"But you see, none of that matters. What goes up and down is one and the same, Nergal. The gods never allow one king or empire to prosper for very long. It is an unseemly affront to their power. What matters is the fact that you and I and the King have been bound together for many lives. Too many to count. None of this is real, of course, and none of this is new. You are caught in a larger cosmological dance, a beautiful and terrible dance—you, me, and Nebuchadnezzar—we are forever playing the same parts, forever circling the same struggles and conflicts. And, moreover, this dance has all been ordained and approved, wedged in the first and last tablet, written by the divine scribe Sîn-leqi-unninni."[7]

"What you are describing sounds like a kind of hell," I said, imagining the three of us in the embrace of the Jackal, dancing to the tuneless monotony of eternity.

"Not a *kind* of hell, Nergal. What I am describing *is* hell."

[Lacuna: tablet damaged;
approximately 45 lines lost.]

A week later, Siduri arrived in my room and fell into my arms—laughing like a wife who had murdered her husband and was now dismembering his body for secret burial in the desert. Her lips were coated the ever-present red paint. Faint scars marked her face. She held a sprig of barley in her hand. In the torch-light, I saw Siduri note the threadbare carpet and the cracked chamber pot under my desk. Alone, she did not seem as heavy as I remembered from when she sat on the star throne in the Great Hall. Yet she was still the almost beauty, still the almost Divine Barmaid. Her sunbaked lips crinkled expectantly as she led me to my bed.

Inwardly, I was dying as her plump bottom perched on my bedroll: Siduri's backside, wrapped in a yellow cotton skirt, resembled one of Slosh's lemon pies. O gods, how I loved lemon pie!

"O Nerggie, I am here."

For a few silent minutes, we sat together holding hands. "I stole this from the King's cellars," she said, pulling a small amphora of wine from under her skirt. "It is one of those wines you will remember all of your life."

At the time, I thought Siduri's remark ridiculous, but I remember the wine that night: it was an ambrosia distilled from the thick lips of Ishtar, a honeyed sweetness that coated your mouth and left you feeling instantly, though not unpleasantly, drunk. I also remember how young Siduri was—her countenance unclouded by grief or fear. If only I could return to that sweet bedroll! Stolen wine: it's an old and sad tale. O Siduri! You would have never found me if you had not belonged to another.

Soon we were drinking wine directly from the amphora, nuzzling our noses as we passed the jug back and forth. Siduri rubbed my head, and I, in turn, rested my head in the soft skin of her neck. We had never been alone together. Outside the contortions of the Three-Legged Jackal, I didn't know what to say or do. Without Nebuchadnezzar and the imperative to seed the land, what was there for us to talk about?

[Lacuna: tablet damaged;
approximately 37 lines lost]

Amid the misshapen bricks of my walls, Siduri caressed my belly. There was the smell of oil in the air from the small wall torch, and I had stolen a freshly baked loaf of bread and a pot of beer from Slosh's kitchen. We lay on my bedroll. She cooed and spoke sweet words to me, lulling me into the trance of love. She rolled over and got down on her knees, smiling enigmatically. She kissed my belly, kissed the stumpie through my wool skirt. When Siduri lifted her head, resting her chin gently on my stumpie, gazing directly at me with her green-blue eyes, a nugget of passion burst in my being and a white light filled my head. That was it: that was when my life of climbing the Ziggurat ended.

And just as definitely, the fever broke and we were gossiping like two harem girls. "Have you ever noted in your tablets that the King likes to keep girls around who have a deformity. Astarte—you know her? She is the girl with the club foot, but she hides it well. You will never see her doing anything but lying on the pillows, smoking Dream Dog on the hookah. Eudoxia? She's missing her left forefinger. Anunit cannot hear out of her right ear. Really, you wouldn't believe it," she said. "Tutu is blind, and Rissi has a limp."

She pointed to the King's taste for suicides. There was Tit-mouse (jumped off the Ziggurat); Bau (stabbed herself with a hairpin); and Atargatis (drowned herself in the river). "Since I have been in the harem, three girls have poisoned themselves—each pregnant with his bastard. The self-sacrificers. That's what they're called. And then the drought came."

That night in my room I learned more than I wanted to know. Although I must admit that I knew as much in my heart, for I had, over the years of my tenure as harem scribe, seen the casualties of Ishtar increase with the King's madness. Each of the "self-sacrificers," as Siduri called them, had been proclaimed the "holy bride," each had been named the Chosen Womb, the concubine who would usher in the new age.

"Oh, Mani was glorious. She had long black hair, played the lyre and sang songs about dying young. She had been quite attached to the man you call your Lord. Oh, he was good-looking ten years ago, I am told, and not quite as volatile as he is now. He slept, you see, and that made a difference in his mood, and he had a quick succession of alpha-girls. But Mani swallowed nightshade. When they found her curled under her bedroll, she had been dead for two days."

The King's honeycomb was more miserable than I had imagined. Siduri said that most of the girls despised her, hated the King, and loathed me, although they hid their true feelings from eunuchs because nobody trusted us.

Siduri, however, insisted that our relationship was "special." She said I understood her, that I listened to her. She also said that I was *special*, and that, in the same way, she was also *special*. We were *special*, and *our specialness* manifested in the dragon of Marduk. "You're not like other eunuchs," she said. I was uncertain what she meant; perhaps she was pointing out that I had not died prematurely, as had so many of my predecessors in the harem. Both the King's previous harem eunuchs—Heel and Tongue—had eaten themselves to death, the former on pickled bull-joints and the latter on fried goat's hinds: they had turned into bloated, red caricatures of themselves before their intestines burst.

And yet, when I tried to kiss her, Siduri pushed me away.

"No, you're too *special* for that."

"But I'm confused," I said.

"More than you realize, my dear Nergal. And I want to be certain."

"Certain of what?

"That you really are the One," she said, her face shining like the harvest moon, revealing pox marks on her cheeks, scars of a youth spent in bondage to men.

"Come on. Let me give you a past-life reading," she said with a malicious gleam in her eye. "I love you, Nergal. But I want to love all of you. I want to love all of the lives you have lived. That is the only way I can be certain. If you are the One—and I think you are—you will have always been the One in ALL of your past lives. You know that we have all lived many lives, don't you?

No? Well, we have. And these past lives will also show me much about you. About us. You want that, don't you?"

"I would like that very much, my sweet," I said, taking her hand.

"Sad to say, but your past lives have been full of failure," she said, laughing, teasing me, as was her custom, twirling a finger on my palm, "and extraordinary boredom."

"I don't believe you."

"Of course, you would be skeptical," interjected Siduri, "as one who has had so many mediocre lives."

"I'm sure my lives have been quite insignificant," I said. "But I can't see how any of this has any bearing on us, on you and me, and what we have here."

"We need to rise above this inferior plane, Nergal. The earth is accursed. It is broken. The drought has proved that once and for all. We are under the tyranny of the heavens, which threaten us with lightning, meteors, and comets. Babylon is falling, Nergal. We need to rise above it. Look upon it as a journey. A journey of self-knowledge. You want to go on a journey of self-knowledge, don't you?"

"But what's wrong with the life we have?" I asked.

"Look at us, Nergal. Look at me. I'm a whore. A sacred whore, a holy whore, but a whore nonetheless. My virginity was sold to a disgusting old man for twenty pieces of silver. And you. Look at you, Nergal. Alone in your room. With your dumb tablets. That's your life most of the time, sniffing around in the past for a clue about your present. What I am offering, dear heart, is a future. Free from a life of deportation and bondage. Free from a life of wedging tablets. Don't you want to change that? Make things different? Aren't you tired of all this"—she said, gesturing grandly to my dusty tablets and cramped room, which seemed infinitely smaller and dingier since she had arrived.

"Think of it, Nergal, as a chance to go beyond the grave. To rise from the canopic jar!"

"But what if I like it here in my canopic jar?"

"Nonsense! Nergal, we both know that you are an old, old soul. Full of gnosis and light. But the key to revealing that gnosis lies in taking a full look at your past. Even if it's painful."

Siduri then spoke of a mad god named Jaldabaoth[8] and the reality of pneuma; she threw around the terms like a seasoned Tablet House seer. She told me that I was a victim of "He who was a Murderer from the Beginning." I was uncertain if she was joking, but unlike most Babylonians, Siduri believed she had some mortality relief. It was well known that she had once been in a prince's harem on the western parts of the Indus Empire, where she had picked up a smattering of Vedic knowledge, which was a queer religion of texts, sacrifices, and cleansings, with a strange belief in the transmigration of souls. Siduri was an enthusiastic advocate for soul travel, and insisted that her spirit left

Nebuchadnezzar's harem every night—attached to her body by a thin stream of green light—to visit her dead brothers and sisters in dusty Irkalla.[9] She claimed she preferred the noise of the underworld to the quiet of harem afternoons, an unbelievable proposition, in my experience, but she liked talking to her sisters.

The smell of old cabbages seeped under my door. Moil was boiling his dinner down the hall. The oil lamp on my desk flickered, and I expected it to go out. Then, in the blink of a camel's eye, Siduri's features changed. Her pupils rolled back into her eye sockets. Her mouth darkened, twisting into an ugly snarl. She adopted her "spirit" voice, one that managed the trick of sounding both sibylline and seductive at the same time:

"O Nergal, in your end is your beginning. Your spirit mark in the heavenly body, that is to say, your soul imprint, is unsubstantial, for you have just begun your cosmological travels. In an early, early life, possibly your first life," she said, "you were a toothless and pox-ridden slave, conscripted by a king to build a ziggurat. You climb the large, bricked edifice, and it is not the largest bricked edifice in the region, but one of the smaller, lesser ziggurats, and this fact bothers you. You are hungry and sick. Your ribs show. I see you digging mud out of a large pit to make bricks. The labor is difficult, and you are not good at your work. I see you breaking rock, clearing rubble, complaining of the food, whining about the heat and dust. For your poor attitude, you are beaten with a stick on the backs of your legs, and your taskmaster is a mean little man with a bad complexion, and he dislikes you. He finds fault with your work and singles you out for special punishment. You sleep on a disgusting little mat with only moldy flatbread to eat. Oh, the dullness of it all! Fettered in boredom, you feel nothing but scorn for your fellow laborers. They gossip and make fun of you behind your back. And oh, yes, your end is not good, not so pretty at all. Lying on your mat, dying of cholera, cursing your luck—I behold the emaciated shanks of your backside. They hang outside the slave hut over an expanse of white sand, spilling your burning insides into the great river. Your sickness lasts for days, and in the end you defecate yourself to death."

Siduri paused to gather her breath. Pudgy, big-breasted, she would be better-looking at thirty-five than she was at twenty-five, if she lived that long. She gave off the aura of an unbroken horse, that wildness that refuses harness or bridle. No doubt it was this quality that made her attractions hard to resist. And while it was a commonplace that Ishtar was the ablest of gods, from the grimace that had settled on Siduri's face, I knew that Siduri was the ablest of seers.

She scanned the tablet of my soul history like a father-scribe at the Tablet House, noting the solecisms of my poorly constructed days, commenting on passages of time that tapered off into gibberish, and marking lives with no sense of an ending at all. My first dozen lives were about what you'd expect, nothing too dramatic, filled with garden-variety suffering and mediocrity, what I would call your average level of insignificance: a scribe wedging a minor booty list, a list that will be lost in a flood. A soldier dying of thirst next to a salt lake. A child abandoned in an alley, howling for his mother. It was this life that I identified with the most. That's it, I thought. That's me. She got that one right.

"Ooweeeee . . . Now I behold the slave called Nergal on a vast battlefield. You toil as a lowly soldier for a minor subcommander in the Aramaean deserts. There is a mighty battle, and I see you running away, fleeing the fighting, and your master orders you to stop. You keep running like a fearful woman, but it is too late—a chariot runs over you and tramples your body, crushing your bones and mangling your flesh. Your mouth has this horrid expression, like you have realized that your whole life has been one long act of cowardice.

"Sickness is upon the unnamed land," she said, lowering her voice to a whisper, "and bodies of the faceless and putrefied dead are scattered along the streets. Plague, pox, fever—who but the gods know the name of the pestilence that has struck the City? Corpses as thick as locusts during the harvest. You are pulling a cart, collecting the blackened bodies. No, wait, you are stealing—robbing jewelry from the dead! That's right. Foolish castrate, you have broken into a wealthy beard's house, a large and luxurious villa full of palm trees and mellifluous sounds of running water. What a thief you were, Nergal! Quite the lifter. Pulling off a ring from the dead finger of a child, cutting a necklace off the neck of her mother. Shame, shame.

"Oh, and here's another life of the slave named Nergal. You and twenty-five other soldiers are captured by an early Assyrian king and immured alive in the brick wall of his palace. Stuck in the mortar of mud, straw and potsherds, you complain about the heat and moan about your thirst. You bicker with your fellow victims over the cramped space. Tsk, tsk. Grumpy, very grumpy indeed. With nothing to do, you wail and lament your fortune. Death comes after six days without water or bread."

Clothed in the sun and moon, Siduri stood on my bedroll, hands raised to the stars, spittle forming on her lower lip as she rasped out my final lives in a guttural whisper, now declaiming in short, staccato bursts: "A canker-mouthed cupbearer to a fruit merchant in Smyrna—both of you are swallowed by a typhoon that slams into a city! A beggar sleeping in his own urine, you spend your days begging for a maggoty crust of bread! A darling girl who fell off the roof of her house! A barber who choked to death on a pigeon bone!"

Siduri became a she-wolf prowling the forests, looking for deer. When she spotted her prey, she howled: "A hooded captive being led through the streets of Ur! With a hoop through your lips! The crowd screams for your skin to be flayed and nailed to the City walls. And guess what, my little castrate? They obtain their desire!" Siduri snarled and raged in my empty room—the walls shook, my desk moved, and the tablets fell from their tower on my desk, breaking into pieces at my feet. She fell back on my bedroll, panting and gasping for air. "And that," Siduri said, "is all I see."

A small ray of sun broke through the window and fell on her face, revealing three freckles, which seemed to have been painted on by an impish god.

"I think you have suffered enough, Nergal. I think we have both suffered enough. I think we should make this life different for you. For me, too," she said, touching my cheek with her perfumed hand. Staring at me full in the face, Siduri leaned forward and bit me. Blood flowed from my mouth, tasting like bitter honey. "You are the One," she said, "and you and I are going rule over this City and reap a mighty harvest!" She lunged again, tearing a small piece of flesh from my face. Reeling back on my bedroll, I gasped in pain. She rose from the bed and evaporated out of my room like a spirit of the air.

Tablet Eleven –

Let Us Go to the House of Samas-iddina

Among my friends, only Chib-nezzar, or Chibby, as he was more commonly known, disapproved of my relationship with King and concubine. Once every other month, I would have dinner with the old eunuch. His room was located in an obscure backwater of the City known as the Little Seraglio, where he waited upon the Queen Dowager, Nebuchadnezzar's mother. The former empress, now toothless and fat, spent her days with three of her late husband's concubines, grousing about her accommodations, while scheming of ways to undermine her son's authority and planning his upcoming wedding with Amytis the Mede.

A wedding! Who would have thought that such a politically retrograde act would be possible in Babylon?

It goes without wedging that a wedding would be a flea in the undergarment of Uruk, who despised and feared the King's mother. Directly contravening the principles of *The Fecundity Tablets*—yet being politically and militarily advantageous to Babylon—the prospects of a royal marriage placed Uruk in a bind. It was evident that Babylon needed the Median alliance, but sacrificing his doctrine of Seed the Land for All was too high a price to pay. Moreover, as Amytis was the niece of Harpagus, the wedding would do much to raise the general's growing power in Court circles, which made Uruk and the rest of the Omnia exceedingly nervous. In a wedge, Samas-iddina's machinations sent a dangerous message and signaled to those in the know that my brother had not wholly consolidated his hold over the King. Thus it was that one morning Uruk had tasked me with the job of ambling over to the Little Seraglio to investigate the progress of the Dowager's plans.

The entrance to the Queen Dowager's court was south of the Ziggurat, next to the old palace; it was one of her chief complaints that deer would wander freely on her property. There were three of the animals eating flowers in her gardens when I made my way over that day. Built in an elaborately old-world style, the former Empress's quarters suggested a time when Babylon was slightly less fashionable than it was today. More of a military garrison than a royal residence, Samas-iddina's home was constructed out of heavy Assyrian bricks, the rooms were full of her husband's memorabilia and the odds and ends she had collected in her widowhood, which had been long and undistinguished.

Chibby's apartment, if one could apply that word to a sunless one-room-hovel, had the air of demotion about it. It was in the alleyway, behind the main building. The door was a hole in the ground—I lowered myself down a rope ladder—and the space, like Chibby himself, smelled of dust and neglect. Tablets were scattered in a heap on the floor. Beer cups lay chipped on his table. Asleep in his chair, Chibby resembled a forgotten geomancer whose prophecies had long since been eclipsed by history. It was not clear that I was expected. For a moment, I contemplated picking up a tablet and dropping it to announce myself, but I was reluctant to startle the elderly castrate out of his afternoon nap. He soon awoke and rose out of his chair. Chibby's greeting, after two or three preparatory coughs, was polite, though perhaps a shade defensive. I held out a hand, but he waved it away. Chibby always treated me as if I were an embarrassing spot he had just discovered under a concubine's nose on the night of her initiation into the King's bed.

"I would like to congratulate you on finding us," Chibby said. "Many intrepid souls have tried and failed. But life is like that, eh?"

Having never really been a success as a eunuch in official circles, Chibby viewed his current employment as the Dowager's servant with the equanimity that came with hard experience. At a certain point in life, there is a disposition to regard one's concerns as the only things that matter, and to believe that one's goals, however unrealistic or unattainable they may seem to impartial observers, to be achievable. Chibby was well beyond that point. He had given up. He deplored ambition in others almost as much as he loathed it in himself. He detested himself for having once possessed the desire to make something of himself. His career had consisted of one failure after another. Moil claimed that Chibby was hopelessly inept when it came to matters of intrigue, that he had no stomach for subordination, and was indiscreet about his contempt for the eunuchoid life. Most, but not all, of this was true. I suspected he still had some taste for behind-the-scenes politicking.

"Please, sit down, but be careful that you don't break the chair," Chibby said. "It is not as sturdy as it looks."

An anxious silence descended. Chibby, whose features resembled those of a grizzled steer, smiled. He was obviously enjoying my discomfort; he refused to look at me as if to discourage any possible social exchange we might have. Not willing to go down in defeat and despite Chibby's reputation for being difficult, I made the opening move.

"How are you?" I asked.

"What a stupid question," Chibby said. "How am I? Unlike you—or for that matter, many of today's eunuchs who have made their way in the Big Seraglio—

it took me quite a long time to resign myself to my truncated state."

These sentiments were radical enough in those days, but they did not imply that Chibby was one of those eunuchs who had been caught in a state of compromise within the harem. Chibby had nothing but the strongest dislike for eunuchs who neither could nor would "control themselves" around the King's girls. That such beardless slaves even existed was a deeply kept secret, but Chibby was fully cognizant of such information.

"Most of the beardless think of little but climbing the Ziggurat, so to speak," he said glumly.

For Chibby, who was unaccustomed to company, the generalization required no reply, and I made none. It occurred to me that most of Chibby's remarks were rhetorical. He rarely made a direct statement, and his pronouncements, even if only in an oblique way, were usually some sort of commentary on his own life. I had forgotten that the phrase "climbing the Ziggurat" had originated with Chibby or was at the least widely attributed to him.

"You begin as a boy, of course, and you believe that one day you will be among the King's ladies or, if you are particularly skilled in the arts of officiousness, achieve distinction as an administrator or scribe."

"My brother Uruk is chief scribe and diviner to the King," I said.

"The dual appointment? Yes, your brother's ambition, as well as his remarkable success, is well known. Haven't seen the dual appointment in over two generations. I believe one would have to go back to the inestimable Dudu the Harelip. He was both, too, you know. I knew Dudu, as a matter of fact. Never much liked him, but he could write a booty list with the best of them. He could wedge a slave transaction tablet and divine a bladder simultaneously, which is a harder trick to pull off than you would think. The dual appointment: that's where the real power comes. But the Big Seraglio is filled, from what I have heard, with nothing but careerists. They have no genuine passion for anything but advancement. Not that I count your brother among them. You seem to control yourself well, by the way. Have some beer."

An amphora of good Aramaean beer sat on the table. Chibby, who brooded over the vessel as if it were a demonic apparition, grudgingly poured two cups. It was an accepted fact that all things quotidian vexed him, particularly when they involved pleasure. Any departure from his rigidly defined philosophy of "eunuchoid correctness" was inimical to him. In our past get-togethers, I would occupy the time by attempting to predict which articles of form and precedent I would violate, and thus precipitate one of those fits of cantankerousness for which Chibby was famous. Deploring even the least concession to luxury, he winced when I reached for my cup. His wince was not subtle.

At Chibby's, one poured the beer but did not drink it. To draw him out, I asked him what he thought of the Egyptian problem.[1]

"Not interested in politics. But if Nebuchadnezzar and that thug Harpagus invade—and Babylon always invades—they are fools. Stirring up the Egyptians will only cause trouble. But let's not dwell on unpleasantness, however inevitable. Speaking of the inevitable, what do you think of the King's upcoming wedding?"

"I do not believe the wedding contracts have been signed," I said, genuinely surprised.

Under the impression that I had "climbed the Ziggurat," Chibby delighted in being privy to important Court matters that I had no knowledge of, and his information, however wild, was usually good. That I was alarmed about rumors of a wedding to Amytis goes without wedging, but to say that I was worried that the marriage would actually happen would be to overstate the case. There had been talk of "marriage" and its attendant heresies for years, and nothing had ever come of it. And Chibby, as far as I knew, had never once deployed a salacious or harmful scrap of gossip to his advantage. Such restraint had marred his career considerably, as his present surroundings attested.

"I pay no attention to Court gossip. I loathe all such innuendo. Now that you bring the unfortunate matter up, I fear disaster. Only war or, perhaps, pestilence could be worse than a wedding."

"But I said nothing of a royal marriage. You did."

"Dowager Samas-iddina has fixed the deal. Or at least, Harpagus has done so, and that, as we know, amounts to the same thing. Although he's younger than the King, it will make him the King's uncle by marriage. He's just a dagger or poison cup away from the throne now. How is the King these days?"

"Quite well," I said, remembering the look of murderous joy on my Lord's face as he climaxed on Siduri's gorgeously plump belly that morning. They had gotten back together only a few days before, and I was as exhausted as I was confused by their near-constant love-making.

"That's not the story I have heard, but I have never been one to care about such things. Would you like some dates?"

I refused, as custom at Chibby's dictated. It was not true to say that the fruit at Chibby's was decorative, but he found eating in public uncongenial. I learned of his antipathy at our first dinner, which occurred on the anniversary of Nebuchadnezzar's ascension to the Throne of the Golden Bull. We were sampling from a bowl of plums, or rather I was doing the sampling, and the juice dribbled down my chin. My lapse of manners was a minor one, but the old eunuch treated the incident as if I had ravished the Queen Dowager. Chibby's power, which I had long known to be very real, was a negative one. He set himself in opposition to the prevailing winds of his fellow Babylonians, which included eating fruit at dinner.

"What is Bunt up to? Still the atrocious breath? When we were young castrates together, he rarely bathed." Chibby's voice, which was what we in the trade call "caponish," lowered an octave, as if to indicate seriousness.

"I never see him," I said.

"If you believe Bunt cares a wit for the Median alliance, you will find yourself with the Dowager and me in no time. And what about this new girl, Siduri what's-her-name? Know anything about her?"

Not wanting to betray the Jackal's intimacies, I complimented Chibby on his room. He seemed pleased with his sparse quarters, which consisted of nothing, apart from numerous tablets spread out on the floor, two pieces of broken-down furniture, and a chamber pot.

"Oh, we get by, somehow," Chibby said. "I suppose one always manages, even in these worst of times. Not, of course, up to the elevated standards you are accustomed to in the Big Seraglio, but it suits our humble position. Now, what exactly are the King's current feelings for his harem? One hears all sorts of things, but there is a rumor—how shall I say this?—of unhappiness. I hear he's having problems with his number one girl, and there are nasty rumors and talk of infidelity. With what or whom, I cannot be certain. And there is also talk of reducing the size of the harem when

the King marries Amytis. Apparently, the Queen
Dowager desires it. Badly. No doubt as belated revenge
against her late husband, Nabopolassar. If I recall
correctly, Bunt always referred to him as True Fructifier
of the Earth, whatever that means. But I do know that
he rarely spent a night in Samas-iddina's bed. Not that I
blamed him. He preferred that decrepit sow, Madame
Grape, who, if the truth be told, is as cunning and
dangerous as the Queen. But remember, you did not hear
that from me."

"Nothing has been mentioned in my presence,"
I said.

"Of course not. It is probably the slander of the
envious."

What caught my attention was Chibby's tone,
which had suddenly grown more resigned than usual.
There had not been a harem purge in three hundred
years, and this confluence boded ill for all parties
concerned. No doubt Chibby was aware of the
unfortunate facts surrounding the King's new
relationship with Siduri; he had run the numbers and
concluded that things were not going as well as
Nebuchadnezzar and Uruk had hoped, though he would
never reveal his calculations to me. This explained my
presence in his apartment. He wanted to know what I
knew, to protect himself, or perhaps what was more
likely, to protect the Queen Dowager, to whom he was
fiercely devoted—despite his protestations to the
contrary. Or maybe he was spying for Uruk, querying

me about the status of the King's and Siduri's relationship, but that scenario was an unlikely one, for he despised my brother almost as much as I did.

"I have to finish up a bit of business at the Queen Dowager's. Would you like to come?" he asked.

"Why not?" I said.

"Have you been to the Little Seraglio before? The Queen will be happy to see someone from her son's entourage, or at least I think she will be. You can never tell what's on her mind."

"I hear she has been seeing ghosts. In fact, my impression of her Court is that it is badly haunted," I said.

"Oh yes, the spirits of her six dead husbands preside over the place and practically run the show," he said. "All of them ex-kings, so you can imagine the struggles. You must be the judge of the veracity of their origin. But be careful. She will pick you clean if you let her."

While pondering the meaning of this last statement, we made our way through the back alley that led to a courtyard. The grounds of the Little Seraglio were not extensive, though less plainly nugatory than I had supposed. A few, thin weeds constituted the garden. There were four small olive trees, and a broken-down statue—it's nose reputedly had been scratched off by the Queen—of Nebuchadnezzar's father occupied a back corner. I asked Chibby about the story that blood had spurted from the wound when the defacement occurred, but he dismissed it with a wave of his withered hand.

The apartment rooms had an air of decline about them; one could smell the regret, that musty odor of better days. There were small statuettes throughout the room; these bejeweled deities represented every known god, major and minor, in the greater Mesopotamia. Samas-iddina was fiercely devout. She was known to embrace every new religion that surfaced in the City, and there had been many of these cults, according to Chibby, with thousands of deported souls brought into Babylon each year, the harvest of her husband and son's foreign wars. It was curious how the Queen nailed the figurines to the tables, shelves, and floors of her apartment as if she soon expected a horrible calamity to shake its foundations.

Indeed, a series of apocalyptic murals—the stories can be safely attributed to a Zoroastrian influence that had lately penetrated the Court—had been painted on the walls, violent depictions of fire raining down from the heavens. One detailed a city uprooted, its inhabitants scattered to the four winds. Less extreme, but no less interesting to the chronicler of the royal family, was the collection of Nabopolassar's swords displayed on the altar. The lapis lazuli handles had begun to fragment; the entire tableau suggested the death of kings and the loss of empire.

The Queen Dowager herself sat on her late husband's throne, an artifact dating from the early

Chaldean period: stars and planets were carved in the ivory, and the inlaid gold was beaten with shells and strange creatures from the sea. Samas-iddina's face, deeply wrinkled by time, still had traces of the beauty for which Nabopolassar had married her, although her wig was a ghastly re-creation of a hairstyle that had been considered fashionable in her youth. Still, her eyes were extraordinary: they spoke of a formidable intelligence, as if they were the portals to an infinite mind burning through eternity, and before which I felt myself to be dross. Around her neck and wrists were over a dozen incantatory amulets, small cylinders carved in the shapes of Gello, Lamia, and a number of other spirits whose origins were known only to the Queen. These figurines were, by and large, grotesques to whom pregnant mothers prayed for protection during their partitions. Why Samas-iddina had draped herself in these demonesses was difficult to discern. I wondered what or whom she was tempting to ward off with her amulets. Perhaps death itself.

The Queen's entourage consisted of three elderly concubines. The old girls lounged on daybeds and played Spirits Speak, an amateur divination game then popular among ladies of a certain age. Each, though still impeccably dressed, had aged badly. There was Sin-shamir, an Assyrian whose face looked like she had endured a bad fall. She had been, I was told by Siduri, the most attractive woman of her generation, a master of allure whose sense of fashion was renowned for its power to defeat her rivals. There was also Gula, of whom I knew nothing other than the story that she had, for a year, impersonated a boy during a little-known but vigorous homosexual period of Nabopolassar's reign. But the lady whose fame eclipsed them all was the great Kalumtum, whose knowledge of the sensual arts was said to be encyclopedic. Her corpulence, too, was remarkable. It was difficult to tell just how enormous she was because she covered herself in the most flamboyant garments—bright crimson silks, rare Aryan wools, and cotton skirts of the deepest azure. A glint of her former lasciviousness hung about her mouth.

How the Dowager tolerated her former rivals was part of her mystery. Long-suffering in the field of love, Queen Samas-iddina had endured over five thousand other women in her tenure as the sovereign's wife. A plower and tiller of great distinction, Nabopolassar had collected concubines the way most kings surround themselves with eminent scribes or famous starmen.

When I was a young castrate, a story circulated in the College of Eunuchs that the Queen had once dispatched a dozen of Nabopolassar's mistresses. The death of concubines was not an event that attracted much attention among the officials in the Court, and the Queen, knowing the low regard in which these poor women were held, acted with impunity. One night she ordered her bodyguards to round up the first twelve girls they encountered in the harem, sew them into burlap sacks and toss them in the river. "Drown them like cats!" she was claimed to have hissed. When she was asked why she had had the poor girls executed, Samas-iddina replied, "I could no longer abide their foolish conversation."

Whether this tale was true, I have never confirmed. Chibby had been unusually circumspect when I asked him about the details, but there was an emotional truth to the account. Samas-iddina had outlived most of her rivals and was now said to be waiting out the deaths of these final three concubines, who appeared to be her only friends in life. In their turn, these faded beauties depended upon the Queen Dowager, and, without her generosity, they would have ended their days as procuresses in cheap brothels or begging on the street.

"You are not paying attention, Gula. Stop fiddling with your hair. You must close your eyes and wait upon the god, like this." Samas-iddina closed her eyes and held her hands up, palms facing outward.

In the Dowager's reprimand, I detected a faint whiff of malice and wondered if Samas-iddina was avenging herself for the innumerable nights Nabopolassar had bathed in the pleasure of Gula's expertise, while the Queen found solace in conversation with one of her corpulent eunuchs.

"Oh, Sammy, let's give it up for the day. You look tired," said Gula.

"You're the girl with the bags under her eyes, not me," the Queen snorted.

"You speak the truth, Sammy. We're all not blessed with your beauty."

"I can just perceive the faint outlines of Ra," said the Queen. "Nabbie, get out of the way. You know how bad the sun is for you; no, I have lost him again." Employing the diminutive for her late husband was her way of maintaining her authority among her ladies. Each was said to be still in love with the late King.

"Is that my Nabbie?" asked Kalumtum wistfully, her watery eyes becoming more liquid. "Send him my love."

"It is he, and he wonders why you have become so ugly. Chibby, give me my fan. It is exceedingly hot in here today, particularly since Ra has visited us."

I have always been fascinated by the various styles employed by eunuchs when dealing with a superior personage. The magnificent but scandalously underbred scribe Balasi, a distant relation of mine, I am proud to wedge, has divided the College of Eunuchs into four sorts of castrates: "sandal-lickers, sycophants, idlers, and scoffers." Chibby was of the latter category. To look at him, however, for he comported himself with a remarkable slowness, one would suspect him of the third class. When called by his Queen, he barely moved, slouching forward like a giant sloth. While unreserved flattery was the expected minimum to which all eunuchs aspired, Chibby held to a standard that was wholly his

246

own: he ignored every question, request, or command
that was put to him. Apart from this willful neglect of
duty, it was Chibby's refusal to conceal his distaste for
some of Samas-iddina's eccentricities that impressed me
the most. A eunuch's jawline cannot be described as
pronounced, but when the Queen beckoned him,
Chibby's tightened like an executioner's vice. In her turn,
the Dowager treated him as if he were a former lover,
one who, in his attentiveness and ardor, had been
without rival.

"Ah, there is my sweet Chib. You appear down
in the mouth today. Are you feeling well?"

"Madame, what possible concern could you
have for me?"

"Dear Chiblet, don't be so cross. You know how
I worry about your health. Why, when you were
suffering from that unpleasant stomach affliction, who
was it that nursed you back to your current robustness?"

"It would have been better if I had died," said
Chibby spitefully.

"But who would carry my fan? You know I
depend upon you."

The Dowager was playing with Chibby, perhaps
not unmaliciously. She turned her gaze on me. In her
eyes, which, as I have wedged previously, were
commanding, one perceived a woman who had
experienced the depredations of cruelty, lechery, and
folly firsthand and had roundly defeated them.

"So this is Nergal. Nabopolassar told me you would be coming today. He was the King, you know, and my husband. He's dead now."

"I'm sorry, Ma'am."

"Yes, he was a king, and I loved him, but he was not without his weaknesses, terrible weaknesses."

"Yes, of course, Ma'am."

"They are all dead. All of my husbands."

"My condolences, Ma'am," I said.

"Don't be sorry, for they are all with me now. In the end, I got them."

"Yes, Ma'am."

"It is time Nebuchadnezzar was married. He has been playing too long with the sluts in his harem. He loves his sluts. Do you love sluts, Nergal? You look like a eunuch who loves sluts."

"No, Ma'am. I do not love sluts."

"Blessings be upon you. It was sluts that drove my husband to the grave, you know. I am worried about my son. Do you think marriage might settle him down?"

From fear of giving offense, I refrained from comment. Marriage, an institution the King mocked with regularity and one that my brother had overturned with his reforms, was obviously outside my experience—although Siduri claimed she desired to marry me and have my children, which were two equally fantastic propositions.

"It would do Nebuchadnezzar good to find a wife. Bunt agrees with me. Bunt feels his Queen should be Egyptian, but I favor something reliable—say, a girl like Amytis the Mede. Do you know her?"

"I was present when the King met her."

"Ah, yes. Did he like her?"

Having been barred from the introduction, Samas-iddina was keen for information. The meeting, arranged sometime last year by a partial third party (who was also a front for the Queen), did not go well. It was well known that a royal marriage would do much to shake up the current balance of power in the Big Seraglio, and the outcomes of such shake-ups were unpredictable. If Samas-iddina could successfully arrange her son's marriage to Amytis the Mede, she could, in all probability, orchestrate her return to the Big Seraglio, and, once reinstalled in the Court, she would exercise her considerable talent for making her son's life a series of crises in which she occupied the center. While I was almost certain that Uruk would never allow this travesty to impact the King's freedom—Uruk claimed Nebuchadnezzar was the only truly free man in the Kingdom—I was not sure to what extent he would have a choice in the matter, given my Lord's current malaise, which some in the College of Eunuchs thought intractable.

At the time, I failed to grasp the nature of Nebuchadnezzar's revulsion, which had been immediate and unequivocal. While it was clear that Amytis shared all the negative characteristics of his mother—the vindictiveness masked as concern, the odd ideas about the afterworld, the fear of lightning—she also possessed the Queen Dowager's positive traits. Their resemblance was uncanny. Amytis looked as I imagined Samas-iddina had looked at the same age: the watery brown eyes, thick legs, and severe expression around the mouth. More important than these physical similarities was her unreconstructed piety, for Amytis claimed that she had devoted herself to a life of the soul. That the King failed to appreciate this quality was obvious, but he did understand the benefit of having a Queen who was genuinely religious, who might help him navigate the rocky shores of Babylon's priestly and astrological elite. He was not, despite what Moil or my brother thought of him, a complete fool. However, Nebuchadnezzar was convinced, rightly I now believe, that his mother was trying to avenge herself upon him for the vices of his father. Without doubt, a girl like Amytis would squat on his carnal impulses, take them out to the waters of Babylon and drown them in the river.

"He wasn't feeling well that night. The dinner was cut short," I said.

"What a pity. I believe that a woman with some vigor would complement his rather limited energies. Her mother was a cousin of mine—a horrible drunk but apparently a good mother. Amytis has sense."

It was clear to me that the former Queen did not believe what she was saying. Her eyes narrowed as she bared down upon me, checking my reaction for traces of dissemblance or hypocrisy. I wondered if she had heard

Nebuchadnezzar's celebrated comment regarding the Median Princess's personality, which he had compared to a water rat devouring a corpse. And while his remark was innocuous in itself, Nebuchadnezzar had never had a meaningful conversation with a woman, despite his intimacy with Siduri and various members of the harem, until he met Amytis. What happened that night between them cannot be verified. From where I was standing, it seemed they argued over how much beer the King was drinking. Or perhaps they were discussing Amytis's pet subject, which was her plan to tear down the Ziggurat and rebuild the former palace. This topic should have made the King happy. After all, he considered himself a builder, the restorer of the former glories of our Great Mother Babylon, but the expression on Nebuchadnezzar's face reminded me of the look of a lion that had just been snared by the royal lasso. He curled his lips but snarled helplessly. I would come to recognize that expression frequently in the months to come.

I was not wholly surprised when Amytis the Mede arrived in the Queen's apartment. This was exactly the type of thing Uruk might arrange when he wanted to test my eunuchoid mettle. She made her entrance—bold and a touch too loud—like a woman comfortable with the attention of everyone in the room. Her style was impeccable: that much could be observed in the quality of her dress, a silver-beaded wraparound with a mother-of-pearl tunic. While her hair had been braided in the style of a temple virgin, her round hips were aggressively on display. And, not surprisingly, the cuts of her skirt signaled familiarity with a class of women Samas-iddina frowned upon. While her looks were "pretty," I was drawn to those physical features that were a degree off. Her eyes were asymmetrical, and her mouth seemed too small. But these minor flaws were obscured by the overall impression, one that demonstrated great command of the Babylonian sexual idiom.

Samas-iddina noted with disapproval Amytis' black-shadowed eyes, her bejeweled arms, and her impressive décolletage—which bulged like the tumult of the ocean deep. On principle, the Dowager Queen objected to the obvious exploitation of physical power. She had suffered under the tyranny of court beauty all her life, and been subject to the inclination that the bearded male displays before the smooth leg and the well-chosen feminine accessory. However, because of Amytis's interest in the magical arts, the Dowager tolerated what she would have condemned as frivolous in others. Samas-iddina held out her hand, stretching her gnarled fingers for the younger woman's lips to kiss.

"My Queen, you look splendid! Now I can see why you were so favored in the days of your husband's magnificent reign," Amytis the Mede said, gaily. Her flattery, bordering on the fantastical, had its intended effect. Samas-iddina raised herself from her hunchbacked stoop, and the slight outline of a smile

252

flickered on her parched features. The mood in the Queen's apartment intensified, with the decrepit concubines tittering before Amytis, whom they viewed as one of their own.

"And what do the spirits of your departed husbands think of my new earrings?" Amytis asked, pointing to the gold Ishtar hoops, which dangled languorously above her bare shoulders.

"My husbands have more important things on their minds today, Amytis," Samas-iddina sharply replied.

"More important than earrings, my Queen? What could be more important than the way a woman looks?" she said conspiratorially. Intent on dominating the situation, Amytis flashed her teeth, which were white and strong, and all present save for one minor anomaly: the left incisor was turned inward, marring an otherwise smooth row. Later Chibby confessed that he was surprised that she challenged the old Queen so early in the conversation, and that her strategy worked. Long known among Court circles for her priggishness, Samas-iddina obviously delighted in being treated as a fellow acolyte in the temple of feminine charms. It was an entirely new approach for a woman who had previously relied on moral censoriousness for her power. She beamed with a coquettishness I would not have thought possible.

"Come, shall we roll the rocks?" Samas-iddina offered. "Let's hear what the spirits of my husbands are saying about our marriage—or should I say, your marriage to my son?"

A flat piece of Lebanon cedar lay on a table in the center of the Dowager's room. Picking up four polished stones, Samas-iddina heaved them across the board. The stones, in their turn, tumbled into the holes drilled expressly for divining the future of the player in question. Eyeing the stones, the former Queen puzzled over the outcome and wrinkled her nose over what she saw. She picked up the rocks and tossed them again. "Nots up," she said, indicating either the displeasure of the spirits or a refutation of her wishes, an outcome that was unacceptable to the Queen. "Againsies," she said with determination and threw the rocks down. Rarely, or so Chibby said, did Samas-iddina allow the spirits of her dead husbands to dominate her. She refused to be denied. Having humiliated her in life, they were expected to do her bidding in death.

"Spirit's Speak was all too fun when I was a girl," said Amytis. "We played it every night in the harem with the slaves. Have you heard of Heaven Ordinant? No? You must let me show you. I am told it is Egyptian and very ancient."

"Heaven Ordinant? Isn't that the one that where you take the feathers of an ostrich and steam them in a broth? It never works. I have tried them all, Amytis. Morning Star/Evening Star, Telipinu: The God who Disappears, and War: the Father of the Gods. Do you remember that one? It took me a month to get the bull's blood out of my necklace last time I played."

"Your husbands are unusually quiet. What does the board say?" asked Amytis, a shade too skeptically. Her already hard features crystallized into a diamond-like resilience. She was my kind of tough girl—one that could whip a eunuch into shape, and I imagined myself tied to a rock with her flagellating my back with a cane in keen, wondrous ecstasy. But would she be good for the King and next fall's wheat harvest?

The Queen took up the rocks and rolled for a third time. And then a fourth. And then a fifth. The ex-concubines leaned forward to view the board better, while Chibby contracted within himself, as if he were a city preparing for a long siege.

"Well, what is the outcome? Will I have a summer or a winter wedding?" asked Amytis.

"I'm not getting much here," said the Queen.

"What do you mean? What does the board say?" asked Amytis.

"Nothing."

"But there has to be some kind of a pattern?"

"The only pattern I can see is that there is no pattern," said the Queen.

"What? There has to be. Roll it again. Samas-iddina, south four is not completely in its hole."

"Yes, it is, Amytis, any contact counts as being in the hole."

255

The next roll of the rocks revealed a divided house. Samas-iddina's husbands were split on the issue of the connubial day, or so said the Queen. Something was happening that, either from unfamiliarity with the manners of the Little Seraglio or the innate dullness of my spirit, I could not follow. Apparently, a disagreement was in progress, a conflict of interpretations. Rules were discussed. Precedents debated. Babylonian women, claimed Chibby, were not tablets to be scanned carelessly. They yielded their secrets only after painful and sustained scrutiny. I had neither the training nor the experience to venture a hypothesis to explain the tightness that now was forming around Amytis's mouth or the change in the Queen's tone. There was an analogy, I suppose, to be drawn between the women's attempts to augur the future and my awkward assessment of the motives and intentions of the parties concerned. At any rate, the board was put away, and a hostile silence descended on the Little Seraglio.

"The spirits are being ornery today. They have a tendency to be truculent in the late afternoon—tired from a hard day of reaping and sowing in the fields of our cosmic destinies," said the Queen Dowager, suddenly grown sluggish like a snake who had swallowed a rodent and was now too fat to return to her lair.

Amytis's cheeks reddened. She was unaccustomed to having her will contradicted. Not all women, after all, perceive themselves as potential helpmates to the Throne of the Golden Bull, a throne which the previous week had received twenty thousand gold bars, ten thousand bushels of barley, and eight thousand sheep from Ithobaal of Tyre. Amytis, however, had that combination of looks, intelligence, and birth, which led her to expect a great deal from life, and this, coupled with the disappointment that invariably comes with such expectations, gave her features the toughness of new and expensive leather. Her face tightened into an inscrutable mask.

"Well, my Queen, I can see that our little game has tired you out. I believe I shall retire for the evening. Good night Gula, Kalumtum, Sinny."

After Amytis had departed, a faint trace of her spicy perfume lingered in the room, as if she had been a ghost whose visitation had been cut short by an exorcist whose skill in the black arts had been underestimated. Her relations with the Queen Dowager, I was later to learn, had that contentious quality of rival claimants to the throne, but there was more at stake than earthly power, though there was plenty of that, too. Amytis had much to gain from the marriage: an alliance between Babylon and Media would solidify her family's political fortunes as well as considerably enrich them. That she was willing and able to put up with Nebuchadnezzar's eccentricities in the field of love, which were considerable in a family well known for its unorthodox tastes, was an additional advantage to all parties concerned. Why the Queen had turned on the young woman was difficult to fathom.

Samas-iddina motioned me to her side while Chibby scowled silently in the corner. Up close, her face brightened, as if she had received a supernatural confirmation of sorts, which I, laboring under the burden of mortality, could neither see nor understand. The dilapidated crown she wore took on a renewed vigor; the gold-leaf flowers, arranged in a set of triangular motifs, blossomed in a spring whose province was not of the earth.

"You spend a great deal of time with my son," she said.

"Yes, that's true," I said.

"He's not in the best of health. I never thought he would turn out the way he did, you know. I had hoped he would do great things for Babylon, but he spends too much of his time in his harem getting high on that Dream Jackal or whatever you call it. I lied to Amytis when I said there was no pattern on the board. There is always a pattern if you look long enough. She will marry my son. There is nothing anyone can do to stop their union. But that is not all the spirits revealed. No, I was given the privilege of seeing the final day when the rivers of Babylon will burn and the Ziggurat falls. I saw the strangulation of babies in their cribs, and the bark of the cedar stripped from its trunk. It was dreadful."

Tablet Twelve –

The Canals of Babylon
Overflow with Honey

That summer during our affair, certain theological difficulties arose. Inevitably, what starts as something pure and transcendentally self-evident becomes corrupted by faction and dissent. There were divisions within the larger movement known as Mardukianism, a movement founded on Marduk's tail in the hand of a eunuch. Small schisms and sectarian squabbles followed in the wake of the great revelation. It was unfortunate, but the Big Slump had given birth to a multitude of heresies within the City, a monstrous issue of beliefs, practices, and rituals that advocated everything from a literalist reading of *The Fecundity Tablets* (whereby all citizens took up a hoe and farmed their own plot of wheat) to a wholly spiritualized interpretation that practiced "inner fertility," an esoteric concept designed to flatter eunuchs, and one, much to my dismay, Siduri had embraced.

It was difficult to admit publicly, and Uruk refused to even discuss the matter with me, but the doctrines of the Greater Bastardy had produced a legion of pseudo-Nebuchadnezzars, small beards with messianic dreams and a lot of time on their hands to read *The Fecundity Tablets*. Give a poor and desperate beard a sacred text and the ability to read, and he will proclaim himself Lord of the Fields and a prophet of the One True Divine Substance. Give a eunuch a holy tablet, however, and he will give you the end of the world— where his enemies go down in a conflagration of dung and fire.

Bi-Reed the Heresiologist compiled an extensive compendium of the dangerous heterodoxies that sprouted like weeds amid the late-spring grasses. Alas, the Akkadian original survives only in fragments, but an Aramaic translation contains the full text. While most of their godless doctrines were extracted under torture, the names of the sects were known variously as the Seeders, the Furrowers, the Plowers, the semi-Plowers, and the most pernicious of all, the anti-Plowers, who eschewed physical union altogether in favor of their narrow and, I must wedge, misguided obsessions.

[Lacuna: tablet damaged:
approximately 60 lines lost]

"That's three, four, five," said Siduri triumphantly. "Nerggie, you owe me fifteen shekels. And you," she said, jabbing the King in his belly, "owe me fifty."

"Ooowwwhhh, I always lose. Why do I always lose, Siddie? Can you tell me, Nerggie?"

"You are letting her win, my Lord. You are a generous soul."

"She's a scorpion, that one," said Nebuchadnezzar, eyeing me queerly. "You lost all of your money, Nerggie."

"He can have some of mine," Siduri laughed and wrapped her foot around the King's. He smiled happily and picked up his gold whip and twirled it distractedly in my face.

"Stop that fucking rattling!" the King shouted to Ass, the flayer of skin, who had just tied Taps to a cedar rafter.

I must confess I was relieved that it was Taps rather than I who was going to be flayed alive, and why this was the case I cannot wedge, but it was so. Perhaps my relief was due to a guilty relaxation of the bowels, that sweat-clinched release of the anus before the spectacle of someone else's imminent death, or maybe it was fear, like that twinge in the stumpie whenever I passed the kneeling slaves, wrist-bound and lipped-tied in a row, or when I set a pudgy foot upon the first step of Great Etemenanki, as I did every morning, whispering the prayer, *I have escaped the spittle of your mouth.*

Taps the Grainman was going down. He'd be in Ereshkigal in an hour or two, if he was lucky. I was relieved that it wasn't me because it should have been.

The guilt over my affair with Siduri was overwhelming, and I wasn't handling the situation with the Jackal very well. I felt terrible. Nebuchadnezzar was a god. He was Babylon's god. I was cheating on my god, who was sleeping with my girlfriend, and I was lying about it on the Bastard Tablets. Uruk had to know. He had to.

The whole sad business, of course, was part of a larger problem, a well-known numbers game called Creep, and every beard played the game of Creep. Every beard except Taps. Water levels, the number of lions killed by the King, the list of hands taken in battle, the production of bastards, you name it, they had all crept upward in the past ten years. Every beard lied on their tablets, although perhaps "lie" was too strong a word. Let me just wedge that most scribes tended toward exaggeration. Official statistics meant nothing in Babylon. Bunt's castration numbers never accurately reflected the actual number of eunuchs in the College of Eunuchs, and Enuggi—long before his unfortunate fall in the drinking game—measured the amount of dew deposited on the bricks every morning and called it rain. But not Taps. He never fudged the numbers when it came to grain production. His tablets never tallied anything but what was there, and what was there was dirt. For this, he was awarded the knife.

And Taps's execution was just the type of thing Uruk would do whenever he wanted to give me one of his administrative wag-of-the-styluses. He had always questioned my work ethic, and he doubted my commitment to the Greater Fecundity. No doubt Taps the Grainman, hanging upside-down from the ceiling, spread-eagled and naked, was guilty of some minor act of insubordination, but I was surprised that it was him. I had recognized Taps immediately—from his brown beard and pimply skin, from the way his hairy toes quivered in the torchlight, from his high-pitched groans. He didn't look too happy. Poor Taps.

Taps's arms and legs shook, which caused his chains to rattle noisily. A fly landed on his nose, and he jerked his head to get rid of the insect, but with every movement of his beard, the buzzing devil would dart away only too quickly, and land again in a more maddening spot, like on the inside of his unnaturally large Persian nose, or on the rim of a blood-shot eye. Taps had seen more than a few of these ghastly exercises in his life, and knew what to expect. To be flayed alive was never a pleasant experience, and to be flayed alive before a crowd of hooting and jeering beards screaming for your hide was somehow worse—or so I imagined as I sat among the best of the Babylonian *schadenfreuders*.

My Lord Nebuchadnezzar, looking stoutly bearded and bullish and holding his golden whip in his hand, was a ballast of calm in the frenzy of the Great Hall, and next to him was the divine barmaid. Still ignoring me, she seemed happier than ever in her blue-stone tiara and matching linen skirt. Her plump arm rested over the King's shoulder, and I winced at the greater intimacies that this act suggested. The previous night, for example, I witnessed an appalling cruelty, as post-coital Siduri held the King in her arms, stroking his matted beard and whispering sweet songs of love in his ear.

It was a typical Babylonian execution for the most part. Neither more nor less interesting than the forty or so I had witnessed in my tenure at the Court of the Winged Bull. There was Uruk, furiously scribbling in a corner, checking moon, noting bladder. The odd concubine complained about how stupid executions were. I spotted that Ziggurat-climber Belit (or Nanshe?) yawning and looking at the sundial. There was the fat scribe Ham the Grammarian, who once told me, during an argument about an Assyrian tablet, *The Gods are Just*, "you know nothing! You know nothing!" There was Chibby in the corner. He looked as gloomy as ever: Samas-iddina had ordered him to attend. Skirted slave attendants lined the walls holding their ceremonial artichokes. There were sacrificial deer, sacred goats, and walking birds milling about the floors. Even the protective spirits and demons appeared for the occasion, hovering in the air, the bullmen, snake-dragons, and scorpion-men who adorn the outside walls of the Ziggurat, breathing fire and spitting malice.

Tablet Twelve

Flanked by mage and priest, the Court waited restlessly before the gibbet, a garish platform stained with the blood of innumerable victims. Munching on sugared dates and downing cup after cup of wine taken in the latest campaigns in the West, the beards and ladies of the Court eyed Taps expectantly, wondering if he had the stuff, hoping he had the balls to give them a proper show (he didn't), because the skinning of a living man could be one of the better events in Babylon—a spectacle of blood, viscera and gore, and one in which spectators demanded much of the victim. There hadn't been a decent flaying in over a year, and the crowd was braying for blood.

Siduri, halfway through her second cup of beer, motioned for the King's cup-bearer for a third, and he scrambled nervously to her side and topped it off. It had been my understanding that she didn't even like beer, yet for the last two weeks, she had been hitting the amphora pretty hard with the King, living a life that was a continuous series of dinners and end-of-the-year festivals, barking like a hyena whenever she saw a familiar female face, relishing the attention her beauty demanded from the lesser and greater functionaries of the Court.

Incense burners filled the room with a gray haze, and I noticed, not without a queasy admiration, that Taps's body was coated in grease to make the removal of his skin easier. From the carved stela erected in the middle of the room, it appeared as if Taps—and I could not believe this charge—had been caught "penetrating the harem," which was a capital offense, and rightly so, for the King couldn't have any bastards but his own running around the Big Seraglio. On the first panel, the sculptor had fashioned a crude but more or less realistic representation of Taps the Pretender, as he was now called, sneaking into the harem, pulling back a date branch and leering at the harem girls. They appeared frightened and indignant, which was ridiculous because the only time I saw a concubine indignant was when she didn't get enough hunks of fatty mutton in her soup. Below that panel, another panel depicted the King on his chariot, beard curled and full of wrath while he subdued the interloper with ropes and dogs, proclaiming his dominion over beast and fowl, human and slave. It was a fine piece of my brother's propaganda. The King could not drive a chariot to save his life, at least not without injury to himself and to whomever happened to be in his way. I wondered what crime Taps had committed, if he had committed one at all.

His confession of guilt seemed equally fantastic. Forced by the executioner to read from a tablet upside down, he performed the feat in a shaky falsetto: "By order of the King, Nebuchadnezzar, the high priest of Marduk—*rattle, rattle*—chosen by Enhil and Ninurta, the favorite of Anu and Dagan, who is destruction among the gods, and by the decree of Nebuchadnezzar—the legitimate King—*rattle, rattle*—the King of the world, King of Babylon, son of

Nabopolassar, likewise great King, legitimate King, King of the world, King of Babylon—the heroic warrior who always acts on trust-inspiring signs given by his Lord Marduk—*rattle, rattle*—and therefore has no rival among the rulers of the four quarters—*rattle, rattle . . .*"

Taps wavered and momentarily lost consciousness, much to the scorn and disapprobation of the eunuchs in the room who had little to do but stand against the wall. Bunt, in particular, was aggrieved by this loss of will and threw a half-eaten apricot at the prisoner. Stub and Moil threw whatever was in their hands: tiny bronze figurines, beads from necklaces, the odd sandal. Poor Taps: hit with inauspicious projectiles, while waiting for the hideous knife. There was nothing I could do to save or comfort him, while sitting on my bench next to the King and the concubine, so I took the opportunity to examine my consort more closely. Sad to wedge, Siduri was having a grand time in her red lip paint and slimmed-down figure. Since her return to the arms of the King, I would wager she had lost about twenty pounds, and it was evident to me, and every other beard and lady in the room, that she was excited by her new figure. While the attendants worked on Taps, she and the King drank more beer and laughed, touched each other shamelessly. I admit that it bothered me to see her surrounded by the fawning ladies and lackeys of the Court, laughing at her so-called witticisms like she was the famed harem scribe, Bel-u-ball-it.

An impenitent polyandrist looked up from her exertions. Was Taps dead? Unconscious? She soon lowered her head into the fleshpots of pleasure and became lost in a debauchery that had now become general. Yet, she was right to wonder. If the execution was to go off successfully—and my Lord needed a success—the prisoner had to remain conscious. Despite the Throne's claim of justice and retribution, the whole purpose of the flaying was to create a living bas-relief, a shuddering wall-painting that demonstrated the King's might over his enemies. Scribes and sculptors hunched in the corner of the room for this reason, wedging notes of Taps's reactions on their wax tablets and sketching pictures of his bony torso on papyri. Nebuchadnezzar collected stone portraits of his dead enemies like a concubine collected sandals: the great wall in his palace was full of images of him smiting the Scythian dog or trampling the Egyptian swine. I imagine he wanted a good flaying to complete the triptych.

The attendant slaves fussed over the unconscious Taps—six well-fed Libyans stuck vinegar-soaked rags into his face. Howling, Taps jolted awake. He squinted at the tablet as if it were a demon spirit, and read again, this time with more chain rattling: "By order of the King Nebuchadnezzar, Great King, Legitimate King—*rattle, rattle*—King of the world, King of Babylon, I B-aha-iddina (which was Taps's legal name), so-so-son of-of-of Nabu-a-ballit, descendant of Shim-limmir, ca-ca-ca-caused sin and crime and pla-pla-pla-

planned evil. The oaths of the King, his Lord, he did not ke-ke-ke-keep, but planned treason. Oh Nebuchadnezzar, King of Ba-ba-ba-bylon, the judicious prince, who determines right and justice, examined the e-e-e-evil-deed of Ba-ba-ba-iddina—fuck you, fu-fu-fu-fuck you ...."

Taps's indignation had broken the proverbial fourth wall, and the audience perked up. He was showing some life. One of the attendants holding Taps slapped his face, which the audience applauded. When Taps spat on him, which the audience also applauded, the attendant slapped him again.

"He h-h-he examined Bba-aha-iddina and brought his conspiracy to naught. He is the Prince who established that he committed the despicable deed in the ha-ha-ha-harem."

Poor Taps's chains shook louder, which bothered the attendant executioners. One of them, a short Ammonite with a scar down the middle of his nose, took a long, curled beam of skinny cedar and beat the soles of Taps's feet until Taps begged him to stop. His lips were very dry, and he had trouble speaking. Somehow he steadied his body. In a low, broken voice, he whispered out the end of his sentence:

"Thou art the shepherd to mortals, the Ki-Ki-Ki-King who subdues the hard of heart, the Ki-Ki-Ki-King who always acts upon tru-tru-truth-inspiring si-si-signs given by his Lords, the gre-gre-gre-gre-great gods—*rattle, rattle*—and therefore who has—*rattle,*

rattle—conquered the land between the Tigris and Euphrates, defeated his enemies in Assyria and va-va-va-vanquished Necho at Carchemish. Marduk the great Lord has chosen me—*rattle, rattle*—behold, I am King, and the g-g-g-god makes a pronouncement concerning my wo-wo-wo-world rule from his ho-ho-ho-holy mouth: Nebuchadnezzar is the King whose fame is po-po-po-po-power!"[1]

As Taps finished, the executioner sharpened his knife on a rock like a beard fully content with his calling, pushing the curled blade slowly on one and then the other side of the rock's wet surface. To remove a living man's skin was a messy and difficult business, and it required real execution talent. While Babylon possessed plenty of beards who could scourge the back and tread the neck, few knew how to please a crowd. For that my brother imported an Assyrian to do the job, a beard named Ass, who called his trade, "skinning the hairless goat." Ass, by the way, looked nothing like his name; he was squat and almost greenish like a spring orange that had gone bad. He smiled an executioner's smile at Taps, barely conscious now, and this smile spoke of an immense awareness, of that rare and perfect meeting of ability and opportunity.

To achieve a comfortable working height, Ass adjusted Taps's chain, making sure that the victim's feet and legs were properly spread-eagled. The King approved of this move, slapping me on the thigh and bellowing excitedly at Siduri—"Fucking Schismo!"—

his term for the political and religious factions that had settled on Babylon as so many locusts in the past year. Siduri didn't give a damn about what was happening to Taps; her hands were all over the King: his chest, shoulders, and lap. It seemed to me that the gods had given her a special dispensation to receive the Divine Plowman's attentions with a degree of abandon I found scarcely credible, and I was forced to be present for whole sickening spectacle, this "rediscovery" of their love. It was awful. But not as awful as what happened next to poor Taps

[Lacuna: tablet damaged;
approximately 26 lines lost.]

From a collection of knives on the floor, Ass selected the shortest knife, one with a handle of jade, to avoid tearing into the muscle and viscera. It looked heavy in his hands, which were delicate, even feminine. He was meticulous. "A clean skinning," he said, "is a good skinning," yet I was not sure what he meant by that phrase. Most of the flayings I had witnessed—about two dozen in all—were never clean, but long, protracted spectacles of blood and agony. In the initial phases, it was obvious that Ass was a good technician as he ran the short blade up and down Taps' body, teasing him with suggestions of his fate. He had rhythm. He knew when and where to pause the knife, when to extend the fear, where to place the blade to achieve maximum anxiety.

Taps's eyes bugged out; he gasped helplessly for air. The Court was silent. They were bored before his performance, which, sad to wedge, was underwhelming to a crowd well-seasoned in the offices of cruelty.

Poor Taps. Later, over a cup of hot wine, Moil told me that he had recently been depressed over his sister's death. How Moil knew this, I did not know, but he did. He said Taps and his sister had lived together well into middle-age, and they had been close, sharing their meals, taking morning walks in the tablet-house gardens. After his sister died of river fever, he had experimented with necromancy to speak to her. They would have long talks about his health. His sister worried about his stomach ailments and feared that he would never find a woman to love him.

Chibby confirmed as much. He claimed Taps had extended these rites to the scribal classes for some extra shekels, which perhaps explained his current misfortune—hanging in the air like a gull over the river while hunting carp. It was dangerous to fraternize with the dead. Perhaps he forgot to add the protective spells, and one of the ghosts took revenge upon him. The dead, as was well known, don't like to be disturbed.

Ass laid his knife in a flame for about sixty seconds—a nice touch, the King said, as he explained the move to Siduri, for it extended the excitement of the crowd for another moment. Placing the burning bronze blade on Taps's hip joint, he cut into the flesh, a line of attack known as Pazuzu's Revenge, which was not at all the standard opening when skinning a beard. Normally a good filleter started with a crowd pleaser—say, for example, a big strip of flesh from the chest or thigh. But Ass was unorthodox in this way, and Taps failed to appreciate the beard's subtle art. He wailed in disbelief at what was happening to him. I thought I would throw up. The King, however, nodded his head in approval, expectations happily met. Siduri covered her eyes and dug her nails into my arm.

[Lacuna: tablet damaged;
unknown number of lines lost.]

Once he removed all the skin from Taps's calves, he started on the thighs, working more quickly [. . .]

[Lacuna: tablet damaged;
approximately 40 lines lost.]

Taps ratcheted up [the weeping] and screamed, "ooooh! ooooh! Gods nooooo!" This reaction, while understandable, had the effect of turning the crowd against him. The louder the poor scribe howled, the more the Court began to boo and hiss. To be sure, they [detested heresy], but they [detested weakness] more. Yet Ass filleted on. Taps wept, wailed, pleaded, groaned, shuddered [. . .]

Tablet Twelve
[Lacuna: tablet damaged;
unknown number of lines lost.]

It was about this time that Ass lost most of the beards and concubines for good. Normally a certain stoicism obtained at these affairs, the victim was supposed to be defiant and brave in the face of his ritual decortication. There were expectations. A proper victim hurled impieties, shouted out curses, provided real theater and spectacle for the crowd. But not Taps. He whimpered like a child for his mother. It was, to the blood-hungry hyenas of the Court, an embarrassing performance. He cried for his beloved sister several times, his mouth trembling helplessly, his bowels voiding themselves noisily on the floor. And the crowd grew impatient, disappointed in the lack of drama. They mostly ignored Taps's continued cries of unspeakable anguish and gossiped among themselves.

My Lord's eyes had glazed over like those of a lizard in the sun. His tongue flicked rhythmically, as he cupped Siduri's breast in his hand. Taps's screams had awakened the King's appetite, and I swore that he looked at me for a moment, but I think now, in retrospect, it was probably a bad reflection in the torchlight. The King leaned back, and Siduri curled her arms around his neck, exposing her smooth, puffy stomach, and thus the bruise on her iliac crest, the one my Lord gave her after their nasty fight on the third moon of Nisan.

Tablet Twelve
[Lacuna: tablet damaged;
approximately 72 lines lost.]

When Ass was done, the poor beard hung before the crowd, naked of his epidermal covering and exposed before the stars in the heavens. But the Court could not have cared less.

The crowd booed and hissed and threw bread husks and moldy cheese at Ass, who, in turn, hexed them with his thumb and forefinger. It was difficult to say whether or not the flaying had been a successful one, although I doubted that my brother would be pleased. One thing was for certain. The poor Grainman had been stripped of more than just his skin—he had been transformed, by the expert ministrations of Ass, from to a howling animal hanging from chains to a blubbering and bloody hunk of meat.

Taps's performance was human, shamefully so. A current of relief pulsed through me. I took solace in another eunuch's reversal of fortune, gloried in his ignominy. I was not proud of these bitter, deep-seated feelings of ill-will, but I was willing to acknowledge these feelings—which is more than most castrates would do in a similar situation—as Taps's carcass was dragged off the platform.

[The following is a fragment and possibly
the reverse of the previous tablet.]

After the execution of Taps the Grainman, the mood in the Great Hall lightened. Gone was the inflated pleasure of watching another beard die badly—for the crowd now turned their attentions to their second favorite pastime: fucking and sucking themselves into frenzied oblivion. My Lord and Siduri passed a tankard of beer back and forth. She took a sip and gave its red-stained rim to Nebbie, who placed it into his mouth, and that intimacy surprised me, though it shouldn't have. On Nebuchadnezzar's upper lip rested a canker the size and color of a big fly. But the concubine didn't seem to mind. She finished off the tankard greedily, wiping her lips with the back of her hand. Oh, how the wolf of jealousy gnawed at my insides! Siduri's lips were a bone of contention between my Lord and me, though he wasn't aware of it. Although there was a time when I was granted almost daily access to her holy of holies—a kiss behind a pillar, a peck between screen and bed—Siduri rarely allowed the King to kiss her. It was the agreement that made our relationship possible. Siduri knew this, of course, and she knew that I knew this, and she knew that I knew that she knew this, for in the days of our relationship, we were always talking about what I "could" and "could not" do with her, and in the end, she had granted me this privilege, but there she was—astride my Lord's lap, nibbling on his syphilitic lip as if it were a hunk of well-aged cheese.

"Siddie, darling, can I get you another beer?" the King asked, wagging his tail like a dog with a bone in his mouth. Siduri shook her head, and then my Lord began to rub her shoulders with a seriousness he rarely brought to his administrative duties. Since her return to his bed, Nebuchadnezzar was always touching Siduri; he was never not touching her. He touched her when he awoke in the morning, after his attempted morning bowel movement, and he touched her at night after a strenuous and teary-eyed session of the Jackal. And he was touching her now, tracing her sharp cheekbones with his fingers, whispering secondhand epithets of passion and borrowed love.

Wiping his mouth, my Lord arose from his pillows. Rod of Justice: Scourge of poor Taps the Grainman. Naked, my Lord resembled a baby elephant. Playing the generous host, Nebuchadnezzar outstretched his arms and folded Siduri within his embrace. Waves of agony swept through the bearded and overfed elite; grown men pursed their chapped lips and shifted uncomfortably in their pillows to gain a closer look at Siduri, as she snuggled her head in the King's lap. Even the cupbearers paused in their cup-bearing to glance at her bottom, which was now raised like the killing moon of the harvest.

[Lacuna: tablet damaged; approximately 20 lines lost.]

A line of dandruff scaled along Nebuchadnezzar's scalp, scruffs trailing down his greasy epidermis and settling like snowflakes on his tunic. They shared a hookah, smoking Dream Dog, passing pipe from hand to hand, blowing smoke into each other's mouths. My chance presented itself. He was vulnerable before the mandarins of Babylon, and vulnerable was good. My Lord's small, reptilian mouth beckoned greedily. It was a truism that my sweet Siduri had left a trail of wreckage and heartbreak from Thebes to Jerusalem, and Nebuchadnezzar's harem had been her sixth in so many years. As she wrapped my Lord in her arms, the outlines of the numerous fibulae, vertebrae, jawbones, and skulls of her past lovers became visible. *He was not the One*, nor would he ever be, despite her impassioned ejaculations.

Taking the King's meaty hand in hers, she led him to the front of the room, and there amid the blood and gore of Taps the Grainman, I would make my move. When Siduri asked him if he would like to "shake the cedar tree"—her euphemism for the Jackal—his face twitched like a river mussel squirted with red pepper sauce. He shook me off, the bastard, just as I was about to kneel alongside the couple and assume my place in the ritual marriage. The King's face glowed with stupid animal pleasure. He kissed her lips and coddled my baby acorn in his red paws.

[Lacuna: tablet damaged;
approximately 20 lines lost.]

On his hands and knees, he slobbered up the leg of his concubine. Siduri giggled knowingly, as if whatever he was about to do, they had done before—in fact, had done many times before. And then, carefully, and with real delicacy, my Lord lifted the skirt of my sweet Siduri, and, oh, I could not fathom nor understand what happened next.

With his greasy beard a mere micro-cubit away from the mystery of all creation, he paused dramatically before pushing his face deep into her loins. Siduri giggled again and wrapped her legs around his neck. Is there an ideogram or phrase that describes when the "divine" breaks through the mortal veil and leaves its adepts panting and trembling in its wake? *Growling the badger? Watering the orchid? Eating the peach?* Chibby said that in his day as a young harem eunuch, they simply called it "myrtle snutching" and left it at that. But whatever you call the act my Lord performed upon Siduri of Megiddo that night, no one can say that he did not perform it with all his might. I cannot recall my Lord as happy as he was when he placed his lips and tongue on Siduri's sacred mound—an act hitherto unseen at royal court functions. Like a common field slave, Nebuchadnezzar lapped up water from the bucket of life. For a full three minutes, he licked, kissed, and caressed the concubine's lettuce box, and the beards and eunuchs of the Court responded predictably. Uruk scowled, his thick eyebrows caterpillared across his forehead. Moil, who had been reading a treatise on the famine, frowned judgmentally. Only Chibby, alone among the attendants of the execution that day, seemed to be aware of the dimension of the *scandal* he was observing, and his face crumpled with indignation. Unpredictable Nebuchadnezzar! And the hierophant of Ishtar? She faked surprise over the King's action: her red mouth opened with pleasure as she wailed to the heavens.

My soul—marinated in the blood of betrayal—howled in anguish. Oh, the indignity of it all! Needless to wedge, Siduri enjoyed the King's ministrations immensely, and as I watched helplessly, she never once looked at me. When her final, toe-curling spasms ended, Nebuchadnezzar smiled a royal smile of self-congratulation, and I can't wedge that he didn't earn it. Nebuchadnezzar's act, however, threw me into a pit of doctrinal confusion. My tongue cleaved to my mouth. What my Lord had done was possibly a dangerous heresy, one that would, without doubt, in coming months and years, provoke sectarianism, schism, and all manner of division within the Kingdom. One might well ask—and I did ask myself, in the dark, lonely hours of the night, buried under mud and dung at the bottom of the Ziggurat—why had Siduri not allowed me this favor?

[Tablet breaks off:
unknown number of lines lost.]

Tablet Thirteen –

In the House of Ma-dug-ama-dung the Mage

Before Slosh, before Chibby, before Siduri, there was Ma-dug-ama-dung the Mage. Ma-dung to his friends. Dung to his enemies. Yet I always called him Dugy. We had a history.

Dugy and I had lived together for a brief time in the harem during my first days in Babylon. He had been rusticated from the Tablet House for drunkenness, and because he could not get along with any of the other scribes in his class. In the two years I had known him, he taught me much about life: how to handle the concubines (you didn't), how to behave in the presence of Nebuchadnezzar (eyes closed, rump up), and how to steal food from the kitchen (only on moonless nights).

Good Ma-dug-ama-dung.

He always claimed it was he who befriended me! That was the phrase he used to describe the first day we met. We had drunk too many tankards of beer when we happily recognized one another for what we were: misanthropic castrates who nevertheless appreciated the joys of a good table. He said that I affirmed his unhappiness. That was the word for what we had together—affirmation. Affirmation meant everything to Dugy then, and that was well before he became mired in the so-called dark arts of alchemy and magic.

Ma-dug-ama-dung's shop was a small, mud-bricked shack among rows of other small, mud-bricked shacks. Crowded together along a narrow lane, they were all that was left from the great earthquake of year twelve of Nabopolassar's reign. Wood-beams spanned Dugy's ceiling, and tapers burned on either end of the room, illuminating a series of large frescos of the sun within a circle within another sun. These wall paintings had been done years ago by the esteemed sage, Nabû-nur-sag; now they were faded and chipped with age. Ma-dug-ama-dung was busy at his desk, mixing a cup of his famous elixir—justly named Sirrush's Revenge for the subsequent hangover it produced—a combination of beer and a fiercely alcoholic beverage of an unknown provenance. He jumped when I banged my fist on the table.

"I have been expecting you, Nergal," he snorted with satisfaction. "I knew you would come back. They always do, my old friends. They always need me in the end. What is your need, I wonder?"

"Can't an old friend come to visit?" I asked.

"Old friends come visit me all the time," he said, handing me a cup of Sirrush's Revenge, "but you only show up when you need something. You have always dealt in the world of 'I will scratch your phantom limb, if you scratch mine,' and these are, after all, momentous times. Look around you: the effluvia of influences pours down upon us. Can you feel the effluvia? It is everywhere. Open your mouth, ears, and nose! Let it flow through you!"

"Relax. It's just a dust storm," I said.

"To you and me, it's just a dust storm," Dugy replied. "But I suspect that to the King, and those who serve him, it's a sacred fountain. Let us drink to the sacred fountain! Nergal, let us drink!" he said, finishing off the cup of Sirrush's Revenge before him. Ma-dug-ama-dung favored a voice of mock piety. It suited the simultaneous reverence and repugnance he felt toward his beer consumption, which was formidable, even on days when he wasn't "drinking." On days of "abstention," as he called them, Dugy would consume between seven and eight large tankards of beer and "taper off" with three or four cups of watered-down wine that he imported by the crate from his native Crete. Yet it was beer, above all things, that made Dugy happy. He was serious about his beer drinking, and often argued—drunkenly—that beer was the greatest boon the gods had bestowed upon mankind. "Drink up the cup because tomorrow it will be empty," he always said after downing his tenth tankard.

The middle son of a middle son, he was also a magus of no slight distinction, and we loathed the same things—small talk, the Tablet House, ourselves—and this phenomenon of "shared hatred" formed the core of our relationship. We had been young eunuchs in the harem, and in an act of stupidity or a gesture of love, I had revealed to him the fundamental ugliness of my person—my neediness, my ineptitude, my selfishness. Now, I feared he disliked me for it.

"What have you been doing these past couple of years?" he said, stroking his curly brown beard, one of his proudest accomplishments and no minor feat for a eunuch.

"Oh, you know, toiling in the fields of our Lord," I said.

"So, I've heard. Your eyes are red. And you've lost some weight. When was the last time you put on clean clothes?"

"It's not what you think," I said.

"I don't think anything. But one look at you, and I can guess why you have come to see me," he said.

"And why is that?"

"You want relief from your corrupt and degenerate state," he said.

"I object to your use of the word *degenerate*," I said.

"But not to my use of the word *corrupt*. I find that interesting."

"You know what I mean."

"I don't know what you mean," he said. "But I don't have to. My magic does not rely on what you may or may not mean, nor does it rely on why or why not you have come here. All I know is that you have come to an old friend for help, and I will help you."

"It's good to see you, Dugy."

"Yes," he muttered in the accent of the northern Babylonian region of his birth. "You want some vegetable soup? It's good, yes?"

Like the beloved mother I never had, Dugy always fed me. Whenever I visited, he would offer me home-baked bread, honey cakes in thick syrup, and grilled pork cutlets in a bowl of barley. Something was always cooking in Dugy's kitchen, and often it was a thick soup. Today the big soup pot was hanging over the fire, burbling softly with vegetables and fatty mutton bones. Like Slosh, Dugy was a magnificent cook, and he loved to eat almost as much as I did.

Surrounded by cups and goblets, his secret potions and ancient stones, Mag-dug-ama-dung busied himself with the work of transcending the manifold deceptions of the phenomenal world. He claimed that all we saw and experienced in life was nothing more than the dream of a blood-filled flea on the back of a donkey tied to a plow. He said he could move objects with his mind. He boasted that he had cured himself of his

285

eunuchoidism and, thanks to his magic, was now a fully functioning beard, a healthy and vigorous Babylonian male who had fathered over two dozen children. His complexion was healthy and pink, which surprised me, for he spent his days mixing poisonous elixirs with dangerous metals.

Before his cure, Dugy was that rare thing, a free eunuch, but he never paraded that fact before other castrates, and I liked him for it. When he hadn't been working in the harem, Dugy lived with his mother in the scribal district (as a free eunuch, he was allowed to reside outside the Ziggurat), and it would be fair to say that she dominated him. She was a pious woman from the old nobility who had fallen on hard times, and so she had offered her son to Ishtar as a young boy. She took her religion seriously, some might say too seriously. She sacrificed a chicken every month to Nabû, and made her annual pilgrimages to Nippur for the Feast of the Bridegroom. Often I saw mother and eunuch strolling down Baal boulevard in the early evening. But mostly they spent their nights at home, playing competitive Hounds and Jackals, drinking a cup of warm goat's milk before bed. It was a quiet life, but Dugy seemed happy, or as happy as anyone else I knew. I envied him.

But Ma-dug-ama-dung had a secret life, one that involved what some of his more uncharitable critics have called a private and blasphemous hobby. At first, it was harmless enough. Nobody in the Ziggurat knew that in his off-hours, away from the harem and far from the umbilical clutches of his mother, he nursed a private dream. When his mother retired to bed, he would descend the warn wooden steps of the root cellar, and there, among the rotting celery and old lettuce, practice his amateur magic, mix his beginner's potions, and chant his apprentice's spells. What Dugy was pursuing was unclear to all, even, perhaps, to himself. He felt his way toward his first magical conclusion, visualizing his alchemical goal through a glass darkly.

In the beginning, he practiced his art with insects, mastering the idiom of the thorax, constructing an elaborate grammar with tagmata and exoskeletons. He mixed pupae and larvae, altering egg and adult species until they were indistinguishable from each other: baby larval bees, within hours, became fully functioning hives. He restored wings to a fly that had been tortured by boys, and turned a butterfly back into a caterpillar. Dugy was not a sentimentalist. Frogs became tadpoles. Toads became gelatinous webs of ova. He loved the hard-to-do transformations most of all. He failed a lot. But even his failures were turned into successes, or at the least, examples to contemplate and learn from. During the middle period of his apprenticeship,[1] he attempted to transform a male spider into a female, but the spell was incomplete, producing a hermaphrodite of sorts. The odious beast autocopulated and ate its own legs in a spasm of postcoital tremors. Dugy liked to keep these dual-sexed spiders in a terrarium, next to his beer-making equipment, and he spent many an early morning drinking himself into a stupor, watching the spiders fornicate and fight among themselves.

As a mature magician, Dugy had difficulty assessing his abilities. I would say that he was more than a crank and less than a prodigy, and his reputation as Babylon's most eminent occultist had never quite materialized. His first and arguably brilliant tablet *De Magia Erotica* had not been recopied by the Tablet House, and he was unhappy about it. Yet as a consequence of this perceived failure, he recommitted himself to his magic and gravitated toward the hard-to-pull-off spells and obscure and inaccessible incantations. If he had a method to his art, it was more or less inscrutable, if only because it rarely succeeded.

"No soup?" Dugy asked, waving his ladle in the air. "Suit yourself. I will give you some to take home. It's good. Now let's make you whole again, shall we? Come here. Let me show you something."

Dugy pulled out a series of protuberances— shiny lizard horns, curled antelope prongs, and battered boar tusks—from a bin in his kitchen. Each could be ground up and smoked, crushed and snorted, or turned into a thick paste that could be applied to "the area of concern," as he called the stumpie.

"The spell is not really a spell—although, on some level, it is the ultimate spell—it is more of a procedure," Dugy said. "All of these items are good; all are potent, but what you need is the big one, the first and absolute last of regeneration magic." He paused in his disquisition and smiled, and his broken teeth and black gums widened into a collage of gaps and spaces.

He grabbed a horn the size of Madame Grape's thigh and put it in my hands.

"What is this thing?" I asked.

"A rhino horn. Very rare. Very expensive."

"I don't think that will be necessary."

"You want something that works," he said. "If the rhino horn scares you, there are other ways, other means by which we might obtain the desired goal. For instance, an elephant's tusk is damn good, but it's awkward. I'll admit that. What is important is that you must be convinced of its efficacy. It's all in *Ma-dug-ama-dung's Dream*. Have you read it?"

When I didn't answer—*Ma-dug-ama-dung's Dream* was more or less unreadable, the text mainly consisting of mutilated forgeries, copied out at night by a small coterie of fanatical eunuch scribes—Dugy sighed.

"Oh, don't worry. I don't feel bad. I haven't read it, either. Nobody has."

He dug around some more among his philters and mortars and pulled out a pseudo-phallus, thick and heavy with age, and placed it, with a thud, on his desk.

"This herm possesses a formidable magic. I believe its origin is Ionia, and the Greek who sold it to me claims it has a long history. He has a name, too. He is called Fortunatus. Say hello to Fortunatus." Dugy opened his jaws and laughed.

Taking up a small glass vial, Dugy mixed some white dust in the blood of a strangled rat that I had brought for this purpose. He whispered the twenty-third magical conclusion over the mixture before topping it with mustard seed, cat urine, one vertebra of an Indian cobra, and the mummified head of a turtle. "For luck," he said. "Now you need to lie down there," he said, pointing to a narrow wooden bench. "It shouldn't take too long."

Dugy gently applied the black, thickish, and foul-smelling paste to my stumpie. My old friend handled me with love and care, massaging his callused thumbs back and forth over the scar tissue. I fell asleep on the bench and dozed for a minute or two, dreaming that I was floating in a river barge—that's how comfortable I was in the mage's hands. And Dugy was a professional. When I awoke, he was swinging a gold stone over my loins and chanting, "You are my bull, Nerggie, you are my big bull! Oh, romp through my fields, Oh trample my lilies!" He appeared to be in some kind of altered state or trance, and he had assumed the persona of a lascivious courtesan. His lips swelled. He spoke in husky tones. "I shall feed you bread fit for a god, feed you beer fit for a king. Shamash shall burn his rays on you!" He placed a horned cap on my head. He painted seven red dots on my forehead. "You shall be as the original viper. You shall become the Plant of Life, the Old Man Who Becomes the Young Man."

Outside Dugy's window, along Baal Boulevard, a procession of flagellants, darkly robed and somber, lashed themselves with cedar branches. In an effort to relieve the drought, chanters stood on every street corner of Dugy's neighborhood, calling out the hourly ablutions. First, there would be the cleansings by water and oil, then, the small animal sacrifice, and finally, the killing of a bull at the temple of Ereshkigal.

Stone phalli stood boldly in every merchant stall. A crowd, consisting of mostly naked Babylonian beards and their wives, painted in bull's blood, chanted *Eridu sleeps* and *Ea and Enhil have passed over to the night.* And then there was a multitude of hoes my brother had given to every Babylonian citizen. Hoes on the corners, hoes in the temples, hoes in the marketplace. The tool of the common fieldworker had taken over the City. Soon acts of public copulation would begin, and neighborhoods would descend into general chaos and licentiousness. It was well known that formerly I had been appalled by these ritualized acts of debauchery by Babylon's working classes. But now, I wasn't certain. I wasn't certain of anything.

"You'll have to change this dressing every other day," Dugy said when I raised myself from the bench. "I'll give you some extra mixture." He leaned down and blew on the area in question, a symbolic gesture, he claimed, that would revive the fading embers of the dragon fire that was within us all.

When Dugy had finished with his magic, he took a belt and wrapped Fortunatus to "the wound," as he called it. "Is that too tight. No? Too heavy? It's a little heavy, but you'll get used to it. It looks pretty good. Not bad at all. Now, you must wear Fortunatus for seven days and seven nights, Nerggie. Do you understand me? It will work. Trust me. That's the important thing. Trust is the most important thing we have in this life. Remember that."

[Lacuna: tablet extensively damaged: unknown number of lines lost; when text resumes, Nergal and Siduri are in the Hanging Gardens.]

"Nabû gives wisdom but not gold. Look at me. I'm getting old. When is my spring coming? When shall I sing like a swallow? Where is my cooling stream? And you. Look at you, Nergal. A lonely slave. You who burn with the glory and fire of holiness. You think your precious collection of styluses and tablets matters? Aren't you tired of all this?" she said, gesturing toward the green terraces. Across the garden in the middle of a large meadow, priests tossed small deer weighted with iron collars into the lake as a sacrifice to Enlil. Dozens of small deer, perhaps hundreds, would be drowned that evening.

"I thought you wanted to be with me," I said.

"I do. But you have to remember that our union is not a physical one, Nerggie. It is too special for that."

"But what of all the talk of plowing and furrowing? You would like to plow and furrow with me, wouldn't you? I mean *The Fecundity Tablets* are explicit on that account. You can't spiritualize that, can you? And don't tell me you don't plow and furrow because as harem scribe, I am fully aware of your record with the King. It's a distinguished record, by the way."

"Don't be an asshole. What goes on between me and the King is different. I don't really have a choice."

"But he is allowed to plow and furrow, isn't he? Why can't I? Give me a chance. I thought you wanted to make a bastard. You want to make a bastard, don't you?"

"Of course I do. But the plow you are referring to is a spiritual plow."

"Let's just hold each other," I said, remembering an old trick of Nebuchadnezzar's. "It feels good just lying here with you."

Siduri smiled and sprinkled oil on my forehead. "Now you're getting it," she said dreamily. We embraced, and things felt good again. It felt right— much like Fortunatus, who was happily tied to my loins. The view was magnificent. Before our feet in the Hanging Gardens lay seven carefully sculpted terraces, where my Lord had commanded the planting of every tree, flower, and bush. We had found a small enclosure where we could be safe from the eyes of the court.

Siduri's face and cheeks reddened as we lay in each other's arms, and her nostrils opened: I could see the filaments of her nose hairs. How I loved those hairs! And then I implemented the second part of the King's trick—carefully maneuvering my leg on her leg, then more slowly, my pelvis on her pelvis. Siduri jumped back angrily.

"What is *that?*" she asked, passing her hand over my skirt and gazing hard at me.

"Nothing. What are you talking about?" I said, as I moved away in an attempt to hide Fortunatus.

"It feels like you are sticking something in my oopie," she said, grabbing my arm and whispering our secret word for the lush entrance to her holy womb.

"No, I'm not."

"What *is* that, Nerggie?" she asked, pursing her lips.

"It's nothing."

She yanked down my skirt violently. There was Fortunatus, who peered out from my loins like an Indian cobra. First Principle of All Things.

"What *is* that? What the hell *is* that?"

"He's a good friend of mine," I said, taking her hand in mine.

"I'll bet he is. That's no friend of yours, Nerggie. That's a dildo," she said, pulling her hand away.

"No, it's emphatically not a dildo. It's a herm, or rather, he's a herm. A symbol, if you will, of the male regenerative organ. He's a sacred object from Greece. An

294

island somewhere in the Aegean, if I remember correctly. He was given to me by another friend of mine. Fortunatus is his name, if you must know. Dugy said he would help us."

"It's huge," she said. "It's also disgusting."

"He's disgusting, you mean. And yes, his size is exaggerated, but that is merely a convention. He's the rod of life, after all, the serpent of Marduk, and you have to respect that. I thought that's what you wanted for us. I thought you'd be happy."

"You're just as bad as the King," she said. "Do you know that?"

"But I thought you wanted to have bastards?" I asked. "Lots of them. Don't you want to have bastards? You said that you wanted to have bastards."

"Are you crazy, Nergal?" she asked. And she grabbed Fortunatus from my loins and tossed him on the ground, cracking the base of his head.

[Lacuna: tablet damaged; approximately 50 lines lost.]

Imperial Marduk rode his dragon, the rapist Zeus hurled his thunderbolt, and Nergal the Eunuch drank an amphora of beer with Fortunatus the herm. I don't know how to wedge this without incurring the incredulity of my enemies and the ridicule of my friends, but Fortunatus came alive and could speak.

Two days after my fight with Siduri, he stood on my desk, unrepentant and bandaged—jauntily tilted at a right angle toward the setting sun. His marble head was wreathed in ivy and dried goat's beard blanketed his base. The first words out of his mouth, however, were complaints—he complained that my room was too hot and that the dust from my tablets bothered his allergies. Perhaps Fortunatus was indulging in the customary dramatic irony of the magio-phallic-herm, but I didn't think so at the time. He whined that he was hungry. He said that he was thirsty. He protested his work conditions. "Don't take this wrong," he said in his heavy Greek accent, his voice slightly muffled—for he was uncircumcised—"but when was the last time you took a bath?"

"The gods curse all eunuchs!" I cried. "You *are* a magic herm."

"I don't know why she turned me into a prick," he said wearily. "The priestess said that I insulted her. It was a terrible misunderstanding. She claimed that I refused to make the proper burnt offering to her beauty. She accused me of mocking her. She said that I belonged to a stiff-necked generation. She called me an atheos. That was completely untrue. I believe in all gods and goddesses, and I never mock anybody. I respect and tolerate differences."

"Why the hell haven't you been doing your job? Why haven't you helped me? Siduri won't even talk to me."

"Chaos trumps broad-bosomed Gaia every time, castrate," he said. "Although I am hesitant to speak on matters of Eros, I generally shy away from things mythological. Sad to say, but Dugy and I have never really agreed on the fundamentals. Did you know that air is the originative substance?"

"You're supposed to be a magic herm," I said. "He said that your magic would help me. I paid forty silver shekels for this service. Don't you remember?"

"You know, I don't believe in magic," he said.

"You're a talking herm, and you tell me that you don't believe in magic?"

"It's a problem. I'm working on it."

"If you're not a magic herm, what kind of herm are you?" I asked.

"You can call me a philosopher, if you like."

"A what?"

"A *philo-sophist*, if you insist on a precise definition," he said.

"What are you talking about?" I asked.

"I'm a lover, castrate. A lover of knowledge."

"You are mad," I said.

"I have already been through my cosmological period, and I'm into metaphysics right now. I'm what you call a new metaphysician. Have you heard of the new metaphysics? No? Well, you will."

A tiny shaft of the fading sun reflected off Fortunatus, revealing his bulbous and vein-streaked base. As a more or less typical regenerative object,

Fortunatus was impressively biggish in stature, and I couldn't tell whether he considered his size a curse or a blessing. Whoever the sculptor was, he or she had rendered him with great realism.

My rooms back then were no different than my rooms now—a solitary hole in the bottom of the Ziggurat, a place designed for solitude and the life of a eunuch-slave scribe: dusty but cozy. The flies were bad, however, flitting lazily around the air, landing for a moment on my hands and face, where I swung helplessly at them and accidently hit Fortunatus on the tip of his head. "Hey, watch it," he said angrily. "That stung. Hey, you got any beer? I could use a drink. I haven't had a beer in four hundred years."

I pulled out an amphora that I had stashed behind my tablets, and Fortunatus requested that I pour the beer in the hole at the tip of his "noggin." That's what he called his glans: his "noggin." So I poured him a beer in his "noggin," but the beer didn't really go anywhere; it just dribbled down the shaft of the pseudo-phallus, making a pool of yellow foam on my desktop. But he said it tasted good. "That was spectacular," he said, "really, really, spectacular."

After a few beers, my shock and surprise subsided, and it began to feel almost natural to have him with me. While I worked on my harem tablets—that dank and musty inquiry into the roots and tubers of empire—Fortunatus rested on my desk, emanating a quiet confidence. Without question, the herm had powerful magic, but it wasn't the kind Dugy was selling. As afternoon turned into evening and evening into night, I set my work aside and we talked. The conversation was excellent. From my current imprisonment, I cannot remember everything he told me: his words appear as fragments, as quotations from other works, late interpolations by didactic editors, or unknown sayings found in buried tablets. He spoke of the Orphic rhapsodies, and he compared my love for Siduri to the enthusiasm of its adherents. The earth was the daughter of night, he said, and the sky was like a bowl. He compared himself to a purifier, cleansing the world of superstition and ignorance. He was interested in the Three-Legged Jackal. He asked questions about my technique and whether or not I used special oils, and he was curious about Siduri's reaction to the presence of an interloper in the fields of the Lord. When I asked him about the rains, when and if they would come, he nodded. He said he had a friend, an ambisexual snake, who said that water existed from the beginning. That was all he would say about the possibility of rain. When I asked about his life, he demurred, but after his third beer, he told me his story anyway in his rusty voice.

Fortunatus was getting tight, and he became depressed when he thought about his job as a magic herm. The sun had finally set, and we sat in silence for a while. I lit an oil lamp, and the darkness intensified in corners as his remarkable face flared or seemed to glow.

"Being a pseudo-phallus is a difficult thing in these difficult days," he began. "In this time of eclipse and wonder, there are thousands of us magic stone phalli in the markets. Many of them are just like me—most are out of work, with little or nothing to do. Maybe a few of the luckier ones are guarding fields. Some preside over weddings. Others are doing hard time in the City's brothels. There is no permanent work in the barley and wheat fields, you see. Too many farmers have closed up shop and moved to the City, and we pseudo-phalli were hit the hardest."

Fortunatus said that for a while he put his head down and worked a number of alternative jobs, but found each of them unsatisfactory in their own way. He admitted that perhaps he was too fastidious. He told me—without shame—that his taste for work was decidedly highbrow. Initially, he set up shop in the market—blessing marriages, helping infertile couples get pregnant, advising virgins on how to approach the sexual act—but that was boring.

"I wanted to do more with my life, you know, make a difference." There was a brief spell when he was a phallic lamp in a brothel, but "that proved unendurable," he said because the other herms were "loutish phalli without refinement or education." He did some boundary and signpost work, but those jobs didn't satisfy his desire to help people. "I'm a people priapus," he said earnestly. For a time, he was in a garden to help stimulate its fertility, but found that he was allergic to tomatoes, and the deer, who came in the night to eat the cabbages, scared him. After these jobs failed or petered out, Fortunatus tried the Bacchanal for a time, but found the orgiastic excesses annoying—"all those middle-aged, naked people. It was kind of sad." Then he said "Finally, after months and years of searching for work, I landed the job I believe I was created for—as an apotropaic herm guarding a wheat field against malevolence. My job, if you could call it a job, was to ward off blight and pestilence. I was thrilled at first. Posted at the edge of a field or on a rock outcropping, I channeled my most menacing tough guy. Sadly for the farmer, I was a terrible warder-offer. Despite my so-called magical powers, I was, in the end, an ineffectual phallus. Blight and infestation were drawn to me, like day follows night. I actually attracted locusts. Locusts couldn't get enough of me. They landed on my head, covered my whole body—and, as you may or may not know, my body is extremely sensitive to touch. It was like I wasn't even there. I was invisible, and it was humiliating. And it wasn't just the locusts—my presence drew birds, weevils, and beetles. I saw leaf rot, stalk waste, and seed death. The last field I guarded was decimated by flying armyworms within the hour of my first watch. Fucking armyworms. They are the worst. Not a grain or shoot left standing."

The ultimate point of Fortunatus's tale, I think, was that he was, in his own way, trying to apologize. He was attempting to explain why he could not help me.

The contradictions of his life were evidently painful to him, and he did his best to make me understand. It seems that he rejected the central premise upon which his existence depended—claiming that after four hundred years of being a magical stone phallus, he was now a skeptic. It had been a long time since the priestess had cast a spell on him, and he still refused to believe what had happened to him would have any real, lasting significance. "It's only a temporary situation," he told me with a more or less straight face. "In a decade or two, I'm going to be out of here. I might even go back to selling carpets in Smyrna. I dunno. But for now, I guess, I'll stick to philosophy. I hear you can make some money as a philosopher."

"Sounds like a plan," I said gloomily.

"All is piss," he said.

"What did you say?"

"Oh, I was just trying out a new aphorism. I'm dabbling with the aphoristic style. Brevity, concision. Capturing the essence of the matter in the fewest possible words. You like it? No? Well, all I meant by it was that you gotta settle down, castrate. Nobody gets anywhere with women by looking desperate. And you reek of desperation. They smell it. One whiff, and they're gone."

"My life is a mess. Why do I feel so sad and anxious?"

"Yeah, well, I hear that. You feel bad right now. Your hopes at finding love—as corny as that sounds—

have been dashed. You feel rotten, understandably so. And you know something? You are going to feel bad for a long time, longer than you want. Then, after sorrow dissipates, you will become angry, helplessly angry. You will be angry at the King, you will be angry at yourself, and you will be particularly angry at this harem girl—what's her name?"

"Siduri," I said.

"Yeah, Siduri. You will be mad at her, you know? There will be some indignation, as in how could another human being do this to me? And after the anger and the indignation will come sickening bouts of sexual jealousy. It will be bad. Really bad. So yeah, the next year or two, it will be rough. And this, castrate, is where I can help you. What I'm offering here is some free counsel. If you survive this crisis, and if the King doesn't remove all the skin from your body with a small and sharp blade, you will want to remember what I say to you here and now. Everybody will tell you, don't get bitter, or, if they don't say that, they will talk about you behind your back, going 'Oh, he's so bitter,' like it is the worst thing in the world."

He paused. I could tell he wanted his next point to land hard.

"But you know something? Get bitter. Get really bitter. *I* am bitter. I am *really fucking bitter*. And do you want to hear something crazy? I couldn't give a fuck about being turned into a pseudo-phallus. I'm over it. It's not going to last forever. Another four hundred and sixty-three years, and I'll be a free man again. But do you know what really infuriates me? What keeps me up nights? It's what happened after the spell. That's what I am most bitter about. Yeah, I am one bitter stone phallus."

"What do you mean?" I asked, pouring more beer. A small army of gnats swarmed over Fortunatus, but he seemed oblivious to their presence.

"You may not know this," he said. "But apotropaic pseudo-phalli are not born; they are made—it takes about fourteen years to make one, a good one, one that works. Mages like Dugy—well, maybe not Dugy, but real, honest-to-gods mages, they sometimes spend decades on a good magic phallus, one that can consecrate a field, ward off blight, and generate some sizable fecundity. There are spells that go into it. Lots of solid sorcery. Conjurations, enchantments. Some incantations. And I became one overnight. It was a really, really good break for me, a nice piece of fortune, or so I initially thought—hence my name. I was ready, too. I wanted to do some good. I wanted, believe it or not, to try and actually help people. But you know what. It actually took me seventy-two years to get a job in that field. Seventy-two years! After being cursed by that priestess, and after being transformed from a respectable merchant into a godsdamn marble cock, when I went out into the workforce, there were no godsdamn jobs. Wait, let me amend that, there were no permanent jobs. You'd get hired on a contingent basis. A year in this field, six months in that. The godsdamn drought dried up too many farms, and farmers were not hiring. So yeah, I'm bitter about that. I'm really fucking bitter. So, what I'm telling you is to get bitter. Get *really fucking bitter!* Fuck shit up. Toss *their* asses off the Ziggurat. Destroy the whole gang of thieves and murderers! Climb into their sweet Temple of Babel and take a big dump on the altar—and, after that, get her too. Revenge. It will make you feel good."

Tablet Fourteen –

Drab's Delight

"Cocksuckers!"

Having accidently nicked the bladder of one of the pigs, Uruk cursed his lot as a large pool of urine gathered at our feet, mixing with the blood that had coagulated in pulpy clumps around our toes.

"Cocksuckers!" he swore again. Swollen with anger, puffy with frustration, his face was bathed in the acrid waters of middle-age. He swung his nose in my direction.

"This is your fault."

"The Jackal is working," I said, "just give it time."

"Nobody believes there is time. We need them on board now. Cocksuckers!"

We stood on top of the Ziggurat, which stabbed the sky like a mace whose head had been shorn off in battle. The Tower's walls were crumbling and unfinished, with broken ramparts and sagging crenellations, and yet I had the feeling of transport, of looming over the great City on the plain whenever I stood on its gray stones, grown smooth with the blood of sacrifice. Staring at the heavens, I perceived a divine murder in the order of things. Fear and awe clutched my insides, and for I moment, I was tempted to fling myself off the Ziggurat, experience the vertigo of flight and welcome oblivion of flesh meeting brick, but that would make Moil—and the rest of the pitiful, long armed neuties in the college of eunuchs—happy. Fuck them. That's what our father Drab always said.

Although I was rarely present for the rituals that were conducted on the ultimate step of the Tower, I felt that awful, monumental acts occurred here. The air was thick with the stench of holocaust, and a strong smell of blood and urine molested our noses, the result of seven pigs that had just been cut open for a last-minute divining. Their death squeals clamored in my head, unhappily reminding me of a recent night I had spent with the King and Siduri. Lately, as I have wedged copiously in this chronicle, things were going badly with Nebuchadnezzar and his alpha-concubine. They were engaged in the typical standoff of lover and beloved—who would be master and who would be slave—and the King blamed me. More to the point, since our fight over

Fortunatus, Siduri refused to speak to me. She returned all of my letters, and I was feeling desperate.

"Nobody blames you, Uruk."

"What are you talking about? Everybody fucking blames me! The Illegitimates are threatening to remove me from the Omnia. I can tell you one thing, good brother Nergal, I am sick of their fucking criticism. I am sick of their godsdamn complaining. You have no idea what I have to put up with every day. The Greater Bastardy is nothing but a godsdamn slogan to these bastards. I have one question for them, one question. Why don't they look at the signs? Why don't they fucking look at the signs?"

"Easy brother," I said, placing my hand on his silken robes. Counselor to the counselor—that was my latest job in the Court of Nebuchadnezzar, and one I was performing with diminishing enthusiasm. The steamy unguents of Ishtar had begun to congeal, and the amniotic fluid of my new birth had begun to dry up. In sum—as my father Drab used to say before he wildly applied his cane to my back—I was growing weary of my new role as yes-castrate to my bearded brother, with whom, ironically enough, I was experiencing a renaissance of affection.

"Are you even listening to me?" he asked.

"What signs?"

"All of them! The stars have already confirmed that the Egyptian thing is a go. The sheep stomachs have all quivered in the fourth quadrant. That's right.

Jerusalem is ready for our siege engines. All signs point to another march on Judah. If the Illegitimates continue to thwart me, Nergal, I will fucking bury them!"

Uruk scare-crowed his long legs across the rampart to check the north star, note its trajectory concerning the latest developments along the Syrian-Palestine border, of which, as his hair-trigger temper demonstrated, he did not approve.

"But hasn't your position—correct me if I'm wrong—that we need a genuine sign from the gods *before* we can enact their will? Before we invade? I don't see what the problem is."

"Don't fucking quote back to me my own theory," he spat angrily. These days my brother's voice possessed an unusual ripeness as if it was a fortified wine that had been opened too soon. "I'm familiar with book six of the *Corpus Fecundicum*. You may have forgotten that I have wedged the fucking tablet, but the godsdamn starmen assume the worst of my approach. They keep insisting that we draw the King's birth chart again."

"What about the scatomants? Any help there?" I asked.

"I'm beginning to wonder about their commitment, Nergal." Uruk pulled a strip off his long fingernail with his teeth and flicked it off the Ziggurat.

"That's odd. Scut has always struck me as a reasonable fellow."

"Scut is a stupid twat," he said. "You spend too much time in the fucking harem. I have always regarded

309

Scut as a subversive and a radical. He's a godsdamn crackpot. More to the point, he brought in some substandard camel droppings to our meeting last month. Wholly unacceptable. And Scut's the beard who is always screaming about the lack of rain. He claims that we have been in a drought not for three years but for the last ten. Can you believe that? His sheep scata were shitty specimens, too. Unreadable. It was unbelievable. They were crap! And you know me. I love scatomancy. But the examples have to be sound. They must be sound. But try telling *that* to a scatomant!"

"I think I hear footsteps on the stairs. They're here," I said.

"Cocksuckers!"

[Lacuna: tablet damaged; approximately 72 lines lost.]

"What possible harm could come from deporting a couple thousand Jews?" Uruk asked the scribes and diviners who had assembled before him on top of the Ziggurat. "Before we march west to Judah and possess the good land, we first must put a question to the gods. Who will pluck the ripe grape from the vine? Will our beloved and glorious King possess it? Or that cretinous fuckwad Hophra and his lackey Zedekiah?"[1]

There was a smattering of applause, mostly from the stomach experts, but also from the astrologers, who nodded with the resignation of professionals long

310

accustomed to fixing the King's will around the heavens. Scut the Scatomant, however, frowned. Years of staring at mounds of animal excreta had produced in him a deep and abiding skepticism for all things earthly and had taught him that everything in the Court of the Golden Bull was not always as it seemed. He expressed his enmity by combing his beard, hunting for breadcrumbs but finding only lice, which—once flushed out of their hairy lair—scattered to the floor.

"Tonight is about more than crushing the hydra of Judaean rebellion. Tonight, gentleman, the veil will be removed," said Uruk as the wrinkles around his eyes tightened.

A new moon enshadowed the parapets along the wall. It was the month Nisanu, and we were on the ultimate step of the great Ziggurat, discussing wars and rumors of war against the kingdom of Judah, that noisy flea in Babylon's imperial bedroll. Twenty or so wedge- and liver-men from the Omnia and Star Room surrounded my brother, and it surprised me to see him treated with such deference and esteem by beards who were obviously accomplished in the occult arts. The price of my brother's grain yield may have been down, but Uruk knew how to command a room full of beards who had spent their lives on a bench with a stylus in their hands.

"Marduk has declared that he is the One True Plow," said Uruk, pulling a small garden hoe out from under his robes. "Only He can push the mud aside to allow the Great Seeding to take place. There are big things ahead. Do you know what? We're all going to have a plow in our hands someday. Do you know that? Every beard a plowman. Every eunuch, too," he said, throwing a proverbial bone in my direction.

The ministers nodded and stared dumbly at the garden hoe in my brother's hand, for it was not unusual for my brother to engage in peasant farmer theatrics. On the whole, Uruk's homily on the plow and field—his blatant anagogic reading of our desperate situation—sounded ridiculous. My brother had picked up this kind of speaking style, with its pauses and colloquial gestures, from our father Drab, who had grown up in the northern deserts of greater Assyria, and who favored, after sixteen cups of strong beer, its mock populist rhetoric. And Uruk was borrowing from father liberally, and without irony, an obvious sign that he was desperate. He seemed unusually tired, even sad. It had been a long year, full of botched offerings, bad omens, and worse portents. My brother's grand plans for launching the New Era of Fecundity in the harem, which had begun on that fateful night of the Festival of the Golden Bull with Nebuchadnezzar's union with the Holy Bride of Babylon, had—after their first hopeful sproutings—withered on the vine. The King was still flailing away with no hope of ending The Big Slump. The harem was barren. Drought was universal. Something had to be done, and tonight's ritual was Uruk's last stab at political survival.

Harpagus the Mede waved his hand to hurry on with the proceedings, and Scut the Scatomant, who was holding dung samples taken recently from the bull fields, shifted unhappily in his wool skirt. Scut had requested an audience with my brother over what he called the "superior-quality" of the samples, but Uruk had ignored him. Bunt cleaned out an ear with a fat finger, screwing it clockwise and then counter-clockwise, examining the yellowish putty before flicking it to the ground. Ennugi the Irrigator scratched a scab on his elbow, slowly pulling at its blackish canopy, inching the hard dimple of dried blood away from its craterous sore; and Scut the Scatomant wedged something on a tablet and passed it to Bunt, who read it and snickered. Uruk was not unaware of these small, tablet-boyish acts of insubordination, and he would remember Bunt's snicker most of all when he applied the purging hoe to the Tablet House in the fateful days that led up to the war.

Picking up another hoe—my brother now wielded one in each hand—Uruk continued his discourse. "You know what these are? That's right. They are simple garden hoes. They feel good in your hands, don't they? Honest work, hoeing a garden, cutting out the weeds, removing overgrowth that is choking the life out of our precious wheat and barley stores. As goes the garden, so goes the world. But remember, what occurs in the natural world, the physical world, is merely a prophesy for what must occur in the spiritual world, for that is the only world that counts. No matter what we do in the Big Seraglio, none of it matters. It means nothing. These hoes, here, have the look and feel of hoes, right? They're heavy in the hands. They feel real, don't they? The handle of each is wood, and the end is iron. But they're not real, just as that dead field out there isn't real, and those empty canals aren't real. Your hunger, your thirst: none of this is real," said Uruk as he spread his arms to the stars in the sky. "We have been born out of due season. The fields are no longer ripe for harvest, and the laborers, well, they are malingerers who shall be dealt with in due time."

The bowel and liver men nodded sadly. They knew my brother's fear of the common Babylonian, who was crying for more bread and beer, and they agreed with him.

"We have to fix that," Uruk continued. "I know that. We *will* fix that. We shall smite the Egyptian with the hoes of righteousness. We will be the prince and judge over him. And I know what you are thinking. You think that sooner or later, this drought is going to end. This famine will one day end. The whole godsdamn thing could very well stop tomorrow—the rains could come, they *will* come, and that will be the end of it, right? Yeah, right. We know better. Don't we? I know better. You know better. There is always another drought, always another little dry spell around the corner. If not next year, then probably the year after, or the year after that, right? We've got to end the cycle of drought and deluge once and for all. Now. Tonight.

And that's why, on this night, gentlemen, I am offering you a new beginning." He turned and pointed his hoe in the direction of Drab's Delight.

Stewing in a large vat, Drab's Delight popped and crackled, glowing in the darkness. Named after our esteemed father—an emerald-colored liquid, full of nettles, pricks, stems, stalks and all manner of vegetable roughage—the ritual was not for the faint of spirit. As Uruk stirred its contents with his staff, dark steam rose from the cauldron, and the smell of burnt peppers filled the top floor of the Ziggurat. Earlier in the week, my brother and I had spent hours crushing and boiling seventy-two of the sacred cacti to make the gloopy, green sacrament, and now its stems and spikey branches had been broken down by the heat and turned into a thick soup. My eyes watered and burned from the heat in the air.

While most of Babylon's elites were habitual practitioners of sacred intestinal purges, many had never experienced the Delight. Indeed, the origins of the great and mysterious rite were lost in time's great hangover. Set apart by Nabû, god of the scribes, Drab's Delight was a gamble. When an adept was in the clutches of its terrifying visions, to him, and to him alone, would be revealed the truth about the world. I had only experienced the Delight once, and it was indeed delightful—the Delight was in fact one, extended spasm of bowel-shuddering pleasure.

"Fickle god. Capricious deity, tonight we drink of your sacred fountain," Uruk intoned in the voice he adopted for official occasions. A sandstorm threatened on the horizon. Awash in a reddish glow, Babylon was painted in amber, like a dead ant encrypted in millennia-old honey. He nodded to me: it was our sign that I was to begin our work.

Our work. At the time, this simple phrase sounded good to me—my brother and I working together to bring about the Universal Fecundation, which, of course, required the Expansion West. As little as a month ago, I never would have imagined our partnership, but here we were standing at the highest point in the Mesopotamian valley and about to call down the Bull of Heaven, and I would be lying if I said I wasn't nervous. Egypt knew that our position was weak and our propaganda equally so. We had intercepted a tablet in which Hophra proclaimed himself King of the Levant. It was high time he had his wings clipped. To this end, Uruk had given me the job of administering the Delight, of helping the Illegitimates in their mystical journey, or, if you will, of opening the gateway to the Higher Purification. Anything to do my part.

As the scribes and diviners prostrated themselves before the altar of the Bull, I passed around tubes of sheep gut, each already bulging with the Delight. Designed specifically by my brother to deliver the green sacrament, the sheep's gut shook with the thick, regenerate muck. At their ends was a lengthy bulb-like apparatus that functioned as a syringe to squirt the blessed liquid up the beard's intestinal tract. The tubes were hot in my hands, and I had to shift the bundle back and forth in my arms to keep from scalding myself. I walked up and down the lines of adepts, blessing them as I passed. Each adept—for all who received the Delight were called such—bowed his head to receive the holy liquid. Stopping before each scribe or diviner, I said—again, pursuant to Uruk's instructions—"to thee, who art a worm, may the god appear."

"Fill my bowels!" cried Scut the Scatomant.

"Fill my bowels," rasped Bunt the Eunuch.

"Fill my bowels," moaned Ennugi the Irrigator.

It was my job as administrator of Drab's Delight to help the adepts insert the tube into their sacred gluteal region, for all things Drab's Delight touched with its magic were sacred, but, let me be the first to wedge, it was difficult work. Brutal rite. Somber cult. I felt like a wet nurse in a room of dying babies. Fiddling with the gutting and making a mess of things, I stammered and apologized for any pain or discomfort I was causing the congregants, who lay in silence and expectation.

A hot wind blew across the floor, and the heat of the night refused to dissipate. Coming down the line, Uruk walked past the recumbent beards quickly. "Move it, move it," he urged, because the ritual had to commence before the moon reached its apex in Saturn, which would be in about twenty minutes. Many of the insertions occurred in a blur, and what I wedge can only be fragmentary—there was Naram the Nonentity, Ikunum the Gouty, Bar the Righteous.

Hunching over chief eunuch Bunt, I eased the tube into his posterior, which was peppered with ingrown hairs and pustules the size of mosquito bites, and spilled some of the Delight on his left cheek. He whimpered and begged me to hurry, but it was a hard job to insert the tube. Bunt's backside was called many things in the College of Eunuchs—Bunt's Nates, Seat of the Eunuchate, Caudal of the Castratorium—but none of the names could capture its doughy texture, its immense and unwieldly shape, or the way its consistency quivered under my ministrations. Years of sitting on it had made Bunt's bottom as soft as a giant fruit-filled pastry, and I struggled to insert the tube, pushing it in only to have it fall out again, and through it all, Bunt cried like a child for his mother.

Once having inserted the bulb, I squeezed it good and hard, and a sucking sound blasted out of Bunt's backside. I pushed harder and found success. As the liquid slowly filled his belly, the chief castrate's eyes rolled back, exposing the whites, which were tinged with reddish, spidery veins. Bunt moaned softly, and I asked him if it was too much, and he shook his head, saying, "No, no, it's good, but please wipe my head, Nerggie, would you please, dear boy?" Bunt sweated profusely; clearly the Delight had begun its mystical journey through his bowels. I pressed a rag against his brow and tried to say a few words of comfort, but he didn't hear me, or if he did, he didn't seem to understand their relevance to his pain, which was now acute.

Three rows to the left of Bunt was Harpagus the Mede, hunched over on his knees. Son of Priests. The only child of an only child. Lewd deballocker of boys. When I approached the great Field Marshal, tube in hand—with unconcealed hostility—Harpagus laughed, which recalled me to the day of my gelding. His black beard was still thick, but it was now sobered with streaks of gray. "Our roles have reserved, haven't they, Nerggie?" he said, raising his rump provocatively toward me. "Go ahead, my boy, you won't be the first," he laughed again.

Now, normally a proud and violent beard such as Harpagus would never deign to be touched by a eunuch, let alone submit to the passive humiliation of the sacred but terrible rite, but such were the reputed powers of Drab's Delight that the Mede had condescended to join us for the ritual. Up was down, down was up, and the moon blotted out the sun. Harpagus merely lifted his skirt and puckered his lips lewdly. "Would you like to cut me open and read my entrails, Nerggie? You won't find much," he chuckled. I shoved the tube fiercely into his bottom, but he only laughed again. And yet my action was hard enough to cause his necklace to unclasp and fall on the blank tiles of the Tower. He did not even notice. I reached down and picked it up, and there in my hands was the ivory-headed castration clamp of Harpagus the Mede.

The clamp was heavier in my hands than I imagined, and the ivory ram's head at its base more beautiful. O Harpagus! My stumpie—with its tender scar tissue and round mound of flesh—contracted tightly in its presence. On a good day, the stumpie was more accurate than any snaggle-toothed seer. It was one of the ironies of my life that my truncation did not, despite what my critics allege, cut me off from the heart of life. On the contrary, my castration produced a clairvoyance of the soul, a gift of premonition, an inclination towards the prophetic. Whenever a sand storm blasted from the West, whenever Uruk put a pedagogic thumb on my harem tablets, whenever the King was having one of his untimely bouts of constipation, the stumpie extended and contracted under my skirt. It would begin with a tingling in my loins and work its way toward my stomach and into my throat, where it lodged like a clump of undigested bull meat. My whole being would come alive with possibilities inherent in things. Liberated from the body's demands, I was free to contemplate its mysteries, and as I peered into Harpagus' quivering rectum, I beheld the terror of the universe, and for a moment contemplated cutting off the Mede's cock. I only cursed him and placed the clamp in my tunic pocket.

"I remember when a good enema was as easy to find as a young boy. Still, this batch of Delight is passable," he said, sneering. Moil always claimed that the general possessed many of the subtleties of the

eunuchoid mind: the slothfulness, avuncular manner,
and critical acumen. Yet it was not easy to fix a single
image of the Mede. Of his resemblance to a god with
three faces much as been remarked, but let it be wedged
that he liked young boys—liked to geld them with his
wit before he spayed them with his knife.

"I'd tell you where to put this sheep's gut, but
you're going to stick it up your ass anyway," he
mumbled as he wandered toward the edge of the rampart
to await his vision.

After administering the Delight to the adepts, I
sampled a considerable measure myself—alas that
bastard Harpagus was right, he was always right. As I
squeezed the bulb, filling my insides with a prodigious
amount of liquid, I willed myself to hold Drab's Delight
in my bowels as long as I possibly could. Bloated,
burbling, I found it was more difficult than I had
imagined. I was not alone, of course, for twenty-four
red-faced beards and eunuchs—each responsible for a
key administrative post in the City, each a purported
authority in his respective field of occult arts—were
now laboriously flexing their sphincter muscles,
groaning, and sighing with intestinal discomfort on
behalf of the goddess Fecundity and her handmaiden,
War. You could hear them mutter to themselves, call for
the help and aid of their girlfriends, wives, catamites,
what-have-you. There were splutterings and pops from
their dilated stomachs; each man had swelled to the size
of a water horse with the delightful brew: twenty-four

rotund adepts of the gods, each with their posteriors up in the air, supplicating the spirits and demons that hovered over the Tower.

"Hold it, my good brother, hold it," whispered Uruk, who had sidled up next to me, as I leaned painfully on the wall. He nodded his encouragement, clearly proud of my work on behalf of the invasion of Judah. "That's it, Nerggie. Your face is turning a yellowish purple, and that's a good sign. Your stomach is filling nicely, too, by the way. Soon you will be communing with the gods."

For what seemed like a long time—and this feeling was a harbinger of things to come, because when under the spell of Drab's Delight, ten minutes felt like ten hours—I held on to the stone ramparts, my knuckles trembling. To describe the sensation that was throbbing through my bowels as "bloated" fails to capture the pressure, anguish, agony, and ultimately the joy of the anticipated release. But my brother forced me—forced all of us—to endure the hellish cauldron for thirty minutes. It was an eternity of spiking pain, for he had failed to adequately crush the thorns, and it felt as though my pyloric valve was about to explode in a nasty conflagration of flesh and fire. "Hold it, hold it," chanted Uruk deliriously.

"Rise, rise up and make an appearance!" he said as he added more Delight in the bulb that coiled out of my bottom. Uruk was taking delight in giving me pain. Yet I nodded my head happily and rasped along with my brother, "Rise up, Rise up!" And then a rumbling in my stomach erupted: *Bbbrrrphhh! Srrpphh! Urrummmph!*—a clear sign of what was to happen next.

"Summon the god!" cried Bunt, who had suffered from fecal impactment most of his adult life—a malady with which the King chronically struggled—and moaned with pleasure at the opportunity of relief. It was wedged that the god roused himself slowly, slumbering from his wintery sleep, breaking free from the dry and cold bonds that held him earthbound.

When the twenty-four beards finally released their hold on the Delight, a loud groan broke across the stone floors of the Ziggurat, as the devilish water sloshed and spurted out their backsides: *Errrrrruuuppptttt! Psssooooooooooooooooooosssssshhh! Rrrrrrrrpppphhh!* A great river of muck overwhelmed the scribes and starmen, cascading through the parapet, rising, breaking, and crashing over the ministers, and a collective wail broke out: "Aaaaaarrrrrgggggghhhhh!"

And Uruk cried: "Behold the God Who Comes! Wait upon Him! He appears!"

What occurred that night has become the stuff of legend and rumor. Uruk's triumph. Scut's sorrow. Bunt's disbelief. The Drabine tradition speaks of a warrior-savior who shall be given dominion over the Mesopotamian valley and transform its crags and deserts into fields of corn, fruit, and oil. In my calmer moments, I would dismiss such an idea that sounded like the delusions that have always plagued the peoples of our

region: the end of the desert, the demise of the
wasteland, the beginning of a new age. This controversy
has been expatiated upon at length by Babylon's scribes
and chroniclers in the aftermath of the war and—all too
predictably—little has been resolved. But the Delight
was different. Greater than magic, more precious than
philosophy, more potent than wisdom, Drab's Delight
overwhelmed earthly protest. Each saw what he desired,
each shaped and massaged the god to meet his peculiar
specifications of what a god should or should not be.
Bunt saw a eunuch happily plowing a field. Scut
witnessed a great rain falling on a dead field. Uruk saw
his enemies drowned in a great river. And Nergal the
eunuch?

Let me be the first to wedge: the God Who
Came was a fat boy whose name was BABEL and whose
round belly measured nearly twenty cubits, and whose
uncircumcised member was the size of the trunk of the
great pizzle, swinging back and forth like the scythe of
Time itself. And to the Fat Boy, BABEL, was given the
power to make war with our enemies, and dominion
over beast and fowl and creeping things of the earth, and
the Fat Boy, BABEL, would lead a great army that would
drench the desert plain in the blood of our oppressors
and the multitude of the unclean would be annihilated,
and all things would be made new. Shaped like a cosmic
egg, the face of the Fat Boy, BABEL, wrinkled in a
universal frown. His fat fingers reached helplessly
toward the airy nothing, for the Fat Boy, BABEL, was a

324

crying god, a vomity god, and a god who messed his nappies.

For a moment, the Fat Boy, BABEL, hovered over the group of scribes, who cowered before his wildness and wept before his painful light. A Giant, Fat Bastard Boy! A great and terrible revelation, the Fat Boy, BABEL, was a good son of Babylon who would make the earth yield a prodigious crop. He would cause the vine to shoot forth and the grape to yield its wine. As the sun settled on the horizon and low, black clouds roiled in the sky, the Fat Boy, BABEL, did something naughty. The Fat Boy whose name was BABEL grabbed his Fat Bastard Cock and sent forth a holy stream of piss on the court scribes and sovereign diviners.

An illustrious scribe once wedged that the face of every true god is the face of the world, and the face of the Fat Boy whose name was BABEL glowed with mischief as he poured forth a golden river on the assembled congregants, who opened their mouths as if to receive holy water. Ennugi, Bunt, Harpagus, and Scut—all were seized with a divine frenzy, delighting in the regenerate stream of the Fat Boy, BABEL.

Earlier in the evening, when the mood was skeptical, and during a lull in the dread rite, Uruk had handed out bull horns, and now each celebrant held one up to the side of his bald, age-spotted head. The horned scribes and starmen bellowed like the man-bulls they had become, stomping, snorting, and swinging their horns under the uncircumcised cock of the Fat Boy whose name was BABEL.

Thick drops of rain fell on brick, splattering the stones of the Ziggurat—one, two, three, then five and ten drops landed in front of us.

Rain!

The City had not seen rain in thirty-nine months.

You could hear a shout in the street, the murmuring of a crowd gathering before the Temple of Ishtar.

"Yes, yes, yes!" cried my brother, who wept with joy.

And there was Scut, sitting on his haunches amid a pool of colonic liquid, disregarding the rain that was coming down from the heavens, as skeptical as ever, shaking his head, scowling over the remnants of his dung samples, which had been swept up in the aftermath of the Delight.

Tablet Fifteen –

The Walls of Uruk

After the Delight, my relationship with my brother deepened, became more complicated, even treasonous. Now most of the City's mages and diviners attributed our salvation to the Big Boy Bastard God, and, of course, Uruk took no small measure of credit for the change in our fortunes. I don't begrudge him for renaming the boulevard of Baal after our Father. The rains lasted two days and two nights, filling our canals with just enough water to tempt a melancholy eunuch to cool his tired feet. On the third day the sun appeared, and the bull of Marduk warmed the plains with his caressing rays, and green shafts sprouted toward the sky.

Once again, the cicadas chirped in the afternoon heat. It thrilled my brother to see the farmer-slaves tilling the field anew: the sight of their crabbed and gnarled forms—stooping and sweating in the sun from morning to nightfall—calmed his feverish mind. However, something happened that no beard in the Omnia or Tablet House expected. For just as mysteriously as the rains appeared, they receded again. Permanently. The Bastard Boy God with the Big Prick withdrew his presence. He really was a bastard.

More than a few overzealous scribes dubbed it The Great Rebuke. The windstorms returned, the sun darkened, and the moon refused to rise for an entire month. Fields outside the City gates turned brown once more, and grime covered the walls and mud huts. The happy interval of precipitation only exacerbated our discontent. I remembered the smell and feel of water, the morning dew on the harem tiles and despaired. The drought was back, worse than ever. Something had to be done. My brother tapped me for the job.

The summons came in the middle of the night. I had just sat down to a plate of fresh bread and black pepper lamb slathered in Slosh's green sauce, when there was a soft knock on the door, a knock I should have ignored. Never leave your room, Chibby always said. Had I followed his precept, the fate of Babylon would have been reversed, bursting with wine and clothed in crown and star instead of dearth and dust. Such are the decisions by which empires rise and fall!

Had I taken a pepper out of the sandwich and dipped it in the vinegary hot green sauce for an initiatory nibble—as was my custom—and crushed its flesh in my teeth, I never would have gotten out of my chair. Had I allowed myself to take a first, ecstatic bite of the sandwich and felt its brown juices flow over my fingers, I would have never opened the door. Slosh's mutton sandwiches were exquisite works of the culinary art, the culmination of a lifetime effort by a gourmand and glutton who dedicated himself to gratifying the eunuchoid belly.

Oh, Slosh! If only Siduri's caresses had given me such satisfaction.

Slosh's sandwiches—called Green Dragons by the eunuchs of the College of Eunuchs—began with a half a loaf of fresh, hot bread and a thick spread of crushed garlic. Then, they were layered with large and steaming slices of mutton that had been marinated in parsley, onions, and oil for forty-eight hours—before being finished off with a generous ladle of green sauce. Slosh's green sauce was not your standard secret ingredient or mystery condiment. Oh no. It was a well-known but impossible to reproduce concoction of beer, garlic, onions, green peppers, and yogurt. I was gripping a Green Dragon in my hands that night with the same intensity with which I had performed my duties in the Jackal, fully intent on placing it into my mouth and experiencing the gratifying union of fat, meat, and sauce. Why I did not do so I cannot explain, but I opened the door, and three hundred harem girls disappeared into the deep.

At the foot of my door was a small tablet. It said simply, "Put down your Green Dragon and come to the Omnia. Immediately."

Now, there were many beards in the Big Seraglio who attempted to predict the King's whims: Scut the Scatomant and Uruk were two of the most notable examples of the Babylonian obsession for divining the future, and they, all too predictably, despised each other. Scut bragged he could discern the King's imperial plans in a pile of freshly laid goat dung, while my brother boasted of the visionary powers of a bull's duodenum. However, no beard knew that Uruk used me and my harem tablets as his backup. Uruk denied that this was so, but as harem scribe, you see, I knew differently. The practice of linking the King's desire to the movements of his royal army would, of course, prove decisive in Nebuchadnezzar's decision to go to war the following spring.

I reluctantly put down the Green Dragon, closed the door behind me, and trudged up the Ziggurat. The trip was as slow as it was arduous. I won't bore the reader with too many details, but it was a typically worrisome ascent. Wiping my greasy hands on my tunic, I bumped into a dark and smelly mass. It was Nit, a former eunuch of the King's late father, Nabopolasser. Had the old castrate followed me up the Ziggurat? He was sitting in the center of a stairwell and smelled of the midden-heap.

Homeless and mad, Nit always appeared in the strangest places—the wedding of an enemy, the castration of a friend.

"Nergal, I am so glad you are here. The party is a big one, don't you think?" he said, pointing to a blank brick wall in the corner of the stairwell. "Look at those beautiful ladies dancing around the cauldrons of fire. It's my favorite part of the Festival. Soon the King will appear in his lion vest. How I love the lion vest! It's going to rain soon. Are you hungry? Do you want a bite of my pear? I don't like the defecating monkeys. Never have. They are tasteless. Watch out for that one, look it's shitting in Bunt's mouth. That's disgusting."

Since the death of Nabopolasser, Nit the eunuch had retreated from the Court and withdrawn into a world of his own making. Famously delusional, he spent his days and nights in a lunatic's reverie, usually as a perpetual watcher at one of the dead King's parties.

"Will the King plow the land tonight?," asked Nit, absentmindedly twirling the dirty red feather that sprang from his loins.

"Yes, hopefully," I replied, playing along with him. "Nabopolasser is a mighty King."

"He certainly is. Not like that fuck-head we have on the throne now. Do you think that lady—that one, the one with the whip in her hand—is wearing undergarments?"

I needed to get away from Nit. Uruk's summons, however inane, had to be taken seriously in these most serious of times.

"You're looking good, Nittie. You look good. You seem good, too."

"People seem all sorts of things. You seem good, too. But one never knows, does one? Do you think when they get rid of them, they will get rid of us too? It's only a matter of time before we we're all going to be beheaded. Our heads will be stuck on the walls like common criminals. Harpagus will see to it. He always does. I wonder how I will look? My head sitting on a dirty pike, I mean. Will my eyes roll back? Go all bubbly and white? The eyes of the decapitated always have that certain look. A look that says, 'how did this happen to me?' You know that look? Yes, I thought you might. You won't look so bad because you're younger than I am."

"I imagine you will be as handsome as ever," I said.

"Well, I'm not so sure," Nit said. "The years are very cruel to castrates. But, of course, the years are cruel to *everybody*."

At the forty-second floor, I paused and looked out the window. Three miscreants hung from their ankles on a chain. Ravens stripped them of their rotten flesh. I think I spotted Taps's carcass among them, but I couldn't be sure.

Tablet Fifteen
[Lacuna: tablet cracked;
approximately 80 lines lost.]

In the alcove to the Omnia, the crème de la crème of sheep's milk stood around scratching their beards, talking about whether the rains would resume, gossiping about the latest hires in the Tablet House, wondering when the fresh shipment of goat bile ducts would arrive. The Star-chiselers, moon-wedgers, theo-stomachists, and liver-liners—all the dutiful oxen and asses of the state were present and accounted for. That great flatterer, Rim-Agu, greeted me with a deep mock-bow. He was an impressive self-promoter, and one of the Omnia's rising stars. Although he wedged in a persuasive, readable prose, he could be very testy when his authority was challenged. His prophecies were impressively sycophantic—although it was rumored that of late he had turned against the Fecundity Project. No doubt he had placed a proverbial scribal finger in the wind, and was waiting on whether Harpagus would make a move on the throne. I suspected that Rim-Agu coveted my brother's job and would happily stab him in the back with a stylus if given the opportunity. I proffered my middle-finger, and he playfully returned the gesture, accompanied by his phony, scribal laugh, which sounded like hyenas copulating in a ditch.

Entering my brother's rooms, I found him stooped over a copper bowl, mixing nettles in a reddish black liquid. He added elixirs and salts and applied them to what appeared to be a quivering sheep's liver. Divination was a discipline to which Uruk came late, and he had a wild-eyed faith in his occupation. His chambers were that of a typical but incredibly powerful bowel-man. Torchlight flooded every corner of the room, illuminating the iconography of a sarcophagus in the corner: a bearded man discoursing on the mysteries with a veiled woman. The beard looked exactly like Uruk; the resemblance was remarkable and explained the reason for this strange object in his workplace. Nearly ten times the size of my cell in the College of Eunuchs, Uruk's quarters were elegantly decorated in cedarwood and ivory inlaid screens: mahogany and gold torches stood in every corner, dried gall-bladders, sheep livers, and bull testicles hung from the rafters. Unknown animal gut covered the floors. Next to the cutting knives and divining rods was a large earthenware jar filled with styli and compasses. Above his desk hung a large drawing of the zodiacal sign of Aries with its three decans. The air smelled of Uruk's massive cedar desk, which dominated the room: Upon it sat innumerable tablets and papyri in all the known languages of the world, and in which he was fluent: Sumerian, Egyptian, Akkadian, Greek, and Aramaic. My brother had drunk deeply at the wells of hermetic studies and was now a full-blown inebriate, teetering down the lanes of Orphical magic, quaffing planetary talismans and burping up Sephiroth and the ten spheres of the cosmos. The whole place had the odor of success, of a beard who had "made it" in Babylon, who had climbed the Ziggurat, and once there, schemed against his enemies and rivals, of which there were a hundredfold.

Uruk turned and gave me the full mug of his face. His chin was not strong, but his gaze was penetrating, though he was slightly wall-eyed. He looked away as soon as I returned his stare. He was not bad-looking. He had, after all, our family nose, long and aristocratically rounded like a half-shekel. He also possessed a fine, gingery beard, one that I envied, which had the consistency of a good porridge.

Slave assistants of every nation and race bustled in and out of the room. A slave handed him a missive from the waterworks gallery: an update on canal levels. He read the message, made a few changes, and handed it back. His Omnia headquarters vibrated with importance. You could tell that real decisions were made here. Another slave-assistant mentioned a party he must attend in the evening, a boring affair, according to Uruk, given by Lady Trismegistus, who had a dual interest in astrology and his affections.

"Yes, she's incredibly attractive and quite smart too—you would find her fascinating, Nergal, but I cannot break away. Great plans are afoot, imperial plans. A war against Judah, for starters. And for all of it, I am going to need your help with the King. Right now, he's in poor shape—which explains this latest sandstorm. I suspect he has been 'scarfing' again. Is that the correct term for it? I don't have time to keep up with the latest eunuchoid jargon."

My brother took a drink from his water cup and made a face. Was it possible that he was aware of its substandard quality? An incessant patter of sand hit the walls of the Ziggurat. The canals had become choked with dirt, and the hot wind broke off palm treetops. The desert seemed to be reclaiming the City. Yet Uruk did not flinch. Drab's Delight, which he claimed to be a success, had emboldened him.

"I'm not worried. This is good. It confirms my reading of the tablets. Before the apotheosis of Marduk—there will necessarily be drought, deluge, more drought again, then perhaps famine, maybe even plague. A good plague would be just the thing to tighten the heresy laws. But we'd need at least twenty-thousand deaths. Do you think we'd get twenty-thousand?"

Contrary to my brother's enthusiasm, the arrival of pestilence would do much to erode the King's support. Chibby had always said that plague could kill you politically, and he was right, although Uruk thought differently. I had heard stories of the great visitation of 636 when blackened corpses lay in the street like vermin, fearful neighbors stepped past the dying without regard, and all the tombs were tenanted. Looting and violence were prevalent. Twenty-thousand would be about right.

"What exactly do you mean by heresy laws?"

"I've just drawn them up. The King's enemies must be silenced. Taps was just the first of many. He was ever a thorn in my side."

"That's going to be a pretty long list," I said, remembering the terrible rattle of Taps's chain. Poor Taps.

"We need to get the Kingship moving again. A war with Egypt—or better yet, with Judah—will get Harpagus and his claque off our backs. Despite my objections and against my counsel, Samas-iddina has been pushing forward with the wedding, and one of her demands—or rather one of Amytis's demands—is that the King get rid of—or rather—divorce the harem. It's blasphemous, but she's adamant about the terms. The King and I think this presents him with a political opportunity, if you will. It appears that Nebuchadnezzar and his mother want to—how shall I say this?— dispense with the current harem, although for different reasons. I believe it is the first time in their lives they have agreed on anything, but I must say, it puts me in a tight spot. Let's take a look at this liver, it's a recent one taken from a young ram. See this grouping of fat and viscera on the third quadrant? That's not insignificant."

"And what are the gods telling us?" I asked. "The King's mother wants a divorce and a marriage? Can this hunk of flesh really resolve a paradox such as that?"

"Don't be a fool. You are familiar with our father's pronouncements on gastro-entrailology? You're not? That surprises me. Anyway, do you see that side of quadrant seven? It's discolored, while that fatty bump in quadrant three points north-by-northwest. The two combined make the divorce from the current harem and the subsequent marriage to Amytis a well-considered choice."

"A well-considered choice? Is that the best you can do?" I asked.

I had expected my brother to accuse the harem of witchcraft, blame them for the King's failures and call them malingerers who could pull down the heavens and make the earth bleed rivers of blood, but that's not what I got. Instead, he shrugged his shoulders and said, "It's a risk, but one that has the gods' blessing."

"But that's just it," I said, "how do you know that the markings on a liver or the quivering of a bile duct adequately translates the language of the gods?" I knew I was well outside my remit, but I had begun to doubt the efficacy of internal organs to forecast the future. "I mean, supposedly, if the gods speak a language, I mean, if we could hear them gossiping or talking or saying whatever they say, I mean, how would we understand them? If they are gods, presumably, they speak in 'god-language,' if you catch my meaning here."

"That's actually a pretty good question," Uruk said, without the usual condescension or anger he assumed when challenged. He was flattering me, and I did not know what to make of that.

"Tek, please come over here. Tek, my brother Nergal is skeptical of our methods. What do you say to a scoffing eunuch?"

"To understand the will of the heavens," he stammered, "one must first understand the will of one's heart."

That filthy little shit, Tek, had been cleaned up and clad in the robes of an astrological aspirant. There were moments, like this one, where Uruk surprised me. He had a taste for the personal relationship, for bringing on board a young scribe or acolyte to pass on the tradition, particularly if he was an attractive street boy or "grubber." There were a half-dozen of these grubbers running around the room, pulling in animal carcasses, carving up cavities, taking out and cleaning the viscera from the organs. They were disgusting little criminals-to-be, and, in my opinion, did not belong in a place such as the Omnia. One could only imagine what Uruk saw in them—I had often wondered what lanes my brother's sexual tastes wandered into, but with Uruk, one could never be certain. What Uruk called his "scribal responsibility" was an act he justified by saying that he liked to develop and place his students in top posts around the Kingdom. Unsaid was how the scheme expanded his own reach into the local politics of Babylon's many provinces, duchies, and mini-states. When I asked him about it, he patted Tek's greasy mop of hair and said, "It's the best way to stay on top of things. I also like forming young minds. It seems I have a gift."

"But if understanding the movements of a liver or lung rests on understanding our own hearts, then I believe we are lost, more than lost: we're doomed," I said.

"Yes, that too is a good point," he said, displaying his pointy teeth, "but that's also where your castrate pessimism gets you into trouble. You assume that I will bring to the job all of my prejudices, of which, admittedly, there are many, that I will see in the entrails merely what I want to see, and that all of the answers from the gods will simply be echoes of my own questions. But you underestimate the soundness of our method, my dear brother. Because when I look at a bull's kidney or explore a sheep's bowel, it's not the sound of my own voice I am looking for. No, I enter into a kind of imaginative sympathy with the sheep's bowel; that is, I begin to see life from the perspective of a sheep's bowel. And do you know something? It's an incredible experience. The gods honor that kind of effort."

"And what if the sheep farts? Do the gods honor that too?"

"You are wearily predictable, Nergal. It is that kind of remark that has kept you in the harem all of these years. Now, shall we look at a sheep's bowel?"

Tek pulled a sheep from a backroom pen. Sheep were supposed to be docile creatures, but not all lambs go down happily under the diviner's knife. This one dragged its hooves and snorted its nostrils in panic. The animal's anxiety at first affected me deeply, pulling at the psychic hangnail that currently defined my relationship with my brother. While I was aware that Uruk worried over the killing of animals for religious purposes, he could be surprisingly flippant with a knife. Yet he claimed that every stone, tree, and animal were sacred to him. All life, he told me frequently, had spirit, a fact few acknowledged in the divining business. But I felt that the sheep knew that his entrails would soon be steaming on Uruk's altar.

Uruk said a short prayer to the Moon, asking her to guide and bless his knife as well as to preserve Nebuchadnezzar's health. He sprinkled juniper and myrrh over the blade and asked Tek to hold down its legs and hooves. The beast refused to relax and wait patiently for the final moment. But my brother was not ruffled by the animal's fear. He leaned down and petted the sheep's neck, stroked its nose, and whispered a question into its ear. He then quickly cut the sheep's throat, and the blood flowed into a smooth stone gutter that led to a bowl on the floor. With his typical efficiency, Uruk divided the sheep's gut with one stroke of his blade. A moment later, after Tek had hauled the irrelevant parts of the carcass out of the room, Uruk placed the sheep's entrails on the gray table.

"While every cup-bearer in the kingdom knows that Marduk wedges the future on the intestines of a sheep," he said, "few appreciate the subtleties of the art.

For example, you saw me ask the sheep a question before I cut its throat? I asked the sheep if the King should invade Judah—for ultimately, that is what will happen if the King is serious about carrying out the plans we have made. Now observe closely the animal's answer: there on the duodenal tract, we behold the machinations of the gods, witness their caprice, await their wisdom. See that breach on the pyloric valve, right there? That could be quite significant."

Uruk turned to the surface of the sheep's stomach. He examined it for abnormalities; he ran his hands over the veiny, gray membrane. Peering closely, his nose almost touching the steaming warmth, he breathed in its pungent odors.

"The first incision is always the most important," he said, cutting open the stomach. "Aaah, do you smell that?" Uruk palmed the invisible presence toward his nostrils, querying the numinous odor for clues about Babylon's geo-political future. "We are going to have a quick and decisive victory in Judah."

"I don't understand," I said.

"The sheep was pregnant." Uruk sliced open the womb, pulling out a quivering, bloody fetus. It was a tiny lamb, no bigger than the distinguished hermeneut's hand, a near replica of its mother in miniature, save for one portentous detail: the little thing had two heads, two, still-born heads.

"That can't be good," I said.

Now in Uruk's line of work, or so he claimed, morphic irregularities were commonplace. A legless pig or bird with a vestigial limb were often welcome surprises because the physical abnormality made the burden of interpretation easy. And when it came to political or spiritual questions, Uruk liked easy. He embraced easy like most beards embraced women or wine. But easy did not necessarily mean wrong-headed or slipshod work. This was one of the great lessons I learned from my brother. In Uruk's experience, easy— in this case, a monstrous birth—often predicted someone or something very important was on its way— like the fall of an empire or the heralding of a new god.

"Let's not make any pronouncements just yet. Tek, hand me that bucket of water."

Uruk washed the fetal lamb carefully and laid it out on the table for closer inspection. "Bi-encephalitis. When you combine that with the obvious mental deficiencies, well, I'm not quite sure what we have. A two-headed sheep could mean anything. It could mean that the war with Judah will give birth to some kind of prodigy, either in the military arts or something else. All I am certain of at this point is that all signs point to something queer or eccentric. Obviously, the rains have to return. It's a real problem, Nergal. People have become used to the comfort of having enough water, and now that the drought has returned, and with a vengeance, they're horrified, and they're angry, and they're blaming us. We must do something to appease the gods. A sacrifice must be made."

"What do you mean?" I asked.

"The current harem must go."

"What do you mean by 'go'?" I pressed him.

"Ahh, 'go' means, well, 'go'."

"It does?"

"Yes."

"Go—where?"

"Do you know what I see in this two-headed sheep? I see the happy convergence of immense profit and divine will here, my good brother, and you know what that means."

"No, I don't. Not really, I mean—" I stammered as I began to comprehend the full import of Uruk's nefarious plans. "I mean, you're not really suggesting . . ."

"Yes, I am suggesting that very thing, but we have to build a boat first—a large ark, and the specifications have to be exact. It has to be big enough to carry the harem, but if it's built too big, it won't float. This is going to be tricky. But what are we going to do? Marduk will not always strive with man, Nergal. That's the message I am getting from the sheep heads."

"You're not serious?"

"Well, the time has come," said Uruk. "The moment is auspicious. The Delight bought us some time. The rains gave us just enough water if my calculations are correct. I believe that this move will appease Marduk, and thus calm the sand-winds and allow the rains to return to our upland grain fields. We need to settle the Egyptian question once and for all. It's the thing to do, Nergal. You understand that, don't you?

"Oh, I understand it.' I said. Swinish Uruk. He used to box my ears at the dinner table for eating too loudly. And, like Enlil, he planned on sending a storm over the earth to drown its inhabitants. "We have to convince Nebuchadnezzar first. He's with us, but you never know with him these days—ever since his affair with Siduri, he has been dangerously unpredictable, and I hold you partly responsible for that. Getting a new harem will cheer him. If he is with us, we can make our move against the powers of the West. Incentives can and will be provided. The difficult part will be breaking the news to him that he has to get married first."

"Get married first?"

"Yes, the wedding with Amytis looms over our horizon," said Uruk. "And we cannot really afford to alienate Harpagus right now. But don't despair, Nergal. What if there was a way for the King to avoid marrying Amytis the Mede *and* get a new harem?"

"More divine paradox?"

"Exactly," he said. "There were, after all, two heads on that sheep. Next week is the scheduled feast for Amytis the Mede. Everyone will be there. Harpagus, the Illegitimates, Samis-iddina. And you know what the King is like at these things. Do you remember what happened last year at the banquet for the prince of

Basara? When he defecated on Bunt's lap? Do you remember that?"

I remembered. It was I who was tasked with the job of cleaning Bunt's tunic. He was a cold one, my brother. He divined the heavens, and the King's army marched. When he stuck his nose in a sheep's guts, our chariots rode out of the Ishtar gate and six months later returned with a train of deportees following in their blood-stained wake, each soul tied lip-to-lip, trussed up like plucked chickens. I also remembered another time, another calamity. Nineveh in smoke and flames. The city in ruins and terrible things happening to the people. *Terrible things*. Women and children lay piked and bleeding on the temple steps. I remembered rapine and rape, grief and woe, and enslavement and deportation. I remembered. A city denuded of life. Bodies and burnt flesh. I remembered the look on his face. My brother and I did not know it at the time, but we were victims of larger forces. The girls, my poor girls. Who would remember them?

Tablet Sixteen –

At the Celestial Table

"Oh gods, what a lot of vomit there will be to clean up tomorrow," Chibby moaned.

"I count one-hundred-fifty amphorae of beer," I said.

"Do you think they will drink them all?" asked Moil.

"They always have in the past," said Chibby.

The feast for Amytis the Mede had commenced with ox-tail soup served in gilded ram's heads and would end with filets of ostrich stuffed with spiced pig. In between these lavish, over-produced dishes, members of the King's inner Court gorged on game-boar, poached river fish in cream sauce, blood-thickened lamb, a dozen sweetbreads, six types of cheeses, and other fare too numerous to tabulate—all of which was washed down with rare Phoenician wines and the finest Babylonian beers. For twelve hours, courtiers, generals, officials, scribes, and ladies-in-waiting dined on dishes of roast horse hind, boiled elephant's liver, and goat hooves marinated in wine and fish sauce. Slaves cleared emptied plates and presented new courses to the murmured approval of the eaters. A tremulous sound, which started low and built to a crescendo, filled the vast recesses of the Great Hall, a sound that brought pleasure to Moil and filled Chibby with disgust—the sound of masticating men and women. Two-hundred mouths moved up and down, thousands of molars and incisors ground bone and cut gristle. The sound was not unlike a horde of locusts buzzing through barley field after barley field, and I thought Chibby was about to go mad from the noise, but then a group of singers—wide-eyed mendicants who would be given slops after supper—broke into song:

> At the sacred table, at the celestial table,
> He welcomed the holy Ishtar!
> And Enki, side by side with her in his Temple,
> Sang the praises of beer and gulped down wine,
> Their goblets full to overflowing,
> Vying with each other in toasts to Heaven and Earth,
> Savoring, without haste, goblets as deep as boats!

Long accustomed to these affairs, the eunuchs along the wall endured the feasting of the bearded with an ambivalence that was customary for our truncated race. Moil, Chibby, and I—we made a hapless trinity—stood behind the second table and watched the Court stuff and swallow its way through two hours of heavy eating.

As a talisman against food-lust, I placed a half-shekel under my tongue. One could never be too careful at these things, for the royal dinners were always the hardest on the neuties along the wall. According to ancient decree, we were not allowed to partake of the eating, but as members of the Court, our presence was required. It was just one of the many paradoxes that made living as a castrate in Babylon difficult. One had to convince oneself that a hungry belly was better than a full belly, that water was superior to wine.

And yet feast nights were never pleasant. It goes without wedging that I was also nervous about my brother's plans to get rid of the harem. Whatever form it would take, this "getting rid of the harem" would be nothing less than a sacrifice, although a repellant one, but one that would remake the world anew. What kind of world would this act conjure up? A nasty one, no doubt, as all worlds are. What could I do? All things must pass into oblivion. Their end would be sooner than ours, that's all. Siduri gone. No more embraces. No more filling our bellies with the bread of love. That night, now six months ago, when she gave me a past life reading, she nudged something deep within me, unraveled a stray piece of wool in my castral being, left me uncoiled and bleeding. Chaos shrieked in my ears from the morning bell to the evening sacrifice. It was unfathomable to me, but such was the power of Uruk's will. He feared that without some kind of appeasement the heavens would dry up altogether. What could I say or do? Uruk had already drawn up the heresy lists. And yet something had to be done. To save Siduri. To save the girls. But what or how?

The King and Amytis sat at the head table, looking uncomfortable in their stiff wool robes. My Lord appeared sullen, sunk deeper into himself, hitting his golden whip against his shins. No longer the Dragon of Marduk, the scourge of famine and drought, he was merely his wrinkled and pock-marked self, a tired and earthly emblem of Babylon's patron deity. And yet the three, sad hairs that curled out of his wax-filled ear did not diminsh the power of his presence, nor did the plantar warts on the soles of his feet lessen the intense emotion I still felt for him. Poor Nebuchadnezzar. He did not know what he did not know. It would be up to me to tell him. The little dog would stop wagging his tail. Expose the farce for what it was.

Moil, who had slept on his feet through preliminary wines, groaned audibly. The steward had just cut steaming slices of moist roast-boar and laid them before the King and Amytis. Unable to conceal his envy, Moil turned pale with hunger and meat-lust. A formidably large castrate, who had almost eaten himself to death on at least two occasions, Moil was an accomplished feast-watcher. He gasped "oh no" when the steward ladled out a thick brown sauce on the boar steak and croaked "oh yes," when the cook added a dollop of orange jelly, as a side. As my Lord cut voluminous bite after voluminous bite and placed them slowly into his mouth, Moil cried, "that's right, now another one, this time with more sauce." This drama was repeated another five times, as Nebuchadnezzar quickly polished off the steak, and then he asked for another. Another boar steak was given to him, and it was thicker and juicer than the last, and Moil's hands trembled wildly.

I wondered what my friend, the old eunuch Chibby, thought about Moil's display, but the scowl on his face said it all. Chibby's personality, constructed through years of suppressing his true feelings, manifested itself in an obscene grin before his masters.

"The King's appetite overflows like the Tigris, yet his eyes burn as the desert sand," Moil remarked, fingering a cheap bracelet on his wrist. "Who can reconcile such paradoxes?"

"That's a pretentious way of putting it, don't you think?" Chibby said.

"Of course, it's pretentious, my good Chibby, but it also has the merit of being true."

"We've had seven sandstorms since the moon of the Rising Bull," Chibby sneered.

"The gods are blessing us," Moil said.

"Or the demons are cursing us," I interjected.

"Would you two cut the crap? I have a headache," sighed Chibby.

While the feasters tucked into their fourth course, Uruk entered the Great Hall and took his place at a feast table. He appeared perplexed, even worried. While there were a number of physical manifestations of Uruk's enthusiasm that annoyed me—his Ziggurat-climbing, the oversized hoe he usually carried, his halitosis—the black serpent he pulled out of a basket unnerved me. Curling around his arm like a forgotten and unknown script, the snake bobbed up and down in the air. Dark snakes, spotted with tiny red triangles, were purported to commune with the invisible world. I suspected that my brother was using the snake to check contingencies and plan for unseen disasters in his move against the Dowager Queen.

Suspicious of the Queen Dowager's back-harem dealings to orchestrate a politically expedient marriage—for the old ostrich had allied herself with Harpagus—Uruk planned a preemptive strike. He did not want Nebuchadnezzar to join hands with the Median woman, as he called her, a marriage that would do much to shore up the practical power of the King while weakening my brother's control over the throne. He hoped to check the old Queen once and for all. It was a plan, if you could call the transfer of large quantities of beer and wine from the amphorae stacked next to the royal high table into my Lord's large and receptive belly a plan, designed not so much as to thwart the alliance with Harpagus as to alienate Amytis the Mede, who had a reputation for abstinence.

"Slather, stuff, snort. Stinking beards shuffling gobs of hot meat. It's always the same: us watching them enjoying life's delicacies," Chibby said, twirling his quail feather, trying to hide his disapproval from the beards whom he had served for fifty years.

"Harpagus's really putting it away. By my reckoning, he's had at least ten," said Moil as the carcass of the boar, stripped of its steaming slabs of meat, was taken away by the servants, and another put in its place on the long table. The Mede paused to sniff the air; his thickly-lidded eyes blinked, and blinked again. A song drifted over the hall, a tale of love and heartbreak, sung in a strong contralto voice. I learned later that the singer was a slave marked for execution in the morning.

We watched in awe as the Mede tucked into his eleventh boar's leg with a zeal wholly in keeping with a general of the far western corps. His ears, broad and elephantine, vibrated with satisfaction as he tore the meat from the bones and savored the juicy bits between his teeth. Everything about Harpagus was larger than the average beard. His arms, well-muscled and scarred from his numerous campaigns, lay against his heavy sword belt, and his hands possessed real heft. The Mede disdained fancy dinner feasts, what with the sandal-licking and my-Lord-this and my-Lady-that. He preferred the wind of the blasted plain, the sound of the chariot trampling old women and children, and the pleasures of defecating on the open sand.

Cracking open the bone between thumb and forefinger—pig's marrow gelatin was thicker than bull's and harder to extract—the general bore his displeasure with patience. If the marriage to Amytis went through, Harpagus the Mede would benefit handsomely. He knew Nebuchadnezzar was weak. He recognized the expression on the King's face. It was the fear of a soldier who was in battle for the first time, the panic of a beard who knows Death is upon him. As Amytis's uncle and guardian, he would be in a position of influence in the Court, perhaps, even become generalissimo of the army. Then Babylon would wage war like it was supposed to be waged: viciously and without quarter. Eliminate the swine and dogs; that was Harpagus's motto.

It was an open secret in the Court that Harpagus the Mede despised Nebuchadnezzar and planned on moving against the throne as soon as he could muster the support from the Illegitimates. I was told by Chibby, who was told by Moil, who was told by a traitorous concubine who had secretly slept with the general. The Mede thought the King was an incompetent bungler put on the throne to appease fanatical elements in the priestly hierarchy, of which my brother was the prime example, and unfortunately for Babylon, he was right on all counts. It was said that Harpagus the Mede distrusted my brother, envied his power over the stars, and dreamed

354

of killing him. One day, perhaps soon, he would carve him up like the hunk of meat sitting on his plate. He would think it good to have revenge on this omen-scribe who controlled the King like a pet on a leash. Having dispensed with his boar bones, Harpagus the Mede surveyed the table for the next piglet or capon to crush between his paws.

After the boar had been eaten and the plates cleared, long-limbed slaves scurried among tables. From bulging wineskins, they poured generous amounts of Persian Serpent into raised cups. Simultaneously light and tenacious, the vintage was guaranteed to accelerate digestion. It was also dangerously potent, and few could survive its depredations for more than a round or two.

"Oh, what a delightful wine—tastes a bit like the field after plowing. It reminds me of my first husband," said Samas-iddina, smiling awkwardly. Her breath smelled of the fish oil she had favored before bedtime every night for the past sixty years.

"Yes, yes, yes, that's it exactly," said Chief Eunuch Bunt, who always applied just the right amount of obsequiousness to his encounters with the Queen Dowager. As head castrate, Bunt was exempt from the decree prohibiting eunuchs from participating in the feast, and this privilege made him more servile than ever. And yet, as vast as his powers of pleasing his superiors were, Bunt always feared that he might lose his ability to praise the bearded, that one day the wells of his flattery would dry up. He confined himself to a snort and a giggle. There was a long night ahead of him and much royal posterior to be massaged with a head castrate's expertise.

"Look at Harpagus," he seems to be having a grand time," said the old Queen.

"By Marduk, he's taken an entire skin of wine from that slave," said Bunt.

"My, what a loud burp," she said without disapproval. "I like a good burp in a man. It suggests a strong spirit."

"Oh look, here comes the camel! I haven't had roast camel since my husband was alive. I wonder who the rider is," said the Queen Dowager, gesturing toward the large sooty figure.

"The King's cook did the selecting, my lady," Bunt interjected. "I am told he goes down to the prison with the executioner and chooses the right man for the job. Sometimes it's difficult to find a slave with enough meat on him, which is a shame, because I am told bread encrusted riders are delicious, that is, when eating them is permitted."

The castrates along the wall shifted in their sandals. Moil craned his neck forward, and even Chibby appeared interested. His long, dried frame tittered as if a brisk, hot wind had suddenly blown through the Hall. It was the moment they had been anticipating, for the dish of the Camel-with-Rider was a rare event in the Big Seraglio. They wanted to savor every nuance, soak in each detail, if only to torture the other castrates in the

College of Eunuchs with an exaggerated anecdote or two.

"It's a particularly large camel," commented Moil, "and its hump, I'll wager, has plenty of meat in it."

"Camel meat is too tough," said Chibby. "I could never abide it."

Like the Sacred Marriage, the Eating of the Camel was an old Sumerian ritual, and one in my opinion that had been superannuated by time. The consequences of this basic fact were not always acknowledged. From our great ancestors, we had inherited a variety of rites and practices, and not all of them were equal. The Camel Feast had no practical function, at least as far as I could tell, other than to titillate the eunuchs along the wall who loved the dish.

"It's Taps," said Moil. "I recognize his hand. He's missing a finger."

"No, Taps's corpse is hanging from the fiftieth floor of the Ziggurat," I said with a heavy heart. "It could be Wart. Doesn't he have a clubfoot? That rider has a clubfoot."

"You are both part of a stiff-necked generation," said Chibby sadly.

As fourteen servants wheeled out the roasted camel on a cart—its long legs and prodigious torso were still sizzling from the heat of the fires—Moil took bets on the identity of the rider. The fat castrate took two shekels from Chibby, but I preferred to keep my half-shekel under my tongue, wisely as it turned out. The camel was over five cubits tall, and along the sides of the beast were small minced pies of quail and partridge. On top of a blanket made of veal fat sat the bread-encrusted human rider, some poor beard whose meaty haunches had doomed him to an ignominious end. His roasted form crouched in mock-stirrups, which were made of mutton bones, and an ostrich leg baton was stuck in his blackened hand. There were the expected oohs and aaahs from the eaters, and one or two sighs of disappointment from Moil who had wagered with Chibby on the identity of the rider and lost—the poor beard was unrecognizable in his tunic of buttered breadcrumbs and belt of parsley leaves. The head steward carved up the camel quickly and expertly, but not before the throwing the rider to the King's dogs who quickly consumed him, bones and all.

"Ooooh, what a delightful surprise! The King, in his wisdom, has out-foxed me," Bunt whispered excitedly to Samas-iddina, as the mutts crunched the bones and swallowed the crumbling flesh of the rider. "He's given the rider to his dogs. Intriguing. And most kingly. Your son is quite generous to his animals."

"He takes after his father that way," said Samas-iddina, raising her painted eyebrows, hoping to imply something scandalous about her dead husband and failing, because Bunt was too busy stuffing camel meat into his mouth to listen to the old woman.

The King's dogs—large, thin animals that looked like wolves but were not—pranced with the remains of the dead rider. One hound gripped a thigh bone between his teeth, while another gnawed a section of the lower vertebrae. Nabu-zer-iddina the Cupbearer played fetch with one of other dogs: tossing the head of the rider, kicking it under the feet of the banquet eaters. With the charred skull in its mouth, one dog ran up and down the Hall, wagging its tail happily, looking for another beard to play with him.

"Behold Harpagus! Worthy beard!" Bunt shouted with admiration, his mouth full of camel meat.

Harpagus reached fiercely for a plate of steaming camel joints. He pulled out the largest, surveyed its fatty, greasy length, and broke it over his thigh—the white end of bone cracked open, oozing its brownish marrow. A camel joint was something the bronze-armored beard could wrap his mouth around. Camel hock after camel hock piled in front of Harpagus the Mede. Nibbling the sweet, meaty marrow, he squinted at his fellow guests like he was about to order their summary executions. He would do it, too. Happily. While Harpagus despised all of the King's courtiers, he particularly loathed his fellow Illegitimate, Enuggi the Irrigator. Enuggi was like the rest of the bench-minded priests: soft, miserable little beards with soft, miserable little jobs. Cut off their hands, the lot of them, was his view. Harpagus spat out a bolus of barley-stew on his plate. "This fucking shit is too salty. Godsdamn it,

Enuggi, I thought you were supposed to take care of this?"

"What do you think Nebuchadnezzar is up to?" asked the Irrigator, ignoring the general. "We haven't been feted like this since the Siege of Tyre ended. Remember that? All those starving children looking down from the walls as we consumed an entire roast ox. What a day that was!"

"Godsdamn it Enuggi, answer my question."

"Or perhaps I am thinking of a different time," replied Enuggi smiling at the Mede. "Yes, I remember, it was three years ago, during the third campaign, the one that came after the drought had decimated the winter wheat."

"Fucking water-beard!" shouted Harpagus, who pounded his fist on the table.

"I remember when a good cup of wine was as easy to find as a young boy," snuffled Enuggi, whose eyes flickered with a carefully calibrated hostility. "Still, the drink is almost passable. And I must say the King is looking surprisingly vigorous these days. I think he did a splendid job with the feast tonight. Quite splendid. And unexpected too, wouldn't you say, Harpagus? The man is a grand host."

Clever Enuggi. He was waging a subversive counter-attack against Harpagus and was, at least temporarily, winning. He knew full well that he had offended the King's former castrator to the core of his heart, which, if the truth be known, resembled a bowl of old fish. To praise the King was simply not done in the company of the Illegitimates in these days of high bread prices and salty barley stews—he of all beards knew this basic political fact. I have often wondered what caused him to oppose Harpagus in such a manner, and to disregard the Mede's murderous impulses, which were renowned at the Court.

When Harpagus hit Enuggi over the head with the broad side of his sword, sending the Irrigator's skinny frame to the floor, Enuggi was surprised, but I wasn't. He didn't expect this kind of reaction from a fellow Illegitimate. Apart from his feelings, Enuggi was not visibly hurt. He got up and cleaned the dirt out of his beard, pulling out a few stray crumbs of camel meat while he was at it. Smoothing the wrinkles from his second-hand wool tunic, he looked at Harpagus like a beard who had never experienced violence to his person, who did not understand its physical logic or its demand for retribution and its need to shock the uninitiated. Yet no one was hurt, and apart from a snicker from Moil, who was suffering under the pressures of hunger and exhaustion, Enuggi's humiliation went unremarked, particularly by Samas-iddina, who had nodded off, as she often did from the rich fare at Court feasts. Yet, it was a great mistake to think, as Harpagus did, that smallish, intellectual men like Enuggi the Irrigator lacked physical pride. Enuggi was more than aware that he had lost in a game whose stakes were large. Inwardly, he vowed revenge.

[Lacuna: tablet damaged;
approximately 20 lines lost]

Sitting on imperial chairs, as if they were two awkward teenagers, Nebuchadnezzar and Amytis the Mede made an unhappy couple. The King's public style, a bumptious insecurity that some found mildly charming, was making him more reticent than usual. Nebuchadnezzar looked down nervously over his plate of camel meat and uttered one inanity after another. How did she find Babylon? Were her rooms comfortable? Was the weather to her liking? Did she like camel meat? He loved a good camel. Would she like some sauce with that? He particularly liked a little sauce on the side of his camel. Did she know this was camel?

Amytis said little. She merely looked about the room at the other eaters, who were gobbling up the delicacy. Watching the King with Amytis the Mede was like observing a spoiled child trying to behave with a strict and unforgiving parent. Her natural imperiousness was formidable. With her hair braided in a high, narrow cone, she towered over him. As the King was defensive about his height, he felt this discrepancy keenly. He downed a cup of wine, frowned, and wondered out loud—for all the Court to hear—if the wine tasted as good as the steward said it did. Even taking a bite on a leg of camel—its length almost took up the entire table—made him nervous; he was afraid of slapping

Amytis in the head with its toe. He anticipated her
disapproval and, when it came, suffered under her
recriminations. He seemed sick in her presence. Nothing
he did pleased her. Usually, the King delighted in
imposing his boorish behavior on his companions,
playing the rogue to their peasants, but not tonight, not
with Amytis the Mede. She cast a negative spell over
him, and one saw this in the shake of her too-large head
as she declined to eat the smallest portions of the single-
humped delicacy or to sip her wine. She repudiated each
gesture of his politeness and pretended not to
understand his jokes. His greasy beard and gold-plated
chest were plainly repulsive to her, and as a princess of
the realm, she could not disguise the fact.

The ideograph "no," Chibby had always
asserted, was the creator of worlds, the only true deity in
a pantheon of false gods. Watching the King with
Amytis, I understood the truth of this metaphysic for
the first time. She was unmovable as only a woman with
eighteen thousand pairs of sandals could be. Her tyranny
over her ladies-in-waiting was the thing of which myths
were constructed. It was said that her favorite jewel was
the ruby, and that she once had a lady-in-waiting
banished to the desert for having the gall to wear one in
an earring. Quick with a snub or a sneer, Amytis thrilled
to the withering gaze, reveled in the haughty remark.
Nebuchadnezzar trembled before her. It was the sort of
imperiousness the King had never encountered in a
woman—not even his mother Sammas-iddina—and

both Chibby and I were impressed by how she thwarted, so consistently, and in such a short time, his attempts to pacify her. With each refusal, Nebuchadnezzar tried harder to please her, checking in on every shift in mood like it was a battle with his mortal enemy, Necho of Egypt, a battle he was losing. If Amytis continued in her tactics much longer, Chibby believed they would be married in no time.

The King stood. It was not unusual for him to speak in the aftermath of a feast. There were a number of feasters who did not survive the fifteenth course—a fine dish of quail eggs mixed with mutton steaks—and were sleeping under their tables. Others—the barber Ur-Nabu and Cup-bearer Nabu-zer-iddina—had equally predictable ends, slouching off to dark corners to disgorge their meals before collapsing in a pool of bodily excretions. The King held his hand up for silence.

"We all know why we're here today, I mean tonight, here in this room. We're in this room, here, today, I mean tonight, to honor Princess Amytis. And I would like to thank Amytis, here, today, I mean tonight, in this room," he stammered, "for bestowing her lovely presence on our Court with the hope that our two kingdoms can work together in peace." Nebuchadnezzar raised the royal cup and emptied it quickly—and three reddish drops fell on his white tunic, a small detail, but one that Chibby read as an omen.

"Bodes ill," he muttered.

Great applause burst from the crowd, who usually disliked having their feasting interrupted by the mention of politics. With the drought on the City and the grain bins empty, I was startled to see this public display of optimism. Like everything else in the Court of the Golden Bull, there were always three or four explanations, and all were plausible, and each was mutually exclusive of the others. What was actually going on was difficult to discern.

It was obvious that Harpagus would have made a better King than my Lord. It had something to do with brute physical intelligence. Utterly ignorant in matters of state, unable to even maneuver a chariot competently in war, it was hard to believe that Nebuchadnezzar had survived the first six months of his reign. During his first campaign against Egypt, he failed to recover his foot-soldiers, who had become bogged down in the marshes of the lesser Zab. He retracted his promises of help to his generals in the field and fell off his horse at the bridge of the two rivers. Because of a misspent and profligate youth, he knew little about how to wage a successful war, and this incompetence had long been a joke among soldiers. From the army's point of view, it would have been better if Nebuchadnezzar had never been born.

My Lord's preferred method for combating his feelings of inferiority and incompetence before Harpagus was to propose a drinking competition. Indulging in his extraordinary capacity to consume beer and wine, the King truly enjoyed his life as staff of Adad during these competitions. While my Lord was a dangerously stupid King, he was not without his successes as a beard-about-the-Ziggurat. It was well known, for example, that he could out-drink any man in the Kingdom. He had genuine drunk-talent. And, he thought, quite wrongly as I would later learn, that Amytis would enjoy the spectacle of a half dozen beards and eunuchs vomiting into a pit or defecating into a potted plant. It was another one of the thousand little things he got wrong with her that night. He announced the drinking contest, and a return to self-confidence, by throwing an amphora up in the air and letting it break into a dozen pieces, and the wine flowed promiscuously on the floor.

Tablet Seventeen ~

Ninkasi is Like the Reed Swamps that Cannot Be Traversed

"Tonight's drinking game is open to all comers," the King announced. "All are welcome. Beards, eunuchs, concubines. Anyone who wishes, slave or free. If we do this properly tonight, we shall waste the night, waste the stars, waste even the gods themselves—for a wasted god is a well-pleased god!"

There was a moment of unhappy silence from the guests—these men and women knew that the outcome of such contests usually ended with a sword drawn and a feckless courtier quartered. Yet not all were worried by this development. Some, like the eunuch Moil—his heavy lids blinked rapidly when he was excited—relished drinking immeasurable amounts of beer under any circumstance and hoped to accept the King's invitation. Most of the other beards fidgeted on their benches and stared at their sandals; more than a few had fallen asleep in their ostrich soup. If Nebuchadnezzar desired, he could order the entire Court to drink itself to death, and had done so once, early in his reign.

Harpagus the Mede stood, rising to his full height. He smiled through a mouthful of camel meat, and the Queen Dowager beamed proudly. Uruk tried to mask his worry and failed. Alas, I knew my brother all-too-well. A wall torch illuminated his countenance, which resembled our father's in early middle age: it had that same bony didacticism, the same diffident sneer, but the torch also exposed that which lay behind the scribal façade, and for a moment, and it was only for a moment, I thought I glimpsed his soul or what-have-you. It was the texture of a delicately pungent sheep's cheese.

"We thank you, Lord Nebuchadnezzar," the Mede said, "for your elaborate dinner, and we look forward to raising our cup in the royal drinking game. Your performance in the vanguard of Babylonian legions is well and justly celebrated. It is impossible to do justice to your skills as a charioteer, the swiftness of your sword, and the accuracy of your spearmanship. Your horsemanship is without parallel. When Babylon's enemies have threatened the City with starvation, you, and you alone, have brought abundance. The fields are ripe with harvest, and the granaries are full. You have lowered our taxes and increased our safety. You have rebuilt Babylon and restored her position as Queen of the Cities and Destroyer of the Enemy. Let us praise the might of Nebuchadnezzar, Lord of Marduk, Father of our Country, the Divine Plowman!" Harpagus clutched at his cup and drained it to the dregs as the Court cheered.

Little the general uttered was true, and the Court knew it—that is, the courtiers, ladies-in-waiting, and scribes knew it. I *thought* Uruk and Nebuchadnezzar knew it too, though, now from my vantage in my prison cell, I am not sure. My brother, who believed in *The Fecundity Tablets*, insisted famine was a theoretical impossibility, and yet here we were: the water levels were precipitously falling, and harvest had failed for the third year in a row. However, the King was a good drinker. A peerless drinker. Harpagus got *that* right. Knowing that the two beards despised each other, and that there was a solid chance that Harpagus would depose the King, the Court applauded his speech loudly. The complete fraudulence of the performance shocked even Chibby, who had heard and seen more cant and hypocrisy than anyone in the recorded history of Babylon.

"Godsdamn thumbs up their asses, all of them," he whispered.

In all, there were four participants in the drinking game: Nebuchadnezzar, Harpagus, Moil— who was notorious among eunuchs for his love of drink—and lastly, Enuggi the Irrigator. I was not

369

surprised by the Irrigator's decision to enter the field of competitive dissipation. Having something to prove to Harpagus, Enuggi would be a dangerous antagonist. The black-haired Irrigator stood proudly next to the King, unabashed to have volunteered for this uncouth game, the aim of which was twofold: the last beard or eunuch conscious would win, if, and only if, he had drunk the most beer.

A short prayer was said by the priest Agag (who just yesterday corrected my pronunciation of the Hittite word for "flattery"): "O Adad, Lord of the Cloudburst, who brightens lilies for Nebuchadnezzar, King of the world, King of Babylon, King of the land of Sumer and Akkad, builder of the Ziggurat, bring, O Adad, the rains from heaven and the floods from underground in good season. Garner grain and oil in his leas. Make his subjects lie down in safe pastures amidst plenty and abundance. Make firm the foundations of his throne. Let his reign endure!"

It was the only direct reference to the drought of the night, and I thought it in poor taste and unnecessary of Agag, particularly as the King was preparing himself to vanquish his rivals.

How to describe the King when he was drinking competitively? Did the great Lord appear as he was depicted on official cylinder seals: prodigiously bearded, his long hair clipped back with an expensive, jeweled headband, his rectangular skirt hiding the mighty trunks of his legs, as he offered a twig of barley to the ready mouth of a goat? No. Let it be wedged that Nebuchadnezzar resembled exactly what he was: a short and repulsively fat drunk. His nose was crimson and bulbously large, and his great and numinous belly had that bulk that took most beards a lifetime of indiscriminate eating to obtain. The King looked like he was pregnant, carrying a demonic, little drunkard in his belly, one who demanded continual offerings of beer and wine.

As Lord of the Deluge, the King elected to drink the first amphora of beer. He picked up the round vase and poured it into his mouth. It took only a few seconds for him to drain it, and with a wipe of his beard, he smiled provocatively at Harpagus. It was a happy truth that Nebuchadnezzar relished the drinking of the Creature, as he liked to call the potent beer he imported in great amounts from Assyria. Nebuchadnezzar dispensed with his second amphora of beer with ease. Three slaves scurried up and down a pyramid of amphorae, handing the King a new beer as soon as he finished with the old one. A vein on his red neck bulged as he gulped down one after another. It was an impressive demonstration of the fecund spirit, and I hoped for a rout.

The crowd was restless. Samas-iddina had awakened from her nap. Her face brightened as if she had received a supernatural confirmation from a dream that I, laboring under the burden of mortality, could not fathom. The headband she wore took on a renewed vigor; the gold leaf flowers bloomed in a spring whose province was not of the earth. Samas-iddina smiled enigmatically. She was rooting for the Mede.

The King ran through twelve amphorae of beer quickly, too quickly I feared, though I must wedge that even Chibby was impressed by the facility with which they were dispatched. The next twelve were not as easy to consume, but they were by no means hard, and it was apparent to me, as it was to everyone in the room, that Nebuchadnezzar relished the feeling he got from drinking large quantities of beer—the burning fire banished his great resentment of his Court and generals, of all those beards who were more talented with stylus and sword. Various theories have been proposed and rejected over the years by scribes and Court hangers-on alike, which attempted to account for his ability with the amphora, but I never was persuaded by any of them. Nebuchadnezzar drank not to vanquish his enemies, nor to smite the soldier's pride, nor to undermine the scribe's arrogance. He drank because he liked it. He liked it a lot.

Fan-slaves fanned and piper-slaves piped while Harpagus and Enuggi knocked back one amphora after another. Poor Moil was the first to fall. It has been wedged that the singular vice of the college of eunuchs was sloth. Laziness, apathy, idleness—these were the gods in which eunuchs trafficked. But not Moil. Not when it came to drinking beer. However, he had made the mistake of drinking on an empty stomach, a dangerous thing to do with the King's beers, and now he flopped loudly in a thick pool of his own regurgitate. Babylon's largest castrate collapsed after a jug of the decidedly inferior beer from Hattusa. He rose up on all fours, only to retch until the contents of his stomach had been disgorged. He heaved, heaved again, and then heaved some more. The scene was distasteful, and I turned to Chibby to tell him so, but he, unable to watch, had turned his back.

"I used to be able to bear these contests without so much a flinch in my stomach," Chibby said. "But no longer. By my reckoning, Enuggi is at least one amphora ahead of both the King and Harpagus. That shouldn't make your brother happy, or Sammas-iddina, for that matter. But that's how these things always go, isn't it? It's the genuine glutton who always wins. I've always taken Enuggi to be an imposter in these matters of milk and honey, but clearly, I underestimated him. The King is doing well but not quite up to his usual standard of violent drunkenness, which is a surprise. And Harpagus the Mede, he's very impressive indeed. I've seen him drink for three days straight without so much as taking a piss."

"You don't think they will let Enuggi win, do you?" I asked, realizing it would be I who would have to clean up the vomit, regardless of who won the competition.

"It's possible, but not likely," said Chibby. "I don't see how your brother could allow it. A victory by a scribe, albeit an Illegitimate, would contradict the principles of his *Fecundity Tablets*. What rubbish! As if you could codify lechery! Capture revelry in a tablet! The whole world has gone mad. The only person who isn't fooled is the Dowager. She is awake again and looks to be in a dangerous mood. She appears happy, which is a bad sign. She's only happy when somebody is about to suffer. Not that I take comfort in her maliciousness, mind you, for I shall be the one who shall have to pay for it later in the night."

"But look now, there's Enuggi," I said. "I believe he's gone ahead by two amphorae."

Enuggi had surprised the Court beards. Even that steer Bunt, whose genial manner masked a cold ambition, seemed genuinely happy for the man. When it came to chugging the King's beer, Enuggi bowed to none. Amphora and vase, cup and goblet, the short, hirsute Irrigator downed everything that was put within the vicinity of his mouth. His hands were covered with leprosy scars, which made grabbing onto the amphorae difficult, but by the thirty-sixth jug of beer, he was holding on to it with his forearms, finishing off the beer with relish. The Court was on its feet, urging Enuggi to grasp victory from the more illustrious beards, an act that amounted to treason, but nobody ordered the guards to do anything about it.

Nebuchadnezzar and Harpagus had both weakened in the late rounds and were resting on one knee. They had underestimated the water-man, and were

now powerless before his swinish capacity for drink.
Chibby thought that Enuggi was at least three solid
amphorae of beer ahead of either competitor when he
finished. The Irrigator put down the jug and looked
around the room, grinning like a dog who had
swallowed a hind of mutton. And Chief Eunuch Bunt
stood up and did something that he would later regret:
He waved his cane in their air, crying, "Glory to the
Illegitimacy! Glory to the Illegitimacy! We have a
winner!" Enuggi, pale and bloated from drink, held a
finger to the air and crashed to the floor.

There was confusion. Enuggi had clearly won,
but the beard now lay recumbent on the tiles. My Lord
and Harpagus the Mede were still standing, however,
looking relatively strong and fit. Each of these beards
had drunk three amphorae less than Enuggi and
therefore could not technically be declared a winner.
Without a victory, the competition was a sham,
potentially a political and spiritual sham. How could the
King of the world or the general of the far western corps
cede victory to a man who spent his days sitting on a
bench with a stylus in his hand? They could not. And
Enuggi's victory was a clear violation of the rules. A
victor could not be declared when the winner was no
longer standing. That would be heretical. These and
other paradoxes would occupy Court scribes in the
weeks to come.

Behind the drinking competition, I smelled my
brother at work. Chibby was right. The whole spectacle

had the feel of his willed libertinage. A fickle bunch, the gods of hop and grain must be approached obliquely. Controlled anarchy—for that's what the feasts and orgies of Marduk were—cannot be invoked just because the star student of the tablet-house desired it to be so. No, this was what my brother had always misunderstood about his grand vision. He believed in the principles of Fecundity—fertility, proliferation, abundance, expansion, life—without ever experiencing them himself. You could tell how he held his cup (tightly without the anticipation of pleasure). And it was this inner tension, more than anything else, that lent a second-hand quality to his talk about Ishtar, Ashtoreth, Baal and the half-dozen other minor deities who might regenerate Babylon and awaken her from her slumber. My brother was nothing more than an administrator of debauchery, a clerk of the divine madness, and this was what I found so reprehensible about him and his ilk.

What happened next was missed by most of the Court, which was too busy staring at the sight of Babylon's head of canals lying in his own excrement. Sprawled like a dead cow on the riverbank, drowned after a rough crossing, Enuggi was grotesquely bloated. One of his sandals had fallen off. The calluses on his foot were yellow and hard, the consequence of a lifetime of moving up and down the Ziggurat.

Walking over to Enuggi, the general placed his hand on the hilt of his sword and nodded at the King, who gave him the sign. Harpagus pulled out his long sword, an instrument he had stripped off a defrocked priest on the plains of Burqa. The general raised the pointed blade high over his head, carefully measuring his target, aiming for the direct center of Enuggi's belly. He would have to stab very deep into the bloated Irrigator to reach his goal, which was now obvious to both Chibby and me. He plunged the broad sword into the water-man's belly. A stream of beer flowed out, arching like the falls of the greater Zab. There was a collective gasp from the crowd as Harpagus placed an empty amphora next to the bloody spout. In all, the Mede collected seven amphorae of the liquid, enough to nullify the Irrigator's victory and prepare for a final round with the King.

Poor Enuggi!

Once in Eshnunna, on a tour of a silver mine with Nebuchadnezzar, we were feted by the overseer with beer that had been fermented in the belly of a large pig. He told us that the process created a highly potent vintage, one that could kill a man who was not used to drinking it. The King laughed at the man and told him that he was not afraid of drink—that wine or beer never aspired to your throne or stole one of your concubines. We drank two cups, and I had never been so drunk. Reds turned into oranges and oranges into blues, as the All revealed itself to be One, and the One revealed itself to be All. Stars fell from the sky. The round moon squared itself. I fell asleep and dreamed dreams and beheld visions: Nebuchadnezzar turned into a bird and flew to the sun, spinning around the golden orb two rotations before crashing down to earth. When I awoke, the King was raving about a child who appeared to him in the desert and cut off his beard.

The King and Harpagus finished off three amphorae of the Irrigator's beer—for what else can I call it?—tying Enuggi's number. A single amphora sat on the high table, and the question the whole Court was asking was who would drink it? I wondered if Harpagus thought about seizing the amphora and breaking it over the King's head, or perhaps he contemplated drinking the beer and declaring himself King of Babylon. He stared hard at the last amphora. I thought his hand moved, as if he was reaching for his sword. In the end, Nebuchadnezzar merely laughed and handed him the amphora, a kingly gesture and one that brought a resounding cheer from the Court. What Harpagus did next was clever indeed. He bowed on his knee and offered Nebuchadnezzar the beer. The King laughed— he was never one to refuse a drink—and accepted the general's homage, finishing off the jug of Enuggi's beer, as quickly as if it were his first of the evening.

Having consumed forty amphorae of beer, four of which had been taken from Enuggi's belly, Nebuchadnezzar betrayed neither fatigue nor drunkenness. He walked merrily over to the royal high table where Uruk and Amytis sat. The victory over Harpagus was his alone, a triumph that neither scribe nor soldier could take away from him. My brother grinned happily. The night had gone according to his plan. The Median general had been vanquished, and it was likely that Amytis was sufficiently shocked by the spectacle to never again grace the Great Hall with her gray presence. Not a bad outcome for a night. Perhaps things were looking up after all. Then the King, Nebuchadnezzar, Master of the Four Rims, Lord of Deluge, and King of the Plow vomited in Amytis's lap. Now, a King ejecting large amounts of regurgitate on a guest of honor is not necessarily a problem. In fact, I believed that the act was planned, or if not planned, at least, hoped for by my brother, but the gods do not always gratify our desires, and when they do, beware.

A formidable woman, a formidable enemy, I had to admit that Amytis would make an ideal wife for the King. It was hard to fathom, but I had come to believe that there was no possible way she would let Nebuchadnezzar's ignorance, his lack of conversational skills, or his casual cruelty stop her from her quest to become Queen of Babylon, Mistress of the Moon, and Handmaiden to the Stars. The King was ripe for a woman such as herself, a woman with vision, a woman who could get things done. Amytis did not quiver a lip, did not stomp out of the room, did not do a dozen of the little things that might indicate her displeasure. She simply and elegantly wiped the vomit off her ruby beaded skirt and quietly looked the King straight in the eyes: her dignity impervious, intact and unsullied.

However, my brother was not one to be underestimated, for he never relied on a single stratagem. What happened next had his scribal hands all over it.

"Let the Holy Bride of Babylon be brought forth!" shouted the King with a surprising robustness for a man who had just vomited up twenty-some amphorae of beer. And, as if the moment had been pre-orchestrated as the *coup de grace*, Siduri of Megiddo was led in splendor into the Great Hall before the assembled Court.

When I saw her enter the Hall, blood surged in my temples, my knees weakened, and I thought the earth would open up and swallow the Ziggurat. That godsdamned two-headed sheep! Uruk was going to impose his will on Babylon, with or without me. The harem was surely doomed now. And what happened next—much to my regret—settled the affair.

O Siduri! She who pressed the grape and culled the vine!

Beckoning the King toward her with a perfumed hand, the Divine Barmaid smiled, and an urgent look appeared on Nebuchadnezzar's face. She ambled over to a musician and picked up his lyre, plucking out a song for the King. Her finger movements were delicate and displayed her beautifully manicured nails to singular advantage. She had hands like a true queen. It was as if she were a magician of fire dancing around a small bundle of faggots, coaxing the glowing embers, blowing on the incipient red coals.

My Lord's small, reptilian tongue—the tongue that had licked Siduri's breasts a thousand and one times—flickered with lust. It was a truism that my sweet Siduri had left a trail of wreckage and heartbreak from Thebes to Jerusalem, and Nebuchadnezzar's harem was her sixth in so many years. As she undid the ties on my Lord's skirt, the outlines of the numerous fibulae and vertebrae, jawbones and skulls of her past lovers became visible. *He was not the One*, nor would he ever be, despite her impassioned cries.

Taking the King's hand in hers, she led him to the pillows on the floor in full view of the assembled Court. When Siduri asked him if he would like to "fuck her"—his face twitched like a river mussel that had been squirted with pepper sauce.

He nodded to me, then called out, "Nergal, a little help here!"

Avoiding the disapproving frown of Chibby, as well as the scowls and hisses from Amytis and Samasiddina, I weaved my way through the beer and feast tables until I reached my master and his concubine. I knelt down, assuming my standard place in the ritual marriage. The King patted his belly, and his face was pale with a look of stupid animal pleasure. Pushing past the folds of the King's stomach, I placed my hands around his holy member and nodded, our sign to commence the Jackal.

As was his custom, Nebuchadnezzar entered Siduri too soon, and I aided and abetted this premature breach of my beloved, by holding on to the King's member like He–Who–Was–a–Murderer–from–the–Beginning. They fucked hard, too, and sweat began to accumulate on my Lord's upper lip, and with each thrust of his hairy buttocks, a drop would fall on her face, that beautiful face, filthy drop after filthy drop. I soldiered on, holding on to my Lord's sacred instrument, disregarding the antinomies of Siduri's behavior, as she moaned her gnostic pieties and mocked my heart with her jiggling hips. I was about to finish them both off with a quick jerk when I realized that Siduri wasn't even aware of my presence. She was leaning back on her haunches and closing her eyes dreamily. She never so much as gave me a look. Her performance was *wantonish*, as if all the doctrines of *the One* were so many lies to be spat on. And so I did it. I upset the balance between the *pneumatic* and *hylic* which is necessary to perpetuate this World of Corruption and Lies. Yes, I did it. I did it for her, I did it for me, I did it for him: I released my hold on the King.

My release, gently loosening thumb and forefinger, lasted for only a moment, but a moment was all it took. Nebuchadnezzar faltered. A whimper of the seven evil winds could be heard all the way from Nippur, dribbling through the temple, through the outer Court, the holy place, and into the holy of holies—and soon my Lord Nebuchadnezzar waved me away.

The King's beard hung over his chest, and he was breathing heavily, too heavily. Siduri and I lay on the pillows in awkward silence. Both the Queen Dowager and Princess Amytis, who had sat with gritted teeth in compulsory observance of this holy rite, smiled victoriously. It goes without wedging, I think, that the "Great Deflation," as it was called later by Court wags, was upsetting to Nebuchadnezzar. I became aware of the depth of the King's distress when I heard him utter a curse—a blasphemous construction of a Sumerian pictograph I dare not repeat—but which translated, more or less, as "I have caught the eunuch's disease!"

The King continued to sweat and pant, and Siduri looked at me curiously. She knew, of course, what had happened, but she said it was all right. She said it was "no big deal." She said I was probably tired. She said maybe they could try again in a half hour, but if I didn't feel like it, that that would all alright, too. [. . .]

[Lacuna: remainder of tablet damaged; unknown number of subsequent lines lost.]

Tablet Eighteen ~

She Who Went Down to the Deep

As the full moon rose to its apex, the King's ship lurched down the canal of the Euphrates, a sewer of sorts for greater Babylon and our only route out of that august and terrible City. We were part of a large entourage, twelve vessels in all, filled with harem concubines and the King's guards, scissoring our way across the shallow waters. Our ship, the *Gate of the Gods*, was a pleasure barge, fifty cubits long and with planks constructed of Phoenician fir trees and oars of Bashan oak that stroked the black water in rhythmic unity. Palm groves lined the banks, and lemon orchards blanketed the nearby countryside. Decorated with purple and gold flags, the procession slipped out of the canal and past the final bricked wall of the City. A cloud of water sparrows lifted from the marshes, winged up and down the dark sky and disappeared around the bend in the river.

Making his way down the planks, which had been smoothed by decades of royal drinking parties and gallons of spilt wine and beer, Uruk checked and rechecked the angle of the moon. The concubines had been told by my brother that they were going downriver to a midnight execution party (mine)—and the mood was giddy. His commission took him past the heavy cedar masts, past the laughing concubines grown indolent by years of smoking Dream Dog and lounging on soft pillows, and past the drummers tapping their palms on donkey-skinned drums. He settled on a bench at the sternpost, intricately carved in the shape of a dragon.

Uruk bowed low and handed a tablet to the King, who sat with his mother, the Queen Dowager Samas-iddina, and his fiancée, Princess Amytis the Mede. Clad in a simple peasant's tunic, an affectation he had recently adopted, Nebuchadnezzar was sober, and he was rarely sober. He had trimmed his beard in the month since I had last seen him, and that had the effect of making him look more serious.

Since Uruk had reluctantly agreed to the marriage, the King was spending more time with his Median princess, and there were other small but noticeable changes in his comportment. Rarely now did he place his hand on my rump when we met; today, I received only a cursory nod when he had boarded the ship. He merely said, "for my parts are not your parts, and my love is not your love." Obviously, he had not forgiven me for throwing the Jackal. But it was more than that, too.

O, how I missed the King's clammy touch of condescension!

Counting the burlap sacks (whose purpose was mysterious to every slave but me), Amytis placed them in neat rows at her feet. Samas-iddina smiled approvingly at her future daughter-in-law, for the victory of the impending marriage was hers. Having long dreamed of vanquishing the harem, the old Queen was about to witness the manifestation of all her hopes and desires. Her face, however, was difficult to read—like a badly damaged tablet full of spiritual gaps and emotional lacunae. Was she reflecting on the nights spent alone in her bed—14,520, according to the official harem tablets—and transmitting her calculations to her dead husband in the netherworld? Samas-iddina fingered a statuette of a pregnant camel, and her face was a mixture of anger and exultation. Having grown accustomed to disapproving of Nebuchadnezzar's every word and action, she found genuine praise difficult, if not impossible, to express. The creases on her face became more defined, and she could not bring herself to say a word of encouragement, or even something remotely noncommittal. The King felt his mother's negativity keenly and refused to look at her.

Nebuchadnezzar pointed a stubby forefinger to the night sky. I could not hear what he said, but perhaps a wayward star had flown across the heavens, auguring bad luck for tonight's river rite. Or maybe the King was discussing one of my brother's pet mathematical calculations that had gone wrong, for there were many things that could go wrong tonight, and Nebuchadnezzar, long acquainted with failure, wanted to be careful. They huddled over an astrology tablet, the King only half-listening to my brother's observations. Being the only genuinely tall man the King abided, Uruk towered over the Royal Beard, and he seemed confident in the evening's portents. He showed the King a line from the star tablet and offered a bold reading, one that undoubtedly overturned more complacent and traditionalist readings.

That was my brother, always overturning things—such were my reflections as I hung upside down, tied to the ship's mast. When I had boarded, Wart had surprised me with a blow from a sword hilt to the side of my head, and now I was pinned to the wood, upside down and bleeding from a cut on my forehead. Apparently, one of the harem girls had ratted me out to Uruk for my affair with Siduri—my half-shekel was on Pea, who had caught me lingering too long in the undergarment room once (yes, the harem had an entire room dedicated to underwear, breast bands, and night-shirts, where the girls would hang out and try them on and off). And yet any one of the concubines might have betrayed me, for I had ever been a tick on the collective head of the harem. It was hard, however, to despise the Daughters of the Moon, and I would mourn their deaths, and when I wedge this statement, I am aware of how condescending it sounds, but such feelings could not be helped. My fate had always been joined to theirs, and while I was the last to be served at state banquets, eating only the tepid leftovers, overcooked rice or burnt goat that nonetheless was a degree too raw in the middle, I never held it against them. It was they—and not I— who ate the choicest cuts of lamb and quaffed the best vintages, and that was as it should have been. We were of a piece, the girls and I, and so, hanging upside down that night, and listening to their giggling chatter, I was almost glad that I would be joining them in muddy death at the bottom of the Euphrates. Note the wedge *almost*.

Along the rows of benches, which split the royal barge into two sections, some forty concubines sat drinking beer and munching on cucumbers and onions; the other girls—two hundred and fifty or so—were on six other vessels, which followed in our wake. Isis tried to catch a moth, but the insect flitted in her hands and was gone on the air currents, rising and falling past the torchlight until it disappeared amid the reed marshes. Mater stroked Anunit's hair with a thin ivory comb, while Anat lay in the lap of Ninsun, who read from a tablet of poetry. Tiny, throaty-voiced Astarte—who almost missed the outing, for she had been ill with a slight fever—was wearing an expensive indigo wrap, a gift from Uruk, who was not so secretly in love with her.

And then there was my sweet Siduri of Megiddo. Her ruby-studded dress was cut broadly at the back, revealing a narrow scar down her spine. It is sad to wedge that even hours before her death, she was engaged in working over Nebuchadnezzar. Since the end of her affair with the King[1]—if you could call one hundred and thirty-three days of anxious insanity an affair—she had made it her mission to pull every beard she encountered into her planetary orbit, and, once there, spin him on his heels. When I looked at Siduri, I was reminded of a remark that Chibby once made in a particularly disagreeable mood: "Good-looking people," he said, "are different from you and me." I scoffed at this generalization, typical of middle-period Chibby, and he immediately added, "they're dumber." Like many of the old castrate's generalizations, it was a hateful thing to say, but the remark was not without truth. Siduri indeed appeared dull-witted to the ignorant observer, but with good reason—any hint of intelligence would alienate the King, who was generally thought, even by his priests and counselors, to be an imbecile. The reality was more complicated, as I now realize. The King's intellectual limits, real they were, did not matter in the slightest. What mattered was his relationship to the gods, his ability to call down the anointing from the heavens. So too with Siduri of Megiddo. Siduri was a shrewd judge of the world around her. And she knew the oily ways of beards, as her costume today suggested.

Still angry at Nebuchadnezzar, she hung about in the back parts of the barge, sitting on a smooth cedar table, kicking her legs lightly back and forth over the water, as a ploy for the attention of the King's bodyguards. The soldier Wart nodded predictably and walked over to where she was sitting, for it is not hard to thread the needle of the average beard's lust. Adjusting her anklet with her hand, she tilted her mane of brown curls and opened her freshly painted mouth wide to display her fine but imperfect rows of white teeth. Her exposed shoulders and soft brown back moved with the ship, quivered with the pull of the oars, and were flecked with the spray of water, as the wood of the deck creaked and groaned.

Along the sides of the river lay a community of Drudgers, small villages filled with the unwanted of our slums, the outcasts of our shantytowns, the big losers in the game of climbing the Ziggurat, but denizens who were also wholly necessary for maintaining our empire. During the drought and subsequent famine, these makeshift villages had spread down the riverside, a seeping wound upon the body politic of Babylon. A group of Drudgers gathered now at the edge of the riverbank: broken men and women, scuffed and blistered by want. A small, dried-up old hag scuttled across the sand like a bed crab, pulling up her skirt, revealing two withered flanks of brown flesh, which she shook up and down in the most disgusting manner (the King had been infested by bed crabs in the years 3, 6, 9, 12, 15, 16, and 20 of his reign). A young beard exposed his hairy and large testicles to the royal boat and made a gesture that suggested a goat copulating with a donkey. They formed a pulsing mass, shouting epithets at the King, which, fortunately—because he neither spoke nor read Aramaic—he did not understand. Genuflecting with their bottoms and obscenely pulling on their arms, they laughed and mocked the royal barge as it slid past them.

"Moonies for the slimbos, moonies for the girls!" said Wart, as he and Bat-et-al strolled down the aisle, passing out small bags of coins for a game of Bean the Drudgers.

"Your beard is touching your armor," Mater said to Wart. "Let me trim it." She pulled out her manicure kit and grabbed his chin flirtatiously. Wart leaned in and slapped her large bottom, which prompted squeals and squawks from the soldiers and other sounds too vulgar to catalog.

During royal river parties, there was an old and venerable tradition of throwing coins at the Drudgers as a demonstration of imperial beneficence, but in the past couple of years, the game had degenerated into a free-for-all of cruelty and malice. Astarte bounced a coin off an old man's pocked nose; its gold-rimmed surface skipped over the sand. Mater deliberately looped a coin into the drink just before the riverbank and then watched the kids scramble over each other to wade into the dirty water. The Drudger children splashed into the shallows, wearing no more than thin strips of rag, only to be pelted by more coins. Mater yelled "Dungers!" a derogatory nickname for the Drudgers, and the other girls in our boat laughed.

From my awkward position on the mast, I watched the King, who was in the middle of consuming an entire crate of small Lebanese oranges. He ate away happily, as if this were a regular royal outing. No doubt Amytis approved of the fruit, although not the indigestion it caused the King. While Nebuchadnezzar sucked on orange wedges, seeding them with his fingers, dribbling juice down his chin, I caught his eye and cried out, "My Lord, it's me, Nerggie, your little dog! My Lord! My King!" I pleaded with him, begging him to remember my long service, asking if he would spare me for the sake of our intimacy, of the many nights I slept in his bed when he was afraid of his night demons, and I would tickle his back until he drifted into sleep again. He just licked each of his long fingers clean before grabbing another small orange. Peeling away the thin skin, he commented on the fruit's sweetness, took another bite, nibbled away at the arc, and dismissed a slave bearing a cup of beer with a wave of the hand.

"There have been seven great ages of the earth, Nerggie," said a calm, Tablet-House-inflected voice. It was Uruk, standing over me. He spoke in his most officious tone—the voice he used in council meetings in the Omnia, but with a note of genuine disappointment.

"Seven dispensations in which the gods have dealt with foolish and small-minded beards, and we are living in the final one. The Great Dragon is coming to sweep the land with his horned tail. A Big and Final Sweeping. I'm sorry to do this to you, my good brother, I really am, but the time has come to say farewell."

"You don't have to do this, you know," I said.

"Oh, but we do." And now he came close to me and looked me in the eye. "You thought by throwing the Jackal, you might save the harem? I don't think you give a damn about the harem. That was an extremely foolish thing to do."

"This is madness, Uruk."

"You think they are innocents? They are heretics and malcontents. If the King is incapable of seeding the land, it is not his fault. It's theirs. And Siduri? She's a drunk and an apostate. The King is well rid of her. We badly need a new harem, Nerggie. Can't you see that? I'm just sorry that you won't be there to enjoy it with him."

A nasty wind from the north blew dust across the ship. "Your burlapping was the King's idea, by the way. You know, Nergal, he genuinely likes you, always has, but he's looking for a new beginning, and, I'm sorry to say, he no longer needs your particular talents. There has been some rather unflattering gossip coming in from the College of Eunuchs, more than gossip, actually: let's call it an established rumor that you have not been entirely faithful to the King's efforts to improve himself."

"He knows?" I asked.

"He knows," my brother replied. "He found your letters to her. They were some of the most embarrassing things I have ever read. The one about the 'one heart' was touching. I like how you called yourself the son of Ishtar; that was almost in line with the *Fecundity Tablets*. I say almost, because, well, you obviously jumped the Ziggurat for her. I'd say you were unmanned by the whole experience, but that would be redundant, wouldn't it?"

I glared at him—for that last remark was wholly uncharacteristic of Uruk. It was a matter of brotherly courtesy between us that he never mentioned my extirpated state.

"The burlapping wasn't his first choice," he continued, "but it is, in my opinion, quick and merciful. You should see what he originally planned for you. You've heard of the Lily that Caresses the Intestine? Yes? I thought so. I spared you that. One last and final favor. You don't have to thank me."

"Thank you."

"Don't mention it. And in case you're worried. Moil is going to get your job. Moil has the right work ethic, I believe, and in the harem tablets that I've seen, captures your tone quite nicely. Of course, he lacks your imaginative abilities. But then, we all do."

Tablet Eighteen
[Lacuna: tablet damaged;
approximately 50 lines lost.]

"Girls, girls, please be quiet," said my brother. "We have a special gift for you. I am not unaware that many of you have expressed a desire to wear a certain material—what's the word for it? Yes, thank you, Melqart, the 'rough sack.' Well, we have it for you." Melqart, looking waxy and bulbous, frowned at me. There dozens of sacks, neatly folded by Amytis. One for each girl.

Shouts of disbelief and excitement punctuated the air, for the concubines were predictably surprised by the King's generosity. They had been clamoring for the material for weeks. Indeed, since they saw the Persian dance in the harem, the fashionable reach of the gray, wool sack had touched every girl and lady in the Big Seraglio, free and slave alike. The concubines laughed the laughter of the innocent when they realized that these awful garments would be theirs. Mater, Isis, Ninsun and the rest threw off their clothes and climbed into sacks, thinking they were slipping into the latest trend of Babylonian fashion, but in reality, they were putting on rather tactless death-shrouds. Awkwardly squirming in their bags, the girls looked more like unshelled peanuts than the sacrificial gazelles. There would be no poems wedged about the drowning of the three-hundred, no hymns or prayers sung in the halls of Shamash, and frankly I did not know what appalled me the most: their egregious lack of taste or Nebuchadnezzar's cruelty.

[Lacuna: tablet damaged;
approximately 20 lines lost.]

The scene was grim. On each of the six boats, four dozen girls, muffled in sacks, stood along the deck. They were anxious but had little idea that these were their final moments. No soul ever recognizes her own death, not even when that thug Melqart prods her back with a spear and barks out nasty things at her. The girls were no exception to this rule, except perhaps Isis, whose pale blue eyes deadened in horror. She was always a thin girl, and her wispy arms tried to push against the sack, which hung generously around her skeletal figure. Refusing to move, she fell to the deck and howled a scream that was heard up and down the river. The Drudgers, curious about the girls' shrieks, congregated along the shore, but the guards drove them back with their spears and arrows.

The soldiers came and picked Isis up, holding her by her thin legs, and she put up a fight, kicking through the bag, screaming bloody Ishtar. Three girls attempted to escape—I was almost certain Eudoxia was one of them—and jumped off the barge and into the water, where they quickly drowned. Rarely out of the Ziggurat, many of the harem girls had never been around water, and I doubted they knew how to swim. Loud splashes sounded in the night. Having been granted absolute power over the girls by Uruk, Melqart threw them into the water—one, two, three, four, six, seven, and then there were too many to count. The remaining girls on the boats began pleading for their lives. It was chaos. They wailed the deaths of their sisters. Loud cries rang out for several leagues and in several languages. Astarte broke from her sack and ran down the barge's planks, only to be speared to death by a soldier. Another girl followed her and threw her body over Astarte's, and she, too, was dispatched by the guards. Pea opened her mouth in terror—and nothing came out. She crumpled into her sack, as if she were refusing to come out. Two guards picked her up and hoisted her over the bow.

The girls sank to their watery ends quickly. From my perch, they appeared as mummies in a crypt. Some struggled; others merely drifted helplessly, but most sank to the bottom; their milky necks that had been adorned with gold-leaf necklaces, their billowy figures that had gleamed under plundered linens and silks, their horsey laughter that had been the envy of the Court, drifted into the darkness. I saw the girls for what they were: slaves whose lives were, more or less, miserable—cut off from their roots, bereft of their sources. "I wish I had never been born," Pea told me after a painful night with the King," and "My life will never be a life," Astarte said when she realized she would be in the harem the remainder of her days. No wonder they loved their trifles. Many, however, such as Eudoxia, dreamed of a life that might have turned out differently; she had fallen in love with three harem girls in six years. Each of her beloveds was dark-haired and each treated her cruelly. Eudoxia had always hoped to find someone to understand her, to appreciate the way she had of humming to herself whenever the conversation drifted, someone who might adore her for her sufferings, which, as for many of the girls, had been long and difficult.

Then came Siduri's turn. Holding the burlap bag with her hands, she gazed past the horror to the Great Beyond. No blubbering or snotting up for her. The girl was tough. Even in death, she had Nebuchadnezzar and me beat, displaying more courage than I had ever seen the King emote on the battlefield. When Melqart, who had been lurking behind the King, grabbed her, she slapped his nose like the dog he was and told him, "Go fuck yourself." Siduri's face was shell-gray. Still the almost-beauty, the great vanquisher of eunuchs and beards. How I loved her! There was a loud crash; Bat-et-al had dropped a beer jug, its foamy contents pooled on a broken plank. The ships behind us pressed at our stern, flags flapped, and rowers dragged their oars through siltish water. Bawdy laughter spewed from archers and soldiers alike.

While everyone was distracted by the incident, Nebuchadnezzar did something not entirely untypical. He prostrated himself—rump up, head down—before his concubine, his crimson tunic blowing in the breeze. He resembled a traitor summoned from his bed in the

398

middle of the night to face judgment. On his chubby knees, he begged the harem girl not to leave him. "Come back to your Nebbie!" he wept. "Come back," he pleaded. "I'll do anything. I will build large palaces for you, dedicate a new temple to your name, conquer worlds. Anything you want, anything you need, but please, please, come back." His red nose dilated; thick, viscous tears streamed down his face. He opened his mouth as if to cry out, but only revealed a strand of spittle, caught between his upper and lower lip. Siduri turned her head away.

Princess Amytis rose from her seat, walked over to the King, and stood over him in resigned triumph. She checked with the guards to make sure the job was going forward. That Amytis allowed the King to lay himself before his ex-girlfriend should not have surprised me. If the King's mother was the bone of the new Nebuchadnezzar, then Amytis was the marrow. The sun of youth setting on her handsome face lent her a melancholy dignity. She remained firm—her silver-leaved headdress signaled her new authority over the realm. And Samas-iddina—she appeared taller on the deck—twirled an amulet around her fingers. Rejuvenated by her son's debasement before his old concubine, her figure, usually stooped and weighed down by age, grew lighter and emanated an almost pleasant spirit.

Siduri refused to acknowledge the King. My Lord tore off his tunic and exposed his chest. He would have to fumigate his soul with burnt cedar to make it up to Amytis for that move. From a later conversation that I had with Madame Grape, who heard it from Bunt, who had tortured Stub to get the full account, Siduri then said something odd to Nebuchadnezzar, something that didn't make sense. She told him that her "ever-living fire" was in Judah, in the harem of Zedekiah—to which she would soon be returning. "You cannot quench the ever-living," she said, laughing. "I will ascend to the eternal harem and become consort to my Master."

[Lacuna: tablet damaged;
approximately 5 lines lost.]

Wart pulled me off the mast and another guard stuffed me into a burlap bag, while a third tried to tie off the top, getting the knot wrong at least three times, until another guard came over and not so patiently demonstrated the correct method of tying the sack off. While these mad pillagers raveled and unraveled the rope, Wart passed the time by kicking me in the stomach and kidneys. It took the combined arms of all four soldiers to pick me up. Wart's body odor penetrated the rough burlap, a smell of wet earth and mice droppings.

Melqart threw me over the rail. The water knocked the wind out of me. It was my turn to test the gods—to roll the immortality dice and take my chances. Tumbling amid the air bubbles, I struggled with the rough sack, imagining that the knot would break as cold water flooded into it. I noted the strangeness of death by water in time of drought and was not consoled by the irony. Everything that I had hitherto valued in life—my rare tablet of Asiatic epigrams, a braised and peppered mutton shank slathered in goat-milk gravy, the morning sun on my face—now seemed without consequence. Despite the cold, a warmth suffused my being. Was I preparing myself for the expected metaphysical silence? Readying my soul for the final snuff-out? No and no. I was simply and quickly choking to death. A roaring confusion filled the bag. My nose and mouth gulped down water, and I gasped for breath and life. I lurched and writhed helplessly and pushed against the bag, struggling in the murky water. I swallowed more water and clawed the burlap with my fingernails. I fought against the currents that were pulling me down. I begged for more air, but only swallowed more water. Memories assaulted me like a bastard child bloodied by the grief of birth. I thought of my father, the great Drab the Indignant, sharpening his styluses, wetting the mud, and occasionally copying out a treatise on the husbandry of pigs or wedging a long-winded king's list. But father had been difficult. Father had been unhappy. Father smelled of mud and dung. He beat Uruk and me a lot. With a master tablet on his left, he carefully wedged line after line of script, pushing wedge after wedge into "his muds," as he liked to call them. And it was this memory, more than my will to live, that caused me to reach for Harpagus's castration knife—since the night of the

401

Delight, I had kept it around my neck as a memento of my abbreviated state—I slashed the sack, splitting its stiff threading. The clamp was a fortunate instrument and clearly blessed with the gods' favor, for the guards had overlooked it, and now I used it to my advantage. Harpagus's blade cut through the burlap easily. I wriggled my way out and swam through the bubbling current. I bobbed with the waves from the ships and hid in the darkness beyond the glare of the torchlight, so none of the beards on board could see that I had escaped.

Lightened in load, the King's barges rode higher in the water, as they shifted north. I could see the royal barge. Uruk walked over to where the King was kneeling. After much goading from my brother, Nebuchadnezzar slowly got up. Siduri was discoursing on the last things. The Dragon of Marduk wasn't listening. He reached out to touch her lip again. His hands were shaking. She had told him what she intended to do, and she meant it, as I would later find out. *She* told him she was going back to her old boyfriend. *He* threatened to force her to copulate with Wart. My brother gently led the weeping King down the deck, away from Siduri. Uruk shook his head and motioned to Melqart, who jerked at the top of the bag, covering her face for the final time. And then my sweet Siduri was thrown over the bow and into the water—into that sewer our cartographers call the Euphrates. She appeared inconsequential in the bag, a tiny clump of burlap, which floated for a bit and then sank in the dark.

To be loved by a god was death—the most blissful death of all—but death nevertheless. I stopped treading water and let myself sink beneath the surface, determined to die with Siduri. Drifting down into the deep, past the sacked girls who surrounded me like the moons of Saturn, death would be a happy release, but soon, too soon, I choked on the smell of the filthy water and felt the burn of its waste on my skin—a burning that pushed me back up to the surface.

Alone in the wash, I imagined I could save her. Save them. I dove into the murk where Siduri had gone down—but I soon became entangled in an old tree trunk with long and treacherous roots. Caught in the slimy branches, amid the steaming water, I saw the sacks of the concubines floating before me, dozens of fizzing shrouds, a thousand bubbles of air breaking as they rose to the surface. After a struggle, I broke with the branches and scissor-kicked toward the sacks of the dying girls. With Harpagus's knife, I attempted to free as many of the girls as time allowed, but my efforts met little success. It was as if I had descended into the underworld, where, amid the thickening shadows, the queenly Ereshkigal reigned. Cutting and punching at the sacks, pulling at the thick stitching, I encountered only water-logged faces, limp limbs, and collapsed chests. Carrot had the stunned look of a poorly rendered statue, as if the sculptor had created a being from an unfathomable realm, unknown and unknowing. Slicing into a second bag, I discovered poor, sweet Isis, her matted hair covering her flat, broad nose and full lips; she moved effortlessly in the water with her head hung down, gazing at the reeds like they were a Cretan skirt or a beaded bracelet she just had to have. Anat popped out of her bag, a lifeless arm pointed upward to the sky. I couldn't find Siduri. I tried to visualize her face in death, but couldn't. Swaddled in mud and black water, would she retain her vivacious charm, her lip-painted mouth?

I surfaced and gulped air before diving to the muddy bottom, moving through bag after bag, liberating dead girls from the sartorial insult my brother had devised. Bodies wavered and rolled in the river; some traveled to the banks, others drifted downward only to become stuck in the watery earth. One poor girl, no older than twelve, was caught in a whirlpool, spinning continually in a tight circle; another floated on her back, her face staring quizzically at the full moon. Cutting sacks, opening bags, I beheld dead face after dead face. The unnatural oddness of the human figure was something I had never before considered. Each girl possessed a unique attitude in death—Pea had a mole on her neck; Tutu had bit her fingernails; one of Urshe's front teeth turned inward—and I realized the girls were more alive and individuated to me in death than they had been in life.

I never found my Siduri. Like her gnostic verbosities on the "ineffable" nature of our love, she was gone, and I was left to contemplate life without her and Nebuchadnezzar. Pale white bodies floated in the torrent, faces beckoning me to join them. The moonlit surface of the river sparkled with bracelets, earrings, tunic pins, a variety of harem trinkets that had floated up. In the depths of the river, the girls had found quiet at last, free from the slavery that spawned such trifles. It was a poor consolation, I thought, as I swam up the river, following the drift to the left bank. I was exhausted from my labors and weary of the river. The barges had turned upstream, past the big bend, and were creaking their way back to the City. *Back to Babylon!* The very phrase stank of royal discord and confusion, of want and excess, and of the imperial cant in which my brother trafficked.

Tablet Nineteen ~

Are You the Womb Goddess Who Decrees Destinies to People?

In the seventh year: In the month of Kislev, the King of Akkad mustered his army and marched to Hattu. He encamped against the city of Judah, and, on the second day of the month of Adar, he captured the city and seized its king. He plundered and sacked the city. He turned it into a ruin heap.
— *The Babylonian Chronicles*

Outside my window, the wind applies the whip more cruelly than one of Nebuchadnezzar's henchmen. I suffer from the tedium that no draught of beer or root of vine can cure. I feel as if I were a man slain in battle, my entrails picked clean by birds. Lice fornicate on my scalp. I am bored of recording Babylon's misfortune, of chronicling the King's misdeeds. I am flea-bitten and in no mood to play sentinel to the end of days.

Life is not particularly pleasant for a sluggishly middle-aged eunuch. I have become so tired lately, so weary of time and its depredations, that imprisonment—as well as my imminent demise—is almost a boon. My back hair, relatively light in my youth, has thickened considerably and now scurries up my neck to tickle my ears. I actually shaved it once, or Ma-dug-ama-dung did, and that debacle is something I will never repeat again. We were both drunk, as usual, having split an amphora of pomegranate spirits, and in a fit of eunuchoid brotherhood, he suggested we shave all of the hair off our bodies. "Screw the beards and their hairy, bench-minded asses," he slurred. "Let's have nothing to do with *them!*" As he scraped my well-oiled back, amid the generous and thick steam of the public baths, I had an attack of heartburn. It was a fucking Green Dragon—we had eaten three that night—returning to thrash my gut with its peppery tail. Soon my chest became a conflagration of small and large fires, and my throat swelled with heat. I jerked from the wooden bench that I was lying on, causing Ma-dug-ama-dung to slice my upper shoulder. The stars were out that night: bright spots in the heavens that glared with disapproval upon our endeavor. With the help of a looking glass, I saw the wound. It was deep and about the width of a child's hand. It bled for a whole day, and

I still have a nasty scar that looks like I was attacked by group of venereal ring-worms. But I learned something about shaving your back while drunk. It's a damn foolish thing to do. Shaving my back, getting inebriated with Ma-dug-ama-dung, falling in love with kings and concubines, these are things I have foresworn.

And yet my unhappiness is not a monolith. The life of a poor scribe—for that is what I am, here in my cell—is not all bad. At least I am not trapped like Uruk in urgent omen meetings with contentious colleagues or under the thumb of venal temple administrators. Beyond the reach and pressure of a panicked King and Court, I am at liberty, free to scratch my ghost balls, and wedge whatever I damn well please.

[Lacuna: tablet damaged;
approximately 80 lines lost.]

"I have jumped the Ziggurat, Boxie. That's what I have done," Nebuchadnezzar said.

"The Army of Babel is an impressive bunch," I said, shifting sorely on my saddle.

"They sure like you," he said, tugging playfully at my vermilion skirt. "They've taken to you like a beetle to elephant dung, and I shall crucify them for their insolence. Just say the word."

The smell of the barley cakes cooking drifted over the walls of Jerusalem, which—I had been told by the King—were twenty-five feet thick. Trapped within the city, the inhabitants doled out water by the measure, and their reserves of wheat, barley, and millet were rapidly diminishing. Yesterday morning the King's men interrogated a lone deserter, a skunky old beard who wailed, "Happy shall they be who take our little ones and dash them against the wall." Whom or what he was addressing was unclear, but his interrogators had him skinned alive on an outcropping below the city gate as a warning to those still within the walls. The poor beard died badly, and there was a lot of blood.

Jerusalem. City on a hill. Place of peace. Or, what the more cynical wags of the Court called that cluster-fuck of contention and war. Lying snugly between the valley of Hinnom and Mount of Olives, the city was perched on the edge of a desert waste, one filled with snakes, scorpions, and all manner of unsavory, crawling beasts. As the Army of Babel prepared to storm Jerusalem's walls, capture its god, Yahweh, and scatter him to the four winds, I contemplated my Lord's plan to destroy the rebels.

The march from Babylon across the desert to Jerusalem had taken a toll, for it had been long, violent, and bloody. Casualties had been high. Dysentery and desertion had exacted a price, and, in the early days of the campaign, raids by Marsh Arabs had decimated our left and right flanks. Drunkenness was rampant, and the general violence of the men had surprised even Madame Grape, who usually liked the rougher sort of beard. Despite these setbacks, it had taken Nebuchadnezzar's army only sixty days to reach Jerusalem, and now the city stood before us like a whore in brothel, daring us to look under her skirts.

As my Lord and I rode through the camp, soldiers raised their tents, laying out sheepskins and hoisting them up with their swords and javelins. The inlaid bronze of the cohorts' shields glittered in the sun; a hot gust blew through the soldiers' armor. Line upon line of spears jutted from the ground like a forest of black timbers shorn of leaves by fire and wind. The camp consisted of dried animal hides and a host of men building fires, cooking dinner, drinking beer, and defecating noisily over the latrine trenches. Many of the boys crawled out of their tents to greet me with hooting, jeering, and catcalling. That faithless brute Rad-ad-iddina said something unwedgeable, and I blew him a kiss. He had a large pimply nose and didn't know what he was doing in his bedroll, but he was sweet, and his hairless chest was pleasant to the touch. I had to admit that I enjoyed playing the role of a wanton harlot. The power was seductive, and I would be lying if I said I didn't like it. Eyes followed each step of my mount's hooves, the greedy leers of the unwashed before the winged seraphim of Marduk: "Heeeeyyyy, Sweeeet Ishtar, come here for a bit of the old topping!" and "Good darling, do you want a drink from my beer straw?"

My enemies accused me of witchcraft. It was a lie, of course. Despite what Ma-dug-ama-dung the Mage proclaimed in a tablet wedged and lined for the Society of Unassociated Mages, I would always be a eunuch, but that summer—as the King's Army of Babel cut and thrust its way across the plain—I had followed the tenth legion disguised as a whore named Box Rose.

The Drudgers alone witnessed my resurrection, and they kept their distance.

After the dreadful river rite, I crawled out of the muddy waters, choking on grief. O, dark, O, dark, they all had gone into the dark! Without Siduri—without Nebuchadnezzar—I felt like a ghost. I twitched like an ox while maggots gnawed at my inward parts. I vowed revenge. But upon whom? After I had climbed from the river, gasping and babbling like a mad castrate, I slept in the marshes for seven days and seven nights. I crawled through the mud and slop of the bank and wept some more. I wept for poor Tutu, I wept for sweet Anat, but most of all I wept for my cruel Siduri.

Along the banks, spread over rock and branch, lay the trinkets, skirts, and blouses of the drowned. A bracelet that belonged to Pea glinted in a small pool. I fished it out and placed it on my wrist. A muddied sash of Eudoxia's hung on a branch, still smelling of the cinnamon oils in which she bathed every night. I tied it around my waist. Cheap silver rings and tiny earrings that Rasp had traded for backrubs in the harem were scattered among the leaves. I placed them in my pocket.

After seven days and seven nights of mourning, I gathered the fragments of the dead concubines and made my way to the City. Madame Grape—she who had birthed Nabopolasser's seventy-two bastards—found me in the back room of a tavern, surrounded by rogues and idlers. I had shamefully traded a brooch of Anunit's for an amphora of beer and had drunk myself into a stupor. She touched my cheek and said, "Oh, Dove-Cuddles, this won't do, this won't do." Even in my drunken state, I felt her look me over, from the sash around my head to the rings around my toes, and appraise me as I had never been appraised before. I saw in her eyes what I can only describe as possibility. She sneaked me into the Ziggurat in a crate of melons, and there I bided my time in the empty harem for six weeks. In the silence of the King's honeycomb, she fed me, applied healing balms and mustard rubs, and within a month, Madame Grape had transformed me into a whore named Box Rose. "Together we will cross over the waters of death, Dove-Cuddles," she had said, "and we will trample the worm of regret."

And yet my disguise was a painful one for more reasons than I care to wedge. Madame Grape, as an act of love or treachery—I wasn't sure which—had fashioned an outfit for me from some of Siduri's old clothes and jewelry: a maroon scarf to cover my laryngeal prominence, a snake bracelet around my arm—bulging with fat and grief—and finally, a thin, gold thumb band that I wore inconspicuously around the little finger of my right hand. It is difficult to say which item caused me more pain, for the clothes and jewelry of the dead carry a potent magic, and I felt my beloved concubine's absence with every swish of my custard-yellow skirt and each wave of my be-ringed hand, and I grieved mightily.

On the outskirts of Jerusalem, our brothel was just outside the army camp, and we could hear the faint and bawdy laughter of beards relaxing over their beer rations, the raucous intimacy of men alone together. I spent most nights with Madame Grape, and those nights were the closest thing to happiness I had known in a long time. Eunuchs, too, dream of paradise, and mine sat imperially on a bed wrought of the finest boxwood.

Every night for the past fortnight, our ritual had been the same. We always began early after our dinner of lamb sandwiches, but before our late-night board games. It was a consolation to be pampered and dressed, to have my wig plaited and my toes painted by Madame Grape. It was a way to both forget and remember that horrible night when I had watched the three hundred sink into the black mud, but Madame Grape had a way of putting it all in perspective. "All lives end badly, Honeydew. Some end more badly than others. Some end less badly. The last chapter in someone's life is always a sad one. There is really no getting around it."

Madame Grape. Lady of Abundance. Her teeth were black but, for the most part, intact, as was her heart. She was that rare thing, someone I could talk to, and she had spent unaccountable hours listening to me detail my sadness and misery. I confessed all to Madame Grape. Why I could talk to her, I cannot explain. I opened up to few people in my life. She had that ability to see and understand, to place another person before her, without preconceptions, without judgment. Manifold were the divine powers with which she consorted, and one crossed her will at risk to one's life and fate.

I have spent most of my life alone, despised for being a eunuch of the Court, castigated by my comrades for my scribal tendencies, misunderstood by my enemies for my religious yearnings, and ridiculed for my misanthropy. However, in the past month, under the tutelage of Madame Grape, I became the most popular whore in the tenth legion. I'm ashamed to admit it, but it was awesome to be the center of the world, to know that men and beards talked about me in hushed tones when I wasn't around. When I held a beard in my arms, he would sigh and mumble about his loneliness, and I would scratch his back lightly, just like I used to do for Nebuchadnezzar. Other boys, and these were legion, spoke of how they missed their homes, the one-donkey villages that populated the provinces, and how their mothers would make barley meal with honey and nuts for breakfast. The beards in the King's army were more complicated than I had hitherto imagined in my life as a eunuch; they shared things with me that they withheld from each other, and none of the beards surprised me more than Nebuchadnezzar.

[Lacuna: tablet damaged;
approximately 20 lines lost.]

How I became the King's favorite girl is a fairly dull story, and it all too typically involved another of my Lord's strange habits, but, by my penitent scribal buttocks, I swear the following is a true account. One evening, I found myself in a little-used backwater of the brothel where a young prostitute named Insatia lived. A low bunkhouse on wheels, Insatia's room was normally filled with a half-dozen girls gossiping or smoking Dream Dog when they could get a hold of the happy plant. I lifted the tent flap, peered into the haze, and slipped onto a cushion in a dark corner. There, I found Insatia. She was explaining to a lowly but corpulent soldier that on the seventh moon, one must bathe one's face in the urine of a strangled dog.

An avid follower of the mysteries, Insatia offered all the pleasures of the spiritually adept while maintaining a powerful erotism. Looking no more than a child in age, Insatia was a wan creature with swollen eyes, and she barely reached the soldier's waist. She poured the dog urine into a cup of beer decorated with the wolves of the northern steppe. Insatia then placed it before the sad beard, who nervously fiddled with his sword buckle. His fingernails were bitten and bruised.

"I give you the flux and reflux of all things, the ebb and flow of the great Mother," she said in a low and throaty voice. "That which is always manifesting and disappearing."

As he sat on Insatia's cot, the corpulent soldier took the cup and drank, swirling the mixture in his mouth and dribbling it back into hers. They repeated this gesture three times. It was a curious ritual, one that claimed to invoke Ninhursag, goddess of the earth, and one that I had once witnessed before in the deserts of Basara, where an old procuress had waylaid the King on a visit to the slave markets. The first time I was surprised and shocked by what happened in the ceremony. I was ready for it now, or thought I was.

The soldier asked Insatia to "just hold me." She nodded, beckoning him forward. He moaned and crawled into her arms like a child, whimpering, "hold me, hold me." In my limited knowledge, no Babylonian King had ever asked a mistress or concubine to "just hold" him, although my poor, illustrious predecessor, Bel-u-ball-it, had used the strange ideograph "love embrace" in a footnote to Nabopolassar's memoirs. What did the poor soldier mean by the phrase "just hold me"? I wondered if it was a perversion imported from Egypt, but the look in the soldier's eyes told another tale: the vulnerability of a sad and tired beard. He curled up on the bed and wept before his newfound deity. It was as if the experience of holding Insatia had flayed him open, as for a divining, and I could peer into the cavities and organs of his being, which had the texture and consistency of a bloody veal kidney pie. After forty-five minutes in the skinny harlot's arms, the soldier said that was all he wanted; there would be no coupling that night.

Insatia shrugged her shoulders, and that was that. But I recognized the voice of the beard. He was Nebuchadnezzar, the Maker of Corpses, as needy as ever. And it was this neediness that I would exploit in the coming weeks, to my advantage. On the way out of Insatia's room, he stopped before me and said, "I know you."

"The heart is a gentle beast," I said, curtsying low.

"And one must be gentle with other people's beasts," he replied. It was an old joke of Siduri's, and I knew he would fall for it, and he did.

Our relationship began innocently enough. He fantasized that I was the Megiddogian's younger and fatter sister, although we never discussed the particulars of our fatal recognition. In the days and weeks to come, as the army sharpened its blade to decrown Jerusalem, the King would stop by the brothel one day a week, and then one day became a week, and a week became a fortnight. Soon we were spending every night together. The King would oil me up with war talk and chariot-know-how, and I would smile and gossip about the other girls. He would make his standard rape move— the ever-reliable forearm around the neck—and I'd bob and duck, giggling the harem giggle, a feint that sounded like honey dripping on the edge of a rocky crag. It was the expression on the King's face that I enjoyed most, the slight dilation of the eyes, the biting of the lip, the disgruntled shaking of the jowl as he realized that he would return to his barracks without satisfaction. However, I would allow my Lord to hold me, and I held him in return, for I knew what he liked: back rubs and the soft caresses of his forearm. I always wore Siduri's favorite perfume, a combination of orange-blossom water and the blood extracted from a living spider, always donned a dark curly-haired wig from the early period of their relationship, and I had Madame Grape tattoo the Hebrew letter samekh on my good front tooth. And yet we were not an attractive couple. The King looked more like my father-in-law than my boyfriend.

It was something of Father's pedagogy that I brought to my relationship with Nebuchadnezzar: the unpredictable violence, the humiliation, but, more importantly, the art of speaking in a secret and holy language. Our first night together, Nebuchadnezzar hand-fed dates into my mouth. He *hand-fed* me dates! It was one of my supreme achievements. I watched him pluck a date from a bowl while I mouthed an intimacy, "Ooh, my Lord, your favor is delightful," and I swallowed the morsel as if it were a hated rival in the brothel. To capture Nebuchadnezzar's heart, I had to become someone else, *something else*. My father's hermeticism in this regard was a great boon. Dressed in Siduri's lion-fur skirt and matching sandals, I became the star of the morning, the girl who destroyed the earth.

Tablet Nineteen
[Lacuna: tablet damaged;
approximately 40 lines lost.]

"We need to inspect the troops, Box Rose," Nebuchadnezzar said. "Take a look at the siegers, make sure they have fortitude to reap the harvest. It shouldn't take too long. Follow me."

Together we rode through the soldiers' camp, me bouncing on my donkey, and the King astride his magnificent black horse like a man born to depopulate the nations of the earth. We rode past lines of infantrymen who sharpened sickle-shaped short daggers on wet rocks, through groups of charioteers brushing down horses, and among the conscripts and mercenaries who would be deployed as rock slingers and bowmen. The men washed and trimmed their beards, cut toenails, rolled dice, and joked with each other. Some officers roasted goat meat on skewers, while the men slopped their barley gruel, and everyone guzzled the weak beer that they had been given with the rations.

All through the morning, I had endured the lustful catcalls from soldiers who slapped their swords on their thighs or made disgusting sounds by sucking their tongues between their toothless gums. And no wonder: I looked incredible in my cornflower-blue skirt and matching blouse, embroidered with yellow suns. But it was the earrings that did the trick—big, blue, double-looped crescents of Siduri's, which the King had given her by way of apology right after their big fight over their respective "lovers lists," and which I had pulled from the mud.

It was difficult to explain, but before the King had chosen me for his girl, no beard, not even the commonest thug in the infantry, had bothered to spit in my direction. Now I was "fighting flies off shit," as Madame Grape said, and I was a desirable creature. I'm almost ashamed to admit that this desirability, like my new profession—however provisional, however fantastic—felt right. I now possessed "kuzbu," what the girls in the harem used to call "allure." I attributed my newfound power to Siduri's earrings. The soldiers gazed upon them in awe, for they made my soft and round face a tad less chubby, more angular, more Ishtarish. It was not hard to fathom, when I thought about it, but each piece of Siduri's jewelry—and I possessed over sixty of her various rings, trinkets, anklets, and pendants— possessed considerable magic. Her copper toggle pin that held my cloak together erased my loneliness. Her gold double-spiral pendant banished my remorse. Her lapis lazuli tiara vitiated my despair. Her silver embossed breast band commanded the hearts and minds of beards—and in their plenitude, I discovered worlds. This confidence, more than my fabulous clothes and biting sense of humor, spoke to the hearts and loins of the men of the tenth legion.

Nebuchadnezzar's expectations for an easy victory were high, as was his desperate need to please me—with gifts of gold and silver, livestock and booty, and a round-the-dial debasement before my fashionably thick ankles. As we rode through the lines, he kept looking back at me, smiling, nodding his helmeted head in my direction. The King's desire was palpable and oddly familiar, of course, and in many ways we simply repeated the emotional geometry of the Three-Legged Jackal. I should have been kinder to the Beard, because I knew all too well what it felt like to be on the receiving end of a cold lover, but I couldn't help myself. I was paying her back by exacting revenge on another. It's a sad, old story.

We rode on, and when we reached the officers' tents, a great "Hurrah!" went up from the troops. The men loved their uncouth King, saw him as one of their own, which, I suppose, he was. And, as if to acknowledge this fact, my Lord scratched his testicles, rousing the men to even more greater levels of approbation. The troops clapped their swords against their legs, demanding my Lord to recognize their love for him with some gesture, but he merely waved them away with a warty hand. There were many in the Court who argued, correctly, I believed, that now that the King was to be married to Amytis, he was more able to rule than ever. On the question of who possessed the real advantage with the people in matters of peace and war—Harpagus or Nebuchadnezzar—it was difficult to determine, but as to who possessed greater favor with the troops, that was obvious. The King ate, drank, fought, and fornicated with his men, and they loved him for it. He operated from the position that because he had a talent for disemboweling priests on their altars, he also had a talent for philosophy, politics, divination, irrigation, grain accounting practices—in short, a talent for all human discipline under the sun and stars. And he never hesitated when called upon to give his opinions, which were usually wrong. That he despised the scribal class goes without wedging, and his beer-drinking abilities were legendary among his men (as well as for a few fanatical eunuchs in the harem, such as Moil), but in the past few weeks of our intimacy, I put my finger on the proverbial chink in the otherwise impenetrable armor of his philistinism: Nebuchadnezzar was capable of love.

When the King and I reached the final mound construction, we dismounted. Like a small ziggurat, and composed of straw, broken bricks, and shards of pottery, the siege mound rose slowly from the ground. Men dragged carts of dirt and hauled buckets of rock taken from the hillside. The mound had to be wide enough to hold the siege towers and a full company of fifty or sixty men, and the workers had spent months extracting dirt and rock from a giant hole in one part of the desert and laboriously carrying it to the mound in front of the city's wall. It was dangerous, spine-ruining work, and the men moved with that quiet despair of enslaved laborers everywhere. I followed Nebuchadnezzar as he inspected the mound. He talked to overseers and joked with diggers, and in general, proved himself to be the beard-about-the-slave-camp I had always taken him to be.

After climbing a short hill, the smell of rotting flesh nearly overwhelmed us. We were near the place of execution, and the wind had picked up, carrying the foul odor our way. Under the mantle of darkness, the enemy had made multiple sorties to destroy the siege mound. These incursions, the King explained one night on his knees before my cruel heart, had been repulsed, and the saboteurs' heads had been impaled on pikes, while their limbs and bodies had been broken on wheels. Three of these wheels stood on the hillside, surrounded by a pile of skulls and bones—tall, thin posts that were topped with platforms to hold the remains. A scattering of crows and vultures flew about the wheels, some of which had alighted on the flesh and had picked away at their feastings. Perched on a moldering head, a black crow gloated over its luck, its claws entrenched in the forehead and beak picking at the scalp, tearing the pulp of an eye, a meal the bird seemed to enjoy heartily.

"These attacks have been surprisingly effective in slowing us down," said the King. "I admit that sad fact, but it's also true that our counterattacks are not without their effectiveness." He spat on the ground to punctuate his point. "And that, Box Rose, is just the beginning." He pointed to the now eyeless head. "They shall pay handsomely for their iniquity." He remounted his great black horse, and then he turned to scan the thick walls of Jerusalem one more time. "You see that, Box Rose? That's the wall I'm going to breach for you."

I remounted my rough-haired donkey, and Nebuchadnezzar squeezed my fat thigh. Lately he had been taking more and more liberties, kissing me in public, groping me in private, and making me do things that I was not altogether comfortable doing, but it wasn't that bad, either. Nebuchadnezzar was about the size of a small red, hairless, mountain bear, but he had a sweet side to him, which I exploited to my advantage. Violent, illiterate, capricious in will and temperament—I still felt the whisker burn on my cheek from our first night together—he would as soon strangle me as make love to me, and ideally, I suspected, he desired to do both.

I had a good view of the west wall, where the enemy prepared for our attack. (Box Rose's buttocks hurt like hell, by the way, as she rode over rock and hill and forded stream and river, because not only was her reddish sheep-hide girdle last year's model, it was also too tight, but such inconveniences, and there were others, came with the job.) Row upon row of Judaean archers stood with their bows raised and ready, eyeing the work of the tower builders with loathing, and a dozen oil boilers heated iron kettles with large fires. Missile men stacked large piles of stones every other cubit for tossing down on the besiegers of the wall—that is, if and when the King gave the order for the wall to be breached.

That's the wall I am going to breach for you, he had said. I wondered why the King hadn't yet given the order. And even as I formulated the question the answer came to me. He thought Siduri was alive somewhere within Jerusalem. Rumors abounded in Madame Grape's brothel which supported his suspicions. Lilith claimed that she had seen Siduri on the ramparts, and Sybella relayed a story—told to her by Beltis—that when the wind died down at night, Siduri could be heard singing to the moon from the ramparts. Nebuchadnezzar believed Siduri was in there—she had to be—and the King needed her to be in there, the idiot. That's why he was waiting to give the order to attack. He was hoping she would come back to him, praying she would walk through the city gates and say those words that beautiful concubines, after they had dumped you and were riding in the gold-plated chariot of another beard, never, ever said: "I was wrong. I've made a terrible mistake. Please take me back."

Tablet Twenty ~

Your Mother is a Gazelle and Your Father a Wild Donkey

He went into action against [. . .] and scattered its people.
— *The Babylonian Chronicles*

"There is a plant that looks like a boxthorn," Madame Grape said. "The Plant of Heartbeat, they call it. Kings would sacrifice whole armies—in fact, have sacrificed whole armies—to get it. To no avail, alas."

"Well, how can I get it? And what does it do?"

We were lying on Madame Grape's old wooden bed in the soldiers' brothel.

"Honeydew, come closer," she said as she leaned over and painted my toenails, an Ionian blue that matched my double-looped crescent earrings and was the old concubine's favorite color. "You begin with the large toe first. That way, it will be dry by the time you finish with the small one," she said. She dipped a brush in an unguent of citrus and palm oil and delicately swabbed each toe with paint, after placing a knot of rough wool between each one. One did not interrupt the Great Mother. I knew Madame Grape would come back around to answering my queries in her own time: She of the Ancient Earth—one did not move Madame Grape. She hummed while she worked, and I recognized the song of the "dum-dum bird" from my childhood, a ditty that my father Drab used to sing after his second cup of beer. The song always calmed my nervousness, and I soon fell asleep. When Madame Grape finished with my last toe, she nudged me awake. "There, there. Aren't you a pretty one," she said. "I'd pay twenty shekels for a bite out of you, Honeydew. Maybe even twenty-five. Now, where did I put that skirt of yours? You can't go around camp without a skirt. What kind of whore walks around without a skirt? Not one of my whores, that's for sure."

When I responded to this by impatiently bringing up my questions again, Madame Grape laughed, "Pssh! *Ligo skata! Ante gamisou!*" [1] Nabopolassar's ex-alpha had the habit of slipping into her native Greek whenever she affected seriousness about anything other than her relationship with Nabopolassar. The old King was on my mind that summer of burning cities. Nabopolassar, that rube from Bit-Yakin who stormed and destroyed Nineveh, that place where I first heard the dum-dum bird sing in my father's garden. He took every brick from every wall and brought them to Babylon to restore the great Etemenanki. Leveler of cities, builder of Ziggurats, destroyer of Carchemish— those were a few of his kingly epithets, and Madame Grape never let me forget that he was also a "fabulous lover."

"Oh, I can see you've got that frowny face again. Don't be threatened by old Nabbie. I love you now," she said, cracking a pistachio between her teeth. "He certainly had his soft side, though. He gave me gifts of apricot and fig for my garden. I'll never forget that day he sacrificed a thousand bulls for me. It was on account of his victory over Sin-sharra-ishkun. I know, I know that is a touchy subject for you, but it was wonderful, and look at it this way, if not for the sack of Nineveh, you and I would never have met. Did you ever think of that?"

I nodded like a glum child sent to bed without dessert.

"Come here, Boxie. Come closer to old Grappie so that I can see you." Madame Grape's eyes were as old as the earth itself, pulling me into their gentle orbit, an atmosphere of old-woman smells and hard-to-apply unguents. She smelled like lemon and vinegar soup. When I came within hand's distance of her, she clicked her tongue and licked her fat lips. "Beneath the earth and waters, that's where you must go. To the darkness and dust is where you must travel."

"But I don't want to go anywhere. I want to stay in our tent and read my tablets."

"The time for reading and wedging tablets is over, Dove-Cuddles. We can't sit under the wall of this city forever. The King has to decide what to do. He has attack the city or find a way to make peace. You must help him decide. And with some luck and the Plant of the Heartbeat, which makes a man forget—among other things—the pain of love, he will decide to make peace. I'm going to help you, Dove-Cuddles. Together we shall trample the worm of regret, and then you'll be ready to cross over the waters of death."

"What are you talking about?" I asked.

"The dead—they're different than you and me," said Madame Grape, cracking another pistachio shell between her teeth. "They have The Knowledge; they speak the language of the gods. If you want to know the will of heaven, if you truly want to penetrate the nature and character of all things, Dove-Cuddles, that's where I would go. The dead. Under Apsu. Beneath the earth and waters, to the darkness and dust: that is where you must travel. Like our lady of heaven, the dead possess *gnosis*. They are also sitting on some excellent real estate: Irkalla. That's what they call it, my sweet," she said, brushing the lint from a skirt she pulled from a bin. "The land of dust. The place of sighs. It is a country you will know or recognize as familiar when you arrive. Lots of dust and bones. An immense sea of bone, bleached white by heat and blackened by time. The stories are true."

"Stories are never true," I said petulantly. I was impatient for my back rub.

"Stories are always true and untrue. Like truth, but not truth. You might even meet the queen of the dead, Ereshkigal. They say she's a beauty. I'm told I resemble her when the dusk light falls a certain way on my hair." Madame Grape turned her head, and her hair, dyed red and blue, fluttered in the wind. "I thought I saw her once when old Nabbie passed over to the other side. We had wrapped him in a shroud for the cremation fires, and I felt a gentle breeze through the lime trees. And that's when I saw her, or thought I saw her. But I was mistaken. It was only an old whore from the temple come to pay her last respects."

"But visiting the dead, that's bone conjuring. Witchcraft," I said. "You have to be a manzazu, don't you? Only manzuzu are allowed to summon the spirits."

"Let me comb your hair," said Madame Grape, crunching another pistachio nut in her mouth. "It's become so golden in the last few weeks. So pretty. Such a pretty girl you make. You will have to look pretty when you meet the ferryman, Urshanabi. I'm told he likes pretty girls." She combed my hair, caressing the locks with the silver teeth of the comb. It was a wig I pulled from the bottom of the river, Sweet Pea's I think, but Madame Grape, who knew it was a wig, was committed to the fiction that it was my hair, just as the yellow cotton skirt, which she wrapped around my waist, was now mine.

"There, there, Honeydew, I know you better than you know yourself. Tabletish, melancholy young eunuch. My Little Stumpie. You can't be sad for the rest of your life. It's no way to live. You feel you have let down your King, and now you want to make it up to him. And you will. You will. You are not listening to me. Irkalla. The dead. You must go. And to get the Plant of Heartbeat for him. Then we might be able to stop this war. Now, wouldn't that be something!"

"You mean, I must travel to the land of dust and find the Plant," I said worriedly, "and then, and only then, the King might release his grip on the hammer?"

"Well, that, yes," Madame Grape said, "but you must also see if she's alive or with the dead. The dead alone may be able to explain that mystery. I am not going to pretend it's going to be easy—few beards have traveled to Irkalla and returned to tell the tale. But, as we both know, Dove-Cuddles, you are no beard. Certainly not now, and sad to say, not ever. But that is why you must go."

To calm my anxiety, we passed the rest of the evening by playing board games: Mistress and Slave, Spirits Speak, and Madame Grape's favorite, Aggravation and Regret, a mean dice game that involved drinking large quantities of beer and became emotionally complicated quickly. After rolling a combination of six and one, and only after rolling a combination of six and one, you would have to name something in your life that aggravated you—such as, for example, the disgusting way Moil used to use a toothpick after polishing off a camel steak; or, as another example, my brother's face. But if you rolled a combination of five and three, or some configuration that led to eight, you had to reveal an event or action that you regretted—such as the time that I made what was considered "defeatist" remarks at my first Festival of the Golden Bull or—Chibby's favorite—the night I was caught stealing an amphora of beer from the Pig and Offal.

Now, there are those who believe that there is no need to dwell on one's past mistakes or errors of judgment. That's not how Grappie saw it. She was big on excavating the past, examining the whys and wherefores of our present circumstances. She ate my pain, as well as my sorrow, for breakfast, lunch, and dinner.

"More regrets," she said. "We must share all." So, I told her of spiking the King's beer with anaphrodisiacs, of making faces during orgies, and about the time I cast the vulture's stone (designed to invoke impotency spirits) over the King while he slept with Siduri. I told her about wedging necromancy rituals on the side for a few extra shekels. "More regrets," Madame Grape commanded. I confessed my despair and belief that life was a cruel joke of the gods, but she merely said again, "More regrets." I told her how I stole omen tablets from the temple of Ninurta and buried them among the jawbones of the dead. I told her about that first night with Siduri, the night when it all began, the night when I fell in love with her, the genuine thing, the thing that led to the destruction of cities and men.

"That's it. That's exactly what it was," said Madame Grape. "Siduri awoke you from the dead, and now she is dead, and that is the regret part."

"Five, six, seven, eight—that's Endsies," Madame Grape said triumphantly at the end of the game. "You know what that means," she said, crunching another pistachio between her teeth. Madame Grape was good at Aggravation and Regret. I suspected her of cheating, because most nights ended with me on my knees before her soft, billowing flesh and giving her a foot rub. She lay on her bed, covered in sheep blankets, sipping beer. Her feet were surprisingly small, and I rubbed a lemon-scented oil over them, beginning with her heels and working my way up to her toes, though I spent most of the time on the heels, pushing on the callused sides. It was impossible to push too hard, she said, for the pleasure was directly proportional to the force applied. "Lower to the left: that's it. Now harder. That's it! Push, push!" We continued in this mode and talked until the early morning—we talked about a lot of things. We talked of kings and eunuchs, of prophets and war, of the flight of blackbirds and the interpretation of sheep stomachs.

The early morning winds stirred up spirits that only Madame Grape could sense, restless spirits that whispered the secrets of the dead, for her powers of divination were strong. After I finished her foot rub, she sighed deeply and kissed my forehead.

"Death's a sad thing, Dove-Cuddles, but we all go into the dark. It's the terrible truth about the world. Life goes on until one day, it's over. Everybody—and I mean everybody—goes into the dark. You, me, your brother, even your new sweetheart, Nebuchadnezzar," she said with a laugh. "That's the comforting part, I suppose, if you can call it comfort. Everybody has to do it."

She lit a candle to Mer and sprinkled a crushed sprig of parsley over a small altar.

"I can't promise you anything. But it would be interesting for you to make the journey. Talk to some people. Who knows? You might find a way to solve the King's problems, your problems, all problems."

"But how do I go?" I asked. "You said that those who go never come back."

"Yeah, it's tricky. You need another plant to cross safely over the waters of death. It's called the Plant of Dumuzi, but it only grows across a great sea, in the low mountains of the West.

"Then how does that help us? It sounds impossible to get," I said.

As the night star ascended to its apex, the desert air became colder, and Madame Grape wrapped a blanket around our feet. We were huddling closely on her old wooden bed.

"Well, you see, that's where being Grappie is a good thing. I once had an old boyfriend who got hold of some of the Plant of Dumuzi in a tablet deal. He was a tablet man in Nineveh of the old school. He claimed he got it in a collection of tablets from a dead colleague. It's a long story, but I'm sure I have some of it somewhere. It's in my little red jar—do you see my little red jar anywhere?"

Rummaging around her things, Madame Grape picked up a statuette of Baal, then peered under a figurine of Marduk. In her tent—which was as capacious as the King's—were a collection of eye-shaped idols, small humanoid figures with elongated necks and stylized eyes like rotten fish eggs. These black clay idols covered her bed stand, her incense burners, her torches.

"I'm being watched by the seven demons," she said. I also am being watched by the King and your brother and probably the old Queen. She's got spies here, too. So, I watch 'em back."

It was as if Madame Grape was warding off the malignant spirits of the earth, but when I asked her about it, she said she just liked having them around.

"It's more of a hobby, if the truth be known. Unlike you, I'm not afraid of death. When he comes for me, I'll just wiggle my bottom at him. Here it is," she said, holding up a tiny red jar about the size of a small tax tablet. "Now, I must warn you, if you happen to find that old girlfriend of yours, don't grovel, whatever you do. Don't tell her you're sorry and that you love her. She'll only despise you for it. You'll look like a blubbering ex-boyfriend, and women can't stand that kind of male weakness. When we're done with a man—or eunuch, sorry, sweetie—we're done, and we never give him another thought. On the other hand, if you really want to talk to her, and you may need to talk to her, for your fates seem to be connected—you need to be prepared. Whatever you do, don't speak first. Let her speak first. Oh, and ask what her secret was with the King. I'm dying to know. She's the only thing that made him happy, as far as I know and for what it's worth, and it may be worth something in the end."

"How will I find the Plant of the Heartbeat?"

"You'll meet the shade of someone familiar to you there, and that shade will help you. You'll know once you're there." Madame Grape lifted one of her immense legs and urinated into a clay pot. "It's okay if you look. In my day, eunuchs were not afraid to take a peek now and then. I'm used to it. Come here. I'll show you a scar on my belly."

Tablet Twenty -One -

When Shall the Dead See the Sun's Rays?

On the fifth day of the month of Nisan, the queen mother died. In [...] the prince and his army were in mourning for three days.

— *The Babylonian Chronicles*

Dog Star in the heavens. Moon rising. Amid the desert cold, we sat in a cemetery outside the city, about two leagues from the soldiers' brothel and at least seven leagues from the front, where our siege engines and ramps, our battering rams and catapults gathered to breach the walls of Jerusalem. To access the entrance of Irkalla, Madame Grape and I performed rituals that I frankly didn't pay much attention to, for I was nervous about my meeting with the dead, and excited about the possibility of meeting you-know-who, and I was already composing in my head a grievance list.[1] There were plenty of diseases and maladies out there that can kill you dead—apoplexy, flux, fungal warts—but love can make you wish you were dead.

At dawn, we smoked the Plant of Dumuzi—a smallish black piece of crud the size of a dung beetle in a green glass pipe. Madame Grape lit the plant with a firebrand, pulled and sucked once or twice to make sure it was lit, and then embraced me in her full bosom, while pressing her lips—still like two fat grubs—against mine and blowing the smoke into my mouth and lungs. Her breasts were about the size and consistency of Slosh's custard pies, and I felt a warm wetness flow down my left leg. The smoke was harsh and sweet. She repeated this gesture four times, chanting: "When She above the heaven had not been named, when She below the earth had not been called a name, ferocious dragons She clothed in terror."

Madame Grape handed me a torch. Two black rams stood next to her, and I have no memory of where they originated, or how they came to the desert with us. Such was the magic and power of the Mother of the Earth, source of all life and death. And there appeared a hole in the desert, and within that hole were numerous mud steps about half the size of my foot, spiraling down to the place of darkness, winding round and round into an omphalos of silence. Stepping slowly at first, and leading the two black rams, I made my way amid the dark. The rams bleated and moaned as they ambled down the narrow passage. Strange smells assaulted my eyes and nose. Old bones have a sickly odor, a sourness that takes thousands of years to ripen, and my gorge started to rise. Death smells like failure, I thought. Death smells like losing. *Death is for losers.*

My small torch, which illuminated the pock-marked and bloodstained walls, confirmed my thoughts. For on the wall, the newly dead had scrawled maledictions, anathemas, imprecations, and obscenities, and these curses were composed in every conceivable language by the innumerable souls who had preceded me on that final journey, and many were directed toward the gods. It was theological graffiti, mostly, final gasps of indignation and helplessness. Some words looked like they had been carved by desperate hands, bloody grooves dug into the recesses of time itself. Others appeared to be slashed with the bones of animals, which littered the stairway. While most of the imprecations were little more than heretical gibberish, others were clear. Some were cries of vengeance; others cursed the creation of the world, tying down the gods to the chthonian powers, damning their limbs and bones to destruction. An entire wall was devoted to ridiculing Enlil, mocking him for his attempt and failure to destroy mankind. Kore, the Moirai, and Pluto were damned, as were Adad, Ea, and Shamash. The whole pantheon of the greater

Mesopotamian river valley and beyond had been cursed and blasphemed by the dead—an ecumenical gesture I was happy to observe. Other messages were more pedestrian:

Ittii-ddina loves Tusa.

Bel-wart was here.

Hey, honey, if you get this message, you're dead too!

Hey Ripi, you borrowed my tunic and never returned it. Fuck off!

Winding down the narrow mud stair, I descended to the abode of the all-powerful Queen. The air became colder and smelled of cat urine, and the steps became smaller, until finally there was little but rubble to walk on, and after a final, broken step, a vast sea stretched out before me in the dark heat. Nothing moved. No mangy cur crawled over sand; no bird fluttered in the air. I grabbed a bone from the ground, there were many strewn about, and carved a circle in the dust. Then I coaxed one of the rams into the ring and cut its throat. Blood slowly filled the ditch. As the holy substance congealed and bubbled, I heard a rumbling of thunder in the distance—and a host of dead souls rose from the midst like a swarming army of termites who had abandoned their mound and Queen, flowing out of every nook and pouring out of every hole, covering the dust and rock, tiny shadows weeping about the shortness of their lives.

Beckoning the dead toward me, I had hoped to question them about Siduri of Megiddo, her whereabouts or presence, but soon, too soon, the numerous dead gathered around me. Arms grabbed my arms, while hands clutched at my hands. The dead wanted something from me. At first, I wasn't sure what that something was, but I realized quickly they were looking for help or relief from the boredom and suffering of their dead lives. A mother offered me her emaciated baby, wrapped in his shroud, his lifeless eyes open, his small, white, lips parted in a final sigh. Never again would his little mouth suckle her breast. I walked nervously among the sick and ailing dead, as a toothless, old woman grabbed my skirt. "I've got rickets, I've got rickets," she cried. Overwhelmed by their sufferings, I would have bolted in fear if I had thought it was possible. All of that death! I could not fathom it. The list of the dead I witnessed that day was long, and it wearies me to record them all. It was as if the god-scribe had set before me the tablet of grief and suffering, line upon line of the ailing and indisposed dead, those who died of pigbum and swinesore, the paralytic and blind, the diseased and bespotted, the mad and lunatic, and the drooling dead who ruled the netherworld. A woman with a goiter grasped at my tunic, moaning "save us, save us." A maker of bricks prostrated himself before my feet, asking for relief from a toothache. A brother wept silently, his sister in his arms. I moved among them all, over crag and under rock, among the old dead, the newly dead, and the forever dead, looking for Siduri, but she was not there.

O the rite of the dead was a terrible rite!

At the thought of Siduri, I heard familiar voices. The concubines! And they were talking about me, Siduri, and even the King. I am ashamed to wedge it, but they painted my portrait with cruel and deep brush strokes. Voices manifested in the dust. Pea, Tutu, Eudoxia, Cucumber, Biscuit, Urshe, and the rest of the arm-bejeweled and bottom-beaded crew: *He's a pompous fool. His breath stinks. Do remember the time he stole the amphora of wine and got caught? Thirty strikes with the rod! Oh, that was a good day! Gods be damned, one day I will get mine. I'll cut his throat when he sleeps. Nergal never tells the truth; he's incapable of it. Siduri runs that show; she's the one in charge of that house. There is something just a little bit off about Siduri. Something missing. Nergal acts like he's the smartest person in the Ziggurat. By gods, does she have the King on a short leash. She won't let Nebbie out of her sight. But who could blame her? I remember when he snouted everything under the sun and moon and stars. And the eunuch Nergal talks too much, and he laughs at*

442

*his own jokes. You know how he'll tell you a story and
you think it is going somewhere, but it is not, but he tells
it anyway, completely unaware that I am absolutely
murderous with boredom?*

It was a sad and bitter fact, but only in death had
the concubines found their voices. Oh, it was a horrid
thing to hear the thoughts of the King's concubines! My
father Drab was fond of saying that if we knew what our
friends said about us, there would not be but two friends
left in the world. I was pained and relieved by Siduri's
absence from this ritual lamentation. Could it be true
that she wasn't dead? She might well be alive.

I slaughtered a second ram, and as his blood
seeped into the sand, a small, broken-down mud hut
manifested, and above the mud hut's door was a sign
that read, "Used Tablet Shop." It was a humble edifice
with low ceilings, poorly made, and filled with dead cats,
the kind of used tablet shop one might see in the scribal
district of Nineveh during Ashurbanipal's reign. I
entered the shop and nearly choked on the dust from the
tablets, coughing and spitting the grime onto the floor.
When my fit subsided, I understood the magnitude of
what was before me: all the tablets ever wedged in the
world by every scribe who had ever stuck a stylus into
mud. Tablets on shelves, tablets on the dusty ground,
tablets on the rocky outcrops of the netherworld, tablets
on the vast banks and shoals of time. And there, in the
midst of the shop, a dead scribe, stacking tablets in dead
languages on a table. It was my father, Drab the

Indignant—the old, violent pedagogue himself, pricing, organizing, and categorizing tablets by author and genre, and fighting his old enemy, the giant killer, Boredom.

O, Father! How I loved the old scribe!

In life, Father had been tall and cadaverous, and in death, his features had changed little: his eyes were still rheumy and swollen, his skin pasty white. He stooped over the stack of tablets, wheezing hymns to Nabû, and his callused fingers caressed the wedges and lines. Drab looked as if the twenty-odd years he spent in death had made him gravely ill.

"How are you, Father?" I said.

"How do I look?" he said with something of the old menace in his voice.

"You look good, better than I would have expected," I said, hoping for his approval, which he rarely gave.

"I'm fucking dead, that's what I look like," he said, and swatted me across the shoulders. *Swat*—and I was happy to note that his beloved cane of Nabû had lost none of its viciousness. It still hurt like hell.

"How's the job?"

"It's not bad, as far as it goes, which isn't very far. The pay is dreadful, but you can't beat the job security. She's a tough one, though, that Ereshkigal. You might have seen her? No? She usually hangs out by the riverbed. Well, if you stick around, you will. She tolerates no mistakes in pricing, and she also has a pretty good eye for the tablet that will sell—not that we sell many tablets down here. Although, the stock of our tablets is big and getting bigger every day. She has figured out a solid business plan—that much is obvious."

"You seem good, Father," I said, and kissed him on his dead forehead, which still smelled of old soap and dry skin.

"Oh, I get by somehow. But you, Nergal, you look funny," he said, pointing to the garments given to me by Madame Grape, which had been ripped in my descent to the house of the dead. "That's no way for a respectable scribe to dress." *Swat. Swat.*

I flinched in the old manner before his onslaught, and the pain returned me to my childhood, before the fall of Nineveh. I was in my Father's study, reading a long poem about a god named Nergal who visited his consort in the netherworld. She was upset with his lateness, of course, and I was profoundly touched by its themes. While I was reading, Uruk entered the study and cuffed me on the head for breathing too loud.

"If you have come to steal tablets, I must warn you that the punishment is a severe one," Father said, his bushy eyebrows rising. "As you are no doubt aware, every good scribe is a good thief. That's how I got my first good collection of tablets. I stole every one of them from the Tablet House, including an excellent copy of *The Bridal Songs of Inanna*. I suppose it's payback of a sort. We have awful problems with theft in this shop—

the few customers that I have mostly come just to steal tablets. They sell them to other shades for food offerings."

Whistling as he moved through the stacks of tablets, Father picked up a tablet, scanned its contents, assessed its quality, noted its rareness and put a quick price on the corner. Father was a fast tablet-pricer. I must note that Father did seem happy—happier, in fact, than I had ever seen him in life. He moved with grace among the stacks, arranging the tablets, putting them on their shelves.

"No, Father, I have come not to steal," I said, clasping his hand in mine. "It's nice to see you."

"Then what have you come for? And what have you done with your life? You didn't make it into the Tablet House, did you? You always wanted to stay inside and read a tablet instead of doing something productive, which is no way to go through life." *Swat.*

It was good to be abused by the old tablet man.

"Well, I don't have much time. Another scribe died—and his widow brought in a collection of Hurrian theogonies that need pricing. They are in *very good* condition. Come here and help me. Here's a stylus. Everything is going for about a half-shekel down here." How the poor scribe's widow made it to the Used Tablet Shop of the Dead was a question that begged to be asked, but when I looked at Father, he merely shrugged and said, "Ereshkigal gives them a special dispensation. It's good for business."

"Anything decent in the collection?"

Looking over the new tablets, Drab demurred, his chin doubling around his neck. Nothing that ever came into the Used Tablet Shop of the Dead was ever good enough for Drab the Indignant. And, as a used-tablet man of the dead, he had seen it all: the hard-to-find tablets that tablet collectors had urgent dreams about, such as exquisite copies of proto-Ugaritic word lists or rare Cretan hieroglyphs of olive oil consumption in drought years. After ten minutes of pricing, Father turned to me and said, "Nergal, your father may be dead, but he is not a fool. And let me preface what I am about to say by saying that I promise not to beat you. What did you come to see me for?"

"To get the Plant of the Heartbeat. An old woman told me you had it."

"Did she now?" Father laughed indignantly and, despite his promise, swatted me with his cane. *Swat. Swat.* "And what did this old woman look like?"

"She's short and fat and makes a good lamb sandwich."

"Uh-huh. So I expected. Well, you're too late. I smoked that stuff up ages ago. It was crap, too. Didn't do a thing." Father poured himself a cup of tea, a special brew of ginger root and date spice. He drank the stuff whenever his sinuses flared up, and he said that in death his allergies were even worse than they were in life.

"But I really need the Plant of the Heartbeat, or at least the King does. I need to stop him from doing something terrible. From razing a city, if you really want to know."

"Razing a city? Ha, ha. What do you take me for? An imbecile? That is what kings are born to do. Well, I have got something better than the Plant of the Heartbeat, as you call it."

"What's that, Father?"

"It's a tablet without a name. Well, there is a name, but it's a foolish one—it's called *The Tablet of Destinies*, and it is the origin of that most loathed and seductive genre: the end-of-the-world or apocalypse, as it is sometimes called. But, being the lazy scribe that you are, you probably don't know this simple fact. However, the obsession with 'the end times,' or as my dead colleague Bit the Wedger likes to say, 'the hindquarter of man's history,' has been scribal sport since the invention of the first pictograph," Father observed sadly, and he returned to pricing his tablets.

Not for nothing was Father called the Indignant One. Resentment, he said, was endemic to the life of the scribe. There were times, it seemed to Father, that as soon as a man picked up a stick, he began scratching out visions of the end of the world, dreaming of the ways and means by which the gods would destroy his enemies. Most of Father's fellow dead scribes in the House of the Dead were secret apocalyptics. "Each of these wedgers," he said, "has his own pet theory on exactly how the Ziggurat will come crashing down. Zagmuk insists that—due to human decrepitude—the earth will one day be destroyed by water. Urshanabi prophesies that a great fire will rain from the sky and incinerate the race of man, an all-purpose oblation that would appease the gods' wrath. And that idiot, Ul of Um, predicts that there will come a day when men abstain from intercourse with women and effect, within a generation, the extinction of the earth." Such were the theoretical speculations—laughed Father condescendingly—of his peers. He took another sip of ginger root tea.

Father spun the cane in his hands and swatted me on the side of my head. "Shall we have one more lesson?" he asked. "Reach over there in my mud bucket and pull out a handful, would you, boy? A little bit of mud, that's it. Now we will add the grass of Akkad, a bit of goat dung, and there it is—a blank tablet. What shall we wedge, Nerggie my boy? That's the fundamental question, isn't it?"

Despite the severity of the beatings, I was genuinely happy to be back in Father's tablet-house, even if it was in the House of the Dead. Pain from my Father's cane was the surest sign of love I had in the world, and the rhythm of the tablet-house year always consoled my anxious spirit.

"Now let's wedge this so-called *Tablet of Destinies* for you, shall we?"

"How can we do that? I thought you said you already had the tablet?"

Father Drab let out a long whistle. "Well, I once possessed a fine copy of *The Tablet of Destinies*, as it is sometimes called, but I sold it long ago to you-know-who," he said, pointing to a dark rocky riverbed where the Queen of the Dead purportedly had her throne. "But no matter, anybody can wedge *The Tablet of Destinies* if he has a mind to. But I must warn you, Nergal my boy, that nobody just wedges *The Tablet of Destinies*—no, *The Tablet of Destinies* wedges you. You may hold the stylus, and you may push it into the mud, but it is Nabû who works the magic of the scribe, and in this case, doubly so. Sad to say, but you are just a bit player in the larger drama of the world. You may *think* you are the hero in a hero's tale, but you're not. Now, tell me, what's really driving the King to war?"

"He wants to go back to an old girlfriend," I said.

"Oh, that. Why didn't you tell me? And yet, if I hadn't gone back to an old girlfriend ..." And here, Father paused and picked up a tablet, as if he were remembering a good meal he had consumed secretly and in haste.

"What are you talking about?" I asked.

"It's not important. Now I have a question for you. The doom of doom, the fate of fates," said Father, raising his eyebrows ironically, as if he were not wholly serious, "*The Tablet of Destinies* is reputed to be written in a transparent language, a divine idiom that needs neither interpretation nor translation by scribe or haruspex. It is reputed to provide access to the inner

450

penetralia of reality. A universal grammar, if you will. Do you think you are up for it?"

"What do I wedge first?"

"Well, what were the last one thousand years like?" he asked.

"Wars and rumors of war," I said.

"Exactly. It's a safe bet. A no-brainer. Let me show you some of the work I did for Ashurbanipal when I was a young man. You might be familiar with it, for I believe I used it in our lessons with your brother a long time ago. And, come to think of it, what I am about to show you is like *The Tablet of Destinies*, or one version of it."

Raising himself from his chair, the good pedagogue shuffle-stepped over to an old and dusty canopic jar in the corner. Holding the jar to his ear, he shook it gently. "Can you hear the music of the spheres? If you listen closely, you can just make out a tune." He sat down with a sigh and placed the red glazed jar on the table before me.

"I have been saving these for you," he said, dumping out dozens of tablet fragments on the desk. On the table's surface—scratched with an eternity of dead scribal graffiti—lay a pile of broken shards from a King's List or chronology. They smelled of the garden behind our home in Nineveh, of old grass and goat dung. I heard the shouts of Babylonian soldiers, remembered that look on Uruk's face as he was assaulted by a goon in Nebuchadnezzar's Bull Legion.

451

"Normally," Father said, speaking slowly and carefully, "these jars hold the organs of the dead: the livers, hearts, and, if the dead soul is Egyptian, stomachs. This particular jar came in with a decent collection of lyric poetry from a scribe I knew in Nineveh. The poor man was a chronic masturbator but a *very good* copyist.

"Babylon's future," he continued, "lies somewhere between the deeps of the sea and drought of the desert. The King's future. But also your future. We must gather up the fragments and make our tablet. Let us gather the fragments! Come, Nergal, we don't have all day." *Swat.*

Laying down the cane of Nabû, Father began to work quickly and efficiently, as was his custom when there was mud in his hands. "Let's see, that one shall go there, and here is this, and that piece—no, no, that's a corner piece. Good, two more, and then, well, it's close. Yes, there we have it. What do you think?

I, ASHURBANIPAL, KING OF THE FOUR RIMS, BUILT A PILLAR NEAR THE CITY GATE, AND I FLAYED ALL THE CHIEFS WHO HAD REVOLTED, AND I COVERED THE PILLAR WITH THEIR SKIN. SOME I WALLED UP WITHIN THE PILLAR, SOME I IMPALED UPON THE PILLAR ON STAKES, AND OTHERS I BOUND TO STAKES ABOUT THE PILLAR. AND I CUT THE LIMBS OF THE OFFICERS, OF THE ROYAL OFFICERS WHO HAD REBELLED. MANY CAPTIVES FROM AMONG THEM I BURNED WITH FIRE, AND MANY I TOOK AS LIVING CAPTIVES. FROM SOME I CUT THEIR NOSES, EARS AND

FINGERS; OF MANY I PUT OUT THE EYES. I MADE
ONE PILLAR OF THE LIVING AND ANOTHER OF
HEADS, AND BOUND THEIR HEADS TO TREE
TRUNKS ROUND ABOUT THE CITY. THEIR YOUNG
MEN AND MAIDENS I BURNED IN THE FIRE.
TWENTY MEN I CAPTURED ALIVE AND IMMURED IN
THE WALLS OF MY PALACE. THE REST OF THE
WARRIORS I CONDEMNED TO BE CONSUMED
WITH THIRST IN THE DESERT OF THE EUPHRATES.

Good old Drab. Ever the reliable pedagogue.
Father had somehow gotten his hands on the fragments
from the tablet Uruk and I had been working on during
that last day of Father's life. I brushed my hand over its
broken surface and marveled at how clear the wedges
appeared.

"The style holds up pretty well, don't you
think?" Father said with a smile of scribal satisfaction on
his face. He smoothed out his tunic and took another
sip of tea.

"Yes, but the story's a little depressing. Isn't
there something that is, I don't know, more hopeful?"

"Oh, hopeful. Well, there is a second approach,
although it's less interesting," he said.

Reaching across the table, Father re-scrambled
the fragments—and the world of the cruel and mighty
King disappeared as if it had never existed.

"Here's a little something I sent to your mother
one day," he said.

Moving the fragments around in a quick, circular motion, Father tried one combination and then another. "How did it go now? 'Let me,' something, something, something, 'for love is,' something, something. Oh, that's right." Taking the last piece, Father placed it in the middle part of the square. When he was finished with the new tablet, he pushed it forward in front of me. "Nergal, why don't you read it aloud for us?"

> *Set me as a seal upon thine heart,*
> *as a seal upon thine arm;*
> *for love is strong as death;*
> *jealousy as cruel as the grave:*
> *the coals thereof are coals of fire,*
> *which hath a most vehement flame.*
> *Many waters cannot quench love,*
> *neither can the floods drown it:*
> *if a man would give all the substance*
> *of his house for love, it would*
> *utterly be contemned.*

When I had finished reading the poem, I had to suppress my tears. Foolish Nergal! I had supposed that Father would proclaim that the wolf would lie down with the lamb, or that swords would be turned into plowshares, but it was not to be. He had given me a love poem! And I—and sadly, I am aware of how hackneyed this sounds—loved a good love poem. Call it a weakness of mine, an embarrassing crack in my eunuchoid colossus. Perhaps Father knew his son better than I had thought. Now there are many magic tablets in the Tablet House of Babylon. Most of these are apotropaic in nature, that is, they tutor the adept in methods of warding off evil, and teach him to protect himself from the malignant spirits and demons that stalk the desert steppes and live in our ruined buildings. But there is one tablet that details a necromancy ritual, and it is this tablet I wish I could lay my hands on as I wedge my addendum to Uruk's history of our City. It describes a series of incantations in which the ordinand invokes the spirits of Ereshkigal who appear and counsel him on his troubles with love.

And yet, when I looked at the tablet to read the poem again, it was blank! Without wedge or line! The mud appeared the same, but where wedges and triangles and lines had been was now as smooth as my bottom after a good sesame oil scrub from Madame Grape's firm hand. Something had been there, but now there was nothing. A nothing on a nothing. And I remembered that Father had always dreamed of wedging a tablet without word-signs or ideograms, a tablet that would mark the end of tablets. It was his revenge on his scribal enemies—who, he would say when he was drunk and in his cups, "don't know fuck all."

"Where has the good poem gone, Father? There is nothing on the tablet!" I said.

"Ha! I can't send you up there with that sentimental rubbish. After all, I have my reputation to keep. There are spies everywhere. Someone might report back to Ereshkigal. She doesn't like visitors, and she doesn't like surprises. My secret script vanishes as soon as it is wedged. Call it a form of self-protection. The critics hate it."

"But what will Nebuchadnezzar see?" I asked.

"He will see what he wants to see," Drab said.

"But that is a terrible way to read a tablet."

"Exactly," Father said, laughing, and he struck me a final time with his cane. *Swat!*

[Lacuna: tablet damaged;
approximately 8 lines lost.]

I left Father—my ears stinging, my journey to the House of Dust nearly over. Father and I never wedged *The Tablet of Destinies*, although I had placed the fragments of the blank tablet in my pocket. I never met the Queen of the Dead, nor did I encounter Siduri of Megiddo, but I left with the hope that she might be alive, and if she was alive, she was living within the walls of Jerusalem.

Tablet Twenty-Two ~

Gog of the Land of Magog

An Aramaean usurper ... he removed to the wasteland ...

— The Babylonian Chronicles

Memory is an edifice built by a tyrant and defaced by time, a tablet smashed to bits by illiterate beards, rampaging their way through a burning library, pissing on shelves, defecating on rare treatises, and we're left to grope with the fragments, fill in the gaps as best we can with our own inventions, however fantastic or implausible. Every Tablet House boy knows that I was nervous about Uruk's plans to flatten Jerusalem—and I admit to a certain eunuchoid pessimism here—but he said it would be easy; he said it would please the King who wanted to find his Megiddogian girlfriend alive and ready to return to him or expunge all memory of the place. The leveling of the city happened fast. The de-bricking of the walls took about three days. Soldiers dropped by the hundreds, and I won't bother the reader with unnecessary details. Most will be familiar with this particular bas-relief or that victory stele celebrating this or that conquest: bowmen on the wall, tumbling down, buttocks forward to their deaths with spears stuck in their chests and throats, arrows perforating life and limb. The soldiers poured through the walls, a thick, teeming mass of arsonists and thieves, murderers and rapists. Behold the subsequent flames, hear the blood and cries. We all know what a city looks like when the walls come crashing down. But the smell. Now that was the thing. It smelled like blood. And blood smells like a dog.

The King bragged about his exploits for a week: he strutted up and down his tent, sticking his chest out, declaiming his might under the heavens. Below is the exact copy of the booty list Moil made of the victory:

9,000 talents of sliver
870 golden rings
710 golden daggers
17,000 talents of bronze
60,000 talents of iron
400 adolescent girls
2,420 bronze pails

Tablet Twenty-Two
86 beds of boxwood
3,560 dishes of boxwood
    inlaid with ivory
900 linen garments with purple trim
93 elephant tusks
72 chariots of polished gold
I golden couch with inlay

Nebuchadnezzar also took 374 horses, 5,439 cattle, 2,543 sheep, the enemy king's sister (one Rachel of Judah) and 10,000 of his subjects to be used as labor. Not to mention, and the King did mention, additional gold and silver ingots, brass bars, baskets of grain, piles of linen, and stacks of cedar that filled six palaces.

Nebuchadnezzar! I have witnessed you and Uruk, during long, cold winter nights, fingering the stars, searching for omens. How did you do it? The sheer volume of celestial objects is enough to thwart the mind. How was it possible to interpret the heavenly flux? How could one read the chaos?

[Lacuna: tablet damaged;
approximately 18 lines lost.]

After the campaign in the West, the King and I returned to Babylon. We resumed our life in the Great Entemenaki, more or less: daily sacrifices to Ishtar and nightly feasts devoted to Marduk, where the King got sloppy drunk and complained about his enemies. Outside the walls of the City, two dozen, sun-blackened hides—the flayed epidermises of subversives, complainers, malcontents, and other sectarians who had broken with Fecundity over the drought—flapped in the breeze. My brother had seen to that. The wind had picked up, and the sandstorms were worse than ever.

It was a relief to live in Nebuchadnezzar's apartments after the long campaign in the deserts of the West. Amytis was away in Media, visiting her sister, and we had the place to ourselves. As I have wedged, the King's apartment was located on the top floors of the tower and was crowded with recent booty from our latest military campaign. There were boxes of silver cups, bushel after bushel of wheat, wood chests inlaid with ivory, and all of it lay on the floor as if it had just arrived from the front. As a gift to my Lord, Uruk had filled the rooms with the conquered images of foreign deities—for the King always became a teensy-weensy bit depressed after a big victory. And, more to the point, the drought had not relented; each week delivered a new sandstorm, more virulent and destructive than the last. Re-Osiris, Telepinu, and a minor divinity called Ba'al Zebub stood in the apartment like a divine rebuke to Nebuchadnezzar's melancholy. Deaf and mute, the stone figures refused the King solace. He would talk to them every night, asking questions about the drought, pleading for answers, for some hint or speck of information that would help him—and Babylon. But they never replied, and the winds kept blowing sand into the City. The days of rainlessness seemed without end.

"Box Rose, come here. Like a faithful ox that plows the field, only you can relieve my burden," he said. "We need another sacrifice, I'm afraid. Something to quiet the voices in my head."

Poor, maudlin Nebuchadnezzar. He was sinking into the lower valleys of his melancholy. Blood demanded blood. I tried to cheer him up. "We could kill a camel and bury it in the desert. That was the gold standard for sacrifices in your father's day," I said.

"Did that last week at the dedication of the temple," said the King, sighing. He disliked anything associated with Nabopolassar.

"How about slaughtering one of the horses?" I offered helpfully.

"Boring."

"We could immolate an old woman," I said. "You always liked that. Remember how you warmed your hands over the flames last year at the Tukulti-Ninurta festival?"

"I'm getting married next week, and I'm so fucking depressed. Have you met Amytis? We're engaged."

"She's a grand lady, and her beauty should bring glory to the City," I said.

"She's a vicious one. And I'll tell you something else. She's got *plans* for me."

461

His face looked as if it would crack into pieces. I had never seen him so sad.

"She demands that I get rid of you, that we end our affair. It's one of the conditions of the marriage contract. A final test, of sorts. Uruk's against the idea. Strange to say, he likes you. He also thinks it will undermine the Fecundity Rites. However, Mother is for it. So is Harpagus," he said, gripping my buttocks fiercely. "But I'm going to thwart them all. Together, we will thwart them all."

I nodded my head, shaking my freshly cut bangs—just the way Siduri shook them after a particularly strenuous bout of coitus with my Lord.

O Siduri!

Where are you now? Your pronounced overbite stabbed my chest! Your lazy eye caused me to write a dozen minor but emotionally significant epodes in the dark of my room! Your fingernails, when you were not biting them, were long enough to scratch my back just the way I liked it—with just a hint of malice.

I knew what had to be done. I had resolved to give the King what Siduri had never given him, what she had never given me. I would become the Great Summoner: In the Temple of Bulls, I would awaken Dumuzi, and together we would trample the field, make the deer and goats multiply, and the wheat shaft sprout.

My approach would be one of caution: one could never be too skeptical when it came to breaking down the King's whims. It was well known in the harem—that is, back when he had one—that Nebuchadnezzar's tastes were narrow. I checked my hand glass quickly: my mouth exuded the proper kind of animal spirit and friendliness that a King had a right to expect from a concubine; my hairdo was ringed, oiled, curled in the Babylonian manner and held together in beautiful gold bands. My eyes were thin and elongated. The Great Bull liked that saucy Egyptian look. Cheekbones prominent. Teardrops painted fashionably below my eyes. Yes, my Lord appreciated the teardrop motif, generally. I had become a coquette of the old school, a real come-here-come-here-get-away-get-away expert. I thrilled to the dance of beard and skirt, the ritual glance of the eyes and accidental touch on the arm. I was no longer nervous about the final seduction of my Lord.

"Good Box Rose, come here and let me embrace thee!"

"You are my gentle shepherd," I said.

"Scorpions, frogs, and creeping things have invaded my City," he said.

"You are hierodule of An."

"Hierodule of An, ha!" he said, dropping his skirt to his ankles. "Behold, I shall show you a mystery. This is it. The thing itself. The Holy Aardvark of Babylon. The Royal Snout of Sippar. What do you think of the beast?" He had pulled his flaccid member out and now stood stretching it up and down and back and forth with his hand like it was an elastic bow. "Ha!

You see that? The aardvark is tired. Without life. I'm afraid he has snuffled through his last anthill."

"He looks to be a formidable enemy, my Lord, and yet also a friend of mankind," I said.

"Foolish girl. I'm afraid I will disappoint you. I'm what my priests call 'fucked out.' I cannot even sack a city anymore. Fucking Harpagus. He's the One now."

Beckoning my Lord forward, I lay coiled on the sheepskin and placed myself in the shadows to lend the right light to my figure—and to hide that nasty scar caused by Harpagus's knife. I massaged my Lord's shoulders, and he moaned as I ran my fingers down his back. Given the terrible success of the Mede, Nebuchadnezzar was ambivalent about the obliteration of Jerusalem. The King was nervous. He lay on his bed as if he were a corpse being prepared for burning, but soon the beer began to take effect, and there was laughter, and more beer, and more laughter. I applied copious amounts of unguent to his back and listened to him complain about Harpagus's ferocity and mutter about the criticism he was facing from the Median faction, and how his mother had always disliked him. So far, all was as good as could be expected. Not the garden of paradise, but not bad.

The Last Vintage. I poured more beer into the King's cup and drank more myself, for we would need the intercession of the God of the Barley and Hops that night. I touched his arm lightly, and he sighed at my touch. I smiled coquettishly and dragged my fingernails slowly over the hairs of his forearm, just the way Siduri used to do in the early days of their relationship. Her magic was now my magic. "I want to make you happy," I said in my best imitation of her voice.

The sun broke through a thin window, speckling the tiles with shimmering light. My Lord needed me. His impotence, his incompetence, his violence, his stupidity, his callous indifference to the agricultural blight that had smitten Babylon: it was all by way of divine plan. And there had to be a plan. That was the important thing. That our ratiocinations on the gods and their ends would make sense. That the chaos and noise of the world would dissipate. That the confusion of my heart would be gone. That the shrieks in my head would be silent. All would become One. All would become Visible.

The King purred like a big cat. To exorcise a demon, said Madame Grape, you must be possessed by another. He jerked back warily, like I was about to slither up his leg and sink my fangs into his thigh. But then Nebuchadnezzar nodded, reached for my arm, and pulled me into his embrace. I felt the hard bump between his loins and moved away, just like Siduri had taught me to do. He responded with predictable ardor.

"I have never met a whore who was so bold as to turn down a King. Did your parents sell you into slavery?"

I smiled at my Lord.

The skins on the Ziggurat walls flapped in the wind. Another sandstorm was brewing.

What happened next between Nebuchadnezzar and me was spontaneous, I swear on the sacred haunches of Madame Grape. Something within my chest broke. I wept. Though my tears were real enough, the tale I gave Nebuchadnezzar wasn't mine. I told him a cock-and-bull story, one that I had borrowed from Siduri, for I had heard her tell it at least a dozen times. It was the part about the young Siduri being raped repeatedly, as the soldiers took turns violating her with their lust, that bothered him the most. It was ugly. My mascara ran down my eyes and cheeks. My lip paint smeared. I blubbered about whatever came into my head. And *I meant it*, or I thought I did at the time.

Wrapping his arms around me, the King whispered, "There, there," and then he hummed a tune I had never heard before. "We build our houses," he softly sang, "we make our nests—and then the river rises and floods, and nothing is there. All is gone!"

"Three hundred young women disappeared off the face of the earth!" I sobbed. "Three hundred young women who climbed on the riverboats that night and never returned to sup at the feasting tables."

The King listened to the story like it was a fable, a tale that pained him but had no connection to his person.

I told him of Eudoxia, Pea, Gashansunna, Astarte, and Anunit, for they were in my boat, and although there were dozens of others, those were the ones I tried to save from their watery shrouds. He never questioned me about the hows or whys of how I obtained this knowledge. I told him of Gemeti, who used to talk to me late at night, and Iltani, who was kind to me when I first came to the harem, sharing her rations of bread and cheese with me. I told him of sweet Anunit, how she laughed at my stupid jokes, and said that I was clever and deserved a better life. I told Nebuchadnezzar that I frequently awoke from bad dreams—choking on water in a tangle of blackthorns, twisted limbs, and the pale flesh of the drowned, digging with my hands in the sand and rock of the riverbank, feasting on the worm of regret. And my Lord began to weep, too, first gently, then harder, as we both grieved over what he had done. Our cries rose and fell with the wind as we sobbed on each other's shoulders.

"Ah my little partridge," he said, wiping the tears from his face. "We shan't ever let anything like that happen to you."

"Don't ever leave me," I said, and to my surprise, I meant it.

Nebuchadnezzar, Lord of the Four Rims, the Divine Plowman, the Master of the Deluge, took my cheeks in his stubby hands and placed the softest kiss on my lips that I had ever experienced. His eyes, bloodshot with war and killing, took the whole of my being into their watery saucers. "Box Rose," he whispered hoarsely, his voice bursting with emotion. "*You're the One.*"

Like a hardy, bulbous perennial, my Lord's lust sprouted. And let it be wedged, I was not incapable of experiencing pleasure of that sort: we the castrated have our ways of gratifying the so-called baser instincts. Nebuchadnezzar whimpered with desire as he unclasped the back of my tunic and began caressing my chest and stomach with his big beard. All along I was careful to hide you-know-what.

As we walked up to the edge of our consummation, my Lord used his beard as if it were some prehensile and extremely sensitive erogenous instrument: exploring, weighing, and measuring his pleasure. Vibrating in the half light of the fire, the hairy appendage seemed to have a life of its own. At one point, early in the seduction, his beard lay around my neck like a small ginger-colored rabbit, collecting dust from the floor. We shifted positions, and then my Lord's heavy weight rested upon my back. "Oh, Boxie," he said gently, and I raised my rump, and with my hand guided my Lord expertly, and, I might add, gently into my *locus amoenus*,[1] that path which no fowl knoweth, that secret lane where no thistle grows. I relaxed and let the warm feeling flood over my being. A white light filled the room, and the dust motes in my Lord's beard accumulated on my shoulders with every thrust of passion.

The whole encounter lasted no more than a minute, maybe a minute and a half, and the curious thing about our union was that my Lord exhibited no embarrassment at all. He giggled like a child upon climax, wells of laughter burst from his chest as if a primal happiness had been dammed up within his soul and only now had found an appropriate outlet. We shared a few jokes, drank another cup of beer, and he fell asleep. He had done this before, you see, or so he told me, laughing off our intimacy as if it was no more important to him than relieving himself in a back alley after drinking too much beer. But I knew differently: our night together was a big deal, *a very big deal*, for the King had not managed a successful coupling with beast or fowl for the better part of three years. He had accomplished with me what all of the women in his harem had failed to elicit from his loins: genuine, singular passion, lust, or whatever you want to call it.

That evening Enlil, the god of the raging storm, poured down the rains. Rain! The god of thunder drowned the gate of the gods in a sea of dark water. Oh, how the scribes gnawed on that bone of contention for decades to come over *what* or *who* caused the heavens to finally disgorge its ill-digested contents! Of course, contrary to what my brother claimed, the human instrumentalities of Divine Purpose can never be settled. Bunt, in a tedious translation of a stolen monograph, argued that it was the animal skin up his own fat bottom that did the job, while Pir-igmi the Petulant claimed that the King's prostration before Siduri at the second feast of the Golden Bull was responsible for The Deluge, as it was then called by the anti-Nebuchadnezzar faction.

The knot that holds the world together had come undone. Torrential rains! Green shafts began to sprout on the plain, and, once again, cicadas chirped in the afternoon heat.

O Ishtar! If only you had treated me thus! Thick sheets of water fell, filling cistern, canal, and lake. It was a sign, the foolish priests said. Healing sap. Wondrous balm. Abûtû.[2] Water poured out of the sky in glorious plenitude on Babylon. The rains lasted for forty days and forty nights. Rain fell like hard pellets, rain dropped in fat drops, rain transformed the dusty streets into a thick, black sludge. Mud was everywhere. Brown muck sucked my sandals into its stinky maw, and each step pulled me deeper into my own terrible powers of love, and filled the folds of my being with earthy, black globs. It was reported that the streets of our fair City had turned into a swamp. Rain, rain, and more rain. I saw a horse drown while crossing the road in the soldiers' camp; carts sank in the muck; chariots were abandoned before the City's sagging walls; everything was mired in the general chaos and noise of The Deluge. Needless to wedge, Uruk and his cronies were happy, and he spent his days rubbing his enemies' faces in the scata of the scatomants, but I knew better, and so did Nebuchadnezzar, if he would only admit it. The rains had come because the love between a King and a eunuch's backside formed a potent magic.

Our affair had sent forth the winds from the plains: the fourfold wind, the sevenfold wind, and the whirlwind blew across palace and temple. As the rain turned into torrents, and the torrents into a flood, opinion among the Illegitimates became once again divided on the King. Having raised the flood-storm with his new favorite, Nebuchadnezzar did not know how to control it. But he didn't care. Prodigious rain. The holy union that was my relationship with the King had been formalized, and it was as beautiful as it was terrible. We had exchanged bodily fluids, and while this was not the first time, it was the most significant. In that slippery act, Nebuchadnezzar had been transformed into my slave, while I had become, for a brief moment, his master. And the gods? They didn't give a damn about either one of us.

The showers did not stop: Utnapishtim end-of-the world showers. A blessing turned to a curse. Every morning, reports came in from Uruk that Babylon was underwater. Streets melted into sinkholes. Whole bridges collapsed under the rush of water, and things went from bad to worse for the citizens of Babylon. Our people were stuck in their homes, watching helplessly as their small garden plots sank into the muddy abyss. Many stooped and aged beards stepped among potholes and pools on the street, while trying to stay dry. The Babylonian peasants pointed to the sky. Filth floated in the streams, which was infused with a ghoulish light of the universal gray that had descended on our City like an occupying army.

One morning, while I was perusing my old harem tablets, I noticed that the Ziggurat had tilted northwest. The people of the City trudged through the water, some on makeshift boats, and assembled around the Ziggurat, begging the priests and scribes to do something. Uruk panicked. Two days later, my brother issued an encyclical on the abrupt—and potentially disastrous—weather he called The Fortunate Deluge, which was little more than a labyrinth of secret hatreds, a dank, subterranean tunnel of remembered humiliations and protracted grievances pounded and crushed in the mortar of the diviner's psyche. He said that floods, which were now destroying the land and drowning livestock, were the gods' way of purging sick cattle and sheep, eliminating fields not fertile enough to serve greater Babylon.

Paradoxically, the rains only made Nebuchadnezzar fall more in love with me. With each congress, with every union, with every declaration of love, the dark waters rose higher and higher, and the foundations of the Ziggurat weakened. A hurried copulation behind the throne, whose silver panels depicted Tiamat slithering through the waters, caused the floods to overrun their limits, and water crashed through the Ziggurat, filling the first ten floors with its dangerous alluvium. A quick fellation in the empty harem caused the outer gate to the tower to collapse. One could feel the Ziggurat sink deeper and deeper with each shudder of lung and heart. When I flagellated the

King's backside with a cane, the water flooded the next ten floors of the Ziggurat. Every time my Lord pawed my backside, the rains rained down harder.

After the third week of The Deluge, the foundation bricks gave way. The evidence was slight at first, a crack on the south wall of the King's apartment, a tremulous window, doors that would not open. One of the wings on the winged bulls—those eternal guardians of the Great Hall—fell off. As the winds continued to blow and the tower trembled, I was struck by a terrible thought: what if I had been sent by an angry god—Enlil or Siduri's Jaldabaoth—to drown the earth and end all creation? I suspected a terrible witchcraft was at work, but soon realized that it was something even more malicious, more insidious in its intent to destroy the world. That's when I knew, or thought I knew. It was Siduri! *She* was causing the rains to fall—or rather, she was causing the rains *through me*. Nebuchadnezzar was *in love with her*, and she, by force of pure, fanatical will, was using *my* imitation of *her* to get back at *him*. She was manipulating me to do her bidding—to destroy the City of the Royal Beard who had enslaved her in the harem and who had violated her nightly against her will.

When the water levels reached the thirtieth floor, Babylon's—or should I say Uruk's—worst fears rose before the mind's eye: the time when the tower would tumble down and the empire collapse into the mud-puddle of history. And that is exactly what happened. Etemenanki, with its ascending seventy-two spirals of brick and mud, wobbled and sank into airy nothing. The fiftieth-floor and the mercantile floors were the first to go under, followed by the grain floors. When the beer rooms collapsed, panic and screams could be heard throughout the Ziggurat, as priests and scribes abandoned their posts and rushed down the stairwells.

And Nebuchadnezzar did nothing. Large chunks of the Ziggurat continued to crumble around us; you could hear them splashing in the deep below. He merely lay on the floor and stared at a mosaic of Ishtar on the ceiling, smiling his dumb post-coital smile. I grabbed him by the hand, and said, "the Ziggurat reaches the heaven, my Lord, rise up," but he ignored me. He was humming a tune that I didn't recognize; it may have been one of Siduri's compositions that she wedged and shared with her fellow harem slaves. Always pay attention to the songs that make their way into your lover's heart when you are not around, for they only mean one thing: your lover is in love with somebody else. As the waters ascended up and past the seventieth floor, I began to compose a tablet on the end of my world, the end of our world, the end of Babylon. The Ziggurat was falling! I threw myself over the King's body and awaited the end, my proverbial barge to the underworld. Servants and slaves ran in and out of the Great Hall. Bunt jumped from the window. Scut disappeared in a sinkhole of brick and mud. Cup bearers, barbers, the chief baker, the major domo, and the overseer-of-the-slaves evaporated.

And then there was a roar. I don't know how or what happened. I remember falling, falling, those seven seconds were much quicker than I had imagined. The water hit me hard, and I spun in the roiling waves. When I finally surfaced, I beheld the gray gloom. I had been here before: Enlil, Lord of the Storm, must hate me, I thought. And yet, I was still alive. I had not sunk into the Deep like the three-hundred. Two divine bulls made of wood rocked on the waters. I swam over to the panels and grabbed a wing. In time, I shimmied on top of the delicate carvings. The rains had subsided for a moment, and the fog lifted. I saw the tip of the Ziggurat, now in ruins, amidst the waves. I searched the waters—evidence of things not seen that would somehow bring consolation but saw nothing. I spotted Uruk. He was hanging on to a broken scribe's bench, his dreams of misrule now unhappily manifest among the high waters and debris. Where were his auguries now? Red slabs of meat at the bottom of a lake. A helmet bobbed, catching the sun's weak light. It was the Mede's. The destroyer of Jerusalem, butcher of many cities, and castrator of boys had disappeared into time's great, silent libation.

While I hung on the winged demons, bobbing up and down on the cold waves, I beheld a vast midden floating on the waters: debris and garbage as far as my eye could see—a broken body of old cups, forgotten beakers, rotten turnips, crusty bull joints, rancid mutton shanks, crushed eggshells, stinking old carpets, discarded garments, sandals of old leather, cracked pottery, bits of

perfume jars, splintered bowls, shattered pitchers, old
jewelry, parts of chariots and carts, wheels of every size,
burned-out torches, rubble from brick and stone. It was
as if all the detritus from Babylon had risen from the
depths and reassembled. All hierarchy gone.

The midden grew bigger and bigger until it
consumed the sea, cubit upon cubit of waste spread
before my eyes, a watery dump that covered the earth in
scrap and rag, junk and bone. And tablets. Tablet upon
tablet of petition and letter, tablet upon tablet of
horoscope and edict, stack upon stack of bill of debt and
debt of bill. Chronicles and hymns floated on the swell,
water-damaged archives of lamentation and song.
Words had bubbled up from the drowned City: every
tale wedged by master and slave; every love letter written
in the desperate loneliness of night; every King's List and
slave transaction tablet created by weary scribe. On the
waters of The Deluge, I beheld the record of human
tongue and voice, tablets of struggle and mirth, stories
of relief and sorrow, accounts of endless transactions
and bureaucratic minutia, little marks made by tired
hands. All that transcription. All that transmission. All
that heralding and prophesying, proclaiming and
declaiming. The hopes and aspirations of life unrealized.
All that chatter. All that noise and, sad to wedge, all that
dirt—the slander and tips and tattle and blab, the
confessions and revelations, the disclosures and rumor
and talk and gossip and innuendo and whispering and
criticism, all that fucking criticism.

Tablet Twenty-Two

And in the middle of the noise, I spotted my Nebuchadnezzar, Despoiler of Nations, with his head peeking out from the waters, and there was the familiar panic in his eyes and sadness, too. He was covered in filth and stink and waste and rot. I felt a new, powerful affection for him, and was happy that I could save him. I thought about my reward for this act, how he would embrace me and receive me back into the royal circle, and he looked at me hopefully. Then he saw the scars on my loins, that strip of hard, melon-colored skin between my legs from where Harpagus had stripped away my boyhood in the basement of the Ziggurat, and his face collapsed in rage and pain and disappointment. And Nebuchadnezzar did something surprising, but something that, in retrospect, he must have wanted to do for a long time. He reached up and grabbed my arm. His touch was hard and mean. He called me "Nergal," and he said my name again, this time with more venom, and he pulled me off the raft, and he rubbed my face in the midden of the City, baptizing me in the waters of Babel.

MAY ANU AND EA DESTROY THE SONS
OF WHOEVER DEFACES THIS TABLET OF MINE,
AND CURSE HIM,
AND OBLITERATE HIM FROM THE LAND,
AND THROW HIS OFFSPRING
FROM THE RAMPART TO BE DASHED TO PIECES,
AND ALSO THE SONS OF HIS SERVANTS.

MAY ADAD, THE LORD OF HEAVEN,
AND ERESHKIGAL, QUEEN THE NETHERWORLD,
AND ALL THE GREAT GODS,
MAKE THE PROGENY
OF WHOSOEVER CHANGES OR ERASES MY TABLET
DISAPPEAR FROM THE COUNTRY.

MAY THE GODS LET THE WORM AND CANKER
EAT UP YOUR WHEAT
AND GIVE YOUR BARLEY OVER TO LOCUSTS.

MAY THE GODS SQUASH YOU AS A HEAD-LOUSE
IN THE HANDS OF YOUR MOTHER-IN-LAW.

AND JUST AS THE DUNG OF A DOG STINKS,
SO MAY YOUR BREATH STINK
BEFORE KINGS AND PRIESTS.

IF ANY SCRIBE OR PRIEST ALTERS MY WORDS,
MAY NABÛ, WHO HOLDS THE TABLET OF FATE,
ERASE HIS NAME AND   [. . .]

[Final tablet broken:
all subsequent lines lost.]

Notes on the Text

Introduction and Note on the Translation

I "The history of phallicism is the history of religion." George Ryley Scott, *Phallic Worship: A History of Sex and Sex Rites in Relation to the Religions of All Races from Antiquity to the Present Day* (London: Luxor Press Ltd., 1966): xvii.

2 **Kittelsby has called the work "obscene."** S. Kittelsby, "Reading Poole's *The Eunuch* : By the Waters of Babylon, We Sat Down and Wept," *Duluth Divinity Bulletin*, 41 (Winter/Spring 2021): 87-96.

3 **"a sad effort by a sad, little man."** G. Thorson, "A Complete and Unexpurgated Review of Henry Poole's Translation of *The Eunuch*," *The Chisholm Literary Review*, 19 (Spring 2021): 24-36.

4 **sold on the black market.** The number of antiquities taken from the Museum is believed to be approximately 15,000, including the Warka Vase, thirty panels from the Balawat Gates, and countless royal seals and tablets. While some of the objects have been recovered, many, including *The Eunuch* tablets, fell into the hands of unscrupulous dealers, who sold them for extraordinarily high prices. For a detailed list of antiquities lost or missing, see *The Moose Lake Post*, March 19, 2004: 3.

5 **Poole adopted Steiner's notion of "literary enhancement."** George Steiner, *After Babel: Aspects of Language and Translation.* (London and New York: Oxford University Press, 1975): 323f.

Tablet One

I **A eunuch's backside . . . potent magic.** The eunuch describes a strange and esoteric form of Mesopotamian divination. It is a ritual whereby the King—in his sacramental role as Divine Bull—receives news from the gods vis-à-vis the hindquarters of a eunuch. See Ole Mohn's, "On the Reading of a Eunuch's Buttocks" in *The Ely Quarterly*, 4 (Spring 2006): 3.

2 **Hounds and Jackals**. A board game originating in Ur in which wild dogs battle jackals to the death. Its later iteration as a Babylonian board game was more sanguine, and players played for a half-shekel a

point. For an adumbration of the historical evidence of the origins of the game, see O. E. Hoyme's, "An Evidentiary Survey of Non-Immolative Pastimes in Ancient Babylon," *The Keewatin Journal of Ancient Near-Eastern Archaeology*, 43 (Summer/Fall 2012): 67-84.

3 The beard. The Akkadian term *saziqui* refers to "the bearded," a word-sign designating the establishment of an elite warrior and priest class. See Karin Jakobsson's, "It Shall to the Barbers with Your Beard: Re-examining the Evidence for Social Caste Fluidity in Ancient Mesopotamia," in *The Biwabik Journal of Near Eastern Studies*, 23 (November 2019): 79-92.

4 wedging errata. The tradition of scribal commentary in the Babylonian Tablet Houses is long and storied. *Errata* is the eunuch's term for this extra-textual work, which includes criticism, endnotes, addenda, marginalia, and appendices. See G. Mellby's, "Drudgery Preserved: Scribal Life in Ancient Babylon as Inferred from Recovered Tablets Archived in the Musée de Louvre," *The Mont Du Lac Review of Books*, 2 (July 1997): 16-48.

5 ghost balls. According to Poole's journals, (later destroyed in a fire) the phrase was originally a compound ideograph, consisting of the Sumerian "gidim" ("gig" for "sick" and "dim" for "demon") combined with the Akkadian "ishku" for "testicle." See Arvid Kildahl's monograph, *Spøkelse Testiklene i Akkadisk* (Oslo: Utgraving Oppslagsverk Forlegger, 2004).

Tablet Two

1 holy bride. The eunuch refers not to an actual wedding but to a ritualized mock-marriage union between the King and a chosen harem concubine, which will take place during the Festival of the Golden Bull, and which, it is hoped, will usher in a new age of fertility and abundance for Babylon.

2 aardvark's tongue. Taken from a Sumerian term that is suggestively ambiguous in the original. The logogram combines the half-syllable sign that refers to a possible power vacuum during the second half of Nebuchadnezzar's reign (605-562 BCE). Poole's unusual choice of translation—much to the disapprobation of Pekka Nilsson and Odd

Anderson—originates from an Aramaic proverb found in a tablet of unknown provenance. See Leo Ellingson and Sigge Holland, *Vox Populi: Graffiti in Antiquity* (Askov, Minnesota: Finlayson University Press, 1998).

3 Papyrus! C. Wilson has argued that clay tablets and papyrus existed alongside each other in many of the Tablet Houses of Babylonia and Assyria. It is a point that has been contested, most notably by the American-Swedish Lutherans, who argue that little or no evidence has been found in the surviving libraries. See Wackernagel, *Sprachl Unters* (Munich: Buch Trocken Verleger, 2015): 304-326.

Tablet Four

1 winds are symbolic. This sentence is an amplification in vague metaphorical terms that Magnus Karlsson characteristically misunderstands. The term "wind" can signify both futility and hope. See Ohnstad's general discussion of "wind" in *Akkadian Participles* (Nashwauk, Minnesota: Keewatin University Press, 2004) 78ff.

Tablet Five

1 Festival of the Golden Bull. The eunuch is referring to the Sumerian Sacred Marriage Festivals originating in the city of Uruk of which the Golden Bull is, in all likelihood, a neo-Babylonian derivative. See the Rev. J. Swanson's study of "Poem of the Holy Coupling," *Verstopfung Seminary New Review*, 52 (2005): 220ff.

2 the most officious castrate I had ever known. In a fragment from one of the Gustavus Adolphus tablets, Nergal recounts a story involving his fellow castrate: "I once found a whole and freshly peppered river fish in Moil's room—baked black in a marvelously complex, spicy sauce made from ginger, black peppers, and tamarind. A real sinus cleaner. I ate it in a closet in the College of Eunuchs, for I was afraid to be surprised by my fellow castrates, who were, at least in public, always quick to censure the illicit food act. The sauce was creamy, and as I sucked out the eyes (arguably the most delectable part of the fish), nibbled away the soft, pliant meat along the gills, and with my forefinger pushed out the gill meat, those two, tender rosebuds of flesh, and laid them out on my tongue, where they melted in intense burst of creamy goodness, butter, and black pepper, I was completely and fully happy for the first and only time in my life. Baked fish was one of life's great boons, but baked fish that belonged to another eunuch—not unlike a concubine who belonged to a king—was even better. I cleaned the bones off that fish on that warm spring day with my usual alacrity, greedily sucking the last cream sauce off my fingers. Moil never really forgave me for pinching that fish, although he never accused me openly of the theft. But he talked about it behind my back all of the time to anyone who would listen: Bunt, Chibby, even Siduri knew about it."

3 Wrath of Humbaba! In *The Epic of Gilgamesh*, Humbaba is a monster who guards the cedar forest and is subsequently slain by Gilgamesh and his companion, Enkidu.

4 my wool is lettuce and he will water it. According to Nesheim, lettuce is an attribute of the Egyptian fertility god Min and seen as an aphrodisiac. The Greeks, however, viewed lettuce as clearly "phallic" and, as such, was a symbol for both male potency and impotence. "In Sumerian texts," he writes, "lettuce is generally associated with the female organ, and the metaphor is less obvious, in that it refers to the need for frequent watering." See also D. Hansen's "Agricultural Symbolism in Ancient Religion," *Mankato Quarterly*, 83 (1994) 117-142.

5 Ea. "Lord of Water," a name for Enki, Sumerian god of wisdom and civilization.

Tablet Six

I The load. Reidar Hilleboe attributes this proverb to an Akkadian scribe of the third period, but Johnston and Pierson, in their magisterial study of Neo-Babylonian rhetoric, argue that it is a recension of a scribal saying from the royal *edubba* of Nabopolassar. *The Northfield Review of Near Eastern Studies*, 74 (Autumn 2017): 37-54.

Tablet Ten

I bull ballocks. A well-known visionary stimulant of the late Sumerian and early Babylonian period and associated with a minor religious subculture. The Sumerian eunuch Utu composed a tablet on this sect which reveals the potency of this practice: "They were more than my favorite delicacy. Three times a day I would ritually stuff a giant animal testicle in my mouth, masticate its sinewy flesh for seventy-two—seventy-two being the number of perfection—compressions of my lower molars and experience the gods' blessing. Boiled goat or, on occasion, camel balls became a personal sacrament, and when I ate them, the godhead of Anu was evoked, a silent presence that tasted of milk and honey and filled me with a quiet joy." Quoted in Svein Hoyme's, *Anthology of Sumerian Love Songs* (Twig, Minnesota: Hestkuk & Skitstövel, 2007) 428.

2 goat jewels. Nergal's reference to "goat jewels" is preserved in a short extract from an earlier damaged version of the text. The motifs associated with goats are typically centered around their high fertility and reproductive rates but also emphasize their cunning and guile. Earlier editions of the chronicle omit this reference. See Thorbjorn Boe, *Die Philosophie der Kastrat.* (Frankfurt: Verlager Schwanzstucker, 2018). 367-383.

3 horse rounds. Horses were domesticated for chariot warfare in the Eurasian steppes. This paradoxical state of domestication and aggression became a rallying cry for the eunuch's rebellion during the reign of Amel-Marduk in 564 BCE. Kveldulf Vigness and Snorri Thomforde rightly remarked on its importance in *Evnukks Deres Krig* (Nimrod, Minnesota: Runketryne Books, 2004).

4 My ghost balls attained a reality that was difficult to deny. This statement is not particularly surprising given Nergal's conversion to Mardukianism, whose cultus, according to Torbjørn Foss, denied the distinction between Being and Not-Being. See: Fett Poulsen, "Die Fragmente der Haremswächter," *München Tagebuch von Studien Mesopotamian*, 67 (Summer 2009): 73-96.

5 Spirits Speak. Early in the second and third millennia, lamentation poems sung by a priest chronicled the gods' wrath against a city and its subsequent destruction by its enemy in war. In later periods, these poems turned into a kind of court game of prophecy, whereby the participants asked the gods directly about their fortunes. Spirits Speak is likely a game springing from this tradition. See the first two false letters of Baltazar in Kurt Bell's *Doxographi Babylonia*, 9th ed., (*The New Ulm Assyriologist*, 1975).

6 Snout Head!!! Vegard Johnson argues that there are four extant versions of this tablet. Three exist only in fragments that are too slight for connected translations. Substantial portions are available in the Neo-Babylonian and Aramaic recensions. While there were a great many lacunae in this version, it is the most complete to date. The middle section, in which Siduri catalogs her lovers, is fragmentary, and it is not absolutely certain that this piece belongs to the letter. See "Ode to Ishtar," in *Dorknott Tidskrifft*, 7 (April 2004): 51-76.

7 Sîn-leqi-unninni. The scribe who compiled the most intact version of the *Epic of Gilgamesh*. He is said to have buried himself in filth before he wedged the final copy. There is no reason to doubt the genuineness of this story. See Helene Halverson's, "The Scribes and Scholars of Ancient Sumer," *Papers Presented to the XXIII Recontre Assyriologique Internationale*, Ed., Trond Tostrud. (St. Peter, Minnesota, 1988).

8 a mad god named Jaldabaoth. Gnostic Demiurge or "son of chaos." In a tablet fragment, Nergal refers to Jaldabaoth as "that dickhead." This interpretation is rightly accepted by D. G. Winden, who correctly chastises L. Simonson for his remark on "puluhtu" (meaning "fear") in their *Cultural Atlas of Mesopotamian Gods*, (Sleepy Eye, Minnesota: Drittsekk Books, 2013) 235.

9 Irkalla. The house of the dead. Sometimes referred to as the "house of dust." In a late and greatly damaged recension of the text, Nergal complains that Babylonian culture had "no mortality relief." See Gilgamesh's visit to the underworld, where Siduri, the divine barmaid, consoles him over this fact. See also G. Hansen, "Der Gesellschaft und der Wissenschaft zu Bardame," in *Essays in Honor of Professor Pompøs Rompehull* (Pine City, Minnesota: Lykkelig Kuksuger, 2006) 91-117.

Notes on the Text

Tablet Eleven

I the Egyptian problem. During the years of Nebuchadnezzar's reign (604-562 BCE), small states such as Judah were caught between the imperial aspirations of Egypt and Babylon. In all, Nebuchadnezzar and the Babylonian imperial regime invaded northern Syria eight times to maintain control of the region. Sections of *The Babylonian Chronicles* detailing Nebuchadnezzar's incursion into Palestine were lost, that is, until the discovery of *The Eunuch*. Poole's translation of this fragmentary text suggests that "the Egyptian problem" remained a proverbial thorn in the King's side. Upon the rebellion of Zedekiah, Nebuchadnezzar's forces invaded Judah a second time and turned it into a Babylonian province. For a more detailed discussion, see Amelie Kuhrt, *The Ancient Near East, c. 3000 – 330 B.C., Volume II,* (New York: Routledge, 1997) 590-593.

Tablet Twelve

I Thou art the shepherd . . . power. Taps's confession is a rather standard pronouncement of kingship and power, and one the royal scribe apparently cribbed almost verbatim from Ashurbanipal. See "The Banquet of Ashurbanipal II" in James B. Pritchard, ed., *The Ancient Near East, Volume II* (New Haven, Connecticut: Princeton University Press, 1976): 99ff.

Tablet Thirteen

I his apprenticeship. The Northfield Tablets, also known as the Homye Tablets after their first editor, or as the Moose Lake Tablet group by its present location, refers to a master that Ma-dug-ama-dung the Mage studied under—a female hierodule named Bau who lived in the Zagros Mountains.

Tablet Fourteen

1 **Hophra and his lackey Zedekiah.** The kings of, respectively, Egypt and Judah. See also note 1 to Tablet Eleven.

Tablet Eighteen

1 **Since the end of her affair with the King.** Siduri's break with the King—reconstructed from two tablets, both in the Moose Lake archives—is, for the most part, missing from Nergal's chronicle. The first and principle source is from Amel-Marduk's library. It consists of seven different fragments and each has been defaced by an early redactor. F1 begins with a confession: "with the possible exception of Chibby, Siduri knew me better than any soul in the Ziggurat. She had dug deep into the regions of my spirit, those dank and must-filled nooks with the faint and acrid odor of misanthropy, and sadly, sadly, of love." F7 ends with "few harem girls said 'no' the way Siduri said 'no.' She could say 'no' to a good joint of braised mutton in the midst of famine or a cup of cold barley beer on a desperately hot day, but most of all she liked to say 'no' to the King in the harem. Nebuchadnezzar would propose a night of carnal indulgence—say, binge-eating fried locusts or a group beer enema—and she would wrinkle her nose." On the rest of the surviving fragments, see Kuktryne Peterson's monograph *Sumerian Erotic Magic* (Biwabik, Minnesota: Blatnik Books, 2016).

Tablet Twenty

1 **Ligo skata! Ante gamisou!** Attic Greek for "Go fuck yourself, you little shit."

Tablet Twenty-One

1 **a grievance list.** Possibly an allusion to the fragment of tablet 204d in the Moose Lake Archives, referred to by scholars as "A Eunuch's Lament." For a discussion of this fragment, see Rompehull Magnusson's "The Historical Backstory of the Eunuch's Lament:

Demonstrable Injustice in Castrate Life," *The Loring Quarterly*, 13 (2014) 6-19.

Tablet Twenty-Two

1 my *locus amoenus*. Here the eunuch, perhaps out of fear for the political realities of the era, departs from the Akkadian to render the act with the old Sumerian *edin*. Poole chooses the Latin phrase for "lovely place" to convey Nergal's political and religious intentions. For a discussion of Poole's translation choices, see H. Bigg-Wither's introduction to *The Collected Papers of Henry Poole*, forthcoming from the University of Two Harbors Press.

2 Abûtû. "Rain flood" or "cloudburst." For a complete overview of the term and its importance in Babylonian literature see Hammond Best's "Weather Gods in Ancient Babylon," in *The Hibbing Review of Assyriology*, 14 (1980) 64-89.

About the Author

Charles H. Fischer lives in Seattle, Washington.